"Given the cultural and political crisis in which we find ourselves today, James Roseman has written a most timely and engaging novel that should speak to us all. *Habits of the Heart* summons us to encounter again traditions and values that are a vital part of our common heritage—regardless of race, creed, or origin—which can point us once more toward our rightful destiny as a people."

—J. LARRY ALLUMS
Executive director emeritus, Dallas Institute of the Humanities

"C. S. Lewis said, 'Reason is the natural organ of truth, but imagination is the organ of meaning.' Philosophical truth becomes 'real' through metaphor and story. James Roseman has demonstrated this beautifully. This is a captivating, vibrant, compelling story. Yet it left me with so much more: a visceral understanding of and a deep longing for the good 'habits of the heart' that are essential for our thriving as a person and as a people. Marvelous!"

—FRED DURHAM
Director, C. S. Lewis Institute—Dallas

"This book is unique and unusual. It is life lessons and character building in the form of a novel, a novel of messages delivered via a family saga. It's full of sadness and realism, yet still a story about hope and perseverance. It's tragic in a way, uplifting in another. And that's the way real life is: bittersweet."

—ANN HOWARD CREEL
Author of *The Magic of Ordinary Days*

"James Roseman's *Habits of the Heart* is a significant, autobiographical story of the way in which a child of the sixties, a wanderer across the confusing terrain of modernity, claims his own past, the story of his forebears, confident in their own epic and sure in their faith."

—JAMES PATRICK
Chancellor emeritus, College of Saint Thomas More

Habits of the Heart

Tim Brennan

Soli Deo Gloria

2023

Habits of the Heart

A Novel

JAMES M. ROSEMAN

RESOURCE *Publications* · Eugene, Oregon

Habits of the Heart
A Novel

Resource Publications
An Imprint of Wipf and Stock Publishers
199 W. 8th Ave., Suite 3
Eugene, OR 97401

www.wipfandstock.com

PAPERBACK ISBN: 978-1-6667-7332-3
HARDCOVER ISBN: 978-1-6667-7333-0
EBOOK ISBN: 978-1-6667-7334-7

VERSION NUMBER 092723

Scripture quotations from The Authorized (King James) Version. Rights in the Authorized Version in the United Kingdom are vested in the Crown. Reproduced by permission of the Crown's patentee, Cambridge University Press.

THE TIMES THEY ARE A-CHANGIN'
Words and Music by Bob Dylan Copyright © 1963, 1964 UNIVERSAL TUNES Copyright Renewed All Rights Reserved Used by Permission. Reprinted by Permission of Hal Leonard LLC

THE UMBRELLA MAN
Words and Music by Vincent Rose, Larry Lawrence Stock and James Cavanaugh Copyright © 1938 Larry Stock Music Co., Larry Spier Music LLC and WC Music Corp. Copyright Renewed. All Rights for Larry Stock Music Co. and Larry Spier Music LLC Administered by Downtown Music Services. All Rights Reserved. Used by Permission. Reprinted by Permission of Hal Leonard LLC

THE UMBRELLA MAN
Words and Music by VINCENT ROSE, JAMES CAVANAUGH and LARRY STOCK. © (Renewed) 1938 WARNER BROS. INC. All Rights Reserved

RISE UP! RISE UP, CRUSADERS!
Creative Commons Attribution-ShareAlike 4.0 International License (CC BY-SA 4.0) for Edward Van Zile's, Rise Up! Rise Up, Crusaders!

Artwork: Book cover and black and white sketch images of Treasure Chest, Anvil, and Howell's Highway Grocery, by Rick Roseman and Joseph Burns.

To

Laura Dean (née Howell) Roseman, my ninety-six-year-old Mom

Mores, properly so-called, [are] Habits of the Heart. . . . [A]t the same time that the law permits the American people to do everything, religion prevents them from conceiving everything and forbids them to dare everything.

ALEXIS DE TOCQUEVILLE

Contents

You Are What You Love

Prologue

1987

After my father died, I went looking for the old tapes. Rummaging through boxes in the attic, I found them. I was transported back to 1967 as I wiped the dust off the two reel-to-reel discs. The recording my father made that spring of an interview with my then ninety-six-year-old great grandmother, Mama Howell. And the one I recorded when I interviewed her son, my grandfather, Daddy Claude, later that summer. I remember so well listening to my dad elicit Mama Howell's stories of the frontier in south central Illinois, and how her life came to life for me that day. Her stories cracked open a door into a world I never knew. That crack in the door led to a world I never imagined later that Fourth of July of the "Summer of Love," when Daddy Claude told me his extraordinary saga.

When I was a sophomore in college back in '67, I remember thinking about how much the stories Daddy Claude told me had shaped him when he was young. Holding those tapes in my hands, I realized just how much they have shaped me. In them I came to see that we *are* our stories. They are the fabric of our lives; woven together by the ones we're aware of and those, if we're lucky as I was, we discover buried in a past we never knew. I came to see in Daddy Claude's story how true it is that education by habit comes before education by reason, and the virtues come to us in a potential form first, when we're young, as Aristotle said so long ago. And how they are forged in us later when hammered out on the anvil of life as it comes to us, revealing our character. This was certainly true for Daddy Claude.

In the simple telling of his story, I found a world of adventurous courage enabled by the kind of habits of the heart that Tocqueville famously declared made America work. Habits of virtue and faith handed over from generation to generation and down to him. The kind of habits that proved necessary for my grandfather to persevere and endure through the triumphs and tragedies of his life.

I plugged the old recorder into a socket on a roof truss in the attic, gently threaded the tapes, pressed the button, and listened. Oh, how I miss the voices of those whose stories changed my life.

Late that afternoon I sat at the old oak table downstairs and began to type.

One—Serendipity at the Oasis

Spring 1967

The rushing waters of change and conflict deluged the campus, the whole country it seemed.

The frenzy of spring break plans was palpable. In our dorm room, my roommate John urged me to come to San Francisco with him and some buddies. To the heartbeat of change at a place called Haight Ashbury, he said. I was curious and in some ways was inclined to go. But I was so conflicted inside by all the noise of the world that I also wouldn't mind a rest from it all.

Just then, someone hollered out, "Jim, you got a call!" I went out into the busy hall, grabbed the receiver, and covered my open ear so I could hear. It was my mom, saying everybody's gathering in Little Rock for Easter—our whole extended family had always gathered at my grandparents on holidays as far back as I could remember. Mom had mentioned it before, hoping I was coming. But I hadn't made a commitment, a bad habit I'd developed. There was no doubt she wanted me there.

Thinking somehow it might help me make sense of what was going on in the world, I thought maybe I should go to California. But I could hear the subtle plea in Mom's voice on the phone—she never seems to just ask straight out, but you can always tell what she wants. She wanted me there with her and Dad and my brothers and everyone else. I was torn.

I threw a few things in a bag before going to bed. I'd head out to Little Rock the next day.

* * *

The purple haze of nighttime slowly gave way to an early red-orange sky as I began the long drive from my dorm to my grandparents' house in Little Rock for our family gathering at Easter. Large patches of wildflowers along the highway surfaced before me as the sun came up, and I recalled that ancient phrase, "Consider the lilies of the field, how they neither toil nor spin but are arrayed with a beauty greater than Solomon's temple." How wondrous the providence of God. But my mind drifted, this time to "flower child" and "flower power," monikers silkscreened on T-shirts and displayed across campus, symbols of hipness and protest, against war and all-things-traditional. The tranquil landscape before me belied a cultural storm, one with universities and my generation at the epicenter. The chaotic world around me stood in stark contrast to the ordered constancy of the one I knew in my family.

Dylan's truism came on the car radio, "The Times They Are a-Changin'." That's certainly true, and it's hard to catch a breath above the waves. But I wondered if he's right that "mothers and fathers throughout the land" should not "criticize what you can't understand." That "your old road is rapidly agin'" with nothing more to say and if "you can't lend your hand" you should get out of the way. I struggled to make sense of "the times," for a rope to grab to make it through.

I stopped at the top of the hill and stared straight ahead, across the grove of trees on the deep slope where I'd spent so many days on the old bag swing. Is it still there? Then I saw it, secure if tattered, hanging from those long thick ropes. I cherished the memories of the days of innocence.

I turned left and heard the gray gravel crunch under the tires as I inched slowly to my grandparents' place on the steep decline of the dead-end street. My '66 VW Bug leaned sharply to the right as I parked in front of the house next door.

There it sat, not a grand mansion like those just over the hill, the modest 1400-square-foot split-level pier and beam: 3412 I Street, the comforting oasis from the storm of my confusion.

I walked down the uneven stones to the front door, pushed on the well-worn flat brass tongue-latch, bumped my shoulder, and it opened. The noise from the crowd was deafening. Everyone else was there. Dad saw me and came over as I dropped my bag on the floor. He extended his hand, and as I extended mine, he grabbed it and pulled me close, wrapping his other arm around me. "Good to see you, son. How was the trip?" he asked rhetorically. Across the sea of relatives, I locked eyes with my brothers Ricky and Bobby, and we nodded. Mom came and gave me a big hug and a kiss on the cheek. She smiled. Her boys were all here now, and she was at home.

I made my way through the small living room shaking hands with uncles, kissing aunts, and shoving a few cousins just because—we knew each other like brothers and sisters. I saw my grandmother Mama Helen sitting in her chair, as she stubbed out a Herbert Tareyton. As I got over to give her a hug, she wrapped her arms around my neck and pulled me in so tight I almost lost my balance—the taste of tobacco gathered on my lips from her full cheek. Squeezing my cheeks in her hands she smiled into my eyes. "It's so good to see you, Jimbo." Yes, so good, the feelings of home. I squeezed on through the sardine-packed space to the tiny dining room in the center of the house and stood scrunched with my brothers between the table and curved-glass china cabinet next to the evaporator cooler.

As we caught up, my eyes fixed on the spread in front of us on the old oak claw-ball dining table—a gift to my grandparents long ago I would learn—laden with platters and big bowls of food, with a space left in the middle.

Then I smelled the aroma coming from the kitchen, just back from where I stood. I leaned and looked in and there he was, wearing a stained white apron, long knife in one hand and sharpening rod in the other. Daddy Claude switched them back and forth with the precision of a master chef—so rhythmic and balanced he never lost the extended ash on the cigar that hung as a fixture from his mouth. It was classic. The preamble stopped and the ritual began, one I would discover he first began to perfect on Hoggin' Day back in 1904, carving the two big hams before him into multiple mounds of flawless sandwich-thick slices. The informal Easter luncheon was ready.

I hadn't yet seen my ninety-six-year-old great grandmother, Laura Carroll "Mama" Howell. She'd been back in Daddy Claude and Mama Helen's bedroom. Just as Daddy Claude placed the porcelain platter of sliced ham in the empty space on the table, Uncle Charles helped Mama Howell into the crowded dining room. She stood next to me, shrunken by age to about five feet tall and roll-shouldered. Her heavily wrinkled face was soft, like her wispy white hair, cheeks colored with a bit of rouge. The blue print day-dress she wore was partly covered by an old embroidered shawl. She turned and glanced up at me through her wire-rimmed eyeglasses—one lens clear, the other fogged to avoid vertigo. I stooped down and gave her a kiss, and she smiled.

Placing his hand on his mother's shoulder Daddy Claude said, "Let's return thanks. Thank you, Jesus, for this food. Amen. Let's eat!" I'd heard it so many times before, and as usual many chuckled. "No need to waste time," he once told me. "He knows we're grateful, and we are."

Cousin Laura Ann prepared a paper plate of food for her namesake. She put a small spoon of sweet potatoes and green beans on the plate, looked at Mama Howell and asked loudly, "Do you want some of this ham?"

Mama Howell looked up at her and responded excitedly in her now soft voice, "Oh Yeah! I love Claude's smoked ham." Just as Laura Ann was about to add some more sweet potatoes, Mama Howell stopped her saying, "Oh no, honey, that's aplenty."

Everyone filled their plates, got some iced tea, and spread throughout the small house to take their Easter lunch. With no intermission, the vast array of desserts was tapped—fresh apple, peach, cherry, and even rutabaga pies, each with a handmade pinched-edged flakey crust, and gooey delicious homemade banana pudding, along with an assortment of brownies, white chocolate dipped pretzels, sugar-gum candies, and chocolate-covered cherries. It was a feast.

Never stopped for long, Daddy Claude headed back into the kitchen and started cleaning up and washing dishes. The younger kids began to slow down, and the older folks caught up and reminisced about when they were young.

Slowly the local families began to leave, the bustling house settled down and got quiet.

I was struck again by contrasts, the savory and sweet of the table, the clamorous and quiet of the crowd in the little house: how the whole gathering reflected the ties that bind my family like the thick ropes that hold the old bag swing versus the fraying fabric of the world at large.

My dad had disappeared after dessert. He was back in Daddy Claude and Mama Helen's bedroom where Mama Howell was resting again after lunch. He'd set up the reel-to-reel tape recorder he brought from our home in Dallas. He tested the recorder and the sound. I stretched out on the floor along the bed's edge in the small, cramped room. Mama Howell had moved to the tufted chair in the corner and got comfortable, holding some old papers in her lap.

"Are you ready, Mama Howell?" Dad asked.

"What's that, Warren?" she responded.

"Are you ready?" he repeated.

Dad pressed two tabs at once on the reel-to-reel and said, "Alright, now."

"My grandfather Raford Carroll was born in North Carolina in eighteen-eight," she declared. "Grandfather Carroll had some of the blood of the Carrolls of Carrollton in his veins. You know who he is, don't you, honey?" she asked my dad, the pitch in her voice rising proudly.

Dad smiled curiously and said, "What's that, Mama Howell?" She repeated herself and explained who Charles Carroll of Carrollton was, a signer of the Declaration of Independence. So began many varied stories Mama Howell told about the family and when she was young.

After listening to her stories for almost two hours, my attention was piqued by a new sound from another room. My grandmother Mama Helen had begun to pick out the first seven crystalline notes and then the chords of Debussy's "*Clair de Lune*." I knew it at once. Surely this is one of the most beautiful pieces ever. So fully here as she strikes the ivory that spreads the soft sounds through the little house, lingering, then faint like a voice calling from far away, a place so beyond here. I read somewhere that Debussy once said, "music is the space between the notes." The sounds of silence that somehow make the story whole. As I listened to Mama Howell's stories against the background of "*Clair de Lune*," I wondered if this might also be true of life somehow. That there might be life in the sounds of silence in my past? That, once told and heard, a past that until now I'd only known as empty space might blend into a thick rich melody?

Mama Howell's life on the frontier in Seminary Township near Vandalia in southern Illinois came to life for me that day and cracked open the door into the kind of story that history books miss.

That Easter Day was just the beginning. Later that summer, the day *I* pressed the two buttons and Daddy Claude began to talk, I discovered how good habits of the heart are formed and how important they are in life's perilous storms.

* * *

Fourth of July Weekend 1967

Silently, he stood and stared out across the lake through the screen walls on the porch. Pulling a single wooden matchstick from the small box, he struck it, held it up covering the flame with his hand from the gentle breeze, and re-lit the half-smoked cigar. I wondered what he was thinking.

I asked Daddy Claude if he'd brought the reference material he said he would. He pointed to a large chest that my Uncle Charles had put behind his chair. It had old clippings and memories he would pull from as we talked— the same chest, I'd discover, that Daddy Claude's great uncle Jim put on the wagon for him when they left Illinois, and which he'd added to through the years. It was quiet enough now to have our follow-up conversation. The sequel to the one my dad had with Mama Howell at Easter.

Daddy Claude took a seat in his chair.

This time I asked, "Are you ready?"

"Sure," he answered.

"Maybe you could begin with some of your earliest and most important memories growing up in Illinois and some of your dreams when you were a boy," I suggested.

He began.

Inheritances, Part One:
At Home in Illinois

. . . how good habits of the heart are formed . . .

Late Autumn 1904 through Spring of 1905

"Education by habit must come before education by reason" and the virtues
are "bestowed on us first in a potential form."

ARISTOTLE

Two—So Important, So Permanent

Late Autumn 1904

It had been an amazing day!

I held my little brother Bill in my lap as we bumped along home in our wagon, his eyes half shut. Lost in my thoughts and dreams, I quietly reveled in everything about my first hoggin' day.

Until in the distance, rising above the foggy moonlit silhouette of our house, Papa saw smoke. He yanked on the reins and the mare took off. We got closer and suddenly my otherwise quiet and soft-spoken Papa yelled, "FIRE! Claude, run NOW over to Mr. Johnson's and tell him our place is on fire. Hurry!"

I quickly shuffled Bill from my lap over to Beth who was holding Maurine.

As Papa rapped the reins again, I jumped from the fast-moving wagon, fell, rolled, and took off across the dark pasture as fast as I could go. I got to the Johnson's farm just as they'd gotten home. Gasping for breath I hollered,

"Mr. Johnson . . . our house is on fire! Papa asks you to come and help, and have Clarence go to the next farm over and gather as many others as he can get, and as much water as you can carry!"

I took off running back home.

I saw it at a distance, it grew bigger and bigger the closer I got. Our home was ablaze.

I ran past Mama clutching Rachel in her arms, well back from the house as I arrived, with Li'l Bill and my two other sisters hugging her dress. The heat was intense. And the smoke.

I saw Papa shovel buckets of water from the cistern and throw it on the fire. But it didn't seem to help. I grabbed a bucket, dunked it, and helped Papa throw water at the fire. It was no competition against the ravaging

9

flames. Bucket after bucket after bucket. The blaze grew larger and hotter. Tall columns of flames shot into the cold night air.

We stood back.

The neighbors began to arrive. But it was too late.

The scorching hot inferno made the luminous late autumn night descend into the darkness of full midwinter. We stood and watched our home slowly collapse into charred rubble.

My tall and strong papa stood hunched over exhausted, gazing at the fiery furnace in stunned silence—his full head of dark-brown hair now wet from sweat and gray from the ash. Mama cried softly holding Rachel, as Beth, Maurine, and Bill huddled around her with their little faces buried into her soft middle. I walked over and wrapped my nine-year-old arms around them all.

I got them back in the wagon as Papa asked. After clearing it with Mr. Johnson, Papa summoned Clarence to drive them back to Grandfather Bill's place while I stayed with him.

I stopped for a moment, stared across the shadowed meadow, and followed the dark edges of the tall trees into the starry heavens above as I had early that morning from the porch. But this time through a haze of dense smoke and flickering cinders floating in the air.

How could something so important, so permanent be gone in an instant?

* * *

The Beginning: Hoggin' Day

A pack of coyotes was hollering in the distance as I stood on the front porch, hands stuffed in the pockets of the fur-collared half jacket Mama had made me. They got 'em a deer or something. The moon was bright in the western sky—enough to paint eerie shadows with giant limbs on the darkened ground below, the leaves all but gone. It was late November, and the morning was crisp. It always was in Southern Illinois that time of the year. Despite my autumn excitement, I could see winter was not far off.

It'd been cold long enough—two-weeks straight—so it was time.

I woke early that day, so early the sun wouldn't break the horizon for another hour and a half—everybody in the family always kidded me about being industrious. Uncle Jim called me *indefatigable*, a word I'd never heard.

With the moonlight to see by, I decided to drain the big watering trough I knew we'd need. Though eager, the way I felt on Christmas morning, I decided to wait till Papa was up to gather the other supplies. I came back to the porch and sat tipped back on two legs against the wall in his ladderback chair like a grown-up. With anxious anticipation I stared across the moonlit meadow into the quiet, peaceful morning.

It was a big day for me, a rite of passage of sorts at age nine. The first one I'd get to apprentice butchering the hogs, not just the chickens as I'd done for a while. Hoggin' Day was something special. And that year especially, being held at Grandfather Bill's place—the old homestead first settled by my great grandparents Raford and Sarah Carroll way back in 1829. Our family, along with many cousins, aunts and uncles, and a few neighboring families, brought four fattened hogs for that year's annual event. It'd be an extra-hard day's work, everyone knew, from sun-up to sun-down. But a great feast for all at day's end.

Still before the sun came up, after gathering the newly sharpened long-knife and hog-scraper and other tools from the barn and the emptied hundred-gallon watering trough for bringing the pork meat and extras home late that night, Papa told me to tie our mature hog, big old Jesse, to the wagon. I'd known him since he was born, a little bitty thing. He followed me everywhere when I worked with Papa, but especially as I did my chores early in the morning before school. When it came time to feed him and our two sows and the chickens, he'd throw his snout up and down all excited and grunt and snort out loud. At a huge waddling 350 pounds now, Papa said it was time.

"Come on Claude," Papa said, "it's time to go."

We all climbed in, Papa and Mama with baby Rachel up front and Beth, Maurine, Bill, and me in the back. Mama told Beth, then eight, to hold Maurine who was four, and me to hold Bill, who was barely two and a half. Papa rapped the reins gently and all of us began to bump up and down on the hard wagon wood as old Jesse lumbered slowly behind, as if he knew where he was going. We made our way the short mile and a half, though with the load we had, it must've taken us a full hour. That early-morning trek was unusually cheerful, as barely out of sight of our house Mama and Papa started a sing-along—sounds of joy and laughter lifted into the silent still air, and I imagined we were a family of traveling minstrels off to our next performance in the village down the road.

When we arrived most of the others were already there. The atmosphere was carnival-like with all the activity just as the sun began to break.

But as I came to realize, it was more like a well-organized three-ring circus than a carnival. There was order and purpose to everything.

The men had already built the slaughter pens and dug bleeding pits under the log-poled Y-stanchions with medium-sized logs stretched across to hang the heavy slain animals for gutting. The three one-hundred-gallon metal wash bins were in their place—we would add the fourth we brought. The women prepared the freshly picked vegetables and placed them near the fire pit.

The all-day gathering was for slaughtering, processing, and butchering the hogs for the winter, and for the great feast of thanksgiving that followed in the evening, filled with fun and festivities. All the preparations were well underway.

My best new day had begun.

Maurine and Bill had found their cousins and were running around under the big trees with glee, squealing and yelling as they chased one another. I saw Bill trying to keep up, but he was unable to move fast and kept falling. He fell and began to cry, and I went over, lifted him up, and dusted him off. No sooner did I have him upright than he was off chasing after his sister and cousins again. Back and forth like cutting horses, the teenaged caretakers corralled the younger ones, and kept them away from the sophisticated process set up for the day's work.

Grandfather Bill walked me over to a butcher table where his older brother Jim stood prepping for the first hog. That day I was assigned to apprentice with the seventy-three-year-old Carroll family patriarch, Mama's uncle whom she cherished like a second father, but who'd always scared me a little. I was excited but nervous. I'd known Uncle Jim for as long as I could remember, and I loved him—but always with a respectful distance as the head of the family and a kind of fear of giants since Uncle Jim was a tall and big man who towered over me like a huge oak tree. I remember him looking solid as a rock and stern-faced. His outward appearance was even unsettling to me, always well-kempt with his white, closely cut hair only on the sides and his white well-trimmed goatee. With trepidation, that day I would be trained by the best in the county. But to my surprise I quickly came to know my great uncle in a way I never expected and learned things about life I'd never even thought about.

Uncle Jim walked me around to each station and explained things in detail—there were four swine, a lot for the six-family crew and cousins available. First there was the slaughter pen, for hanging, cutting, gutting, and bleeding. Then there was boiling and scraping, with the scraper we'd brought, followed by the slain hogs being placed on the butcher tables for processing and extracting lard—which was used for making soap and cooking and baking as well as for other things. The cleaver, the saw and various knives, including the long knife we brought, were laid out on the big table. That's where we would work, and talk. Everybody talked while they worked. And to my surprise, so did Uncle Jim and me—I even got the courage to ask questions.

"Uncle Jim, when did you first learn to do this? To slaughter and butcher the hogs?"

"Well, let me think, Claude. I reckon I was about your age, nine or ten or so. That would have been back around '42, I guess. I remember being plenty excited, just like you. What do you think of it all? What do you like about it?"

It struck me how easily Uncle Jim and I began to talk. How openly and with unexpected gentleness he talked with me. As if I was grown, at least it made me feel that way. I quickly responded excitedly, "I like it *all* . . .

"I really like farming with Papa, doing all the work of planting, harvesting, taking care of the animals, and repairing things in the barn. Then taking the harvest to the market in town to sell what we don't need at home. And the chickens too, I like getting them ready for Mama to cook, butchering them, cutting them up into the right pieces and all, for use at supper . . ."

The words just flowed out of me like I'd tapped one of those hundred-gallon troughs.

"I like it all but . . . but sometimes it's hard to see those chickens break out of their shells, grow up when I feed them, only to have to take them. I felt that way a lot when I tied big old Jesse to the wagon this morning and as I look at him now on the table. You know, Uncle Jim?"

"I do know, son. But that's the way God made things. We all live from the bounties in this world. That's the blessing of the mandate we've been given, to cultivate the world and the parts of it we're given responsibility for.

"As we do that and receive the rain that allows the seeds to take root and sprout and gain the strength to weather the storms and come to maturity under the sun, we accept the fruit of our cultivation. The same is true with these animals. Once cultivated and cared for, with the fortunes of providence we take the harvest and receive the bounty and are provided for in the process. But it's okay to feel close to the animals, and to the land, too. That's as it's supposed to be. We should be thankful to God for our provisions but also to the critters God gives us. We're thankful for them and to them just as we are for the rain, the sunshine, and the harvest that sustains us. That's a good and natural thing, Claude. That you loved old Jesse shows you understand the order of things, how we all depend on each other."

I still remember how startling it was to talk with Uncle Jim that day and how he could explain things. What he said stuck with me. Almost everything he ever said did.

Uncle Jim showed me how and helped me cut the animal into its useful parts with great precision and caution. How to tend to the innards and even the head. There was little left unused.

As we worked at our butchering table some of the experienced women and their young apprentices worked at a processing table to prepare for sausage-making the next day.

Some of the other women worked at another table gathering and dicing the fat and putting it in large cast-iron pots hung over two small, separated fire pits. The younger women would stir it down to fresh lard. Some was potted to make lye soap on another day, and some rendered into crackling that would be fried in another iron pan as pigskins for snacking on later.

There was a steady rhythm to the work—a joyous dance between the different pits, pots and tables, each person with their own job, butchering, scraping, slicing, dicing, and boiling, yet all acting in concert as one. It was a strange but wonderful scene—one I'd never taken notice of before that day. Made even more so by the rhythmic waves of sound rising and falling from the cracks of cleavers, convivial chatter, and the high-pitched squeals from the kids. It was amazing!

As the day got long and the bulk of the work dwindled, many of the women moved to the large pots over the white-hot fire pit. There they cooked the backs, neckbones, and leftover bits, and roasted the spareribs, and tended to the vegetables, the white and sweet potatoes, and the ear-corn. Then they boiled the greens and made hot-water cornbread in the black iron skillets for the upcoming feast. I overheard Mama say they had also fried up some fresh apples. To top it all off, three big, skewered hams were slowly rotated by the dedicated teenagers. The fused aromas made my mouth water.

The younger ones who'd been cleaning the worktables began setting the long, big one with forks and knives, platters, plates, and bowls, and glasses and large pitchers of water drawn from the well. Then there was the coveted apple cider, a treat no one could resist, poured from large pottery jars taken from the winter storage part of the barn.

As the sun sank behind the large elm and walnut trees, the lanterns were lit across the big yard in front of the old Carroll family homestead. Everyone began to move slower. Little Rachel had fallen asleep in Mama's arms. Even the bigger kids slowed down. The men had parceled, wrapped, and packed the pork for the families' smokehouses, covered the blood pits with fresh soil, and cleaned and washed all the tools and tables. The work-day drew to a close and the feast of Thanksgiving was about to begin.

A few of the men had gathered some of the coals from the big fire-pit and built two new ones over closer to the long supper table brought out from the log house—the old table Great Grandfather Carroll made when the house was first built. With nightfall it began to get cold again.

Everyone had taken their work gloves and aprons off, washed up in one of the cleaned and refilled hundred-gallon bins, and gathered to sit along the big table. Grandfather Bill sat at one end and Uncle Jim at the other. Uncle Jim stood, raised a glass of cider, and declared loudly,

"Good, successful day everyone! Now, let's return thanks. We thank you, Lord, for all your good gifts, and for life itself. Please keep us with these provisions for another year and continue to bless our family and friends. Thank you, Jesus, for this food. Amen. Let's eat!"

The feast was great that night. I felt closer to becoming a man than I'd ever felt before.

As the coals in the two nearby firepits turned gray and the younger kids fell asleep in the laps of their mothers, aunts, and cousins, I looked around at everyone sitting about the table. I'd grown close to Uncle Jim that day and I felt at home among my big family like never before.

Papa and Mama and I gathered everything together in the now almost pitch-dark night and loaded our crew in the wagon. It was time to start home. Without old Jesse lumbering in tow but packed in the back, as we pulled out, I knew it wouldn't take long.

A light, smoky fog was descending, but through a break I saw the moon again.

God, it'd been such a great day. If I had a dream back then of what my life would be, I'm sure it was simple. To become a man and someday assume Papa's role on the farm, eventually to have a family of my own and take care of Papa and Mama in their old age. That's probably what I and all my nine-year-old cousins imagined our future to be. That's the way it was and always had been as far as I knew. It was impossible, then, for me to see life any other way.

Until the fire. That fire changed everything.

Three—Amid the Embers

That terrible night Papa and me and the neighbors who'd come to help, kept watering the remains of our house. Little was said by anyone. But the sadness on our neighbors' faces told what wasn't said. Mr. Johnson came and put his hand on Papa's shoulder, and they looked at each other. In a stoic daze I watched the silent exchange and saw a deeper sadness in Papa's face.

When the flares were finally out, Papa thanked everyone and quietly they went into the night.

He motioned me to get Betsy from the barn. I settled and bridled her and brought her out without a saddle. Papa gathered her mane as I held her at the bit, and he jumped to climb on. She allowed it. He swung his leg over, took the reins, grabbed my arm, and jerked me up. Still, in the darkness, this time from the height of old Betsy we both stared across the smoldering embers. With a gentle kick we headed back to where we'd had such a good day just hours before.

It was late when we arrived, well past midnight. Grandfather Bill met us with a lantern and helped get the mare watered and stalled for the night, and Papa and I washed off a little in the trough. Mama had gotten my sisters and brother asleep in the long side room where she slept as a little girl and met us just as we were coming in.

Standing in the open doorway as he shuffled up, I saw her look up at Papa and hand him a cup of water. He threaded his still wet hand behind Mama's neck, leaned down and kissed her softly, and went on inside.

She stopped me as I stepped up on the porch, wrapped her arms around me and pulled me tight, pressing a kiss on the top of my head. Saying nothing, she lifted my face away with a hand on each cheek, looked in my eyes and kissed me on the forehead. The day came crashing down. I buried my face back into Mama and the tears began to flow. Unsteadily, she held me, then pulled me away again and gently wiped back the matted hair from my eyes, and with the water from my hair mixed with the tears on my cheeks she washed the remaining soot from my face.

How could such a good day turn so bad so quickly? Again, I questioned how such permanent things can become smoke in a moment. I'd thought I made a big step into manhood that day. That night it didn't feel like it. My body was numb and tired, my mind so confused.

We got little sleep that first night. Early the next morning Mama's sister Aunt Ollie came to help Beth with Maurine and Bill and take care of Rachel while Papa, Mama and I went back over to rummage through the remains. Papa wanted to see if he could learn why the fire started. He and Mama sifted through the ashes, but they didn't find a cause. We began to see if there was anything left to salvage.

Looking across the debris of what was our house, I saw small circles of smoke spiraling up from the tiny cinders that still burned. The bottom of my boots got hot as we walked through the blackened residue of wood and stone. Under one of the large fireplace stones, I found the big family Bible, burnt on the edges, and a small history book my teacher Miss Jennie gave me. I tripped over a piece of charred hardness and looked down. It was the stock of the rifle Papa had given me at Christmas the year before. My heart sank.

I saw Papa's chair, the one his papa, Grandfather Isaac, made for him when he and Mama got married, now broken and charred black. The canvas-covered, straw-and-down-stuffed-pillow Mama made for it was like flat flakes of incinerated paper. Papa crouched down and lifted a broken and burnt part of the wooden rocking cradle he made when I was born—the one all of us kids slept in as babies, the one Rachel slept in the night before. All of it just used up kindling.

I looked up and saw Mama stoop down and delicately pick up pieces of some broken dishes. Hunched over, tears fell from her eyes as she inspected remnants of a few cups and saucers of chinaware. Keepsakes, I learned, from her mama, Grandmother Mary Ann, who died when Mama was only three and a half years old. They had been kept by Grandfather Bill's sister, Mama's Aunt Beth, my sister Beth's namesake, for eighteen years and given to her the day she and Papa married in '92. Only when I heard this story did I understand. The loss I saw in Mama's tears that day was not from broken dishes but from broken dreams at the loss of the mother she never really knew.

All I'd ever known as home I could see through Papa's chair, Rachel's cradle, and Mama's dishes. Everything gone but for the family Bible, a history book, a few toys in the yard, and the stuff in the barn. All but the memories. Oddly, I could hardly remember the anxious excitement and high hopes I'd had on the porch the morning before—that so familiar place where I and my sisters and brother played, and Papa and Mama sat. I was overwhelmed as I stared across the wasteland where I'd spent my boyhood, a place I never imagined was anything other than permanent. Where would we live? What would we do? Would things ever be the same again?

I couldn't make sense of it all. It'd be hard, I thought, but we would just have to rebuild.

* * *

Suddenly we all lived at the family homestead with Grandfather Bill. It surprised me how quickly Mama settled in. She moved around with a familiar ease, made the meals, took care of Rachel and us kids, Papa, and Grandfather Bill as if we'd lived there forever. I guess I knew but had forgotten—this was where she was raised after her mama died by Great Grandmother Sarah.

Maurine and Bill settled in quickly too—after supper, most evenings they played on the old rug that stretched across the biggest of two main rooms, in front of the large stone fireplace that opened onto both. Everyone settled in, it seemed. Grandfather Bill, Papa, and Mama sat in three big chairs like the one Grandfather Isaac made for Papa—Grandfather Bill with his pipe and Papa his cigar sitting next to Mama holding Rachel. They relaxed, talked, and watched the kids play. Beth sat on a floor pillow and fiddled with long needles and yarn Mama gave her.

But not me. It made me mad! It was all too relaxed, too much like we were there to stay. I was uneasy. Back from the others I sat quiet in a straight chair at the big table, the one used for the Hoggin' Day feast, did school lessons Miss Jennie gave me, and thought about things.

The days were different too. The rhythms were off. Instead of school and working the farm with Papa, we'd go over to our place to salvage stuff in the barn and clean up the ruins. He'd give me instructions and I'd do it. We hardly talked—Papa had always been more of a thinker than a talker. I saw that as a strength. But he was especially quiet after the fire. Even so, I preferred the days to nights. The work somehow helped, and it made me tired enough to sleep.

But before I fell asleep, I often heard Papa and Mama and Grandfather Bill talking. I couldn't make out exactly what they were saying, but it seemed like plans of some sort. Then late at night I'd wake when things were quiet and hear Mama weeping softly when she'd get up to nurse Rachel and care for Bill. I became more and more uneasy, anxious even.

Christmas was fast approaching. Before I'd gone to bed and heard them talking, Grandfather Bill told Papa he wanted me to work with him for a few days. Because Hoggin' Day was held at the Carroll homestead that year and then the fire followed, he hadn't finished winterizing the place. Papa told me, and early the next morning Grandfather Bill said, "The Almanac shows a hard winter ahead. Let's get started."

We went to the barn where he gestured at a workbench and told me to gather a small pickaxe, an awl and chisel, and a masonry trowel, while he picked up two large buckets, one full of wood splices and the other full of some mix he'd made. He carried the buckets as we left the barn and stopped to pump a small bit of water in the mix from the well jack, and I carried the tools. I followed as he walked to the north side of the old house where he said the winds hit hardest. He put the buckets down and stirred the mix with a stick.

"We'll do the daubing and chinking first."

He knew exactly where he wanted to start. It was clear he'd left off and we were picking up from there. But I didn't know what he meant by chinking and daubing.

"What's that, the daubing?" I asked.

He rubbed his hand on the white stuff between the logs.

"It's this, Claude. See?"

As he talked, he found a big crack and rubbed across it.

"See here? This is what we're looking for."

To show me, he took the awl and punched into the crack, moved it up and down the length of the crack, and wiggled it. He explained that it opens up the crack, makes it a little bigger and deeper. Then with the pickaxe he chopped gently in the crack and with the chisel removed the crumbled white stuff and debris that clogged it.

"This daubing covers the chinking—that's a mix of clay, mud, and rock between the logs. You can't see that unless this mortar-based daubing cracks, like here. That's what we're doing, repairing the cracks."

He plugged the crack with some of the sticks we brought, pushed the pasty mud from the bucket into the crack, filling it up, then with the trowel threw a big blob of the mud right on the crack and smoothed it up and down and across so that the crack was gone.

"The chinking and daubing helps hold the logs in place, you see, and it protects the inside against the cold winter winds, snow and rain. It's got to be repaired every year because when the rain and snow freeze in the small cracks, it makes bigger ones."

Grandfather Bill and I had already talked more than Papa and I did in a week working over at the remains of our house. We worked our way around the wood cabin fixing different spots.

He had me do the next crack he found, how to dig into it, clean it, and use the trowel to fill in the cracks and worn spots and spread the outside smooth. The work distracted me in a good way, and I learned things.

"This is real different from our house, Grandfather Bill. I mean it's made different."

"Yes, that's right Claude. This old log house was built a long time ago, you see. My father and Mr. Jeremiah Evans and some of his boys built it in '36, two years before I was born. Seminary Township and this whole area was still pretty much frontier then. All houses were built this way back then. But when the lumber mills up near Ramsey came along, many folks in these parts, including your papa, began to use shiplap cladding more than logs and daubing—I helped your papa and mama build their house. Shiplap lumber is easier to build with and the feathering of the boards does some of the same thing that chinking and daubing does, it helps protect from the rains and wind."

Grandfather Bill talked of our house with such ease, as if it was still there, and that bothered me.

As we made our way around plugging cracks in the old place, Grandfather Bill explained how it was put together. Long, large logs about nine or ten inches thick were stretched all the way across the sides of the cabin, stacked on top of each other, up to about twelve feet high, and mitered at the corners—big old logs that had come from huge, tall trees like the ones that now shaded the house. They matched up evenly with the shorter logs across the back up to the same height. It really did seem like it'd been there forever.

I remember thinking how hard it must have been to build the log house so long ago—to cut down those big trees, drag them into place, trim, lift, stack, and fit them together just so. Just winterizing it made me imagine how hard it was to build. It seemed almost impossible.

I'd never thought about how houses were built before that day. I suppose it's just how it is, things can be hidden even when they're right in front of you.

Looking at the old logs I thought about the special boards Grandfather Bill said were used to build our house. The more Grandfather Bill explained, the more excited I became. I imagined working with Papa to rebuild our house.

Almost finished with the daubing repair on the west side, we came upon two gigantic overgrown bushes of asparagus. Grandfather Bill pointed into them and motioned me forward. Stepping through to get next to the house felt like I'd entered a jungle. Those bushes were so big I guessed they'd been there since the beginning, those two huge ferns.

About that time Mama came out with some lemonade. I crawled back through the ferns and heard Grandfather Bill say to her, "Look there Laura, your boy's following in your footsteps, climbing in through those ferns," and they both laughed. We sat down and took a break. He asked Mama if she remembered how they would cut those big leaves when she was a girl and cover the walls and pictures inside when they'd repair the whitewash and do spring cleaning. "Oh yeah!" she said, smiling at her papa. I'd never really thought about Mama working with her papa and being a young girl and growing up like me. If everything had been normal, I think I would have wanted to talk with Mama about that more. But things weren't normal.

The next day we worked on the roof. Grandfather Bill got a log-slatted ladder from the barn and pointed to some shake shingles he'd cut and motioned me to carry as many as I could. He positioned the ladder and we each climbed up and scaled the gabled pitch roof. He told me to move with caution so I wouldn't slip from the twenty-five-degree slope, which he said was to allow the snow to slide off. He taught me how to replace broken shingles we found and how to repair a piece of the flashing on the large stone chimney—that, he said, stood six feet higher than the roof's ridge to give a proper draw.

I learned so much working with Grandfather Bill. It made me feel grown up again. The daily work after the fire with Papa over at our place and especially with Grandfather Bill, helped take my mind off things.

The longer we were there that winter the more often new routines set in. Uncle Jim came for supper almost every night. School was out for the holidays, but each night I sat at the big table reading and practicing my lessons. I'd overhear Uncle Jim and Grandfather Bill tell stories about when they were young in the old cabin, and they teased Mama about things she did as a little girl. There was laughter again. The spirit of the place began to change for me. I came to see that the old place had a life in it I hadn't known. My anxiousness settled a bit, and I found myself more comfortable. I missed being home at our place, but I began to see a kind of home in the old cabin. I started to see that it had stories to tell beyond just how it was built.

I guess I'd always known it was the Carroll family homestead that Great Grandfather Raford and Great Grandmother Sarah built. But until I worked with Grandfather Bill, seeing how it was built and all, I'd never thought of its not being there. More than cutting the logs and the other hardships I imagined they endured to build it, one night I learned how difficult it was even to get the land to build it on. I overheard Uncle Jim and Grandfather Bill talking about how their parents first settled in Seminary Township in

1829, but they didn't get the homestead land until seven years later—when they bought eighty acres from a man named Mr. Joel Thomas for $100. But that was the beginning, not the end. Uncle Jim told Mama they were forced to sell it back to Mr. Thomas because of hard times. They were forced to move a couple of times before they got it back again.

"First to old John Pugh's place for a time, where I was born," Uncle Jim said, "then over to the Crouch place west of Sam Andrews's farm for a time. Only after seven years of hard work and a loan from the bank, did they finally buy the same eighty acres back from Mr. Thomas. That's when they built this homestead cabin, in '36 a couple of years before Bill was born," Uncle Jim said.

That story fascinated me. Hearing of moving here then there, I wondered again about the permanence of things, how what seemed so permanent wasn't always so. How hard life was for my great grandparents and how hard they struggled—it wasn't till much later that their hardships came to mean a whole lot more to me.

The old house was warm inside, and once heated by the river stone fireplace it stayed that way because of those thick log walls and the daubing between them. The separate hearths in the two big keeping rooms spread the warmth around.

Grandfather Bill had a big picture of George Washington hanging in the biggest common room, about two feet by four. He said it'd been there ever since Great Grandfather Carroll hung it when the house was first built. Near the president was a large rack of deer antlers and a picture of a hunting scene that Grandfather Bill put there, of dogs working the deer on the hunt. Mama said it reminded him of hunting with his brothers when they were all young and, as I would learn later, of hunting with her brothers until a tragic accident.

That winter I learned the old homeplace held lots of memories. I caught a glimpse of how there are so many things hidden in places and events that can just pass us by. That old place is where Mama was raised, where her mama died when she was so young, and where her papa was born and raised along with his five younger brothers and sisters. The crevices of that old homestead told stories. I began to see there was life where I'd never seen it before.

Christmas was fine enough that year but different. Mama made stockings for all us kids, hung them on the big fireplace, and stuffed them with walnuts, fruit, and some sugar candy and butter cookies she made. It was fun to be with my cousins, aunts, and uncles. To all go to church together and come back over to what had become "our home" for the family Christmas feast. It was good but it wasn't the same. I was sure we'd start rebuilding soon.

Until one night just after Christmas. Papa and Mama sat me and Beth down in two of the big chairs next to the fireplace, where they usually sat. It was strange. Papa looked at us and said,

"We've decided to move, children."

It hung in the air with a silent pause. I didn't quite get it at first. He went on,

"Not just move to another house but leave Seminary Township—move away."

I heard it this time, loud and clear, and so did Beth. We didn't believe it! They told us we had to sell the land our house was on to settle the debt on it and start over.

Shouting over each other as if in competition, we exclaimed, "*What! Where?*"

"Settle down, now! Both of you. This is what your mama and I have decided. We'll stay the winter with Grandfather Bill, but come spring we're moving to Texas, to Texarkana."

I didn't like it! Not at all. I didn't understand. Everything had gone from bad to worse.

It struck me like a bolt of lightning how big the change would be. Not only would we not have our home anymore, but I wouldn't have my cousins, my friends or school anymore. It was too much to take in.

Where was Texarkana anyway? I wondered. *And what would it be like wherever it was?* Nothing at all would ever be the same again. The ground under my feet felt unstable.

Four—Providence and Promises

Winter 1905

Night after night I stewed in my straight-back chair at the big table flipping the fire smudged pages of Mr. Edward Eggleston's *First Book of American History* I found protected in the rubble after the fire, the one that Miss Jennie gave me for school. Papa and Mama would encourage me and talk about how a fresh start in Texas could be a good thing. I couldn't hear it, I wouldn't. Like a bad echo it bounced in my head with a grating constancy, "We've decided to move . . . ," not rebuild or just move to another house but leave Seminary Township—move away.

The Almanac was right, just as Grandfather Bill had said it would be. The snow came heavy after Christmas and gathered high on the north wall we'd repaired. And it was cold. The big fireplace kept us warm, but I was cold inside. Everything was different.

* * *

After supper one night when the snow had stopped and it was clear, Uncle Jim came to the big table where I sat, shrugged-shouldered with my head hung down staring blankly at the book. I'm sure Papa and Mama had asked Uncle Jim and Grandfather Bill to talk to me, hoping they might have better luck changing my attitude.

"Put your boots on and get your coat and hat, Claude. Let's take a walk," Uncle Jim said.

I'd grown close with Uncle Jim. I liked being around him. His presence made me feel safe. I remember thinking he was just trying to distract me with a walk, take my mind off things, cheer me up a little. But I didn't expect much. How could he say anything that'd help?

We stepped out into the quietness of the cold night air, off the porch, and began to walk.

"Son, your Great Aunt Martha, God rest her soul, and I had twelve children, as you know. And growing up for them was hard sometimes, just like it is right now for you. I know you ponder things a lot. And that's good. But it's hard, I know. I'm old and you're young, but I want to talk to you about some things I've learned about life that'll help make you a man, not straight away, but as time goes along."

I wanted to be a man and had thought I'd taken a big step on Hoggin' Day. But that walk was a bigger one. One I didn't fully understand then—I couldn't really, but it has anchored so much in my life ever since. I remember it like it was yesterday.

"Claude, homes and the land they sit on are special places. They become a part of us and we them," Uncle Jim began.

"They're places where our stories are written—like the ones you've heard in this old place my papa built so long ago. They bind them together like a book, and that's important. But just like with the food we eat, the homes we have come from the soil, from the trees, and other things we use to build them. It's part of what we're given stewardship over, to cultivate, build, grow, all to sustain us like we talked about on Hoggin' Day. But it's all the blessings of Providence, no more or less than the whole of life itself. And it's all up to Providence, what we have and how long we have it. Some blessings we have for a long time and some short. The longer we have them, like your papa and mama's house and their farm you grew up on, the more permanent they seem to us. But they never really are. They're on loan to us to take care of for the time we have them. As hard as it is to accept—and I wish you hadn't had to learn this so young—the truth is, Claude, everything in this life is transient. You know that word, son?"

I listened and shook my head, no, looking down as I watched my boots crunch the snow.

"It means like water vapor. It's here for a while and then gone. Sometimes it seems like *we* decide when to let it go, but the truth is, so much is not up to us. You understand what I'm saying, son?"

I finally spoke. "I kind of do, but not really."

"It's like the gift of life itself, you see. We come into this world without any say and go out the same way."

Then the example he gave led us down a path neither of us expected.

"It's like with your Grandmother Howell's death, whose life we celebrated at her funeral at Corinth Baptist last June. You see, son? It's in God's hands. It's all his, life itself, you understand. He gives us blessings of all sorts, things like land and houses and so much more, like children—they're the best. We have them for a while, hopefully a long while, but sometimes not . . ."

Uncle Jim paused. We stood still and silent, as he stared out into the night sky.

"Why'd you stop, Uncle Jim?"

I was curious. He didn't respond at first. Just stood there. Then after a while, what seemed a long time, he looked down and wrapped his big arm across my small shoulders and said, "My children, Claude. I'm thinking about my sweet children who died so young, Ben, Amanda, and William Raford—he was named for your grandfather, you see. God gave them to your Aunt Martha and me, and we loved them so much, but we lost them, and way too young: Ben when he was thirty-five, Amanda at the tender age of twelve, and little William at only twenty-one days. I think about them often, just as I have now while talking with you, Claude."

I didn't know what to say. What could I say? He stared into the cold night again. I could see he was back with his children in his heart. I looked at Uncle Jim, and my heart was sad with him.

"To be given such gifts for a season is a wonderful thing, and it's hard to let go. But we must trust God. Your Grandfather Bill knows this too, just as your mama does. He lost his three sons, and your mama and her sisters lost their brothers. Two from disease and one in a hunting accident—when he looks at that hunting picture above the fireplace now, your grandfather always sees young Robert, your mama's last brother, who she called Bob. They're all gone now, all before they were out of their teens.

"Here's what I mean, Claude. What we think is guaranteed in life is not. There are times that all we have is to trust in the providence of God."

What? I thought. What he said stuck in my head. Then I blurted it out loud,

"Mama had brothers? I didn't know that. I mean if I did, I don't remember."

"You wouldn't, Claude. Not necessarily. Though I'm sure she's mentioned them if only in passing. Your mama's brothers all died before you were born. Charles from the measles when he was eighteen, John from what folks now call the flu at sixteen, and Robert, the youngest—who was two years older than your mama—at fifteen in that tragic hunting accident."

But rather than talking more about Mama's brothers, Uncle Jim continued:

"Death is always hard, son. It just is. But in a strange way death is a part of life in this broken world. We hope it comes in a natural way after a long and fruitful life. When it does, we can find joy even in the sadness, like at your papa's mother's funeral, your Grandmother Howell. But when it's unexpected, as it too often is, it's very hard, especially in those that are tragic mysteries. The worst of all is when it's out of order, when a child is taken before his parents. There's no joy to be found then. All you can do is trust God."

As he continued to talk, he stared straight. I wasn't sure if he was talking to me or someone else, or maybe himself. Then he looked down into my eyes with gentleness and started again.

"For those of us left to go on, Claude, those of us who still take the breath of life, we must find a way to see each breath we're given as the true gift it is. We must find a new joy, if only by giving thanks for the joy we were given for the season we had them. The first steps are always the hardest. And most often they are thrust on us by the sheer demands of life, the kind we can't shy away from. But that too is a kind of grace—it helps move us out of ourselves toward life again. If we don't bury our grief, hide it away, after a while we find that the fullness of joy comes again. The beauty of life clouded away breaks through just as surely as the dawn of a new day."

He stared at me again and smiled, saying, "It's true, Claude. I promise you it's true."

I thought of Mama and her brothers. How sad she must have been, yet how filled with joy she is most of the time. Even how soon she laughed again after the fire when Uncle Jim and Grandfather Bill told stories about when she was young. She can find joy, even in the sadness.

Something Uncle Jim said stuck in my mind when he talked about Grandmother Howell's funeral. I remember how it was such a joyous celebration, like he said. But then I thought about how sad everyone was at Grandfather Isaac's a couple of years before—Papa's papa. Everybody came to the church but left right after and went home, no meal and celebration. I wondered about the difference between those two funerals, the first ones I'd ever been to, and if buried in there might be what Uncle Jim meant by tragic mysteries.

It was so hard, thinking about death that night. It was all a mystery to me, and so sad.

Then I thought about the sadness I felt. From the fire and on top of that, not to rebuild but sell our land and move. I wondered if my sadness was the same as came with death, or different.

As we began to walk again Uncle Jim returned to talking about the fire and about promises. I was astonished by what he first said, because he seemed to have read my mind.

"The fire that destroyed your home was an unforeseen tragedy—even a kind of death you might say. But death is not all there is, son. Not for those who die in the hope of our Lord and not after the tragedies of life. I want you to see how new days can dawn even when it looks dark. Even when it's dark and we can't see things clearly, we must keep moving. And part of that means keeping our promises as much as it's in our ability to do so. Keeping our promises is part of the demands of life we can't shy away from—that strange grace that helps move us forward after the tragedies. That's what your papa and mama are doing now.

"You see, son, whether short or long the blessings of life come with the responsibility to steward them, care for them. That's the general unwritten oath we have to God, the promise we make to him. We make unwritten oaths to one another too, simple but binding promises, you see. But sometimes we make written oaths to others that can enrich our lives, formal agreements like when we buy land and houses. We must keep both our unwritten and written oaths.

"Your papa and mama made a written oath when they borrowed against their land to improve it and build the house you and your sisters and brother were born in. They must keep that promise now, even though the house is no longer there.

"Settling our debts is about making good on our promises. To keep their promise your parents must sell their land. To make good on their promise. You, see?"

I listened but the truth is, it was all too much to take in then. I wanted to be grown up, but I could see I wasn't yet. Uncle Jim knew it, of course, but he could see it too; how confused I was. Then he told me a story, one that it became clear he'd planned to tell me.

"I'm going to tell you a story, son, that I think will help you understand.

"My papa, Raford Carroll, who built the old log house, died Tuesday February 26, 1856, right in that big bedroom where you and your papa and mama sleep. He died a young man of only forty-seven years, Claude. That's just five years older than your papa. I know you're only a boy—quite grown up for your age but still very young—but try and understand how young my papa was when he died. That's young, I'm telling you. He and my mama, your Great Grandmother Sarah, had nine children at the time. We buried him in the Evans cemetery just down the road the next day.

"What happened following my papa's death is the story I'm gonna tell you, Claude. It helped me understand the importance of promises."

It was still cold out but not so much as we noticed since we'd been walking for a while.

* * *

"It was especially cold the first Saturday in March of '56. And it'd snowed seven or eight inches overnight," Uncle Jim began. "A lot like now. See? Imagine this is like it was back then."

"My brother, your Great Uncle John, and I were up before dawn, gathering provisions from the barn for the trip and mustering the mules and hitching the wagon.

"After my papa died, my mama had us nine kids to be concerned with and care for. My sister Beth and I had already married and were living on our own by then, but Mama still felt responsible for us—that's how mamas are, you understand; it doesn't matter how old you get, they still feel responsible for you. She had all of us and the farm too, and it had $300.00 of family debt attached to it, much like the debt your papa and mama have on their property. My mama said she didn't want to administer the estate with the debt and got the creditors to agree to give her time to dispense of some property to pay the bill. Alone and without the man she loved and came out west to start a new life and family with, she had to make do all on her own.

"You see, Claude, my mama had all these kids, a farm to manage, and a $300.00 debt to pay—a debt, a promise, my father had made but for which she was now responsible. She had a decision to make.

"We had a span of mules, which mama had gotten in good shape. Thinking about the debt she told me to make plans to find a buyer for them. She knew there was no local market in Seminary Township or in Vandalia or anywhere in Fayette County, so she told me to take my brother John and the mules and go up north and find a buyer.

"We left early that Saturday morning. The wagon was heavy with supplies in case we had to be gone for a while and had the further drag of the mule team following behind. It was slow going in the deep snow, and it was cold.

"See here," Uncle Jim said pulling an old paper from his jacket pocket as we stopped walking.

"I wrote this letter to my niece, Juno, the daughter of your great uncle Bill Evans and my sister Mary who moved to California. In it I told Juno of this trip to sell the mules for the same reason I'm now telling it to you. Juno sent the letter back to me so I could keep it in my storage chest where I have lots of old letters and papers I've collected through the years."

He motioned me to raise the lantern I carried as he read the first lines of the letter.

> The dark blueish hue of a moon-lit night bathed the path with a muted light. As the clanging sounds of the flat wagon cutting crevasses and the rhythmic stomps of the mules broke the

otherwise soft silence of fresh fallen snow on the road, the sun began to breach on their right and slowly paint the sky with a tinge of purple and orange. Morning was breaking on the new day, but it would be a slow rugged trek.

"Letters are good things, Claude," Uncle Jim paused again. I could tell he was back to those days long ago when he wrote the old letter.

"They allow us to remember and be more reflective. And how things make us feel. I remember that's exactly how things looked and felt when we left that early frigid morning. Written down, letters preserve our memories, you see."

Then I paused. Storage chest? I wondered if it's the one just inside the doorway of the cabin. As we began walking again and he returned to the story, I noticed the glow of the lantern before us and saw our breath in the cold air. I'd glance up at Uncle Jim and he'd catch my eye and smile. He was clearly telling me the story, but I could see he was reliving it too.

"It's less than a ten-mile trip from this old homeplace to Vandalia, as you know. Once through town things eased up for us just a bit. But the sixty miles from Vandalia to Taylorville in Christian County were slow, and that stretch at times was treacherous.

"I once heard that President Abraham Lincoln joked that the reason he wanted to move the capital from Vandalia to Springfield was to avoid traveling on that primitive wearisome road, as he called it. He was more than half right.

"Roadways were primitive in those days, Claude. Some were well-worn animal paths that became old Indian trails and then primitive roads, you see.

"Most were simply dirt trails where trees had been cut off—the stumps just low enough to allow a wagon to pass over them. With just John and me traveling, if all went well and we had clear weather, I'd estimated it would be at least a two-day trip up and the same back—but pulling the mules, you never know. That first day the previous night's snow had already slowed us down. Knowing the road well, I recall thinking at the time, going over the stumps would be fine for the wagon, even in the snow, as long as we kept in the middle. But I worried about those lagging mules. We needed to keep them from stumbling, or worse, coming up lame before we could make a sale. That was a fear.

"Things were going better than expected in the deep snow, until about five miles north of Vandalia. The ruts under the snow from an earlier rain, made the wagon sit too low. All of a sudden, we caught a stump. I jerked hard on the reins and the team of two yelled a loud bray and tried to rear.

The harnesses held and the wagon stopped dead—the lagging mules all but came up the back, but they got stopped just in time.

"Once settled, I handed the reins to John and climbed down to survey the situation. We were stuck just on the top of an old elm stump about fourteen inches in diameter. But there didn't appear to be any damage to the back axle—it had caught just the top and because the forward motion was carried up and over just enough to land sitting square in the middle of the old stump, raising the back wheels just off the ground. The question was, how to get it off without damage and free things up to continue the trip.

"I hollered at John to tie the reins tight to hold the team and climb down to help me unload the provisions to lighten the load. After about a half-hour we were ready. John got back up in the wagon, untied and held the reins, and I came along the left side of Daisy, the best trained of the team. I got a tight grip on her collar and mane.

"'Okay, now, and *lightly*,' I said. John gave a small ripple on the reins, and I held Daisy's collar. The two horses tried to move forward, but the wagon didn't budge. John gave another ripple, and this time I pushed against Daisy, and she moved forward, but just a bit. 'One more time, on three . . . One, two, *three*,' John snapped the reins harder this time and I shoved against Daisy and pushed. Then *crack!* There was a big noise.

"The wagon dropped off the stump and the axle remained intact. Just as that happened the team jumped forward, but John pulled back hard and brought 'em to a stop. He tied off the reins again, got down. John and I reloaded the wagon. The whole upshot took a little over an hour and a half. Not much lost time. No damage to the wagon and the mules were in good shape.

Captivated with excitement, I asked, "So what happened next?"

"Well, we'd seen only a couple of stragglers on horseback all day, each passing on the left and right of the road headed south. We made pretty good time headed north. But nightfall was approaching, and it was getting cold again. We needed a spot to make camp. It'd been overcast all day, and it looked like more snow overnight. We needed shelter, for ourselves, the wagon team, and the mules. We figured we'd have to build it.

"We'd looked for a site just outside Ramsey, about thirteen miles north of Vandalia.

"Just as we were weighing our options, we saw an old fellow on horseback coming up from behind. He hollered out good greetings, but in a strong accent that made him a bit hard to understand. We slowed the team to a crawl so we could hear better and exchange proper greetings.

"'Where you headed,' he asked us in broken English.

"Up near Taylorville," I replied, "to find a buyer for our mules.

"'Is that so?' the old man asked. He volunteered that his name was John Hunt, and we told him ours. Then he said something like, 'I know someone up there whose mules might like,' though we weren't quite sure if we heard him right.

"'You fellers like some rest, you could do with some, I expect,' Mr. Hunt said.

"We didn't need to give much of a response, he could see it in our faces.

"'I'm home going,' he said, putting the verb at the end as is customary in the German language we learned. 'Not far up above beyond Ramsey. You can put your team and mules in my barn,' he told us. 'Meine Frau will some cooking made for supper. You a warm place to stay.'

"We needed no translation. John and I gave a quick glance at each other. We knew how fortunate we were. That sounds great! we both exclaimed to Mr. Hunt at the same time.

"We really needed a place to stay that night, Claude. I'm telling you, son, it's amazing how God so often provides what we need just when we need it," Uncle Jim stressed with a broad smile on his face. Once again, I could tell his mind was back when this story happened. He continued:

"John and I looked at each other again. Had the old man said he might have a line on a buyer for the mules? We were pretty sure he did, but his thick accent made us unsure. We sure hoped we understood him right, and we found out at supper that night that we did.

"Meeting old Mr. Hunt was indeed a fortunate turn of events. And everything he said was true. He and his wife Maria were most hospitable— we came to find out this was an expression of their religion. They were Dunkards, we learned, 'a peaceful, industrious people of simple means, and plain appearance,' Mr. Hunt explained. Their people were about the first white inhabitants in this whole area. Their church baptism is always by full dunking, he told us, which accounts for the name. Their German descent made for their strong broken English, and proudly Mr. Hunt felt the need to explain his name, that though their surname sounds of English descent, it's only because their family name Hundt had become shortened to the English version since coming to America. The Hunts were good, simple, but proud people we came see.

"Their place was a small two-room farmhouse, including the kitchen, with an open porch on the front, and a barn. All the meager trappings of a small tenement settlement for sharecroppers. They were warm and hospitable. And the beef stew Mrs. Hunt made for supper was wonderful, especially on a cold night—it reminded us of Mama's. And the two batches of hotwater cornbread she made to go with it were perfect—especially with leftover pieces as dessert lathered with apple butter.

"They could not have treated us better. We slept on the floor in front of the roaring fire in the small keeping room, a lot better than the lean-to we were planning just before Mr. Hunt came along. The fire cracked and popped and made the whole house warm. It was an unexpectedly good night on our travels.

"Early the next morning we woke before the Hunts. With their permission, we fed, watered and readied the team in the barn, and the mules, and we repacked the wagon. Now all we needed was to know where we were going. Mr. Hunt came out to the barn and explained who he thought might have an interest in our mules. 'Old Dickerson Whelpton's place go, to talk,' he told us. 'His farm about fifteen miles up. Just south of Pana,' he pointed north. We took note of what he'd said as we hitched up the team and tied the mules behind. We were ready to leave.

"We thanked the Hunts and offered them as much payment as we could for their generous boarding and hospitality, but they declined and wished us good luck.

"Dawn had already broken when we left. The weather was better that second day, and there'd been no new snow overnight. Though still cold the sun warmed things up as we traveled—and it glistened off the earlier snow, a bit like a diamond-studded carpet. Traveling would be easier that day, we thought.

"By late afternoon we arrived just south of Pana. Using the directions Mr. Hunt gave, we found Mr. Whelpton's farm. We turned in and traveled down the long entrance and finally came to a stop at the barn. A tall lanky man came over and introduced himself as Mr. Whelpton. We introduced ourselves and explained how Mr. John Hunt recommended we stop by. That we'd come up from Seminary Township to try and find a buyer for our mules—that our papa'd died the last week of February and our mama had sent us to find a buyer to settle a debt owed against his estate. We told him Mr. Hunt thought he might have an interest but wasn't sure.

"He did, and we struck a deal. Just like that! Can you believe that Claude?"

I couldn't. My mind was off of everything else by then, how cold it was and even that we were moving. It was so exciting listening to Uncle Jim tell how things worked out on their trip.

"Mr. Whelpton said he'd give us $250.00 but could only pay $50.00 at the time. That he'd be able to pay the rest of the money at Christmas. We agreed. It was an unexpectedly simple, successful day. Mama would be glad, we were sure.

"It was getting late in the day, so we camped the night near Pana and started home early the next morning. Without the mules lagging behind and with good weather, we made it close to thirty miles, all the way back to Vandalia.

"Back in our stomping grounds but late, we stayed the night in town with our good friend young Bill Evans—long before he married my younger sister, Mary.

"When we got home and told Mama how we'd done, she was glad. She felt a big weight lift off, though it wouldn't be fully off till Christmas.

"At Christmastime that year, Mama had me go back for the rest of the money. I rode John's mare, and it was cold. A big snow was on the ground again, but with no wagon or mules, I easily made it to old Mr. Hunt's place. Not surprisingly the Good Dunkards invited me to stay the night again. The next day I rode up near Pana and saw Mr. Whelpton. As he'd promised, he gave me the $200 balance he owed Mama."

Then Uncle Jim said, "So you see, Claude, the task your great grandmother Carroll gave to me and my brother, John, was complete. With the money from the mules and $50.00 from savings she paid the debt and stood good on the responsibility she inherited when my papa died. She could start fresh.

"Here's what I want you to see in this old story, Claude. All of us in life are called upon to stand good on our word, and sometimes even the word of someone else. It's just the right way in life.

"And there's something else here too, son. At times the circumstances of life change suddenly and unexpectedly, and our money debts become too large for us. Then we must hope to be forgiven the remaining debts we cannot pay. This is what happened to your papa and mama. They are selling the land your home was on to pay most of their debt, but it doesn't cover it all. The man they borrowed from is forgiving the rest. This is a second important lesson. As we are forgiven, we in turn should forgive others—including debts they have to us but cannot pay. This is the way of grace, you see. When you owe a debt you cannot pay and it's forgiven by the mercy of another, that's the grace built into the patterns of everyday life. We all need it.

"Living up to our promises is just a part of doing what's right, son— standing good on your word. And part of living up to our promises, at times, is a reminder of the grace we all need and always receive from God in his goodness and providence. And with this reminder, when we see others in need, we'll be ready to be merciful to them as we have received mercy, and to forgive others as we have been forgiven."

Uncle Jim stopped walking. I stopped. He turned to me and softly said, "These are the things I wanted to talk with you about tonight, Claude. I know selling and moving from the only place you've ever known is hard. All losses are hard; they're even a kind of death as I mentioned. But try and understand that your papa and mama are doing what's right. It's hard, for them and for you and your sisters and brother, but it's good and true. And never forget, after a time the fullness of joy will come again—more even than you felt on Hoggin' Day last fall. I know it's hard to see right now, but I promise it'll come again."

Thoughts swirled in my head. As deep as a nine-year-old could, I tried to make sense of what Uncle Jim told me. I couldn't fully back then. But that night I did begin to see that life was bigger than my own feelings. How much bigger I could not imagine—I couldn't know then that Uncle Jim's words were but a glimpse into a rich inheritance bequeathed to me on the journey ahead.

Five—Departure Day

Spring 1905

The winter was long and so different. Even so I wanted it to drag on so we wouldn't go.

Papa and I worked the farm all day every day preparing for planting. And late in the afternoons before dark we'd regularly go by the old place to sort and pack things from the barn that we'd take with us, along with the new things we'd been given by family and friends.

We got the fields ready as part of the agreement Papa made to sell our property, settle our debts, and earn some for the trip.

What we'd sorted and packed was for the prairie schooner wagons. The one we had stored in the barn and one Papa's brother John Howell had—he'd decided to go too. I learned ours and Uncle John's were made for canopies—canvas covers coated with linseed oil called bonnets. We hadn't ever used our wagon like that, with the arched, wooden bows to cover the whole wagon and protect the inside from the weather. Papa assigned me the task of learning to install those bows and the new covers we bought to get the wagons ready for loading.

Spring arrived all too soon. We sold the land our house sat on, and the proceeds from the sale and the small stipend we got for the work we did over the winter allowed Papa and Mama to settle our debt and keep a little. With that and generous family gifts, we had enough for the journey and to get settled down in Texarkana.

I had no idea where that was then, except farther west and down south from us. Someone had told Papa it was a good place to farm near the expanding St. Louis Southwestern Railway Company, nicknamed the "Cotton Belt." It ran through cotton country and offered new options to sell and ship the hay, corn, produce, soybeans, and cotton cultivated on the farms down there. Papa and Uncle John saw it as an opportunity, a good place to restart. I overheard Grandfather Bill tell them that farms in that area had recently grown from about three to four thousand.

I didn't understand that way of thinking then. I couldn't see what they saw—new opportunity in the folds of change.

* * *

The day before our departure day was another big festival at the old Carroll homestead. Everyone in the family living anywhere close was there. It was a beautiful spring day—Mama smiled when she saw that the jonquils had burst into full bloom overnight, from the bulbs she'd planted just after the fire in front of the big old asparagus trees. Some of my cousins moved the big table out in the front yard again, and a feast was spread across it. The little kids ran randomly from pillar to post like startled rabbits. You'd have thought it was Christmas, but it was closer to Easter. It was a jubilant day! The feel of it took me back to autumn on Hoggin' Day.

Early the next day the quietness of the cool early morning made the clatter of the final preparations loud. The wagons were packed and ready. It all felt strange, a mixture of sadness and excitement at the same time. Only Grandfather Bill and Uncle Jim were there to see us off.

Uncle Jim tapped me on the shoulder and said, "Let's take another short walk, Claude."

We headed down by the Fish Pond. That's what we called it—a small lake nestled at the bottom of the wide sloping meadow on Grandfather Bill's property. No snow this time.

"Claude, I know you're torn by having to leave Illinois. To leave the only place you've ever called home can make you feel like you no longer have roots. But I want you to know, that's not so. Your roots will always be here, and they go deep. In this land, in your blood-family that remain here, and in the virtues you've learned here. Don't ever forget that."

We stopped and he looked down at me like he had on our long walk after Christmas. He stooped down and put his big hands on my shoulders. I could see he was earnestly telling me things he believed I should hear, but I could also see he was saying goodbye.

"You're not the first in the family to leave this place and settle somewhere new, Claude. As I mentioned before, my sister, your Great Aunt Mary, left for California when she and your Uncle Bill Evans married—you don't really know them, but you remember me telling you about Bill; he's who my brother John and I stayed with in Vandalia the night we came back from selling those mules. Well, about ten years after that night, he and Mary married and they moved two thousand miles from Vandalia to Taylorsville, California, in Plumas County. About a hundred and fifty miles northeast of Sacramento."

I remember wondering why Uncle Jim told me this again. I now think it was the mixed feelings he had about us leaving just as he had felt when his sister left. I had them too. But I came to see it was more than that. Continuing, he said,

"Bill and Mary didn't move because of a tragedy but for opportunity, you see. Now that your papa and mama have settled things, they look at your move that way. I want to encourage you to see it that way too."

Then Uncle Jim's thoughts seemed to wander off. Thinking back, I recall he often did this when he talked to me, as if he was reliving things that happened long ago. I do that now myself.

"As I'm sure you've heard about, Claude, almost sixty years ago now, back in forty-nine there was a Gold Rush that took lots of folks out to California to try and strike it rich. That year Bill Evans's father James and his brother Jeremiah went out there. Jeremiah settled and stayed. James stayed for a year and then came back to Illinois, but only for a short while. In the early fifties he went back, and on this second trip he took a few others in his family with him, and they settled together out there.

"Those moves were for opportunity, Claude. Some hoped to strike it rich and others to put down roots in the soil of a new place, and in new towns that were growing up.

"In sixty-four young Bill Evans went out to visit his papa, and my brother John went with him. They took the Oregon Trail wagon train from Independence Missouri to Fort Hall, Idaho and then south on the California Trail to Plumas County. My brother was twenty-nine years old then, and Bill was about nineteen, I reckon. It took them more than five months to get there. When Bill came back in sixty-seven, he told many exciting tales about Indians they met along the way and the hardships they endured crossing the plains. That same year he married my sister Mary, and they turned around and headed straight back to California. There they stayed and built a new life and had a family—including Juno, who I wrote the letter about the mules, you recall?

"Not everyone became rich in the California Gold Rush. Very few did, none in the Evans or Carroll families that I know of. But the settlements flourished all across northern California because of it, new townships, mercantile stores, and lots of farms cultivating the fertile land. It was a good place to build a new life, and with hard work, they had a chance to get in on the ground floor of new opportunities. That's what Uncle Bill and Aunt Mary did, along with other family members from Seminary Township.

"Often people move for new opportunities, Claude. Many folks came to this country for opportunities before it was a country, many came for religious liberty, and many out of sheer necessity, a whole host of necessities. There's always a mixture. Life's just that way, you understand.

"I just want you to remember that even from tragic events like your papa and mama's house burning down, new life can come about—good things you might never imagine. I pray your papa, mama, and all of you will find this too. No one can read the mind of Providence, but we can always trust it. From that trust you'll find the strength for endurance.

"So, hold on to your roots in this home place in southern Illinois. But look forward to what's to come—on the trip down and as you start a new life in Texas. It'll be exciting if you allow it. You'll learn a lot along the way and new things when you get there. And there'll be more hard times too, that's just how life is—things that'll test you like fire softens iron to be shaped anew on the anvil, allowing you to become stronger than you were before. But always find the joys of life along the way, especially in the small things. Rejoice in the good times and endure the hard ones. You're almost a man now. This trip will help you become one."

I remember wondering why Uncle Jim told me these things. It wasn't until much later I realized he was not just talking about the move to Texas but about my whole life. Those were big thoughts for a ten-year-old. I'm amazed at how he treated me like a man long before I became one.

What he told me that day became the rhythm of our days on the wagons and in the evenings when we camped. Even how Uncle Jim told his stories, wandering off into different tales at times, became our pattern. I've come to see that's how life itself is, the best laid plans and all. There are always so many twists and turns, just like in the stories we hear and tell.

Continuing, Uncle Jim said, "Get your mama to tell you more about the family, Claude, from the stories I told her when she was young, about my parents, and from the family records I put in the old treasure chest for you.

"I love you son, and so does your Grandpa Bill and the whole family. Be strong for your papa and mama. Help take care of them and your sisters and brother."

I hardly said a word as Uncle Jim talked. Just nodded a few times. Absorbed in what he'd been saying and thinking hard about it, I hadn't noticed we'd walked all the way back to the house. It was time to go.

Uncle Jim held out his hand to shake mine, like a man—the firmness gave me shivers. Still in his grip, he pulled me close and wrapped his strong arms around me. I relaxed into him almost to the point it seemed he was holding me up . . . in my memory I can still smell the aroma of his pipe tobacco. I felt special and safe, assured I had a place even though where I'd live would change.

Grandfather Bill hugged me too. I looked up into his eyes and he mine. "Be a good boy, Claude. Take care of your mama and sisters and brother. And mind your papa."

I nodded yes.

That moment saying goodbye lingered with me. It does even now after all these years. I didn't realize it then, but that was the last time I'd ever see Uncle Jim and Grandfather Bill. The last time I'd hear their voices. I've so often wished I could take another walk with Uncle Jim or work around the old log house with Grandfather Bill. I never did, but what they gave me has never left me. More times than I can count, to my surprise and delight I have discovered what they gave me stored up in my heart—and in this old trunk Uncle Jim gave us when we left.

Papa got Mama, Rachel, Maurine, and Little Bill settled in the back of our wagon. Beth got up top with Papa. I climbed up with Uncle John in his wagon. I remember thinking how big and spacious they were when I first put the canopies on. But all packed up they were like sardines in a can, especially for Mama with Rachel, Maurine, and Bill in the back. For Beth and me up top with Papa and Uncle John, it was wide vistas across an ever-changing painted landscape.

I remember seeing Papa looking at maps spread across the big table with Uncle Jim at Grandfather Bill's the night before. Once settled atop our wagon he pulled one of them out of his satchel and folded it into a square. Looking down at the map then up at Uncle John, he began to describe the whole trip, using his hand vertically and sideways to point out which way we'd go. I'd never been far from home. It seemed strange to me, I recall, when Papa told us how the trip would go.

"We'll head southwest first, to St. Louis," he said then, and interrupting himself, he looked at me with a grin and continued, "the fourth biggest city in the US. There, we'll cross the wide Mississippi on the big old Eads Bridge into the big city and spend the day there to see the sights from the World's Fair they had last year."

When he said that, about spending the day at the World's Fair, Papa really struck a chord. I looked over at Beth. Her eyes looked like saucers, as I'm sure mine did too. We were beyond excited! Excited at the very idea of it. But not because we knew, we couldn't even imagine then.

"We'll camp just west of the city for the night, then head a bit farther west and turn south through the Missouri river basin on the Old Southwest Trail."

Papa said that road would take us all the way to Texas. I had no idea how many tales it had to tell, how many lessons there'd be along the way. I didn't know when we started out, I couldn't have known just how much that trail would become my open road schoolhouse.

"We'll edge on down through Missouri along the forested St. Francois Mountains range rising over the Ozark plateau," Papa continued, "and cross into Arkansas. Following on south through northern Arkansas, when we get just east of the Arkansas river at Little Rock, we'll turn west. From there we'll travel southwest across the southern edge of the Arkansas River Valley over into Hot Springs, then turn almost due south through Arkadelphia, Hope, and Prescott to our new home in Texarkana."

I remember wondering why Papa said all that. I certainly had no idea where any of those places were. I now think he was just rehearsing the journey for himself. Two things stuck out to me, though: how easy Papa said, "our new home," and how long the whole trip sounded.

Then, just as I wondered how long, Papa told us. "It won't take us the five months it took John Carroll and Bill Evans to get to California, but it will take at least two to get to Texas."

I looked out across the meadow of Grandfather Bill's farm. Though it was barely light yet, I could just make out the Fish Pond from the perch of the wagon seat. I remember noticing the glistening morning dew on the grass along the sides of the wagon path, just as Papa and Uncle John rapped sharply on the reins. The two teams lurched with the heavy loads, a milk cow behind each, and that jolted me back into the moment—the last time I'd call Illinois home.

We were off on the slow uneven road—I looked back and waved goodbye. I was so torn. I was with Mama and Papa and my brother and sisters, but my heart was so planted in that familiar place we rolled away from. I wondered if I'd ever know that feeling again?

With the first bump I could feel the hardness of the wooden bench. I knew I'd have butt calluses before the trip was done.

"We'll move at a snail's pace with our packed wagons and little ones," Papa said. "About ten to fifteen miles a day." Not bad for wagons like ours then but not anything like being on horseback or a train. He was just preparing us. "It won't be fast and won't be easy. But it should be a fun adventure." I remember glancing over at Papa and Beth when he said that. He smiled.

In a way I was excited, but my heart had a hard time smiling back at Papa then.

Inheritances, Part Two:
On the Trail to Texas

. . . how good habits of the heart are formed . . .

Spring 1905 to Early Summer 1905

You are your stories. You are the product of all the stories you have heard and lived—and of many that you have never heard.

DANIEL TAYLOR

Six—Cornbread and Apple Butter

The rigors of our trip to Texas were not too different from what Uncle Jim told of when he and his brother John went up to Pana to sell Great Grandmother Sarah's mules. There was always something stopping us, muddy ruts to get out of, things that broke to fix, but we never got caught on a stump like they did. Mama was still nursing little Rachel, and with the two other girls and Little Bill, well, there were plenty of times to go slow or stop and use the bucket and other reasons. Being late spring when we headed out, at least we didn't have snow to deal with. The spring rains and storms were enough, they were heavy and fierce at times.

Despite those normal travails, most nights were good, even if short. Papa and Uncle John would build a fire and Mama would cook up something good in the big old copper pot or in a black iron skillet that had survived the fire. We brought a few roasting chickens and got more along the way when needed, and a rooster and mother hens for eggs—we kept them in crates tied to the outside of the wagons and their never-ending cackling from the jostling of the wagon was a constant chorus on the trail. Grandfather Bill packed us a lot of the pork we'd butchered, heavily salted and wrapped tightly in two layers of cheesecloth. Mama's suppers were most often some kind of stew with pork or chicken mixed with vegetables and potatoes that we also brought. But the real treat was the biscuits or cornbread she always made—my favorite was the cornbread, especially with sweet apple butter lathered on a piece of it for dessert. I remember imagining Uncle Jim doing the same at the Good Dunkards' place on that trip with the mules.

"Mama," I asked after our special dessert the first night of the trip, "do you remember when you first learned to make apple butter?"

She responded excitedly, "Oh yeah, honey!" I could see it in her eyes, she was back to when she was a girl. "I was about your age."

I love to listen to Mama tell stories, and how she tells them. She's so funny sometimes. She began.

* * *

"We made that apple butter out in the yard, the same area just outside the old log house where we did the Hoggin', you see. Right there at Grandfather Raford's old log house where we just left. It was cooked in a deep brass kettle hung between two forked poles, like those Papa and Uncle Jim built to hold the hogs. You see, honey? That's where there'd be a fire built under it. That's where we'd do the cider apple butter.

"It took two days to make it. First, we'd have to pick all those apples. Your Grandfather Bill, he'd go to the cider mill the day before we made the apple butter, with a big load of apples.

"I remember how excited I was the first time I helped pick up the apples to take them to the mill. By the time we were done we'd have two full barrels of cider made.

"Six miles we had to go, down to Mulberry Grove, originally called 'Houston' after old Sarah Houston's father way back, you see. We had to go down there to the mill. And we'd bring that cider home to make the apple butter the next day. By then, you see, the cider was perfectly sweet and not yet fermented.

"Early the next morning we'd fill that big brass kettle, but only after we scoured it with salt. With salt, honey, so it wouldn't be poisoned.

"Papa and the others put that big kettle out—well, I'd say . . . I don't know how much it held. Maybe . . . I don't know . . . maybe thirty gallons or more."

The cadence of Mama's voice made Beth and me smile, I remember. I still love to hear her tell this story.

"They'd fill her up with that apple cider and boil it down till it got nearly as thick as, just nearly as thick as molasses.

"And while it boiled down, me and several others, it took several, you see, to peel and slice those fresh apples, you know. Real thin and put them in there raw. And then that all had to be cooked down again, honey, cooked down again until it was pure apple butter, without any sugar. We'd use a long stir, you see, long enough to sit back from the fire and go deep, you know, to the bottom of that kettle—there were holes in that long stir, so it swishes that thick cider and with the fresh apples, you see, and corn shucks tied to it to rub the sides of the kettle with the long handle.

"Somebody would sit way off and stir the vat with that long handle constantly to keep it from burning, till it was pure apple butter. It was all stirred off about ten o'clock at night. But I didn't stir much."

Mama was proud of it when she said she didn't stir much, like she'd pulled something over on her sisters. I could imagine her doing that. Mama is so mischievous sometimes, still. I could see she was reliving it again when she looked at me and laughed before continuing.

"My sister, your Aunt Dean did most of the stirring back then. She's the one that mostly stirred that apple butter, not me," Mama said with a chuckle.

"Then, well, you know how it's always cold at home, honey? We'd put that fresh apple butter in big open jars, so it wouldn't sour. Those great big twenty-gallon jars and ten-gallon jars. I think that big kettle made about thirty-five gallons when it was stirred off. Well, it got fairly cooked about ten o'clock at night, and that's when we'd put it all in those jars and seal them to be put away in the cold-storage barn."

Proudly again, Mama said, "I didn't do any of that then. Aunt Dean did," giggling as she pointed to the two small pots we brought.

"These right here, you see, these old pots are from that barn. They're full of the last batch of apple butter made before we left. We've got to keep them sealed really good after we use them to keep that butter from spoiling.

"That's the first time I remember helping make that sweet apple butter, honey."

Mama's lighthearted story about apple butter started a whole trip's worth of storytelling on the trail to Texarkana.

As time went along, I realized how important that night was, how important Mama's story was for me. It began to melt my troubled heart—the grief from the fire and of leaving Illinois. It tied me to the old place and opened me up to new things.

Mama's after-supper story that night began our routine. We'd clean up—my chore was washing the pots and plates—the campfire would settle to mostly charcoal embers, but still hot enough for warmth, and Mama would get Rachel, Little Bill, and Maurine down to sleep. She'd sit next to Papa on makeshift stools of old stumps or buckets we brought. He'd light his cigar from a stick in the firepit and the smoke would circle up into the night air, and Uncle John would draw deep on his pipe.

Beth and I would just stretch out on the ground close to the coals. We were always close growing up. Partly because we were only a year-and-a-half apart but also because we did so much together. Except for my cousin Forrest Bone, Beth and I were best friends when we were young. We loved exploring together like we were Daniel Boone and his daughter Jemima in the dense groves of white oak, walnut, and mulberry trees on our farm back home; and catching tadpoles and fishing in a small tributary off the Kaskaskia River that ran through our property. She was a shapely, pretty girl of medium height, with silky smooth skin—Mama always told her that. And she became an elegant, beautiful woman with her shiny long, dark hair.

On clear nights I'd look up and see a million white diamonds on the pitch-black blanket above—some nights they felt so close you could reach up and grab a handful. That's when we talked around the fire. At home on the farm there was always something to do right up to bedtime, so I'd never known this kind of conversation or heard many stories. And the truth is, Beth and I didn't talk much around the grown-ups—that's the way it was back then; kids didn't say much unless asked. We mostly just listened and asked a few questions now and then. I grew to look forward to those talks in the evenings. The Trail was a new experience in so many ways.

Mama's story that night opened the door to my new schooling on the trail. A kind I hadn't known much of but grew to cherish more and more the longer our journey went.

Seven—Widening Horizons

The first ten days of our journey took us on what Papa said people call the extension of the old National Road—what many say is the first highway in America, stretching from Cumberland, Maryland, to Vandalia. But the part we were on wasn't really the National Road, he said. "It's natural people would think so, but it was never finished from Vandalia to St. Louis because of the railroads and the war between the states." After that first night it was slow going and rough. That unimproved stretch left deep ruts of dried mud when we came through—the wagons rocked and jumped from side to side, and we had to be careful. But Papa said it was better than wet mud. Just east of the big city it softened up and flattened out. And it was worth all the struggles.

In every way imaginable, St. Louis was truly amazing!

The closer and closer we got to the wide Mississippi, the bigger and bigger it seemed to be. Papa slowly positioned our wagons behind a gathering crowd of other vehicles, and we started across the wide river on that high Eads bridge—I remember looking over the edge to the swirling currents below and got dizzy.

It took us over an hour to get across, with the dense carriage, wagon, and pedestrian traffic. With all the hustle and bustle, the sounds of the big city grew livelier the farther we went—and became almost deafening when a rumbling roar from a long freight train arose from the tracks below us.

Just as we got to the Missouri side, someone hollered out and laughed at Papa, saying, "If you'd been here in February, you could have driven your wagons right across on the river itself because the whole thing was frozen solid." That seemed impossible to me, I remember thinking, as I looked down at the river again. But it was true, we found out.

For us, though, it was springtime, and everything was in bloom. St. Louis itself was, with so many new buildings built for the World's Fair. Once fully across we found ourselves right in the city center.

I kept turning my head this way and that, I remember—it was like I was in one of those mirrored rooms at the carnival where you get so confused and disoriented. There was all the activity and noise from down on the river wharf below, from all the boats, barges, and industry and commercial trade, and then there was all the busyness, buggy-traffic, streetcars, and people in the center of town where we'd stopped. I'd never seen anything like it. I'd only ever seen Vandalia.

The whole year before we left, every time we went into Vandalia, I remember seeing posters all over town announcing the St. Louis World's Fair. They were colorful, with huge, red, block letters wrapped around a big eye-shaped painting of the new city in the center—like it was looking at you. As intended, they made me dream of going. That's why Beth and I got so excited when Papa said we'd spend the whole day there seeing the sights.

Ever since we'd left home, I thought sitting on the wagon seat put me at a high vantage point. But all the buildings and surroundings swallowed us like we were nothing. The size and speed of everything was beyond my imagination. It felt like we were caught in a whirlwind.

We continued west through the city to a place they called Forest Park, where the big fairgrounds were. Papa motioned to Uncle John to pull over to a horse rail and wagon stop. I got down and tied off the teams—there was a water station with buckets nearby and I filled them and watered Jacob, Sadie, Betsy, and Sam. As I did, I saw a small paper blowing by and grabbed it. It had the same printing and picture I'd seen on the posters back in Vandalia, except it was called "Daily Official Program." I was looking at it when Uncle John climbed down, and Papa got Mama and the other kids down. Papa saw it and asked what I'd found.

"A poster, Papa, of the fair, like I saw back home in Vandalia last year. Except it's not a poster, it's called a program. It says, World's Fair, but then it says, Louisiana Purchase. See here?"

Papa inspected the flyer, handed it back to me. I remember because then he began to explain. That always seemed to happen on our trip, one small thing led to another.

"That's right, son. The fair they had here last year was to celebrate the one-hundred-year anniversary of the Louisiana Purchase."

"What's that?" I asked.

"Well, it happened back in 1803 when President Jefferson bought a big piece of land from France, so big it stretched from New Orleans all the way to Canada. It's that purchase by the US that opened the Missouri and Mississippi rivers and allowed the country to expand west—think about it, we're standing right here at the doorway to the west because of what Mr. Jefferson did a hundred years ago.

"That land purchase was so vast and of such importance, it changed the country overnight—it opened the Mississippi to move crops and goods up and down the river from and to New Orleans, and from there to other parts of America and across the ocean. Many people say it was the most important real estate purchase ever made. I can certainly see why they'd say that."

When Papa told me that, I remember thinking about what Uncle Jim said about land, and how it becomes a part of us—and about the story of selling the mules to settle debt on their mama's land, and how we sold ours to settle the debt on it. Until then, I'd never thought about how important land purchases can be for countries too.

"See, son, the Louisiana Purchase not only got more land for America, but it became the key unlocking the doorway to the west. It's what allowed old Lewis and Clark to start up the Missouri River on their expedition to find a way across the country. You remember Miss Jennie teaching you about Mr. Lewis and Mr. Clark, don't you?

"Yes, sir," I told Papa.

"For a whole year they'd been camped on the river up in Dubois—just a short distance west from Vandalia—waiting until the president made the agreement with France. When the deal was done, they headed off on their famous adventure. Their expedition widened the US and opened settlements to the west, like when Uncle Bill Evans and Aunt Mary went to California."

I didn't quite know what to say, so I don't think I said anything. My bottom had barely come to life again from sitting so long on those hard wagon boards, and we hadn't yet taken a step. Already my head was spinning from the sights, sounds, stories, the connections.

The Louisiana Purchase opened a new world west for America and St. Louis was opening a new world to me.

When we arrived in St. Louis that spring of '05, the official fair was over. It had ended in December. But there was still a lot to see at the exhibit halls, just not as many people as before. And there was a new Education Museum that had just opened.

Right after I'd tied off the wagons and talked to Papa, a fancy-dressed man approached us. He welcomed us to St. Louis and introduced himself, saying he'd seen me looking at the program, and he handed Papa a bigger program that explained all the exhibits—I still have it, here. As it turned out, the man was one of the directors of the fair. We all stood and listened as the man spoke excitedly about it, like he was selling something. But he sure knew a lot. I remember it as if it happened yesterday. He took us around and talked about everything.

He said world's fairs go way back, but the St. Louis Fair was the biggest, saying over twenty million people came through the gates and the buildings we stood in front of. I couldn't even conceive of that many people, especially not in one place.

"World's fairs allow people who may never go out of this country to see the world," he said, "because the world comes to them." For us that was certainly true. The whole new changing world had come to St. Louis! And we were standing right in the center of it.

"The St. Louis World's Fair and the Olympics last summer not only did that, but it showed America's growing standing in the world—and advancements on all fronts in civilization, government, military strength, industry and especially modern science."

To show how important the Fair was, the man told us the boyhood cabins of President Lincoln and President Roosevelt were brought to the celebration. That was really interesting to me, because I remembered Miss Jennie telling our class that Mr. Lincoln lived in Vandalia for a time, when the capital was there, and Uncle Jim had mentioned him too when he told the story about selling the mules.

The man showed disappointment when he said that President Roosevelt himself didn't make it to town for the official opening—which, he said, had originally been scheduled in '03, the anniversary year of the Louisiana Purchase. But he got excited again when he said,

"The president *did* open the Fair, though! From all the way in Washington with the new wireless telegraph to showcase a major theme of technology."

Besides celebrating the one hundredth anniversary of the Louisiana Purchase, the man wanted us to know the Fair showed America's growing stature around the world—pointing to the many exhibits drawn from the recent American military success in putting down "the Philippine insurrection," he said.

I had no idea then what that meant, but it was interesting. His whole spiel was.

The fancy-dressed man went on and on about what he called the "international aspect" of the fair and what he called the new advancements in the human sciences.

"See those buildings there? They show the advances in civilization marking the ethnic and cultural differences, in the Anthropology Days and Human Zoos exhibitions, and Special Olympics. They show the differences between primitive peoples—like the Negritos and Igorot natives brought here all the way from the Philippine Islands—and civilized peoples. These showcase the broader US pursuits of the new science of eugenics."

I was confused even then by that word, *eugenics*, and what he called the new human sciences. I had no idea what it all meant. I wouldn't for decades. But forty years later the whole world came to know what it meant in unimaginable horror! The St. Louis World's Fair was at a pivotal moment in time. So much new and so many possibilities—so many things that have brought so much good. But that one the man spoke proudly of led to great evil. I'm reminded of Grandfather Bill's wise saying, "Just because you *can* do something doesn't mean you *should*."

The man directed us as we walked. I remember staring at all the huge white marble buildings, the canals, and lights—even lit in the daytime. I had truly stepped into a different world. The possibilities seemed endless that day we entered St. Louis. Papa urged Beth and me to see how the Fair showed man's ability to cultivate and make the world better. Cultivate, a word I remember Uncle Jim used—a responsibility we have to build, grow, and care for things.

Papa pointed to a big sign. "See, the Fair's overall theme was Technology and Education."

Seeing the words so big on the sign, *Technology and Education*, I wondered to myself.

The Fair was full of new inventions—marvels like the new private automobiles, outdoor electric lighting, wireless and radiophones, X-ray machines, a whole host of new scientific agriculture and farming techniques and tools, and foods from across the United States and all over the world. All of these were new to us. None of us could take it all in or make sense of it all.

As we walked around from place to place, Papa told me St. Louis was a major center of a new industry that was coming about in America. And that includes new ways of thinking about education. The man pointed at *The Palace of Education*. "See there, a teacher named Miss Amelia Meissner leads tours there, in the new museum. The tours are for both grown-ups and kids. You should go." Mama and Papa thought it was a good idea, so we did. It was amazing.

Inside there were what they called living classrooms, with kids doing their lessons right there in front of us as we walked by. In one room, the lady said they learned about those new X-rays, and in another they reenacted the Spanish-American War with toy battleships. I was mesmerized, seeing so many new science things and hearing about far-away wars.

I always did the lessons Miss Jennie had given me, even then on our trip. I liked school and learning, I always had. But seeing the stuff in the education museum and seeing the big city and learning about all the new things made me thirst for more. When it came time to go, Papa had to tug my hand—more than once. I didn't want to leave. At that moment, I wanted to learn everything in the world. For a moment, I forgot about the purpose of our trip.

"I think Claude's in a trance," I remember Mama saying. She was right.

As we left the education museum and before we headed out of town, we stopped at some modern outhouses—like none I'd ever seen, what they called commodious toilet rooms. *How strange*, I thought. They were part of the new technology featured at the Fair. Shaking his head when he came out, Uncle John blurted out, "Even the damn privies are new here." We all laughed about the new outhouses.

We'd barely been gone ten days and a whole new world had opened up to me. It seemed like a dream, but so much bigger than the fleeting one I'd had when I saw the posters back home in Vandalia. But it wasn't a dream. It was all real. It's impossible to describe how big that day was for me.

As we prepared to leave, Mama saw a woman selling some kind of food in a little cart and stopped to talk to her, and Papa picked up a copy of the *St. Louis Post-Dispatch*. None of the rest of us noticed at the time or thought anything of it.

Everyone was extra quiet as we left the big city. Our minds were aswirl, a time for thinking more than talking. I even felt a touch of sadness—not in the same way as when we left home, but a good kind. I remember I kept twisting my head back over the side of the wagon—to catch another glimpse at what was like a keyhole into a world I'd never known.

We headed west toward Springfield on the old Butterfield Overland Mail route and set up camp about two miles outside town. In a place called Webster Groves, originally a Spanish territory, then a French one known as Dry Ridge, Papa said, a fur trading village along Shady Grove Creek. While St. Louis had become an urban industrial hub, Webster Groves was then still a small hamlet, separated from it but almost part of the big city.

* * *

St. Louis was the most extraordinary experience I had yet had in my young life. The impressions it made on me were permanent. I was sure that's all we'd talk about for days.

But once we settled that night and Mama made a small supper and got the younger ones down, the new rhythm of conversations around the fire began. We did talk about St. Louis and the Fair, but as conversations go, that night it began one place and wandered to others.

As we all talked about the day, Papa began reading the newspaper he got. He interjected:

"Listen to this, John," Papa said, referring to a small story in the *Post-Dispatch*. "It's about a Russian revolution called Bloody Sunday." It began, Papa said, on a Sunday earlier in January that year when troops in St. Petersburg in Russia fired on a crowd led by a priest trying to get the attention of the Czar. I'd never heard that word before. Papa said it referred to the Russian king named Nicholas II. He read on, that the crowd had gone to the king's summer palace to raise attention to what the paper said was "the plight of peasant workers and other things that resulted from a war between Russia and Japan and new industrialization."

They called it Bloody Sunday, Papa said, because Russian troops killed so many of the protesters. That triggered huge political and social unrest by the masses throughout the Russian Empire. Some against the government and some against new industries.

It all sounded strange to me, then. How could something so far away have anything to do with us? How could anything be more important than St. Louis and the World's Fair? Papa'd made connections between other events I didn't easily see, and Uncle Jim had done it too. But talk of a remote Russian revolution that night by the campfire was confusing.

As I think about it now, that small story is the first time I caught a shadowy glimpse of how very distant, faraway, and seemingly unrelated events can be connected to me. Not Papa nor anyone else then had any sense of just how much that seedling event would affect the world.

Papa saw my confusion and tried to explain.

"The importance of this small newspaper story is about how the world changes, Claude. Sometimes in good ways and sometimes bad. Some even leading to war. Think of it this way. Going through St. Louis today and seeing all exhibits at the Fair showing the changes in industry, technology, and education was like walking through a big newspaper article. We saw how the world is changing before our eyes in so many good ways. But nobody yet knows what might be the downside of that change, you see? This small newspaper article about Russia shows how there's always tradeoffs. It shows how the world right now is struggling with the benefits and tradeoffs of this kind of change."

I sort of understood but not really. I asked Papa if I could keep that St. Louis paper. I stuffed it in this old trunk, a practice that became a habit of mine following after Uncle Jim.

Papa continued to talk about how the world is changing. Change is what's taking us down to Texarkana, he said. That even though our change started by a tragedy, it could lead to new opportunities and a fresh start with the new railroad hub down there, he said.

"We're trying to take advantage of the benefits of these changes, you see, son. There'll be new ways to ship from Texarkana. It's sort of like how the Louisiana Purchase opened the Mississippi and Missouri to new places and opportunities out west. The kind Uncle Jim told you about that took Uncle Bill and Aunt Mary to California. We're going to make a new start in Texas, like my grandparents did when they came to Fayette County. You understand, son?"

Abruptly, what Papa said shifted my focus. His grandparents coming to Fayette County? That was new to Beth and me both. I asked, "Your grandparents, Papa? They came to Fayette County to start new?" Our conversation took off in another new direction that night.

Seeing he'd piqued my interest Papa told us some about how the Howell side of the family came to Illinois. How his father, Grandfather Isaac, met his mother, Margaret, and how their parents got to Illinois.

As soon as he mentioned Grandfather Isaac and Grandmother Howell, my mind went straight back to the talk Uncle Jim and I had, about how sad Grandfather Isaac's funeral was and how much of a celebration Grandmother Howell's funeral was. I remember wanting to, but I couldn't bring myself to ask Papa about his father's death. Papa continued:

"Well, yes, Claude, they did. Both sides of my family came to Illinois for a new start. But your Grandfather Isaac and his parents were already in Illinois when my mama, your Grandmother Howell, moved there with her father. Her father, my Grandfather James Dugan, moved to Seminary Township from Portsmouth, Ohio—that's where Mama was born, you see, in Portsmouth. Grandfather Dugan—Dugan was Mama's name before she married my papa, you see—well, Grandfather Dugan got to Ohio from West Virginia with his father, who'd gone there from Maryland before the Revolutionary War.

"My papa's parents, Grandfather William Howell and my Grandmother Rebecca came to Seminary Township from Tennessee, where she was born in 1808.

"So, you see, kids, almost everybody in this country came from somewhere else. And once here, moved again, most folks more than once. Lots of folks in our family have moved places for a new start. We're doing the same. Right now, we're living through the change we saw in St. Louis. That's just part of life."

Beth and I listened and were fascinated. I didn't know it then, but even the year that Great Grandmother Howell was born would become another connection later.

I'm not sure if we'd never heard any of that or just never listened. With just that short family story, I began to feel the roots of family grow like Uncle Jim said would happen on our journey. And I began to see that moving to a new place to start a new life could be a part of those roots.

So much to take in, I remember. The whole day had been awash with new things to think about, and that night too.

Then all at once Mama interrupted, starting with a laugh. It was just what we needed to end the night.

"Enough with all that talk. I have a story, a funny one about those new motor wagons we saw in St. Louis, automobiles they're calling them. I remember when I was in town in Vandalia last year," she said excitedly.

"There was a man from Michigan, his name was Ford. He came to town from Detroit with a car named after himself, a "Ford Model A" car he called it. He brought that motorized buggy to Vandalia on the train. Oh boy, was that a fascinating day. I was with Papa, your Grandfather Bill. Your papa wasn't with us. That man, he took different ones riding in that buggy. And when he came back from one of those rides that day and they got out, that new car caught fire and burnt down right there in the middle of the street. That man was so upset when his new car caught fire and burned up.

"I felt bad for him, that man and his new motorcar, but it was kinda funny too."

Mama's eyes glistened as she told that story. Innocent but with a sly malicious grin as she talked of the car catching fire. She started to chuckle, then broke into a full laugh, throwing her head up, saying, "That car . . .," and Papa began to laugh, then Uncle John, then all of us. It was so much fun.

Mama has always had a way of seeing through things. Just like Papa, she saw how the world was changing, and she also saw the two-edged sword of it all—to her mind perfectly illustrated by Mr. Ford's unfortunate but hilarious car fiasco. But she also saw we all needed to settle down and get some rest. She knew we had a long way to go.

It'd been a whirlwind of a day, and we were all bone tired. Mama and Papa got in our wagon with my sisters and brother. Uncle John in his. And I curled up under a blanket by the fire.

As the logs crumbled into an amber glow, my eyes grew heavy. Then, strangely, I saw another amber glow, a hovering light emanating from the big city. Something I'd never seen before—from those new outdoor city lights. *Wow!* I thought. How my world had grown in a day.

I stared up at the stars made faint by the glow from the distant city light and drifted off to sleep.

Eight—Hidden Treasures

The coffee Mama had cooking smelled good.

I crawled out from the warm wagon where I'd moved during the night. Beth, Maurine, and Bill followed just after. Our feet had barely hit the ground when Mama said it'd been over a week, and we had to bathe. We'd have normally done it the day before, but we missed because of the full day we spent in St. Louis. Papa and Uncle John had already been in the shallow slow-moving section of Shady Grove Creek where we camped. Uncle John had kept Rachel while Papa watched over Mama as she waded to the edge and took what she called a spit bath. Papa'd brought a bucket of water and filled the large copper pot, where he'd warmed it a bit over the fire and took it off. Mama had just started giving little Rachel her bath.

"Claude," Mama hollered at me while bobbing Rachel up and down in the pot along with an imperative glance at Beth, "you and your sister take Maurine and Bill down to that creek and get cleaned up—not too deep." Nodding at a bucket hanging on the side of our wagon, she said, "Take some of that lye soap with you and that rag and scrub yourselves clean—make sure you do the same to your brother and sister."

Maurine and Bill took off running, and when we caught up, we all got naked and waded in. It was so cold, but it felt good to wash off the trail dust and the soot from the St. Louis factories. I washed Li'l Bill's back and Beth did Maurine, then we each washed ourselves. As we rinsed off, I heard high-pitched screaming and turned and saw Maurine's and Bill's hands flailing wildly, splashing each other in the cold water—that says about all there was to tell about them when they were young: naturally happy-go-lucky, always full of joy; I've often wished I had more of that tendency, but they bring it out in me. Then like bullets from a gun, they took off, naked as jaybirds headed back toward camp as Beth and I scurried out to catch them, but they were too fast. Still holding Rachel, Mama grabbed them both at once as they came flying by, almost knocking her down. She wrapped them both in

58

one big flour-sack towel and pitched one to Beth and me as she dried them off. Papa took Rachel, and Bill and Maurine fidgeted while Mama put their drawers on. Beth and I put ours on and the rest of our clothes next to the fire. It was a fresh new day.

Clean and reclothed, we gathered around the fire pit and Mama gave us some pan-drop biscuits she'd made—they were big, probably three inches across. And hot, I could see the steam rising when she took them out of the pan. She gave each of us one with butter and sorghum molasses slathered all over them. Man was that ever good. So good we all got messy and had to wash up again, our hands and faces at least.

Papa got out the big family Bible, singed on the edges from the fire, and called us together for our Sunday morning time—an occasional custom that'd developed since we could no longer attend Corinth Baptist back home.

Papa gave a brief introduction to the story we were about to hear, opened the big book, and began to read.

"This is a story about a man who was an outsider," Papa said, "not a part of the accepted circle of the Jewish religious people. Another man had gotten hurt, not just hurt but beat up and thrown in a ditch for dead and the Samaritan helped him. It's a story from Luke chapter ten.

> And, behold, a certain lawyer stood up, and tempted him, saying, Master, what shall I do to inherit eternal life?
>
> He said unto him, What is written in the law? how readest thou?
>
> And he answering said, Thou shalt love the Lord thy God with all thy heart, and with all thy soul, and with all thy strength, and with all thy mind; and thy neighbour as thyself.
>
> And he said unto him, Thou hast answered right: this do, and thou shalt live.
>
> But he, willing to justify himself, said unto Jesus, And who is my neighbour?
>
> And Jesus answering said, A certain man went down from Jerusalem to Jericho, and fell among thieves, which stripped him of his raiment, and wounded him, and departed, leaving him half dead.
>
> And by chance there came down a certain priest that way: and when he saw him, he passed by on the other side.
>
> And likewise a Levite, when he was at the place, came and looked on him, and passed by on the other side.
>
> But a certain Samaritan, as he journeyed, came where he was: and when he saw him, he had compassion on him,

And went to him, and bound up his wounds, pouring in oil and wine, and set him on his own beast, and brought him to an inn, and took care of him.

And on the morrow when he departed, he took out two pence, and gave them to the host, and said unto him, Take care of him; and whatsoever thou spendest more, when I come again, I will repay thee.

Which now of these three, thinkest thou, was neighbour unto him that fell among the thieves?

And he said, He that shewed mercy on him. Then said Jesus unto him, Go, and do thou likewise."

I had always stumbled over the thees and thous of the King James Bible—though since Miss Jennie had us read from it regularly as part of our English lessons, I'd gotten better. But I didn't know who the Samaritans and Levites were. I hardly knew what a priest was—I only knew that because a schoolfriend of mine called his preacher a priest; his family was Lutheran and came to Vandalia as part of a German Lutheran colony way back around the time the Evans family settled in the area. But as Papa read slowly and stopped now and again to explain a few things, my confusion gave way to some new understanding.

"Jesus is talking about who we consider our neighbor. And the truth is, everyone is our neighbor, even if we don't know them, whether they're part of or from our area or not, or even if they look or talk different than us. This is a good thing for us to think about now on our trip to Texarkana, because we're going be strangers to the people we meet along the way, and they'll be strangers to us until we get to know them. We ought always to be neighborly to folks, and that means we should help them out when we can, even doing good to folks in need when others walk on by. Even if someone looks down on you for helping folks different than you."

I remember distinctly Papa saying how Rev. Barber back home told him it's not just about us being neighborly to others. It's also about how easy it is not to see the needs of others because we're too busy or we think other people's problems are not our problems—when we just don't notice. In that story, Papa said, Jesus showed how the Samaritan man did notice.

"The man who people in Jesus's circle considered unclean; the Samaritan, you see. He noticed and stopped to help the so-called clean man—the Jewish man in the ditch—when those of his own people didn't. The Samaritan is the one who was being the neighbor, doing the right thing. The unclean man helped the clean man who his own people should have helped but didn't. They walked on by. And the man in the ditch accepted help from the outsider. You see, when someone needs help, really needs help, he doesn't care who gives it to him, he just wants help. The Samaritan is an example of how everyone should be. It's so easy just not to notice."

Saying it out loud but sort of like he was talking to himself, Papa said it again, "It's so easy just not to notice." He stared into the fire and repeated, "So easy . . .," and got quiet.

I couldn't get the Samaritan off my mind; off what Papa said, and how struck he was at how easy it is to be like the priest and Levite in the story and how hard to be like the Samaritan.

Papa gave a little prayer and said church was done. We quenched the fire with water and dirt and loaded things up to head out. We had a long day ahead of us and a much longer way still to go through southern Missouri, down through Arkansas and across to Texarkana.

* * *

I'd switched and rode with Papa and Mama in their wagon and Beth was with Uncle John. Papa gave directions again. He said it would take us a week to go the seventy miles from Webster Groves to Farmington on the upper Southwest Trail—"the old Natchitoches Trace long used by Indians, and what some called the Old Military Road because of some improvements made by the army during Andrew Jackson's presidency," he said. From Farmington we'd go farther south just east of the Irish Wilderness to Greenville before heading into Arkansas.

Hearing what Papa said, as soon as we got under way, I started in asking questions.

"So it's called the Southwest Trail, but it was an Indian trail, Papa?" I asked.

I'd hardly gotten the words out when Papa pointed at the old chest Uncle Jim gave us and told me to grab the leather satchel stuffed in the front. "Unwrap it," he said. It held a bunch of papers and old maps to help us make the trip. "Right there," Papa declared.

"See there? That piece. It's Uncle Jim's paper about the Kaskaskia Indians. They're the people the first state capital of Illinois was named for before it moved to Vandalia—one of the Illiniwek tribes who gave Illinois its name. That tells about this trail, now called the Southwest Trail but what some folks still call the trail of tears—that's what the Cherokees and other tribes called it. See right there?

Pointing at some letters on the page, Papa said, "See those letters there, nunahi-duna-dlo-hilu-i? I can't say it. Maybe you can."

I remember looking at the letters. I couldn't pronounce the words then and can't now.

"Old Mr. Creely, a friend of Uncle Jim whose family was from the Kaskaskia area, told him those letters mean 'the trail where they cried,' now just called trail of tears.

"Read there, Claude, read what Uncle Jim wrote."

> The name came to be associated with the Indian Removal Act signed into law by President Jackson in 1830 that moved the Cherokee, Chickasaw, Choctaw, Muscogee, and Seminole tribes from their native lands to reservations in the Oklahoma Territory. Ol' Davy Crockett strongly opposed the Indian Removal Act when he was a Tennessee congressman, and its passage and continuation led him to leave Washington, even leave the United States for the "wildes of Texas," as he put it. He did and died at the Battle of the Alamo in 1836.

"Isn't that interesting, Claude?"

"It is Papa . . . but . . ."

The sounds of the rolling wheels cracked underneath us; the wagon shifted and bumped until we reached our slow and steady pace again. Papa heard my hesitation. He asked, "What is it son, what's on your mind; is there something you don't you understand?"

"No, I mean . . . but what about the Indians and their land? Uncle Jim told me how important the land is, that I'll have roots in Illinois even though we've moved. Isn't the land important? And what about Davy Crockett deciding to go to the wilds of Texas?"

"Well, yes, son, the land is important. It was and still is, for us and for the Indians. There's something about land. When you live on it, work it, and it sustains you, it gets in your soul. You will always have roots in Illinois and particularly in Seminary Township. That's why it's so hard to leave it like we've done. That's why the Indians call this the trail of tears. When they were forced to move from their homelands, and walk to their new land in Oklahoma, they lost part of themselves—many even lost their lives.

"I wasn't around then, but if I was, I think I'd have been on Davy Crockett's side."

"What about Davy Crockett? I remember Miss Jennie telling us about him, about how he was the King of the Wild Frontier, and about his stand with Jim Bowie and his big knife at the Battle of the Alamo in Texas. That story's the first I ever heard about Texas."

"Yes, that's such a great story, isn't it, son, the Alamo? I've always liked it too. They were famous and brave men, and all who fought with them there.

"But before Davy Crockett went to Texas, he was a Congressman from Tennessee. And he and President Andrew Jackson got crossways over the Indian Removal bill that Jackson proposed, and Congress was considering. Jackson and Crockett knew each other from when Jackson was an army general before he became President. Davy Crockett served under General Jackson in the Tennessee Territory militia. After the second British war in 1812, Jackson along with some Cherokee and Creek Indian volunteers, led the militia against a small group of renegade Creek Indians called Red Sticks who'd massacred hundreds of settlers, mixed-blood Creeks, and militia at Ft. Mims in Alabama. Crockett volunteered with the militia to help chase down those renegade Red Stick Creeks. His wild frontier tracking experience helped find them in the swamps of Louisiana. Rather than capturing them, though, Jackson ordered a massacre of the Red Sticks. Crockett strongly disagreed with Jackson and told him so. But General Jackson told Crockett to follow orders or face the consequences. It's said it was a real standoff. The general threatened to shoot Crockett on the spot. Against his conscience he followed orders. This was their first disagreement over Indian treatment. And it came up again years later when Davy Crockett served in Congress, when he disagreed with the Indian Removal Act.

"You see, son, even though Davy Crockett saw it right to chase down those Indians who'd massacred a bunch of folks at Ft. Mims, he saw it as wrong to massacre them once they caught them. Old Davy Crockett had a compass in his conscience, a way of seeing right and wrong even in matters of war. That time in the swamps with Jackson shaped Davy Crockett's views about how the Indians should be treated. So when Congress passed the Indian Removal Act, Davy Crockett couldn't stomach it and left and went to Texas."

"Oh, wow Papa, that's so fascinating . . . so fascinating. I never knew that. But what about the Indian's land and this trail of tears?"

"My goodness, Claude, you're just a fount of questions, aren't you?

"It's a complicated story, the relations between the Indian and the White Man. In many ways the Indians helped America to be born, in the Revolution and with land as we moved west. But there was also war between the Indians and the White Man—wars really, not just one, in different places, with different tribes, at different times, like those Red Sticks and Indians who sided with the British in the war of 1812. But there were treaties too, a bunch of them with many different tribes, treaties that allowed Indians and white folks to live mostly in peace. But some of the treaties were broken too—on both sides, by different American presidents, like Jackson, and like those Red Stick Creeks and the tribes who made a compact with the British against America in 1812. Deep divisions came about. Many Americans wanted the Indians moved out so they could settle new western lands. And some Indians didn't want any white man at all on their land, and continued to fight against it, and brutally. The US government did the same.

"As with most wars, memories are long. For real peace to exist, folks must learn to forgive—even if not forget. If they cannot bitterness gnaws and festers, and unbridgeable differences set in, like those between the priests and Levites and the Samaritans.

"You see, son? But just like with the Samaritan man who walked across the street, bridging the long abiding differences to help someone not of his own kind, it doesn't have to be that way. People can learn to do the right thing even when it's hard.

"Well, I'm on a rabbit trail now, a big one. I'll just say, if I'd been around back then, I'd have likely been on Davy Crockett's side, especially with the treaties. We should have kept ours. Promises are important, like Uncle Jim told you. If we had kept ours, and the Indians on their part too, who knows? The conflicts that lingered in various places might have been avoided.

"Anyway, about this trail we're on, imagine how many feet have trod this ground before us. It has been a trail of tears for some and an opportunity for others, as it is for us now."

It was hard for me to imagine. As I think back on that conversation now, it was for me an extension of St. Louis, a cascade of new perspectives on the past emerging into the present and an example of the extraordinary complexities of this world.

After the stories, I remember I chuckled to myself, not at the stories but what happened when I asked a simple question. Papa saw it, and he asked, and I told him . . .

"All that from a question about the name of this trail, huh, Papa?" I laughed out loud when I said it, and Papa did too.

"I guess questions are like pulling a string of yarn. Better watch out, son, you never know how big the ball is and how many different strands are wrapped in it."

My head was spinning again as it had in St. Louis. We would hardly roll two feet in those old wagons before I'd discover something else new and amazing.

The old trail that had so many tales to tell followed the natural break between the Ozark mountains to the west and the Mississippi River delta to the east, where there was a patchwork of forested bottomlands with cypress-tupelo swamps, and oak and hickory like at home, plus willow trees. And the wildlife we saw was plentiful, with many kinds of birds.

Papa and Uncle John pointed them out, and Beth and I played a game trying to name each one of them along the way. On the prairies east of the stone-capped ridges, we saw hundreds of scissor-tailed flycatchers and lots of bob-white quail, pheasant, and turkey. On rare occasions we saw the beautiful painted-bunting and many warblers, vireos, woodpeckers, owls, and other forest birds. We saw lots of birds of prey winding and surveying the landscape for their next meal, and occasionally even bald-eagles and osprey.

One day as we passed along the St. Francis River, we saw one of those osprey dive from a hundred feet up into the middle of it and rise like a dragon with its catch.

At dawn and in the evening twilight, we saw herds of deer, and on occasion coyotes—we definitely heard their haunting lilt every night. We saw red foxes and bobcats, and late at night raccoons and opossums. Once I saw a badger capture a field rat he'd dug up from his burrow. And another time a pair of beavers built a dam on a spring-fed stream—it was to create a pond, Uncle John said, and make a home to protect them from the coyotes, wolves, and mountain lions.

Late one afternoon after we camped near Farmington, Papa let me take a good-sized mule deer with the old Winchester centerfire Grandfather Bill gave us for the trip. We dressed and butchered it for stew meat and some backstrap, ribs, shoulder, rump, and venison steaks. Packed in salt and wrapped in cheesecloth, like the pork we brought from home, this took us quite a ways on our journey.

I'd hunted with Papa many times back home and saw lots of birds and animals, both in the wild and on the farm. But the days on the Southwest Trail were richer somehow. The new scenery and critters opened new places and revealed a world I'd never really paid attention to before, one teaming with life, and with death.

Those days were special. I've so often thought about that devotional Papa gave about the Samaritan, and when he had me get the old paper Uncle Jim wrote about the Indians and Davy Crockett. I began to see this big old trunk as more than a place to store the Bible, old papers, some guides for our trip, and my schoolbooks. I came to see it as a treasure chest, as Uncle Jim had called it when we left, and to see our trip as an adventure.

As we came down through dark forested bottomlands of the river delta one day, my ten-year-old mind imagined we were on a special journey through foreign lands, carrying sacred cargo. Well, what we carried was not sacred treasure as most people think of it. But as the days gathered on our journey, for me the cargo we carried and the places we saw did hold hidden treasure.

Nine—Cain and Abel

At Farmington Papa moved the treasure chest back to Uncle John's wagon. I needed it for my schoolbooks, and who knew what else. I rode with Uncle John till we got to Arkansas, almost two full weeks—two weeks that were so important in my education but still haunt me to this day.

Most days I'd become accustomed to reading and doing lessons up top on the hard plank flat-board seat—I'd learned to put a blanket under me by then, a comforting provision for my backside. One day I was reading Mr. Eggleston's *Book of American History* again and saw a section about Mr. Lincoln and what the book called the Great Civil War.

I'd thought about war ever since St. Louis and that night afterwards around the campfire, and again when Papa and I talked about the Indian wars and the trail of tears. Mr. Eggleston made me especially interested in the Civil War in America—and more about Mr. Lincoln:

> Soon after Abraham Lincoln became president there broke out a civil war, which caused the death of many hundreds of thousands of brave men and brought sorrow to nearly every home in the United States. Perhaps none of those who study this book will ever see so sad a time. But it was a brave time, when men gave their lives for the cause they believed to be right. Women, in those days, suffered in patience the loss of their husbands and sons, and very many of them went to nurse the wounded, or toiled at home to gather supplies of nourishing food for the sick soldiers in hospitals.

Reading this, my imagination took me far away to people, places, and events I'd never thought of, and triggered my two-week-long conversation with Uncle John about war.

The more I read, the more the Great Civil War sounded terrible. *War?* People killing each other, so many hurt and crippled for life. It was the first time I'd ever thought about war involving real people. I tried to imagine that war in Russia, that place so remote that Papa'd read about, where neighbors killed neighbors in the same country. And then to read about people in America doing the same thing during the Civil War. Back and forth my mind went, from those Russians to those in the Civil War.

As we broke camp at Farmington, I picked up a smooth, small, but heavy pinkish-gray stone speckled with what looked like shards of dark glass in it. As I rubbed it and looked close at it, Papa broke my attention, hollering, "Okay kids, let's go." I stuck the rock in my pocket and climbed up on Uncle John's wagon.

I pulled out the rock and was rubbing it unconsciously as I continued reading about the Civil War. Uncle John saw me, and asked,

"Whatcha got there Claude?"

"Oh, just a rock I picked up. I think it's interesting. It's hard, real hard but kinda sparkly too. Looks like it's got broken pieces of dark glass buried in it. See?"

"I do, son. It's a nice stone, don't you think?"

"I do, Uncle John."

"What are you reading?"

"I'm reading Mr. Eggleston about Mr. Lincoln and the Civil War in America."

Just as I answered him, Papa hollered out, directing which way we'd head—a bit farther east from where we'd camped, where the stone-crowned cliffs were, then we'd turn due south.

It was quiet again after the exchange, except for the squeak of the wheels, the jostling carriage, and chirping birds. I grabbed my hat from the back for shade and went back to reading.

Unaware at that time, I could not have known then, I was taking my first steps into the dense dark maze of the world of war and of the human heart.

I remember that morning so well. Confused, I looked up from the book and turned to Uncle John. What came next was so much better than the book.

"Uncle John," I asked, "can you tell me about war and the Great Civil War?"

He looked at me and paused, "Hmmm?" then said, "Yeah, sure, I can tell you some things, Claude. It's a complicated story with lots of dimensions. You know what that means, dimensions?" I didn't then. Uncle John said, "It's like a house with lots of different rooms."

I remember his eyes when he said that. I could see I'd pulled on another string of yarn, probably a long one with lots of shorter ones tied into it.

* * *

"Well, let's see," Uncle John queried to himself. "There's lots to think about when it comes to war, especially the Civil War, but we've got time. Close your book there, and we'll talk about it.

"I guess I'd have to say first, war is terrible, any war. It's about the worst thing human beings can do to each other. War's a last resort, or it should be—we should be slow to go to war, with each other and as a country. Everyone I know on both sides of our family has always taken that view. Best to remember that as you grow up and try and live that way.

"But the hard truth is, Claude, war's been with us ever since Cain killed his brother Abel. Sadly, I'm afraid, it won't go away until the fullness of redemption comes.

"So, despite all attempts to avoid it, war is forced upon us at times. When it is and when it's a just cause as best we can know, we must muster the courage to stand up and stand firm and do our duty, especially when our country calls upon us to serve.

"You understand what I'm saying, Claude?"

Hesitantly, I responded, "I think I do, Uncle John."

But I didn't. Not then. I'd never known or seen anything like war. I hadn't even been in a fight unless you call a scuffle or two with my cousins a fight. I'd had an idyllic life up until the fire. Not much tragedy and certainly not war. I just couldn't understand then, but I would.

Uncle John looked at me and saw I was confused, but he also seemed to see how much I wanted to know more.

"Well, son, when I say war should be the last resort, I mean we should turn the other cheek whenever possible. But there are times in life when we must take a stand. To defend what's right, you see, even when we'd rather not. It takes courage to turn the other cheek, but it also takes courage to stand up for what's right, and that includes doing your patriotic duty."

"Have you ever been in the army? Have you ever been in a war, Uncle John?"

"No, Claude, I never have, but your papa has."

"Really! I didn't know that! When?"

"For less than a year back in '98 when you were not yet three years old. In the war with Spain, helping Cuba get its independence. But that involvement led to the wider Spanish-American war, which resulted in the US acquiring Spain's Pacific possessions, including the Philippine Islands. Remember, at the St. Louis World's Fair, when we saw the kids reenacting the war in the education exhibit, and the pictures we saw of the Filipino people who were brought over and displayed in the anthropology exhibit. You remember, don't you?"

"Yes sir," I told Uncle John. And I did. I remembered everything about St. Louis.

"Your papa was a private in the army, in the ninth Illinois Infantry. The Cuban conflict didn't last long, so he was back home quick, before you were old enough to ever know he was gone. But your mama had to take care of you and your sister Beth with the help of her sisters while your papa was gone. That's how it is when men go off to war, you see. It's hard on the whole family. The women take care of the home front, and that's very hard. There are so many things about war, Claude."

I remember noticing how Uncle John's mind seemed at work when he said that. It was like when Uncle Jim and I walked down by the Fish Pond. Uncle John didn't seem to be just talking to me, telling me distant stories about war. There was a kind of curiosity in his voice. I asked what he meant, and I remember his response—and how struck I was once again by the complicated nature of this world and of people.

"What is it, Uncle John? You just stopped talking."

"Oh, I don't know Claude. War is just such a strange thing. I've talked with your papa, your Grandfather Bill and Uncle Jim, and others about this so many times. As I said, war's as bad a thing as there is but necessary sometimes. But as bad as it is, it so often brings out the best in people—in times of war human courage and noble sacrifice show up in ways they never seem to otherwise. It's such strange thing."

"Is that always so, Uncle John?" I asked.

"No, that's the part that's strange. Just as much as war can bring out the best in folks, the impossible courage and sacrifice soldiers make for one another, it can also bring out the worst. Some men become cowards, and some, like the Clingman gang who terrorized Vandalia during the Civil War, become like parasites, drawing their life and sustenance from war. And some even lose their soul and become like rabid dogs."

"Why is that Uncle John? Why does war bring out the best and the worst in people? And who is the Clingman gang?"

"My Lord, Claude, you're making me think about things I haven't in a long time. The Clingman, well I just mentioned them because you've asked about the Civil War. They were a gang of ruthless men in southern Illinois during the Civil War who terrorized folks throughout Fayette County. They were bad men, really bad, and cruel. Folks like that always seem to come out of the woodwork during times of war. They take advantage of chaos, especially the kind that happens in war. They do it for their own private gain. They're like leeches, you see.

"The truth is, I don't know why war brings out the best and worst in folks. Not sure anyone really does. Men can do very good and even extraordinary things. In a strange way, war can somehow bear the fruit of the good and extraordinary—perhaps it's because it stretches men's courage far beyond what they ever thought possible. But we can also do very bad and even evil things. War too easily opens the door to that, to the underbelly of our nature.

"That we keep having wars shows us how we're bent the wrong way, you see. To Cain's way. Like an unbroken horse, we all need to be trained to the good and to the restraint of the bad in us. It seems to me it's only by the grace of God that we're ever bent away from war and can resist the temptations to evil that so easily summon the darkness within us. Only by his strength can we garner the courage to bravely sacrifice ourselves for others and endure war's terrible tragedies. And only by his mercies can we find our way to live in peace again in its aftermath. It's quite a mystery to me, son. It really is."

I saw it again. As he spoke Uncle John was asking as many questions as offering me answers. That was the first time I'd ever thought of good and evil inside each of us. I remember thinking about how quick-tempered I can be, like I reacted that night Papa and Mama told Beth and me we were moving. How hard it is even now at times to keep it under control.

Time had slipped by fast. I was surprised when Papa pulled up alongside us and said it was time for lunch. I looked and the sun was just east of straight up. He pointed over to a bank of trees next to a small stream. My mind raced with thoughts of war as I got down and tied the teams off and we all got out.

Mama made us all some sandwiches with leftover biscuits and ham. She fed Rachel while Maurine and Bill ran around for a bit. And we all took privy breaks and stretched out under the shady trees for a short while. I laid my head on a rolled-up blanket and put my hat over my face, but I couldn't stop thinking about my morning conversation with Uncle John.

After resting about thirty minutes, Papa called us to load up. "We still need to make about five or six miles today," he said.

I pulled the pink rock from my pocket and was rubbing it again as Uncle John and I settled in and got under way. Immediately, I started in with more questions.

"So how is it, Uncle John, that countries wind up going to war, and how'd America wind up in a war with itself, the Civil War?" I asked.

Chuckling out loud, he responded to me saying, "Young Claude, I'll say this, you're nothing if not persistent. You're like a dog with a bone. Well, let's see . . .

"Take that rock you have there. It's a piece of Missouri granite. Most wars come about like that rock did. They don't just come out of nowhere, out of the blue, though it may seem that way. I mean, you can always find a war's triggering event, the thing that gets it started, but that's the obvious, above ground explosion. Most wars are like volcanoes, you see, like what formed that rock. They explode only after a lot of pressure builds up from deep below the surface. That's the way most wars come about. And that's what happened with the American Civil War."

I looked at the rock. I wouldn't even remember it, that small mindless gesture of picking up a rock, except that Uncle John mentioned it the day we started talking about the Civil War. As I think back on it, likening the way wars come about to the way rocks are formed from volcanic eruptions seems an apt picture of things. An all too sad one, especially in the Civil War between families and friends and neighbors that came about in this country. He continued.

"The Civil War is the worst we've ever had. It killed more men by far than any other war we've had, over six hundred thousand, all among our own countrymen, and it left another four hundred thousand wounded. It was terrible!"

"I can't imagine, Uncle John. I can't. Why? Why'd it happen? Was it the same as why those Russians got in that fight between themselves?" I asked.

"No, Claude. No, it wasn't that. It was about things peculiar to America. Pressures, like in a volcano, as I said, that had built up over a long time, and finally exploded."

We were only a few hours out of Farmington, still in St. Francois County. I remember it well. The sky was blue and the landscape was beautiful. Natural crevices carved in Knob Lick at the foothills of the St. Francis Mountains back to the north and west and the wide vistas of the delta-lands far out to the east. I didn't realize it at first, but the new conversation I'd started with Uncle John led me into one of those cypress-tupelo swamps we'd later see near the Missouri Bootheel.

"Why did it happen? Well, let me see, Claude. I guess I should start way back, before the country came to a boil, in the early days of this country. Just after the Revolutionary War, I mean, when the founding fathers first imagined how the thirteen colonies would come together as the United States and how our country would be governed. I suspect Miss Jennie's taught you about that, the Constitution and the three branches of government and all. Am I right?"

"Yes sir, she taught us about that. But I can't say I know of it so well," I said.

"Alright then. What I want you to see is that the roots of the Civil War go back to the beginning. Ever since way back then there'd been simmering battles, a war of words not guns, over a lot of things. One of the biggest battles was over two big things, slaves and slavery and how much power the states have compared with the federal government."

"I don't understand, Uncle John," I told him.

"What I mean is, if the founding fathers had been able to resolve the simmering battle over slavery and whether states have the right to secede at the beginning, maybe the war would've never happened. But the times and circumstances back then just wouldn't allow it, you see. Sometimes it's the decisions we don't make that result in the most tragic events. This is one of them. The Founders put the country together with what they could agree on and pushed the disagreements to the side. But the battle didn't go away, it just continued to simmer."

"The Civil War is complicated, Uncle John."

"Yes, son, it certainly is.

"So, what caused the war? Well, as the country expanded west and new states were added, the slavery and state's rights questions continued to come up, time after time. There were lots of debates, including between Mr. Lincoln and an old lawyer friend from Vandalia, Mr. Stephen Douglas. In their first debate, Mr. Lincoln shifted the question from whether new states should enter as free or slave states and who should decide, to why slaves shouldn't be entitled to the same rights Mr. Jefferson wrote about in the Declaration of Independence: the right to life, liberty, and the pursuit of happiness. Even though this debate happened two years before Mr. Lincoln ran for president, in it he had laid his cards on the table, you see. He made the question of slavery not just political but moral.

"Lincoln's views scared lots of folks in the South. By the time he ran for president the country was at a boiling point over the issue. His election triggered an explosion."

"But why, Uncle John? Why'd the folks in the South not like Mr. Lincoln?"

"Well, underneath it all it was his views on state's rights and slavery. But more basic than that, it was an argument over whether the government had the right to tell folks how they can live. And several states in the South believed Lincoln wanted to change their way of life.

"I'm still confused, Uncle John."

"It's hard, I know, son. Think of it like this. By the time Lincoln was elected president, America had grown to be almost like two different countries in the same country, one in the North and another in the South. And if you add the frontier out west you might even say three countries. Each area, the North and the South, and the Americans out west, while they were each dependent on one another, they lived in very different ways. It didn't start that way so much, but as the country grew and expanded, it became that way.

"So, when Mr. Lincoln was elected president, he was greatly concerned that the country was breaking apart. As president it was his duty to keep the country together, a union, you see. But the Southern states feared he wanted to change their whole way of life, not least by getting rid of slavery, and they didn't want that. They saw it as their right to live the way they wanted.

"In his first speech after he was elected, Mr. Lincoln sought to assure the Southern states saying he had no plans to end slavery, that he couldn't if he wanted to. But the Southern politicians didn't believe him. They viewed his election as a sign the country was changing. They believed they had the right to withdraw from the Union to preserve their way of life, including slavery. Almost immediately after Mr. Lincoln was elected, they did."

It stuck in my head, so I asked. "There were different countries in the United States?"

"Yes, well, in a way, but not truly different countries. Different in the way they lived, so much so the North and the South seemed like different countries. Not all agree but I think that might be the most important reason the Civil War happened. It's surely one of the most important.

"Think of it like this. Imagine two or maybe three brothers are born of the same mother but get separated when they're young and grow up in different places and live in very different ways, one in the North, the other the South, and you might even say another on the frontier out west. Where people live and when they live have a lot to do with how they live, you see. Folks in the North, South, and West grew to live in different ways and how they lived shaped them and formed their outlook on life. That's the way it's always been."

I pondered out loud, "People live different in different places? I've never thought of that before."

"They do, son. Take our way of life in Seminary Township. The way we lived there grew from the way your great grandparents Raford and Sarah Carroll and my grandparents lived from when they first came to Illinois. It's all you've ever known, and me too. It's the way of life of mostly small farms and small towns. That's how almost everyone lived from the beginning when the first settlers came to America. Consider how you felt when you saw St. Louis. You were so amazed; it was so different. But imagine you grew up in St. Louis. It wouldn't feel so new and surprising; it would just feel normal. You see, where you live and how you live shapes what you think is the right way to live. As the country grew and new things came along, like what we saw in St. Louis, the way folks lived in the North and South grew different and grew apart. And their views of what the right way to live is grew apart."

"How'd that happen, Uncle John? How'd the way folks live in the North and the South grow apart?"

"Well, people's ways of life in the North and the South had always been a little different, but not so much as to create big conflicts. Some of that was avoided in part because at the beginning most folks still lived and worked on small farms and lived in small towns.

"There'd always been pockets of different beliefs on the two simmering battles over slavery and state's rights and such, in both the North and in the South. Some folks in both the North and the South had long wanted to do away with slavery. There had been movements to outlaw the slave trade, and that succeeded in America the year after England did it. England went on to outlaw slavery altogether, and that led France, Spain, and other countries in Europe to do the same. But America didn't. Not then. A big reason why is because slavery had become so interwoven with the way folks lived, most especially in the South.

"But as the North more and more adopted the newer modern ways of living, like what we saw in St. Louis, over time it became easier for the Northern states to change their views. Life in the North grew more fast-paced with big cities and big ports—which brought lots more folks from Europe and other places straight into the North through the port of New York. Drawn by growing railroads and factories of all kinds, as the cities grew and new industry developed, people poured into them from other countries and from the smaller farms. As the way folks lived in the North changed, they grew less and less in need of slavery. It was the opposite in the South.

"Their way of life changed too, but not with bigger cities, industry, and railroads. In the South, the slower paced traditional agricultural life expanded with more and bigger plantation farms. This way of life became more and more dependent on slavery. Giving it up seemed impossible."

"Did the bigger and bigger farms make the smaller ones go away in the South?"

"No, most folks didn't have much, and most farms were small. There were lots of small plantations, and most of them had slaves but only a few. There weren't many really big ones. But those big ones required hundreds of slaves plus all the surrounding small yeomen farms, small towns, and villages to support them. Farming, big and small, and mostly small towns, were what made up the South before the war. There was very little industry in the South like we saw in St. Louis, and they had far fewer railroads than the North. The way of life in the South became more and more reliant on slaves to work the plantations and to do all the service work on them—even more so once cotton became king.

"That's kind of interesting, though. The demand for cotton harvested by slaves in the South increased because of new fabric mills in the North, in Britain, and other places across the world. As this new industry developed, the North and those other places grew more dependent on slavery in the South. So you see, the North and the South grew apart in the ways they lived, but in a strange way they were held together by their mutual dependence on slavery—though most folks didn't take note of that at the time.

"All these things had grown to a severe pressure point when Mr. Lincoln was elected. A month and a half after he took office the guns blasted at Sumter and the war began."

Day after day Uncle John and I continued to talk about the tangled story of the Civil War. He told me about how the North was losing battle after battle for the first two years and morale was failing, until in the third year. At this lowest point of the war for the Union, Mr. Lincoln made a proclamation freeing all slaves. And later in the summer that year, with the victory of that fateful horrendous battle at Gettysburg, the war began to turn in favor of the Union.

Uncle John finally told me how the war ended. The South surrendered and the Union was preserved—in a formal way. Then began the hard task of putting the country back together. I had reopened Mr. Eggleston's book to its part about the Civil War. Uncle John focused on it and said, "See that, son. Read it. What Mr. Lincoln told the country after the war. Read it out loud."

> With malice toward none with charity for all with firmness in the right as God gives us to see the right let us strive on to finish the work we are in to bind up the nation's wounds, to care for him who shall have borne the battle and for his widow and his orphan—to do all which may achieve and cherish a just and lasting peace among ourselves and with all nations.

"You see, Claude, Mr. Lincoln had learned through that terrible war that to have a chance to be one country again, we needed the mercies of God to find our way to live at peace again in the aftermath of war. Some had not learned the lesson though. Less than a month after he gave that speech, Mr. Lincoln himself lay dead of a gunshot wound."

After supper for many nights, I'd mostly read in Mr. Eggleston's book and wrote about my daytime talks with Uncle John. Mama and Papa were confused at first by how quiet I was, until Uncle John explained. I heard Mama say, "Claude's in another trance."

It was all so interesting and all so sad, for everyone—and especially for how it ended for Mr. Lincoln.

But a question lingered in my mind, something I'd asked days earlier. It gnawed at me.

So, as we rocked along during our last full day in Missouri, I asked Uncle John again.

* * *

"Uncle John, I understand so much more about the Civil War, and I'm so sad in my heart about so many papas and sons and friends and neighbors who fought and died in it. You said if slavery could have been outlawed back when the colonies first came together, maybe the war wouldn't have ever happened. Why wasn't it? Didn't folks know it's wrong to own people, even the folks in the South who wanted to keep slavery? Didn't that matter?"

"It does matter, son. Your Grandfather Bill, your papa and I talked about this over lunch with Reverend Barber one day after church. I expressed the same confusion you have now. And I'm still not sure I understand completely, but here's what he told us. Get that Bible in the back and look up St. Paul's letter to the Romans, chapter seven. Look there," he said pointing to verses eighteen and nineteen. "Read that."

> For I know that in me (that is, in my flesh,) dwelleth no good thing: for to will is present with me; but how to perform that which is good I find not.
> For the good that I would I do not: but the evil which I would not, that I do.

"That's St. Paul talking there, one of the Apostles. See there how confused he seems to be. He says the very thing he wants to do, he doesn't. And the very thing he doesn't want to do, he does. That's the confusion of the human heart—the enslavement to sin. The same kind of confusion that, in war, brings out the very best in some and the very worst in others.

"There've been many in our country since the beginning who always found slavery to be wrong, both in the North and in the South, before, during, and after the War. But many others didn't, or at least it'd become so interwoven with their lives they became convinced there was nothing wrong with it. I even heard a man in Vandalia say one day that there are those who honestly believe the institution of slavery is to the mutual advantage of master and slave.

"It's hard for us all to see what's right sometimes. Sometimes when it stands right in front of us. Sometimes we can't see, sometimes we won't.

There's a kind of blindness inside us. It's true for all of us. To see we need a mirror or some powerful event to show us. To make our heart see. Reverend Barber told me that's actually what led England to outlaw slavery.

"The man who led the effort to change the law there was himself made to see the need to outlaw slavery through a man who had himself been a slave-trader. That slaver-trader got caught in a fierce storm at sea and fearing for his life he called out to God to save him, and he did. Saved from the storm, his heart changed. That man, Mr. John Newton, gave up slave trading and became a minister. He later met a young politician named Mr. William Wilberforce, and the old slave-trader's testimony helped set aflame the heart of the young man to end slavery completely. Mr. Wilberforce spent the rest of his life leading England to outlaw slavery, and his efforts there influenced other European countries to end the slave trade and eventually to outlaw slavery.

"Old Mr. John Newton even wrote a famous hymn we sing in church, "Amazing Grace." You remember that hymn, Claude?"

"Oh yes, Uncle John, I love that song," I said, captivated by the new story Uncle John told.

"Well, you see, sometimes we can only see when the eyes of our hearts are opened. We're all blind to good things somehow and our hearts are distorted, often times assisted by the way we live. That's the way it was for many in America, some in the North and many in the South. Sometimes it takes a special awakening brought about by God himself, like what happened to Mr. Newton. Along the way as America grew, such an awakening happened here too, what folks now call the Great Awakening. Many hearts were turned to God and many in turn saw the need to abolish slavery. That helped move our country to change its laws. The heartbreak is that unlike in England where the change happened peacefully with the tireless efforts of Mr. Wilberforce, in America it took a terrible war to bring this about.

"What can we say? Well, partly we can say that just because the law says something is okay doesn't mean it's right. For a long period of time slavery was legal, but it didn't make it right. This country finally aligned the law with what's right. But because the country finally got it right doesn't mean folks in the North or anyone else should feel superior to folks in the South who clung to their way of life. America needed to see and change, and it did. But we're all in danger of blindness. Best we see the speck in our own eye first before judging others."

So ended my long and winding days talking with Uncle John about war. We made camp that night just north of Pitman's Ferry along the Current River. The flurry of activity always needed to set up camp momentarily pulled me out of my deep reflection on the tales about war and the Civil War. The sky turned a pastel orange in the west as things settled down.

As had become my habit, that last night in Missouri I stretched out on a flour sack towel after supper, and I read and wrote late into the night next to the fire. Until it dwindled down, and my eyes burned from squinting.

My mind raced. So much so that I had a hard time falling asleep. I finally did, and had sad dreams about the thousands of fathers, sons, brothers, and friends who died in that terrible war and the sorrow it brought to every home. War? I hoped I'd never have to go to war.

As I think back on my lessons with Uncle John, it was impossible for me then to understand the politics of war. I shudder at them even now. But I began to see how decisions matter, how seemingly small ones are woven into big ones. Harder to see is why we make the decisions we do and how conflicted the human heart is.

But it dawned on me, even then, that nations are a bit like Grandfather Bill's old log cabin. When cracks in the chinking are left unattended, like the crack of slavery when the country was founded, come a hard freeze and it'll crack wide open. Or like volcanos, when unreleased pressure from unresolved conflicts builds up deep inside, they explode, leaving death and debris across the landscape, like the fragmented piece of granite I casually picked up that day.

Ten—Journeys

"Bud, you'd better put on that long underwear; it's cold out today." Bud is Mama's name for Papa—his papa gave him that nickname when he was a boy.

She was up early with Rachel, had the fire going with a pot of coffee brewing, and bacon, eggs, and biscuits cooking. The wafting smells in the crisp morning air were mouthwatering.

"You too, Claude and Beth, and dress your sister and brother."

We'd slept in the wagons overnight—Papa with Uncle John in his, Mama and us kids in ours. We were all crowded together, especially with all the blankets and provisions, but snuggling up kept us warm.

The dew was heavy that morning along the Current. The brisk wind whistled through the densely forested oak and hickory on the eastern slope of the Ozark Plateau, and it made the towering softwood pines dance. Papa said the plateau, and Arkansas too, got their names from French explorers when they met the Quapaw Indians who lived and hunted bison in the area. There were no bison left when we came through, mostly only white tail deer, which we saw every day, and other critters—we were told there were black bear, but we never saw any.

We crossed the river into Arkansas at Pitman's Ferry, a strategic area used by the Confederate army, we learned. They'd gathered troops there before battles in Tennessee and Kentucky, a place of four skirmishes in the second year of the war, we were told. The Current River acts as a natural boundary between the Plateau and the Mississippi delta, what a man in Greenville, Missouri had called the alluvial plain, another new word I'd never heard.

Moving south into Arkansas that spring we saw a carpet of beautiful apple and peach blossoms spread across orchards on the slant lands, and acres upon acres of dark, tilled soil ready for cotton seed on the plains to the east. Farther south were oxbow lakes and bayous that watered the land for rice farming. The landscape was rich with cultivation.

Papa said we'd reached the halfway point of our journey. As had become his custom, using his hands to point this way and that, he said, "From this point we'll head southeast, down through Randolph and three other counties, then cut across the edge of Lonoke, where we'll turn west through Pulaski County at Little Rock."

About a day into Arkansas, we stopped to resupply in Pocahontas. There, I discovered more and more about the rich history of the land we were traveling through. How it'd been traveled and settled long before us everywhere we stopped. In a deeper way, what Papa had said about how everybody in America came from somewhere else, even the Indians long, long ago.

When Papa and Uncle John were gathering supplies in the general store, I sat on a bench outside with my book. An old farmer sat at the other end—at least he seemed old to me, then, and his overalls said he was a farmer. He saw me reading and inquired what it was. I showed him the cover and told him the book was Mr. Edward Eggleston's *A First Book of American History*, part of my lessons. He told me it's good to know things about places and their past and, extending his hand, he introduced himself.

"My name is Randolph Drew. What's your name, son?"

"I'm Claude Howell, sir," I said, pensively extending my hand as we shook. It felt strange to shake a stranger's hand. I wondered briefly, *Randolph in Randolph County?* That was funny. "My Papa's in the store restocking for our trip."

"I see, Claude, where's your trip taking you?"

"We're headed to Texas. We came from Seminary Township up in Illinois, and we're moving down to Texarkana."

"That's a long trip, but I expect it's interesting too, am I right?"

"Oh yeah!" I exclaimed, "I mean, my apologies. Yes, sir. It sure is. I've learned so much, more than I ever imagined, from my lessons but especially seeing so many new places and things and hearing amazing stories from my Papa, Mama, and Uncle John."

"So, whatcha readin' about?" he asked with cutoff words like Mama says sometimes.

"It's about how everybody in America came from somewhere else, even the Indians."

"That's interesting, Claude. You want me to tell you a few things about this area?"

"Oh, yes sir, Mr. Drew. That would be great. I sure would, that'd be terrific," I told him excitedly.

Though my time was short with Mr. Drew on the bench in Pocahontas, I remember it even after all these years. It was something special. What a nice old fellow. Good people make an impression on you. You just can't beat folks like that.

He told me about the Quapaw Indians that Papa had mentioned, and the Osages and Cherokees who all lived and walked this area long before the white man arrived, and he even told me stories he'd heard about how the Indians in America came here long, long ago.

He told me about the first westerners to come through the area, saying a Spanish explorer named de Tonti set up the first trading post in what became Randolph County. That trading post later became Pocahontas, now the county seat, he said.

Then he told me a fascinating story of how Pocahontas got its name, from a real and famous person. An Indian woman named Pocahontas, he told me, the daughter of an Indian chief back at the beginning of America— I learned later it's a famous story, but I didn't know then. Pocahontas became famous after she offered to sacrifice herself in place of an American settler, Captain John Smith, whom her father had captured and planned to execute. Later, when she herself was held captive in the Jamestown settlement, Pocahontas accepted the Christian religion, was baptized in a little church there, and married a man named John Rolfe. Her father was happy at the marriage. It brought peace between the Indian tribes and the English settlers in Virginia.

I thought about how that Indian woman was willing to sacrifice herself for a white man she didn't even know. Then, when she herself was held captive, a white man redeemed her, they married, she became a Christian, and lived a new kind of life. I thought again about the Samaritan Papa read to us about.

The town of Pocahontas, Mr. Drew told me, was once the leading river port in northern Arkansas, and because of that was the site of a few Civil War battles. Proudly, he said that while Randolph County is special for lots of reasons, it holds the prize for one special thing.

"It's been a part of four countries if you count the Confederacy, our town historian Mr. Dalton says. And three territories, two states, and four counties, too. It's older by a year than the state of Arkansas itself. It's a pretty darn good place to be from, son."

Mr. Drew pressed hard on the wooden arm of the bench to stand. Stretching his hand again to shake mine, he said, "It's been a pleasure meeting you, Claude. I really enjoyed our visit, but I must go now." I thanked him for talking to me. He tipped his hat, and said, "Godspeed as you continue your journey," and slowly walked away.

What a fortunate surprise, I thought. Life is fortuitous, Uncle Jim would say.

The stories about Randolph County were fascinating, especially about the town of Pocahontas and how so many layers of folks had come through the area and left their mark on it. The whole area's a rich, storied tale of people who came before us in America. So many people met at this small crossroad, journeying from one place to another.

Learning those things made me think a lot about our journey. That we were even on a journey, and what that meant. I knew for us it meant going to Texarkana. But I recall wondering about how it seems everyone's on a journey somehow.

I wanted to know more about how everyone in America came from somewhere else, and why.

Waiting on Papa, I continued reading Mr. Eggleston. He wrote that all the American colonists came here in pursuit of freedom and opportunity, many for religious freedom, and all for new prospects like what Uncle Jim had told me our journey was about. They all came with a longing for liberty, the book said. In pursuit of happiness in life, something they believed they had the right to pursue as an endowment given to them by God in his providence. So they did, and despite hardships, many found it. But after a while, Mr. Eggleston wrote, the king of England started restricting their freedoms and rights, and the colonists became unhappy.

"Come on, Claude!" Papa hollered, jolting me from the caverns of my imagination.

As we loaded the fresh supplies, I asked him about what I'd been reading. Still focused on loading supplies in the wagons, but with no hesitation, he said, "Well, Claude, when the liberties that people came here for were betrayed so severely over a long time, the colonists felt compelled to act to preserve them. That's in the Declaration Mr. Jefferson wrote," he said. And without even a pause, speaking as if still just giving me his own thoughts, he recited the first part of Mr. Jefferson's words from memory.

> When in the Course of human events, it becomes necessary for one people to dissolve the political bands which have connected them with another, and to assume among the powers of the earth, the separate and equal station to which the Laws of Nature and of Nature's God entitle them, a decent respect to the opinions of mankind requires that they should declare the causes which impel them to the separation.
>
> We hold these truths to be self-evident, that all men are created equal, that they are endowed by their Creator with certain

unalienable Rights, that among these are Life, Liberty, and the
pursuit of Happiness.

"You see, son, the United States was created to preserve our God-given
rights to life, liberty, and the pursuit of happiness."

I was amazed at how Papa just came out with that.

"How'd you know that, Papa?" I asked.

Talking to me while working, the sound of his voice rose and fell
rhythmically as he grabbed and then turned to swing the crates of supplies
into the wagon, he asked what I meant. "What? . . . Oh, you mean what
the Declaration says. Well, next to the Bible that's about as important as
anything to know, Claude. You should, too. I first learned it in school, in my
lessons like you've been doing. But also from my papa and mama. Later, and
quite often really, your Grandfather Bill and I have talked about the founding of America and how fortunate we all are because of what those brave
men did to give it to us."

It struck me when Papa said that. It reminded me of how Uncle John
had told me he and Papa, Uncle Jim, and Grandfather Bill talked a lot about
the Civil War. I don't think I'd ever thought about that before. How learning
things in school and then talking about it can fix them in your mind like it
did with Papa, so that he could just pull it out as if from a well-used drawer.

"It's important never to forget what and who gave us what we have.
The freedoms we have because of them are what allowed my father's father to make the journey from Tennessee to Seminary Township and your
mama's grandparents too. Those freedoms allow us to make this trip, to start
over again. You see, Claude? You might think everybody has the freedom
to move this way and that and live as they want within the boundaries of
reasonable laws. But they don't. It's important you learn what brought our
country about and keep it with you always."

There it was again, what Papa said about his grandfather making a
journey from Tennessee to Seminary Township, and Great Grandfather and
Grandmother Carroll too.

"I want to, Papa. I want to know more about it all," I told him.

Beth and I switched wagons again when we left Pocahontas. I rode
with Papa and Mama as we drove farther south into Arkansas. Mama and
I were in the back with Rachel, Maurine and Bill, and I continued to read
in Mr. Eggleston's book. This time about Mr. Jefferson's Declaration of Independence because Papa recited it and about President Washington when
he was a boy, then in the Revolutionary War, and later when he became
president, and because Mr. Drew talked about it, I read a story in the book
about Pocahontas and Captain Smith.

As I read about President Washington, I thought of his picture in Grandfather Bill's old log house. My mind drifted to Great Grandfather Carroll and to the Carroll family.

I turned and said, "Mama, Papa told us some about his parents and grandparents that night after St. Louis, where they came from and how they journeyed to Fayette County. Would you tell me about Great Grandfather Carroll?"

"Oh yeah, honey!" she said. Mama always got excited about the Carroll family story. This began several stories over several days drawing on Mama's memories from stories told to her when she was a girl and from the old papers Uncle Jim stored in the big treasure chest.

* * *

She knew it by heart but hesitated as she rummaged through the chest. She found the paper she was looking for. Looking at me she said, "See here, honey, here's the story Uncle Jim wrote." She began to read and talk from storied memories at the same time. "'Grandfather Raford R. Carroll was born in North Carolina, November 3, 1808.' Isn't that something, Claude? A long time ago, huh?" She continued talking, reading, and shuffling papers.

"He left there in 1828, when he was just twenty years old, and went to Tennessee. He settled for a short while, just three miles south of the Kentucky border. There he met Grandmother Sarah—Sarah Elizabeth Jernigan, you see—and they were married less than six months later, in the spring of twenty-nine. The very next day, Grandfather and Grandmother Carroll left Tennessee for Illinois."

Mama always said their names slow and sweet, with a lingering lilt in her voice. As if her Grandfather Carroll were right there with her, even though she never knew him, and as if she still sat with and doted on his wife, her Grandmother Sarah in that old house until her death. My mind went back to Uncle Jim's story about how Great Grandmother Sarah sent him and his brother to sell those mules, and I imagined Great Grandfather Carroll putting the chinking between those big logs when he first built that old house. I wished I'd known them too.

"They were the first to settle and own their own farm in Seminary Township, entering the first eighty acres registered there.

"And here's something interesting, Claude, something you don't know," Mama said. "Grandfather Carroll had some of the blood of the Carrolls of Carrollton in his veins."

All of what Mama told me was fascinating, but it caused lots of questions too, and I blurted out a bunch.

"So Mama, where'd Great Grandfather Carroll live in North Carolina," I asked. "What made him leave there, did they have a fire like we did? Why did he go to Tennessee where he met Great Grandmother Sarah, and how did they get over to Illinois? Was there a trail they took like this one? And who are the Carrolls of Carrollton?"

Mama stopped and stared at me with a strange look. Then she broke out laughing.

"You're so funny, Claude. You and all your questions, they never end. But I can answer them. I know some, but we best have a look more in these papers to be sure."

She turned and opened Uncle Jim's chest and started shuffling through more of the old papers to help her answer my questions.

"Hold on a bit, Claude," she said. "We'll get to them. Uncle Jim knew you'd have lots of questions. We've got the time. So, let's see here," she said, looking at the papers and remembering the stories she'd been told when she was a girl. "Here we go; I found it. Uncle Jim wrote down a lot from what his father told him, and we've got it here.

"Grandfather Carroll was born in Sampson County, North Carolina, where his parents James and Francis Carroll came to from Virginia. Uncle Jim was named for his grandfather James, you see, honey.

"Uncle Jim says here that his grandparents and their first four older kids came down the Great Philadelphia Wagon Road from Virginia, around the year President George Washington went back home to Virginia after eight years as president. Grandfather Raford's family originally settled in Duplin County, North Carolina, and a few years later they moved over to Sampson County. That's where my grandfather was born, you see, Claude. Back there in 1808.

"Grandfather Raford and his family back there in North Carolina were yeoman farmers. Same as us in Illinois Uncle Jim says. When they first got there, he says, their way of life was called subsistence farming, you understand Claude?

"That means they owned their own land, like us, you see. But to get by, they ate what they raised, killed, or gathered for themselves, and had little left over to sell.

"Corn was a staple, Uncle Jim writes here, and most people had access to apple trees, from which they made apple sauce."

When she said that, Mama paused and looked up at me, and said, "See honey, they made mostly apple sauce instead of apple butter like us.

"Grandfather Raford left North Carolina in the fall of the year he turned twenty. Uncle Jim and Papa told me he never said exactly why he left, but he let on a few things. Times had gotten especially hard.

"But, it seems," Mama explained, "he was also drawn west by the government's offer of free land for those who'd go settle it and work it in new territories and states.

"Yet, there was an even more important reason he left. He wanted to be married and have a family.

"So, he set off on horseback towards Tennessee. It seems he chose Tennessee partly because he had learned from the newspaper that President Andrew Jackson found his wife there. Dreaming of something of the same, he decided to go there first.

"He rode west from North Carolina, across to Chattanooga, and up through Nashville. And from there, he made his way across the Cumberland River farther north and west, to Stewart County, just south of the Kentucky border. There, just east of Dover, Tennessee, he settled at North Cross Creek.

"There in that small North Cross Creek village at Christmastime, Grandfather Raford met his wife to be, Sarah Elizabeth Jernigan. They married the following March, and the very next day they set off to Illinois in an oxcart. Isn't that something, Claude? That was hard traveling, a lot harder than we have it in these wagons, don't you think?

It sure was, I thought.

"The trip to Fayette County and Seminary Township took 'em about two months," Mama said, recalling the story from memory.

"See, son, that's about the same time it's taking us to go from Illinois to Texas," Papa yelled back.

"There in the late spring of '29," Mama continued, "Raford and Sarah Carroll, started their new life. There in Seminary Township Grandfather Raford finally found what he'd wanted when he left North Carolina. A family of his own and land of his own, and new prospects for a future.

"You see, honey, that's the story of how Grandfather Raford and Grandmother Sarah came to Illinois and started a new family there. Our family, where I was born, your papa, and all you kids, you see. They came out west and settled on the frontier of America and made a new life."

Rachel began to tell Mama she was hungry, and Maurine and Bill were restless. Papa hollered across at Uncle John and Beth and pointed to a grove of trees along a river, this time the Black River. We all had a little lunch, nothing cooked, just some of the leftover biscuits from breakfast. Like on most days, sometimes several times a day, we rested for about an hour or so and loaded back up and headed out.

Once settled and making our way again, I asked Mama if we could continue talking.

"Sure, honey. Let's see. Here's something. Oh, I forgot Uncle Jim put this in here. You're gonna love this, Claude. See here, this right here is the deed to the first land grant from the government that Grandfather Carroll got . . . it's not the deed to that first piece of property, you see, that piece they built the old house on, which they bought. This is the first land grant from the government.

"See here, honey? It's signed by the president of the United States himself, President Martin Van Buren. Can you believe that?"

I couldn't believe it. And that it was in that old trunk—more evidence that it was a treasure chest. Not that having possession of that deed entitled us to land, it didn't. But it was special.

"Uncle Jim told me Grandfather Carroll was excited the day he got this deed back in thirty-nine. They'd worked that land for ten years. That November day they finally got it, and everyone was so excited. Isn't that something? Here, you can hold it, Claude. This is part of your family history.

"This deed was just the first, you see. Three years later they got a grant for another eighty acres, signed by President John Tyler. Then, eight years after that got another one for forty acres, signed by President Zachary Taylor. That's really something, don't you think, Claude?"

I held the old document and was amazed. I could see our family was part of something. Small, yes, small, but Grandfather and Grandmother Carroll helped to build our great country. It made me feel good inside. Proud, in a way, like I'd never been before.

Mama crawled up and grabbed the canteen from the flat-board seat where Papa was and took a big drink—she'd gotten thirsty with all the talking and reading. She handed it to me. I took a drink and handed it to Maurine, and she gave it to Bill.

Then she pulled out some old diaries. Uncle Jim had told her he wanted her to read from them to me. "These are things he wrote to himself, you see," she said, "from when he was a boy."

I still have them. They're musty now and the pages are brittle, but I have them right here.

"When we left Uncle Jim said he was old now and he wanted you to have his old diaries, Claude. Your Uncle Jim loves you, son."

Hearing Mama say that made me sad, but grateful too. I'm even more grateful now.

Great Grandfather Carroll would tell his sons things when they worked the fields together. Lessons, you can say, from his own journey from North Carolina to Illinois, and life on the frontier. Things Uncle Jim learned and wrote down from what his father told him and wanted me to know on our journey.

Mama began to read from the diaries.

> All of us are on a journey in life, small ones that make up our own steps in this world. And each step of the way we are journeying through a bigger story. We should take account of that bigger story just as we do of our smaller ones. And our journeys are not about never-ending wandering but about putting down roots, even though there may be times in life that force you to move.
>
> Papa journeyed from North Carolina and Tennessee and put down roots here in Seminary Township, to make a new life. Wherever you go in life, he said, put down roots in the soil. The place you call home is part of you, and the land and the improvements you make to it are yours to take care of. Yet never forget that the land we have and call our own is ours to be stewards of, caretakers of, just as those who had it before us, and those who'll have it after us.

"You see, honey," Mama stopped to explain, "Uncle Jim's talking here about his papa and mama, my grandfather and grandmother Carroll."

I've so often thought about Mama reading from Uncle Jim's diaries that day, and I've gone back to them so many times in my life. She continued:

> Boys, just as with all the rights endowed to us by God, with all that we have and own, we're beneficiaries of them as the gifts of God. We are his stewards. Our obligation is to have dominion over it, be stewards of it, and cultivate it. Just as we are all to cultivate ourselves, each to his proper end. What we are given and how things work out with it is not always up to us. As farmers and ranchers, you know that. We do the best we can. Then we leave it up to the sunshine, rain, and storms, and the pests to decide how much harvest the crops will yield. The same is true with the animals. We feed them, care for them, bring them in the barns when needed, and even when I have you boys take them down to St. Louis to sell. There are some things we control but not much. Most is out of our control. Farming and ranching make for a good profession. It's been good for us. But what it does best is help us see that we are at the mercy of Providence. Just the same as we are with the Creator's endowments of life, liberty, and the pursuit of happiness that Mr. Jefferson wrote about in The Declaration.

Our duties in this way are not just with land and crops and animals but with our lives too, as individuals, the communities we belong to, and the country we live in—they all require cultivation, by each and by all, those with the most and those with the least. We are men of duty.

"You see, honey, Uncle Jim's papa, my Grandfather Carroll, not only told him important stories of his beginnings but of lessons from life he'd learned. When we left, Uncle Jim told me he saw these as his inheritance, given to him by his papa, and he wanted me to give them to you."

I could almost hear Uncle Jim's voice as Mama read from his diary. It was like I was working with him on Hoggin' Day or walking with him in the snow. I realized listening to Mama read what he wrote in his diaries about what his papa told him, that it was from his own papa that Uncle Jim got a lot of what he had told me. I still hear his voice when I pick up these old books.

I had already begun to see that that old chest was full of treasures. But until then I'd never thought of its contents as a kind of an inheritance. I'd never considered that inheritances might be found in stories of journeys people take in life.

The conversations with Mr. Drew and Papa and Mama those first days in Arkansas were like a wandering journey, going to times and places I didn't know with people I never knew.

Eleven—Deeper Roots

We were well along toward Little Rock, following the Black River south out of the five rivers at Pocahontas. That night we camped along the river. Mama made more of that delicious venison stew with the meat we'd salt-cured and some potatoes and carrots we'd picked up from a local farmer on the trail, plus some wild rutabagas we found at a stop. We all had some. But Papa, Mama, and Uncle John ate most of it because Mama said she'd made something new for us kids.

"Hamburgers," she called them. Something she learned about from a lady who sold them from a street cart back in St. Louis. She told Mama they'd been a hit at the Fair. "They're normally made from ground beef," Mama said, "but since we have venison, that's what it'll be." She'd ground it up from the hand-crank grinder we'd brought and made the meat into circular patties about a quarter-inch thick, like sausage. She fried them in that black iron skillet and put them between two pieces of sliced bread—fresh bread we'd bought in a small village just south of where the Black and White rivers come together.

We loved our first experience with hamburgers. Boy were they a juicy, tasty treat. But I didn't think the name matched since they weren't made from ham, so I asked Mama. She said the woman in St. Louis told her they thought the name came from a town in Germany, but they weren't sure. It still sounded strange to me, has ever since.

When we cleaned things up and Rachel, Bill and Maurine were asleep, we had our regular talk around the fire. I asked Mama to tell Beth and me about the Carrolls of Carrollton she'd mentioned in the wagon but never explained.

"Oh yeah, honey," she said in that jubilant refrain again. "I've loved this story ever since Uncle Jim first told it to me when I was a girl."

She retrieved some more papers from the old chest.

* * *

"Grandfather Raford Carroll had some of the blood of the Carrolls of Carrollton, Maryland coursing in his veins," Mama began, repeating what she'd said in the wagon.

"Mr. Charles Carroll was one of the signers of the Declaration of Independence, you see. We've got some of his blood in our veins. That's something, isn't it kids?"

"Wow, Mama," I said, "someone in our family really signed the Declaration of Independence?" Beth and I looked at each other wide-eyed and back at Mama.

"Yes, it is so exciting, Claude. Your feelings now are the way I felt when Uncle Jim first told me this story—it's been in our family a long time, forever as far as I know. This is how Uncle Jim came to know of it.

"On the December day in '32 when Uncle Jim was born, his papa had gone to town to settle a land purchase and record the deed for a neighbor— that's when Grandfather Carroll was the Fayette County Assessor, you see. The day was memorable to Grandfather Raford most especially because it was his oldest son's birthday, but it was also the day the Vandalia newspaper ran the obituary that Mr. Charles Carroll had died.

"News traveled slower then. The Vandalia paper had just received and printed the news from a month before. It says, 'On November 14, in '32, Charles Carroll of Carrollton, the last surviving signer of the Declaration of Independence, has died. He was in his ninety-sixth year!'

"See here," Mama said, holding up the old clipping Uncle Jim put in the big chest.

"Uncle Jim kept this old clipping because it's what his papa used to tell him about our family connection. He was about y'all's age when Grandfather Raford told him. He kept this and wrote the story his papa told him in his diary. He wanted me to tell you kids.

"Grandfather Raford said Mr. Carroll of Carrollton was a distant relation of ours, you see. Not a direct relation from here in America but way back in Ireland. From someplace near where our Irish relatives had come to America from. The O'Carroll family they're called back in Ireland. With an O in front of their name, you see. They're the ancient ancestors of both Mr. Carroll of Carrollton Maryland's family and our family, too. You, understand, kids?"

"Really Mama?" Beth asked. "Is that right? We're from Ireland? That's so exciting."

"Oh yeah," she said as she continued reading from Uncle Jim's old paper.

Charles Carroll of Carrollton was an American founding father and wealthy landowner—at one time the largest landowner in America. Charles, along with his cousin Daniel, made gifts of land from their estates to help in the building of Washington, DC, the capital of the United States.

Charles Carroll of Carrollton was the only Catholic signer of the Declaration.

She looked up excitedly as she read and talked, showing the clipping to us again.

"The way Uncle Jim tells the story, Grandfather Raford and Mr. Charles Carroll of Carrollton were both pioneers, you see. Charles Carroll and his relatives pioneered the colony of Maryland and helped to form this country. Grandfather Raford Carroll pioneered North Carolina with his family, then he went to Tennessee, and settled in the new state of Illinois, you recall. They were both pioneers, Uncle Jim wrote in his diaries, but not in the same way. See here?

> Even though the blood that coursed the veins of Raford Carroll of North Carolina and Charles Carroll of Carrollton of Maryland was the same, and even though they shared a Common Lord, even if no longer the same church, the courses of their lives in the New World were very different. What they shared is the same steel and virtue forged in them both by their common descent and common faith. That same steel that was required of them both in this land they each called home.

Beth and I were transfixed listening to Mama read and talk about what Uncle Jim said in his writings. I couldn't believe how long ago it was and how far back it connected our families. Yet how close it seemed in a way. Mama read on from Uncle Jim's diaries.

> Both families drew upon their common O'Carroll heritage of the lords of Ely and Oriel in Ireland. And while the path for Charles of Carrollton's Carroll family turned out far more moneyed than Papa's line, they still shared a lot in common. Charles of Carrollton's grandfather lost everything back in Ireland, all their O'Carroll inheritance of land and status. They had to start over, just like my great grandparents did when they left Ireland and came to America. Why the fortunes of the Carrolls of Maryland's turned out one way and my papa's another is not clear to me. Such questions must be left to the providence of God.

"Remember, when Uncle Jim writes about his papa here, he means Grandfather Raford. Your great grandfather."

Papa spoke up and said, "You see, kids, Uncle Jim is talking about how the Carrolls who came to Maryland had lost everything and had to start over again. Grandfather Raford told Uncle Jim and his brothers about how his own great grandparents lost everything back in Ireland and that's when they came to America. You understand? Both sides of these Carroll families lost what they had and were forced to move and start over. Just like we are now. Whether there's fortunes before us, or not, is no more certain than it was for the Carrolls of Maryland."

When Papa said that my mind shifted back to where we were then and why. I felt like I was in some kind of travel machine—one moment in Ireland, the next on the trail to Texas.

Mama handed Papa Uncle Jim's old newspaper clipping about Charles Carroll of Carrolton and asked him to read from it. He took his cigar from his mouth, leaned near the light from the campfire to read, and gave a short preamble.

"This is the obituary of Charles Carroll that Grandfather Raford read in the *Vandalia Whig and Illinois Intelligencer* that December day back in thirty-two," Papa said. "It tells a bit of Charles Carroll of Carrollton's family background, his life and what he achieved." He began to read.

> Charles Carroll of Carrollton was born September 19, 1737, in Annapolis, Maryland, where his father Charles Carroll of Annapolis lived and managed a huge estate. He died November 14, 1832.

Mama stopped him and said again, "Remember, eighteen thirty-two is the year your Uncle Jim was born."

I interrupted and asked, "Where's Annapolis, and if his papa was from there, why was he called Charles Carroll of Carrollton? I don't understand Papa."

Papa gave a short answer, saying, "Those places are both in Maryland. In the old days, if people were wealthy, sometimes they called themselves by the land they owned. You'll see."

Then he continued, but rather than just reading it, he read and talked about it like that night he talked about the story in the St. Louis paper.

"Well, let's see. It says here Mr. Charles Carroll of Carrollton is the third generation of the Maryland Carrolls in America. His grandfather was called Charles Carroll the Settler. He came to Maryland from Ireland by way of England, and folks called him the settler because he's the first in his family to come across and settle in the new colony of Maryland. It says here that when his family lost everything in Ireland a school friend who'd gone to study in France helped him get into school there too. He eventually became a lawyer and moved to England to practice law. And to his great fortune he was appointed Attorney General of the colony of Maryland under Lord Baltimore—see kids, this was when this country was still British colonies.

"'The colony of Maryland was set up as a haven for Catholics so they were able to practice their religion freely, which they couldn't in England at the time,' it says. Charles the Settler was a Catholic and things worked well for him in Maryland at first. He secured property for his services and the future looked bright. But soon after, the Catholics faced the same problem in the Colonies they had back in England. Just when he was on the verge of losing everything again Charles was fortunate to marry well, and through his wife's inheritance they became the beneficiaries of a very large estate.

"This began the Carrolls of Maryland's eventual accumulation of fifty thousand acres, it says here. Can you believe that? Fifty thousand acres. Wow!"

That was hard to believe. I couldn't imagine anyone owning that much land. The story of the Carrolls of Maryland was amazing, like so many others I'd learned. Papa continued.

"Charles the Settler's son, Charles Carroll of Annapolis, inherited his father's estate. And Charles of Carrollton would too, in the end, but not easily it says here."

> Charles of Carrollton was at risk of not receiving his father's estate because of the anti-Catholic inheritance laws instituted in Maryland after King James II was deposed. Because of these laws Charles' mother and father didn't marry before he was born, so he was born out of wedlock, though they did eventually marry.

Papa said, "See kids, it says here, there were severe restrictions on Catholics in Maryland then, even in education, you see. So, the young Charles of Carrollton was sent away to France to study when he was eleven years old."

That's about my age, I thought. I couldn't imagine being away from my family like that. What would it feel like? So lonely.

"He studied there and then in England until he was twenty-eight years old," Papa read. "Because of it, he became known as the best educated of all the founding fathers of America—some called him the American Cicero, for his education and his commitment to virtue."

"Who is Cicero, Papa? Why was Mr. Carroll called the American Cicero? I asked.

"Well, Cicero was a smart old Roman leader, way back in the Roman Empire, you see. But he wasn't just smart. When I was in school, we learned he was known for being a man of the highest virtue. That's why they called

Charles Carroll of Carrollton the American Cicero, because he had such a good education, and, like Cicero, he was a man of high virtue.

Papa continued to read and explain,

"But even when he finally came home, the laws in Maryland still restricted Catholics. He couldn't hold any official office. So as a regular but very well-educated citizen, he wrote things and became very influential in Maryland colonial politics. He became a very early supporter of American independence from Britain. When it came time to sign the Declaration of Independence, he did, even though he had the largest estate to lose of all the signers.

"We should never forget that kids, just how much the founding fathers put at risk and sacrificed for us to have the freedom we have. Mr. Charles of Carrollton put a lot at risk, but he also had great influence on the formation of the new government after the war was over.

"Here it says, Charles of Carrollton and President George Washington became good friends. They wrote letters to each other often, especially after the Revolutionary War. Mr. Charles was elected to the Continental Congress in 1776 and helped persuade the adoption of a republican form of government, where the power rests with the people to elect their leaders but in a way that protects the minority and the majority, and of the three branches of government.

"But it says here, and this is very important kids, Mr. Carroll stressed that for this kind of government to work, the American people must be good enough to maintain the power that rests with them—that means all of us, you see, kids. And that goodness, Mr. Carroll believed, doesn't come from the laws that are passed but from the religion and the virtues of the American people.

"The obituary writer says that George Washington expressed the same beliefs in his Farewell Address. And the writer says a young Frenchman named Tocqueville he met when he was visiting America in February before Mr. Carroll died, witnessed these beliefs in the American people. The Frenchman saw these beliefs in what he called the 'habits of the heart' of the American people, explaining that 'there are many things which the law permits them to do which the religion of the Americans forbids them to do. These habits are what make America work,' the Frenchman told the obituary writer. 'Charles Carroll of Carrollton was a man of such habits. His life and words gave testimony to all Americans to pursue them,' the writer concludes.

"Kids, this story is important and exciting to our family, of course. But listening to what the obituary writer says, you can see its importance goes beyond the family. Charles Carroll of Carrolton, a founding father of the United States, was an exceptional man."

Beth and I were captivated the whole time by what Mama and Papa said and read about Charles Carroll. But it was years before I understood a lot of what they said.

"You see, kids," Mama said, "not only is it exciting to think about our family as a part of the Carrolls of Carrollton, but there are things from Mr. Charles Carroll of Carrollton's life that Uncle Jim and Grandfather Bill wanted you to understand and make a part of yours."

Papa went further, saying to Beth and me, "You see, kids, you share the blood of the Carrolls of Carrollton, and we all share the country Charles Carroll helped bring about. We also share the pioneering spirit of those Carrolls, a common faith in the same Lord, and the same sense of the importance of personal virtue and goodness of the people that make up the country we live in. These all go together to make our country work.

"Even though your Great Grandfather Raford Carroll never knew anything of the life of privilege Charles Carroll of Carrollton knew, and even though he was not from a family of great wealth like the Carrolls of Maryland, your great grandfather knew he and his family could be people of virtue just like his distant relative. He was, and so can you be."

Beth and I looked at each other. We were both proud to know about our family's connection to Mr. Charles of Carrollton, what kind of man he was, and how Great Grandfather was like him in the best ways even if not so fortunate in other ways.

The night got quiet, and everyone turned in. I stared up at the clear moon again.

I wondered about how wealthy one distant part of our family line had become, and how poor another. Like Uncle Jim, I couldn't make sense of such things then, and I can't now. I also wondered about what wealth is. Is it how much money or land you have, or the position you hold? Or is it something different, like Papa said? Something like virtue, maybe even the richness of family?

I wouldn't understand fully until many years later, but that night I began to see what Uncle Jim meant about my roots. That they are in Seminary Township even when we're far away, and they are deep in our blood relations, even distant ones. Even as a young boy, that night I caught a glimpse that my deepest roots are in our legacy of faith and virtues.

Twelve—Providential Junctions

We followed the Southwest Trail south alongside the Cairo and Fulton Railroad on the western edge of Lonoke County through the northern town of Ward. The farther south we traveled the more cotton fields we saw, miles and miles and miles it seemed. I'd never seen farms that big anywhere. It was breathtaking.

When we stopped at the blacksmith in Ward to fix a wheel on our wagon, I talked to a local farmer, as I had back in Pocahontas. I told him I was amazed at how big the farms were in the area, and he nodded yes. But when I asked him about the history of that part of Arkansas, he told me an even more amazing story. About how way back before those farms were there, somewhere between five hundred and a thousand years ago, he said, a whole different civilization covered the area—the whole area, many times bigger even than the farms I saw. "It's what folks who study such things call the Toltec region," he said. "Where a people called a Plum Bayou culture lived." I could hardly believe it and I tried to think about how long ago that was—as long ago or more than the O'Carrolls back in Ireland, it sounded like. I asked about those people.

"They were sophisticated. A people, as the story goes, even the old Aztecs said were the most advanced civilization around. That's something, because those Aztecs, it's said, were darn well advanced, even if they were a strange and brutal people, I'm told. Anyway, the old Toltec people's ceremonial center in this area is just south, near what today is the village of Keo."

Everywhere our wagons passed, there was a new story.

We intersected the first truly improved part of the Southwest Trail as we entered the Little Rock area. The endless fields of cotton and corn spread wide to the north and towering cypress trees jutted up from the water in the winding oxbow lakes to the south.

Talking to some workers along the way, we learned we were in the middle of one huge farm. The Alexander Plantation, part of the older Pemberton Plantation, we found out later that night.

The Trail took a sharp bend to the west at a corner of the big farm. Just after that junction there was a small store on the south side. It sat just off the road in front of one of those meandering ponds, surrounded and shaded by a tall grove of bottomland hardwoods and bald cypress. Papa decided to stop for supplies. It was a simple place but well-stocked. A plantation store, we learned, in what was once Youngs Township—a general store for the big farm.

There we met Mr. Charles Alexander Jr., who was about seventeen or eighteen years old or so, about seven or eight years older than me then. He was the son of Mr. Charles Alexander Sr., he would tell us, who with his wife Blanche Pemberton inherited half of the Pemberton Plantation. They'd merged that big old inherited parcel with Mr. Alexander Sr.'s smaller one and ran it as the Alexander Plantation. Just back from college, Charles Jr. ran the store.

We pulled up and tied off the wagons and got out. Papa took Rachel and helped Mama down and we all stretched and shook the dust off. Papa, Uncle John, and I went into the store. As we entered, Charles said, "Welcome," and stepped over and extended his hand to introduce himself.

"I'm Charles Alexander, how can I help you?"

Taking his hand, Papa said, "Hello Mr. Alexander, I'm William Howell."

"Good to meet you, Mr. Howell. Please, just call me Charles."

Charles and Uncle John shook hands. Then he extended his hand to me, and we shook. I felt grown up again when he did that, but a little different because he was not too far from my age.

Papa asked Charles if we could water our teams from the well-filled cistern nearby. He said, "Oh, yes. Of course, please do."

I went back out and got a bucket and opened the tap to fill it, wiping my face with some of the cool water, it felt really good. I watered the horses and headed back inside. Just as I did, Beth held the hole-ridden screen door as Mama went in with Rachel, and straggling behind Maurine and Bill slowly climbed the three wooden steps and went in, followed by Beth and me.

It was nice to be indoors again.

While Papa and Uncle John went through the store gathering supplies, I looked up at the top of the long curved-glass counter where there was a bunch of jars of jerky and stick candy. Charles saw me and said, "Which kind do you like?" I looked at Mama.

She said, "Sure, honey, but only one apiece for each of you." I picked a yellow one, Beth picked a red one, and we got one each of the same for

Maurine and Bill. "No running till you're finished," Mama instructed us—she looked at me then glanced at Bill. I understood.

Papa and Uncle John finished their shopping, and I walked around with them sucking on my candy stick as they talked with Charles. He and Papa discussed where we were from and where we were headed. And Papa asked about the Alexander Plantation and farming around the area.

Papa paid for our supplies and expressed our gratitude for the water for the teams. "You're welcome," Charles said. And then he said, "Since it's late in the day, if you'd like, you're more than welcome to camp next to the store for the night."

Papa looked at Charles, and said, "Well, son, that's a more than generous offer. It's been a long day, so we'll take you up on it. Now, let me offer you something in return. When you close up, please come over and have supper with us."

"I'd love to, Mr. Howell. Thank you so much."

Papa and Uncle John built a fire and Mama cooked up some of the fresh squash we'd got in the store, and some, what she called, collard greens—something I'd never had before. She mixed them in the big black skillet along with some onions and dices of potatoes we'd bought. Pushing that mixture to one side, on the other she fried some full cuts of the cured ham we brought.

Charles joined us for supper and was beside himself when he tasted Mama's big old drop biscuits, with the last bits of apple butter we had.

It was a wonderful evening under those trees next to the store. Charles told us about his papa's farm, about the soil in Arkansas made rich from the remnants of an ancient glacial flow that made the Mississippi an alluvial plain—that word again, I remember—and about cotton.

"This area in Arkansas is built on cotton," he said, "though we grow lots of other things including lots of corn and rice. We take our cotton down the road to the Cobb Cotton Gin in Keo, the old Cobb settlement named for Mr. Lafayette Cobb."

I remembered that town called Keo from when the farmer in Ward mentioned it. Charles told us it was a small village near a large pecan grove, and that it was becoming a local cotton hub since the Altheimer-Argenta branch of the St. Louis, Arkansas, and Texas Railway was put in place fifteen years earlier. That railroad line allowed shipments to ports up north and down south in New Orleans and over to Galveston on the Texas coast, he told us.

That night Papa and Uncle John began learning about farming in this area, and about the importance of the cotton gin, the railroads, and the geography for the varied crops and for commerce.

But most important, we made our first friend in Arkansas that night. At least as much as one can over a single meal.

Charles could see weariness in our faces, so he thanked Mama for the great meal and all of us for the conversation and took his leave. We settled down.

It was a clear and comfortable spring night, so Papa, Uncle John, and I slept by the coals. Mama and the rest slept in the wagon.

We'd reached a crucial junction that day on our trip to Texarkana. We all slept hard.

We woke early and we didn't dally after breakfast but loaded things up to head out toward Little Rock. Charles said it was about eight miles west. Papa said he hoped to get a few miles the other side before we'd make camp again.

Charles opened the store just as we were leaving and hollered out, "If y'all ever come back through this area, be sure and look me up."

* * *

Looking at his maps, Papa said we would cross the Arkansas River at Little Rock and travel southwest a few weeks over to Hot Springs. From there we'd turn farther south and west for a couple of weeks, through Arkadelphia, Prescott, and Hope, to reach our new home.

Embarking on the east-west path of the Old Southwest Trail that morning, we soon passed out of Lonoke into Pulaski County. At supper the night before, Papa had asked Charles about that name—it was strange to me. He said it came from a Polish army officer named Casimir Pulaski. He came to the Colonies at the invitation of Mr. Benjamin Franklin, who met him in Paris when he was in France rallying support for the Revolutionary War. Mr. Franklin recommended him to General George Washington. He served under Washington and saved his life at the Battle of Brandywine and became an American hero and a Brigadier General.

Hearing that story, once again I thought about that picture of Mr. Washington over Grandfather Bill's fireplace back home. About how woven into our family American patriotism is, and about how woven it is into the places and towns across the whole country.

As we crossed into Pulaski just before crossing the Arkansas River into Little Rock, off to the north and west we saw a high two-hundred-foot bluff, what we came to learn was Big Rock Mountain, part of the Ouachita range cut out by the river. That mountain got its name, we were told, by being about three miles upriver from what an old French explorer had named "Le

Petit Rocher," a French phrase for "the Little Rock," the city's name. On that tall bluff, we learned, was a place called Fort Logan Military Post, a large munitions depot and army base. We heard they'd started building it earlier, but it got interrupted by the Spanish-American War, the one Papa had been in, and had just started building on it again as we came through Little Rock.

I thought to myself how Arkansas was connected to so many things I'd been learning on our adventure, about differences in the land and farming, especially big plantations and cotton, and about war, the Revolutionary War, the Civil War, and the Spanish-American War.

We headed across the big river, the biggest we'd seen since crossing the wide Mississippi out of Illinois into St. Louis. In the city, right where we crossed on the Free Bridge, that river runs almost due west to east. The bridge took us from the community of Argenta on the north side of the river straight into Little Rock. As we crossed, we could see another high point bluff area to the west on the south side of the river, what we learned were the foothills of the Ouachita Mountains.

We passed a streetcar like we saw in St. Louis just as we entered Little Rock. Charles had told us the best route is to turn west along the river road and catch Broadway through the city, where it continues the Southwest Trail out of town. But we made a mistake and missed Broadway but didn't know it until it was getting dark.

We'd traveled about fifteen miles from Charles Alexander's store through Little Rock to just south of the river on the bluff we saw from the bridge. We were in at a heavily wooded grove on the foothills of those Ouachita Mountains, at the base of a place we'd later learn was named Pulaski Heights the same year we came through. We were set for the final leg of our trip.

There we camped in the flats below Pulaski Heights before heading to Hot Springs.

The next morning, we backtracked and connected with Broadway out of town. It took us about a week to travel through the Arkansas River Valley that lies between the Ozarks to the north and the Ouachita to the south. We finally arrived in Hot Springs.

That was another new kind of place I'd never seen before—a natural wonder where underground hot water springs bubbled up to the surface, what the Indians called the valley of the vapors. I found it interesting when we learned that old President Jackson made this place, what he called Hot Springs Reservation, the first national park. People came from across the country for holidays and for special medical treatments in the thermal waters, in what they called public bath houses. I remember that sounded strange to me. I'm not sure there was connection, but the night we camped there, Papa and Mama learned the town of Hot Springs had gotten a reputation for illegal gambling and prostitution. They were happy to pull out the next morning.

Due to a recent flood south of Hot Springs near Arkadelphia, we were advised to head west to De Queen and go into Texarkana from the north. The detour added another week or so to our journey. But there in De Queen, I again saw something new, a new "industry" they called it, the large-scale timber and lumber industry. De Queen had become a central place for this new kind of business, harvesting logs from the lower part of the Ozark mountains and processing them into lumber for local and regional use and for shipment across the US.

We made good time from De Queen, so it took us only three or four more days to arrive in Texarkana, a city split right in the middle of the town between Texas and Arkansas, with Louisiana just thirty miles away. Papa was thrilled. We all were.

Every slow mile of our journey turned out to be an adventure. A journey I didn't want to make. I was a boy when we took it and could not have known then, but without it my dreams would have been too small and my heart too unprepared for when I became a man.

Forged on the Unyielding Anvil of Life

And how important good habits are in life's perilous storms.

Spring 1908 to Midwinter of 1954

The excellent man is urged, by interior necessity, to appeal from himself to some standard beyond himself, superior to himself, whose service he freely accepts . . . it is the man of excellence, and not the common man who lives in essential servitude.

José Ortega y Gasset

Thirteen—New Starts, Travails . . . and Tragedies

Spring 1908 to Fall of 1913

Mama sat in a narrow wooden rocking chair on the front porch in her ankle length floral calico print dress holding baby Theresa. She watched over her brood. Beth and Maurine played Graces, an old game Mama taught them— one she'd played with her sister Ollie, where you have two dowel rod sticks and a circular hoop, and you drop the hoop over the sticks and push them apart in your hands sending the hoop flying in the air for the other player to try and catch. Whoever catches the hoop ten times first wins. Bill dug in the dirt, whisking away the ants that crawled in straight lines, and Rachel jumped to catch a butterfly in the dusty front yard.

We'd been settled in Texarkana for three years. That bustling railroad town nestled on the northeast edge of the great piney woods forest of East Texas, an oak-hickory system of pine and oak and rich hardwood bottomlands. It was not just like Vandalia, but it wasn't all that different, except the winters weren't as harsh. Our new home wasn't buried in the dense forest and bogs farther south and west. It was on a piece of flatland cleared a decade or so before we arrived, with one tiny wooden farmhouse on it and barn just big enough for our horses and the one milk cow we kept.

There, in that little sharecropper's house on Mr. Augustus Allen's eighteen-acre farm about two and half miles out of town on the Texas side, our new start had taken root. New life was sprouting, and not just in the crops we planted, in our family too. I had a new baby sister, Theresa.

"It's that 'Pompeian Beauty Powder and Day Cream' I got for her, I'm sure," I heard Papa tell Uncle John at supper one night. "What she'd seen in the *Ladies' Home Journal* magazine," he said. "That's what accounts for

Theresa, I'm pretty sure," he told Uncle John in a smirky whispering voice. Mama looked up at Papa from nursing Theresa and smiled. "You boys be good now," she said, and they all three broke out laughing. I wasn't quite sure why.

Papa was the head and provider for the family, but Mama was the center of our home. She made it a good one, and with the simplest things filled it full of laughter. The new start in Texarkana was not all they'd imagined, but every morning they saw new prospects.

Life was hard but good in those early days. Each day began well before dawn, as it does for all farmers. Mama almost always got up first to feed Theresa and then gave her to Papa till the rest of us got up. She navigated the darkness of her and Papa's small bedroom, lit a lantern, and went into the kitchen to reignite the stove with woodchips or kerosene. She'd adjust the damper to make the temperature just right for cooking breakfast, head to the outhouse and wash up in the cistern, and come back in to get things started. Papa, Uncle John and me would be up by then, taking our turns in the outhouse. I'd gather the eggs from the chicken coop and a bucket of milk from the Jersey in the barn while Mama got my sisters and brother up.

Breakfast usually meant fresh eggs and sausage taken from the narrow smokehouse section of the barn, fresh brewed coffee, and those wonderful, pan-fried drop biscuits with butter and homemade jams—and if we were lucky some of that sweet apple butter. Finished cooking, Mama filled the plates and all of us sat scrunched at the small round table. Papa'd read a Bible verse, then returned thanks, and on days of drought he gave a special prayer for rain. That was our routine every day, except when we got ham steak or bacon instead of sausage.

Mama made sack lunches for us kids to take to school—me and Beth and Maurine to begin with, then later Bill and eventually Rachel, all at Rose Hill Grammar School in town on the Texas side. Theresa was too young for school when we were in Texarkana. The school calendar lasted six months revolving around the crops, starting just after cotton-picking season and ending just before cotton chopping in the late spring. The subjects were reading, writing, physiology and hygiene, geography, history, arithmetic, and penmanship, girls on one side of the room and boys on the other. I was always good at the first five and got better at the last two over time. For boys ten and over, like me, school let out at noon so we could go help work the fields.

On some days then, after getting us off to school, Mama would take Theresa to the barn in the crib to gather more milk and spend the day separating the yellowish fat and the cream from the top, then the skim milk, and straining the whole milk for drinking and cooking. She'd set aside the cream for churning into butter, which Beth and I helped with on Saturdays. And she'd allow some to culture for buttermilk, which we'd pour over crumbled leftover cornbread in a glass for a special treat. The milk that remained Mama used to make cheese. Not too long after we got to Texarkana, there was an iceman we paid to come by every few days and give us a block for a cold storage bin in the barn. That's where we kept the milk products in pots; it gave them a longer life. Later, that same iceman became our milk man, bringing us fresh milk from a local farmer who'd a made a business out of dairy, though Mama or I still milked the Jersey for the other milk products. That simplified life for Mama a whole lot.

On other days, Mama would mend and make clothes for us all . . . oh, what memories, like that old fur-collared coat I wore on the porch that morning on Hoggin' Day so long ago. Mama was so good at making us clothes back then. Her work never stopped.

Daily she'd make bread and dough for biscuits. In the springtime she canned food from the garden, and made jams, jellies, and preserves, which Beth and I helped her with. On Fridays she made pies and cakes and cookies to take into town on Saturdays with some left for us when we got home. My favorites were the fruit pies, especially the strawberry and blackberry from our garden, and those juicy plum and peach ones from the trees on the side of the house.

Mama took care of everything at home for us to get along, including tending that garden just behind the house, which me, Beth, Maurine, and even Bill helped her with. As I think back it reminds me of Mama telling stories about helping with the garden when she was a girl back in Illinois, out by those big old asparagus bushes where she planted the jonquil bulbs after the fire.

Mama got a short break to sit down after supper when I was tasked with cleaning and washing things up using the water from that big copper pot Mama always kept filled and hot on the thick back part of the steel slab wood-burning cookstove—the same pot she bathed little Rachel in on our trip down to Texas.

Papa and Uncle John left each day just after breakfast, taking Mr. Allen's tractor to the fields. I went with them in the summertime, and after I got out of school in the fall, winter, and spring. We grew cotton and tried sugar the first year as our cash crops—though the sugar didn't work, not good for the Texarkana area—and also corn. We prepared the fields of rich soil for planting with Mr. Allen's tractor in the fall and the spring, depending on the crop, and dug trenches to capture and direct the rainwater to crops that needed it.

Even though the sugar crop didn't work for us, Mama always likes to tell about when she first saw five- and ten-pound bags of white granulated sugar in a grocery in Texarkana. "Up 'til then," she says, "all we ever had was brown sugar. Can you believe that?"

During planting and harvest, Mr. Allen hired a crew of hands to help, mostly local area negroes and some poorer whites that relied on the seasonal work. We didn't have much, not much more than many of the day workers, but we had enough to be tenant farmers, where we worked the land, paid some rent, and earned a half-share of the yield from the harvest.

When the harvest came in, we'd take the cotton on big flat wagons to Mr. M. C. Lively's gin and the corn to the Fouke Grain Company. There we got paid for our yield, and then we'd pay Mr. Allen his 50 percent portion. Since we had a little money saved from working the old farm back home until we left and we had some of our own equipment, we didn't have to draw much from Mr. Allen between planting and harvest, and we didn't have to rely on crop-liens with the stores in town. If all went well, our share of the profits went further for us than for some of the other tenant farmers in the area.

Things were going pretty well, Papa often said back then. We'd made a new start and a new home in Texarkana. "Not much of one," he'd say, "better than some, less than others. But happy." Then he'd smile. Papa smiled a lot then.

* * *

Saturdays and Sundays were especially good.

On Saturday we'd all head to town for the day to resupply and for the festivities. We'd take all those pies, cakes, and cookies Mama made and fresh vegetables from the garden to sell and exchange. The town bustled with families and activity. It was festival-like every Saturday.

Texarkana had long had a reputation, some papers wrote, as a place for "idlers, thieves, burglars, and ne'er-do-wells" as well as "gamblers, gunmen, and other lawless individuals" who were regular patrons in the red-light district down near Swampoodle Creek. It'd been a place made up mostly of saloons, gambling, and crime, where it was easy to escape from Arkansas to Texas and from Texas to Arkansas by simply crossing State Line Avenue or hopping a train to disappear. Texarkana was born from the intersection of railroads at the borders of Texas, Louisiana, Arkansas, and the Oklahoma territory. But it had become a thriving place ever since Mr. Jay Gould, who many people called a robber baron, formed the St. Louis Southwestern

Railway Company by combining the Missouri Pacific, the Texas and Pacific, the St. Louis Southwestern, and the International-Great Northern lines— folks called it the Cotton Belt Line.

When we first got there, we rarely went into town. But after a while Texarkana grew and had lots of regular businesses, new industries, and many churches, even though it was still driven by the railroads carrying farm commodities and lumber north, south, east, and west.

Those Saturdays we'd drive the two and half miles into town from the west across the railroad tracks into Arkansas, on the northern side passing by the new Texarkana Baptist Orphanage. There was a straighter shot that took less time, but Papa often took this route because the roads straight in were all dried out with big ruts left by the wagons from the rains. But that Saturday it was beautiful. Once in town we went just a bit farther south into the city center to the farmer's market. There we parked our wagons and set up a makeshift booth to exchange things and sell our produce. Mama and the girls took the cakes, pies, and cookies over to Mrs. Jenny Simmons, where everyone could test out the many desserts after the sandwiches and fixins most brought from home—though some of the better-off folks bought their lunch and some treats from Mr. McCartney's restaurant on the patio of the Cosmopolitan Hotel.

That day, just as I was about to help Mama with some of the desserts, Bill jumped from the wagon onto my back wrapping his arms around my neck like he was riding a runaway horse, a game we played at home. I spun around like a wild Mustang, but he held on. And as I did that, I saw Billy Mercer, a friend from school, walk up with his little brother Harold. Billy and I'd become good friends, and I'd met Harold a few times but didn't know him well. But I did recognize he had some issues. He couldn't talk very well and didn't seem to understand things and looked strange in the face. But he was always in a good mood. I didn't understand Harold's issues until one day Billy said it was what a British doctor named John Down called "Mongolism." When Bill climbed off me, Harold motioned for me to spin him too. I looked at Billy and he shrugged his shoulders as if saying, "Okay with me if it's okay with you." I stooped down and let him get on, and I spun him round and round. He squealed like a stuck hog and laughed out loud. Billy retrieved him from my back, then we both picked up some pies and took them over to the dessert table for Mama. Billy and I chatted for a bit, then he and Harold headed back to their family's wagon—I knew him from school, but he was also our neighbor. His family farmed next to us.

No matter the time of year, on Saturdays in town the women and girls had their long hair stacked high on their heads, and most had some kind of bonnet on, like it was a spring day. It was a great social time, and we all loved it. That Saturday I heard one of the ladies telling Mama about a new organization they'd started in Texarkana. The Lone Star chapter of the "Daughters of the American Revolution," she called it. Part of a national organization started by Mrs. Caroline Scott Harrison, wife of President Benjamin Harrison. I'd never heard of it before then, but the ladies were excited about it. Talking with them Mama mentioned that our family has some of the blood of the Carrolls of Carrollton in our veins. All the women perked up and wanted to hear more so Mama told them. They were impressed, and that made Mama feel good, I remember. They asked her to join the club and she was pleased. I loved seeing Mama feel special.

I'd taken Bill and gone back over to be with Papa and Uncle John to help sell some of the produce. Just as we got there our landlord Mr. Allen came by. He told Papa about his investment in the new St. Louis Cotton Compress Company. I didn't know what that meant then, and neither did Papa or Uncle John. Mr. Allen explained how the new compresses pressed the cotton together tight and lowered the cost of shipping. Before the hydraulic compressors, he said, workers called screwmen used screwjacks to pack and stow cotton bales by hand. That's all we'd ever seen. The compressors shrunk the bales from gins by about half, so the cost of shipment was a lot less.

I remember thinking how much I'd learned about cotton since we met and first talked about it with Mr. Charles Alexander Jr. that night outside his store back in Lonoke County.

Good weather Saturdays were the best. They were the most relaxing time small farmer-families like us ever had. The younger kids played with all their friends until late in the afternoon, and all of us had a great time. And that Saturday was a great day.

As we packed up to leave, Billy and Harold came back by. They were walking home, and Billy asked if I wanted to come with them. I looked at Papa, and he said, "Sure, just come straight on home. It'll be getting cold after dark."

The sun hung low in the sky just as we crossed State Line Avenue back into Texas. As we walked along, Billy and I talked about the day, the people and things we'd seen, and Harold sang to himself out loud shaking his head smiling all the way. He seemed happy all the time. We were just on the edge of town near Swampoodle Creek, probably a mile or so from home when we were approached by a group of boys. I'd seen one of them around and knew his name, Jack. I recognized a few others from school. Jack was a couple of years older than me, and I knew he had a reputation as a rough kid. They came up and Jack said, "Hey guys, where y'all going?"

"Just headed home," I said, and we kept walking.

Then they started gigging and making fun of Harold. We kept walking.

All of a sudden Jack grabbed Harold and spun him around, so fast he fell down. He looked up at Jack confused but still smiling. Billy stepped forward toward Jack and I stepped in between.

"Why did you do that? Harold did nothing to you," I said, my anger rising. My quick temper was on edge.

Jack started making faces, mimicking Harold, and making strange noises. I got madder and madder at Jack. Then he looked at me and said, "Wha'd ya gonna do about it, shorty?"

I hadn't yet hit my growth spurt and was shorter than many kids my age, but I was stocky. Suddenly Jack shoved me and took a swing at my face. I moved and he missed. With that he took another swing and this time he hit me square in the jaw, so hard it made my mouth start to bleed.

"There you go, stump-on-a-rock. You're a short weakling, dumb shit, ain't you, shorty?"

Without even thinking I took a swing at Jack and hit him so hard he fell down face-first in the dirt. The other boys were taken aback. Jack got up and they all took off, nothing more said.

My heart was racing. I looked at Harold, and he looked back smiling. I saw Billy and for a moment we stood in rigid silence staring at each other. . . then he said, "Wow Claude! Wow, way to go, man. You showed him. One swing and old Jack's flat-out on the ground, his face in the dirt."

I felt proud for a minute but didn't say anything. Then I felt bad.

All the rest of the way home I thought about what Uncle John said about war. That war should be a last resort, not a first resort like pulling a hair trigger on a gun. But that there are times when war is forced upon us. I wasn't sure if this little battle had been forced upon me, or if I'd just lost my temper and let Jack get the best of me. I just felt bad, and my jaw hurt.

When I got home, I stopped at the barn and took some water from a bucket and washed my face before going in. Mama saw me first and rushed over. She could see something was wrong. Papa noticed and got up and came over too. "What happened, son?" Papa asked. And I told them. Mama checked me over to see if I was all right. "Okay Claude, sit down and let's talk about it," Papa said.

We spent a little while going over what happened. He could see I was not proud of myself, as I stared at the floor with my head low. He didn't say too much, but he did tell me something like what Uncle John had said about war.

"Sometimes," he said, "you're put in situations you can't avoid fighting, but whenever possible you should try and walk away. Look at me now, son. See, here's the problem.

"When you get caught up in a fight you can't ever tell what might happen. One thing leads to another, and somebody can really get hurt, often just by accident. Try and stay away from trouble. Just walk away whenever possible, even if you think you're in the right. Always better to be safe than sorry. Always better to turn the other cheek. Courage can sometimes mean backing away, especially when your actions can carry over onto others around you. And in the end, try and never let anger lead you into a quarrel. But standing up for others is always a good thing, son, especially for those who can't stand up for themselves. I'm proud of you for that. Just don't let anger get the best of you. I'm sorry this happened. Keep a watch out for those fellows and stay away from them if you can. You understand? I love you, son."

"I do, Papa," I mumbled. Then Mama pulled me up from the chair and put her arms around me. It was hard going to sleep that night. I'd never been in a fight before.

I've thought back on that little fight many times. And how quick-tempered I am. I don't like myself that way—ever since I first noticed it that night at Grandfather Bill's old cabin after the fire when everything seemed too relaxed, like they'd all just forgotten the whole thing. Then again when Papa and Mama said we were leaving Illinois. I don't know why. I'm mostly calm and easygoing. But some things just get to me, and when they do, I react quickly.

* * *

We'd had a good crop that year, some cotton and lots of corn and soybeans—we even had a good harvest of pecans from a grove along the tree-lined edge at the back of Mr. Allen's property. We made a good profit. Papa said we were well on our way to the new start he'd hoped for when we came to Texas. The slow but steady success of our new venture felt good. I was old enough to be a real part of it, and it made me feel proud. Things really were looking up.

We gathered in the wagon early Sunday morning. This time to go to church at Beech Street Baptist, in its monumental new Beaux-Arts classical building, as Pastor David called it. It had been a good year for us and a good Christmas.

Coming back from town on the last day of December, Papa picked up a copy of the *Texarkana Gazette*. He read that at midnight a 700-pound lighted "electric ball" would drop down a flagpole atop the *New York Times* building in New York City. The first-ever "ball-drop" had happened

December 31 the year before, and they were doing it again to ring in 1909. The paper also said Mr. Wilbur Wright took a nearly two-and-a-half-hour flight in his areo-plane, the longest one ever. The calendar was changing. The world was looking up.

Then came the new year.

We lost all the corn for harvest that spring and most of the cotton we'd planted that spring, but we didn't know that until fall. That was the problem. A bad spring storm tore things up and soaked the ground too much all at once. The corn was ruined along with most of the cotton seedlings but not all. Papa was forced to draw on Mr. Allen and on the stores in town for credit for the first time to replant and carry us to the summer-fall harvest. We replanted the worst-hit acres, worked hard, and it looked like we'd be okay. Then in September the remnants of the Grand Isle Hurricane that hit the Louisiana coast came up through Texarkana and devastated the whole crop. All our bridge credit became burdensome debt we couldn't pay.

Everything we'd built over the past three and half years was gone, all in the blink of an eye. When the weight of the loss pressed down upon Papa, it was too much. He was heartbroken.

What Uncle Jim said about what we do and don't control came to my mind. My heart sunk for Papa and for us all. But it was what came next that made me feel even lower.

Papa talked to Mr. Allen, and they agreed on a plan. Mr. Allen wrote a letter to Herman Dierks on Papa and Uncle John's behalf about jobs at his Lumber and Coal Company in De Queen. Mr. Dierks had bought the Williamson Brothers mill and needed more help. Papa agreed to move our family up there and work labor jobs to pay off our debts, both to Mr. Allen and to the stores in Texarkana. But Mr. Allen made another suggestion, one Papa resisted at first but finally agreed to—I would stay in Texarkana and mind the farmhouse and work at Mr. Allen's cotton compressor factory. That way we'd have three incomes to allow Papa to pay the debt off sooner. And it would allow Beth, Maurine, and Bill to continue with school in De Queen. Mr. Allen said he'd make sure I could go the fifty miles and see everyone once a month or so.

Once again, almost as sudden as the fire took our house back home and as the fight broke out with Jack, our world was turned upside down.

I stretched and wrapped the old canvas cover across the wooden arches on one of the wagons like I did when we left Illinois. And helped Papa and Uncle John load it with provisions for about a week.

I watched the dust clouds gather behind their wagon as they all left that winter morning. The drab brown leaves hanging dead on the blackjack red oaks I saw in the distance in front of them captured how I felt. I squinted until I couldn't see them anymore. There I stood on the same plankboard porch of our small house that had been so active and happy a year and a half before. When Mama sat happily holding Theresa and watching the girls and Bill play in the barren yard. With their absence a new barrenness occupied our front yard and little porch. I was alone for the first time—I remembered wondering how old Charles Carroll leaving his family must have felt. All at once, I knew. When I walked inside the empty, quiet house, the feeling got worse.

Everyone but me moved to De Queen in January of 1910. There they lived and Papa and Uncle John worked as lumber laborers at Mr. Herman Dierks's lumber company for the next two years. That new forestry and lumber industry we'd seen developing when we first came through De Queen back in '05 had become big business in the Ozarks. But Papa and Uncle John were just small cogs in the wheel. The work was steady, though, and paid cash weekly. But even with that and what little I contributed it would take a long while to recover from our loss.

I stayed in Texarkana, walked into town each day, and worked at Mr. Allen's cotton businesses, and took care of his tenant farmhouse at night. Our house.

I had to give up school. But I borrowed books from the school library and continued to read and study a lot at home by myself. It was about all there was to do. Like school lessons, I wrote down a lot of the things I'd learned on our trip down to Texas, the places we saw and how it felt, the people we met and the conversations we had. Things I've kept through the years in Uncle Jim's old chest.

It was a lonely two years. God, it was lonely. I'd never known anything like it. The little farmhouse was so empty and, except in the high summer, most often dark by the time I got home. Billy's papa would come by to check on me now and again, but mostly I was alone. It was sweltering hot in the summer and bone-chilling cold in the winter. My routine each night was to come in, light the lantern just inside the door, light a fire in the winter, fix a bit of supper and clean things up, take my boots off, and settle into Papa's chair. I'd sit reading and writing by the kerosene glow until time to go to bed. Except for a few coyotes howling in the distance, it was quiet—oh, so quiet. Always before, Papa and Mama and my sisters and brother were around filling the house with constant activity and sounds. Until those two years of quietness in that little house, I never realized or noticed just how much my life simply was my family. I missed everyone so much.

To beat the loneliness, or at least delay it a bit, on occasion I'd stay in town after work and meet up with Billy for supper—it was really good to have a friend. His curfew was sundown, though, so most of those times we'd head home together.

But sometimes I stayed and took a walk around town. Texarkana had changed a lot since we arrived. Most places were calm. But some, I can tell you, were still no place for a sixteen-year-old to hang around by himself after dark. I stayed away from those areas except one night. I won't say much about it, but, well, it was one of those life-shaping moments for me.

There was lots of activity in town on Friday nights. And most places were good to have a stroll and kill time. And I had a lot of that. It was a nice night, so I walked up West Broad Street through the quiet after hours in the business district, and crossed Stateline Avenue continuing up East Broad. Just after I crossed, I heard some laughter and lots of noise, so I turned south on Pine over to Front Street into the railyard district. The noise level increased the closer I got. The atmosphere was like one big party. There were people everywhere and nothing but bars and gambling halls up and down the Front. I'd never seen the railyard that way, but I'd never seen it on a Friday night. And I'd certainly never been in a bar or gambling hall. I admit I was curious. Though I could feel Mama and Papa on each of my shoulders saying, "Watch out, son. This is not the place for you," I decided to go in one of the rowdy places anyway.

It was crazy loud, thunderous compared to the quiet of my nights at home during those days. An extremely attractive woman approached me and said, "Boy, your eyes are like saucers. See anything you like?" I didn't know what she meant at first . . . until, as she stared into my eyes and I into her half-exposed breasts, it dawned on me. It was an invitation. Of a kind I'd never had before. I excused myself and walked over to the bar, which because of my diminutive stature was up to my chest. I leaned back against an open spot and stood there looking out across the crowded room trying to make sense of it all. Then like an explosion, suddenly a fight broke out right there in the middle of the place. Men shoved and swung at each other and threw chairs all over the place. Then there was a real explosion. A deafeningly loud gunshot blast went off right behind me. My ears went dull, and everything stopped. I turned to see smoke circling up from the pistol in the bartender's hand. A sheriff's deputy rushed in and arrested the two men that had started the fight. The music and noise picked up as before. In that moment I confronted the truth of the imagined voice of Papa and Mama on my shoulders. This was no place for me.

I retreated through the crowded mass over to the saloon door and left. Hurrying away from the area, I wound up over at the corner of Sixth and Beech Street. I sat down for a minute to take stock of what'd happened. Right there, as it turned out, on the Romanesque steps of Beech Street Baptist Church—I'm not quite sure what that coincidence meant if anything, but it seemed to mean something at the time.

I headed back west toward home, taking the short route Billy and I took the day of the fight, by Swampoodle Creek. Well, that wasn't such a good choice either. I knew people called it the "red-light district" but until that night I didn't know what it meant. While there was a certain subtlety with the woman in the bar, there was nothing at all shy about the women at Swampoodle Creek.

Now it was not just Mama and Papa whispering in my ear, it was also Uncle Jim and Great Grandfather Raford Carroll talking to me about virtue.

I began to run and kept running all the way home. For better or worse, that night I discovered something. Something I didn't want, the life I encountered on my walk around town that Friday night. And something I did want, I wanted more. I discovered I wanted what Great Grandfather Raford left North Carolina for. Someday I wanted to find a wife and have family of my own.

* * *

I was seventeen when Papa, Mama, Uncle John, and everyone came back to Texarkana late in 1912. It was a great reunion. Mama made a big roast with lots of potatoes and carrots, and even those great pan biscuits, something I hadn't had much of for two years—I had gone to visit them on the train when Mr. Allen made way, but it turned out my visits were only a few times, not once a month as he'd promised. The debts were all paid off. I'm reminded of Grandmother Carroll's mules and Uncle Jim and his brother's trip to sell them, and about our land that Papa sold after the fire. We could finally start farming as a family again. It was so good to feel the house full of life again, to hear it full of chatter and laughter again. It was so good to be together again.

The rhythm of our life returned to what it was before, for most of the next year.

Until one morning in late October of 1913 when Mama went out to the barn to milk the Jersey. The first bucket was about half full when she heard a shattering noise in the house and a terrible scream. She rushed in thinking something happened to Theresa, who was then five. There in the kitchen she found Rachel on the floor. She grabbed her and realized she was unconscious with burns all over her little nine-year-old body. Trying to help Mama, we suspected, adjusting the big copper pot on the stove, she'd pulled it on top of herself. The same pot Mama bathed her in as an infant on the road to Texas. The scalding hot water drenched her.

Mama lifted her in her arms just as Beth and Maurine and Bill came running in. She forcefully directed Beth to get Theresa and for Bill to hitch the carriage. "Hurry!"

Everyone frantically got in. Mama and the girls were scrunched together with Rachel in Mama's lap. Bill drove the carriage—fast! So fast it took only fifteen minutes to travel the two and half miles to the Pine Street Sanitarium in town. On the way there they saw Mrs. Jean Craig outside, and Beth hollered out for her to have someone go and get Papa, Uncle John, and me.

When we arrived, Mama sat hunched over in a waiting room chair with her hands covering her face. Beth, Maurine, and Bill stood close around her, ashen-faced. Theresa buried her face into Mama's lap, hugging on her.

The silence broke with the soft sorrow-filled sounds of Dr. Nettie Klein's voice.

My sweet little sister Rachel was dead.

Fourteen—Visions of Tomorrow through Tear-Filled Eyes

Late Fall of 1913 to Early Winter 1914

Rachel's little casket sat atop the Communion table at Beech Street Baptist. Papa, Mama, and all us kids sat in the first pew just a few feet away. Mama sat straight up in a stupor, her arm around Theresa and holding her dampened handkerchief in her lap. Papa sat forward, roll-shouldered with his head tilted up just enough to stare in silence at the five-foot box in front of him. The whole town was there it seemed. Everyone we'd come to know over the past eight years packed the church. Rachel's closest friends and their families sat in the pews just behind us. The muted sounds of the crowded room mixed with the Wurlitzer tremolo that echoed off the cavernous walls as the organist played *Softly and Tenderly*.

Just before the organ stopped, Pastor David stood up, went to the pulpit, placed his Bible on it, and stood silently looking at each of us, then at Rachel's casket . . . Theresa fidgeted and Mama hugged her, pulling her close, stroking her hair. . . He fixed his gaze on Mama and Papa and began.

"Laura and Bud and all you kids, our hearts break with yours this morning as we gather to mourn the loss and celebrate the young life of Rachel taken all too soon in such a terrible accident. Hear these words from our Lord as we remember her today. 'Come unto me, all ye that labor and are heavy laden, and I will give you rest. Take my yoke upon you, and learn of me; for I am meek and lowly in heart: and ye shall find rest unto your souls.' And these, 'Let not your heart be troubled: ye believe in God, believe also in me. I am the resurrection, and the life: he that believeth in me, though he were dead, yet shall he live.' Find comfort in our Lord and lean on Him to help you bear the burden of this terrible loss. And find hope in Him,

Laura and Bud, and especially you sisters and brothers of Rachel and all of her friends here today, in Him who is the sure and confident hope that one day we will all be with her again."

Pastor David continued, and his words hung in the air.

At the end we all sang "Amazing Grace."

We buried my little sister in Texarkana. Mama's heart was broken. Papa's was shattered.

My heart was broken too. I'd never known anything like it. Rachel's absence left a deep dark hole inside. It's still there. Tears still well in my eyes as I think about helping Mama take care of my little sister since she was a baby, and when she squirmed and giggled as I spun her around on my back like Bill. The emptiness I felt in the little farmhouse when they were all away in De Queen didn't compare to the emptiness I felt in it since her death. She'd turned six just a couple of months before they left and was so grown up when they came back—so pretty and tall and only beginning to see the world through her own eyes. We were all so happy then. Her laugh made the little house sparkle again. But it was gone. Like a candle flame caught in a gust of wind, it was out. The silence of Rachel's missing presence and joyous laugh was overwhelming.

As I thought about Rachel's death, I remembered what Uncle Jim told me on a walk after the fire back in Illinois. About how everything in this life is transient, like a water vapor. It's here for a while and then gone. How so often it seems like we decide when to let it go but it's not up to us. It's in God's hands. It's all in His hands. That's true. But it was little comfort.

For quite a while Mama was in a daze most of the time, so often just going through the motions. Even those motions were mostly because she had five kids, a husband, a brother-in-law, and a farmhouse to attend to. Ever since Rachel's death she always doublechecked where Beth, Maurine, Bill and Theresa were, and gave strict instructions before going to the barn for milk—I could tell Mama questioned going to the barn to get milk to make butter the morning Rachel was burned. Her heart longed for things to have been different. But the truth is, that day wasn't unusual. It's what Mama's routine consisted of. We all second-guessed that day—Beth, who was getting Theresa up and going for the day, felt especially guilty that she had not been in the kitchen, but she couldn't have known. Maurine and Bill had the same feelings. I did too, wishing I hadn't gone to the fields with Papa, or at least had stayed home that morning to milk the cow. We all still do.

But despite her grief, somehow Mama has always seemed to have a deeper strength in the face of life's harsh realities. All us kids saw it. Somehow, we drew our strength from her. I don't know where she got her strength from, maybe from her grandmother or maybe from her father when her three brothers died. I don't really know. I asked her once and all she alluded to was God's providence, like Uncle Jim always had.

But Rachel's death affected Papa in a different, harder way. No, not harder—how could any of us miss little Rachel any less? We couldn't. Not harder, but something happened to Papa inside that became completely stifling. He had a hard time even going through the daily tasks. He couldn't seem to start living again.

The days and weeks went on. Papa did follow the day's routine with the rest of us, but it was far more labored for him. He never talked much. His heart just didn't seem to be there anymore.

The little farmhouse was quiet and gloomy, not like it used to be.

I heard Mama and Uncle John talk to Papa every now and then, encouraging him to start living again, as hard as it was for us all. But he couldn't seem to. He was trapped in a despair he had no control over. I later learned that Mama talked to Dr. Klein to see if she could help—she said it's likely bereavement related melancholy or could be a form of neurasthenia, she called it. She recommended rest to reinvigorate Papa, then said we might consider a change, possibly even someplace completely new.

In early December Mama said to him, "Let's move, Bud, and start over again. We must find a way to move on. Our beloved Rachel wouldn't want us to miss all the joy she found in her short life. We must find a way to live again."

Mama had made some pies for the Saturday gathering in town, but we didn't all go. I drove Mama to drop them off, in the same buggy she'd held Rachel on the way to the hospital. On our way I asked Mama about Papa, why he hardly moves or talks. I mean, I understood why he was so down. I was too, as were Mama and Uncle John, everyone was. But Papa was in a different state.

Turning to me as the wagon bumped and shuffled, she said, "Well, Claude, I don't know for sure, but there's some history in the Howell family that might be at work. I've thought about it but hope not. We must keep encouraging your papa. I think he'll recover, especially if we move."

"What do you mean, Mama? What do you mean by history in the Howell family?"

"His papa, son. Your Grandfather Isaac. You were young when he died, about eight years old I'd guess. You were with us at his funeral at the Corinth Baptist church, remember?"

"A little, Mama. I remember Uncle Jim talking about it and Grandmother Howell's funeral after the fire, when he told me about you losing your brothers."

I looked over at her and saw Mama's eyes tear up as she thought about what I just said.

"Yes, honey, those were terrible days. I lost all three of my brothers in a span of three years. My papa lost all his sons, the last, my brother Bob, just two years older than me, in a dreadful hunting accident. That loss almost tore Papa apart, and my sisters and me too."

As I reflected back on when Uncle Jim told me about the death of his children and Mama's brothers so long ago, I also vaguely remembered him saying some deaths are tragic mysteries. I remember being confused by it then and still don't know much about what he was referring to.

"What about the history you mentioned, Mama?"

"Well, by all accounts your Grandfather Isaac had the melancholy, Claude. And it was so bad he took his own life. It was terrible. No one knows why, not even your papa. Everybody in Seminary Township packed that small Baptist church. It was somber, so sad. Folks came and they went with nary a word because they didn't know what to say. Who does at such a time?"

"Surely you don't mean Papa would do such a thing, do you, Mama?" I was concerned.

"No, I don't, Claude. I'm sure he wouldn't. But I love your papa with all my heart, son, and we need to try and help him the best we can. Nobody I know of seems to know much about such things—I talked to Dr. Klein at the hospital about it one day when I was in town. She's the one who suggested we think about moving. We need to get him in a different setting, away from the house where Rachel's accident happened and where she's buried, to someplace new so we can have a different routine and talk again about new things, even happy things. That's why we must move. To help Papa. It'll help us all."

"I love Papa too, Mama. So much. I'm so worried about him. We need to do something to get him out of this stupor. If moving will help, I want to be a part of that."

Papa agreed to consider it.

* * *

Just after Christmas Papa took Uncle John and me to the newly refurbished Union Station in Texarkana. We took the early train to Little Rock to catch the Altheimer-Argenta line down to Keo—the little town Mr. Charles Alexander Jr. told us about that night we camped outside his store when we first came to Texas. The little village where he said they took their cotton to the Cobb Cotton Gin. We'd recently heard Keo had become a thriving central exchange point for shipping cotton and other commodity exports out of the rich soil of east central Arkansas. Maybe it would be a good place for a new start for Papa and all of us.

I'd taken the short train ride to De Queen a few times, up to visit Mama and Papa when they were there. But this was a whole new experience. I'd never eaten in a dining car before or walked between the rickety rail cars when the train was moving.

Mama had tasked me to go find us a new place to live and explore the prospects for new work—some place that would allow us to start over again without the cloud of Rachel's death hanging over Papa so constantly and maybe give him a new lease on life. Papa agreed. But they asked Uncle John to go with me to be a sounding board and watch over me a bit, even though I was eighteen and had previously lived by myself at the farmhouse for two years.

It took us about six hours to get to Little Rock because of all the stops in between, and more time to switch to the Altheimer-Argenta line. Once we got started again, it took us only about thirty minutes to go the twenty-four miles to Keo. I was struck by how different and how much faster this trip was than when we came through Lonoke County back in '05 headed to Texarkana. Sitting in the train seat I was preoccupied with thoughts about Rachel and Papa and Mama and my sisters and brother. Here we were making another move again.

When the train came to a stop, Uncle John and I stepped off with our bags. We just stood there for a minute looking across at the small town. It was small indeed compared to Texarkana. On quick survey, it was a sparse place, a flat railroad-stop and cotton gin and grain elevator town. There were no trees in the town center, and not many I saw nearby, nothing except for a large pecan tree grove that caught my eye behind us, beautifully arched together like a cathedral. To the south and east it was surrounded by good, rich farmland, with some of those snaking oxbow lakes off in the distance. We walked across the street to the Keo Hotel. A tall grain elevator down the street with a cotton gin next to it caught my eye as we got off the train—I wondered if that'd be Mr. Cobbs's gin. But I particularly noticed the remnants of a recent devastating fire that had taken its toll on the buildings on each side of the hotel.

We walked in past the porter who opened the door for us, saying "thank you" as we entered. That was really unusual for John and me, we weren't used to anyone opening the door for us. We headed over to the front desk. I glanced up at the tall ornate plaster-molded ceiling, then straight ahead to the tall dark mahogany receiving counter—measuring on me about mid-ribs high, about like the bar on Front Street in Texarkana. It had a long, beveled cut glass sheet flat across its length. Behind, on the wall was a huge smoked glass mirror stretching the same length as the counter. Below it was an inset block of key-pocket sleeves, and further below, a row of enclosed mahogany cabinets with brass pulls. A lot fancier than the places I was used to being in, far more than I'd ever stayed in.

The clerk introduced himself and welcomed us, asking if he could get us a room. Uncle John and I both said, "Yes, please, sir," at almost the same time. We weren't used to this, nor these kinds of elegant surroundings.

The clerk said, "Sure, any idea how long you plan to stay?" We didn't really know but said we thought a few days. He registered us, gave us a key and directed us up the staircase to our room on the second floor. We went up and dropped our duffle bags off.

It was getting late in the afternoon, more like early evening really, so we came back downstairs and asked the desk clerk where we might get a bite to eat. He pointed and said, "Just across the lobby is the hotel restaurant. It's quite good."

We went over to the "maître d'," as he was called, who stood next to a podium with a curved brass lamp shining on a padded leather portfolio. He asked, "How many?"

Uncle John said, "Two for supper," and the man turned to escort us to our table.

This was all new to me. I mean, I'd walked in the Cosmopolitan Hotel in Texarkana a few times and the Evans Hotel with Papa once back in Vandalia. But I'd never stayed at them and had never eaten supper at them. My life of truly new experiences had largely stopped for eight years, replaced by routine. The new things were back again. We knew eating out instead of at home would be different and expensive. But this was required. Papa had given me money for my part and Uncle John would pay for his.

A waiter came over, gave us each a glass of water and some menus, and left. We looked at them and decided we'd each have steak and fixins, which we expected to be a potato. But instead of that it came with rice and some of what they called sugar glazed carrots. It all sounded fancy to me. The waiter came and took our order and left again.

In a few minutes I felt the presence of someone come up behind me and thought it was the waiter with our food, but it seemed too quick. Then the presence tapped me on the shoulder as I saw Uncle John, eyes peering up to focus behind me. I turned and saw the fellow grinning and holding his finger to his lips asking Uncle John to be quiet. It was Mr. Charles Alexander! We all three broke out laughing. I was amazed to see him at all but especially at our table in this hotel restaurant. He said, "Hello, Mr. Howell. And how are you doing, Claude?" I was surprised he recognized us and that he remembered my name. "I guess you're older now than I was when we first met," he said. "How are y'all doing, and what in the world are you doing in Keo?"

Without hesitation we invited him to sit down at our table and have supper with us. He said, "I'd love to, but would you mind one more, my brother-in-law will be down in a minute." We said sure. In a couple of minutes, Charles's brother-in-law Mr. Lewis Gaston arrived—Mr. Gaston had married Charles's sister Margaret, and with that marriage they assumed running her portion of the Alexander Plantation. We had a great supper that night in the Keo Hotel, a good steak, good rice, grown just down the road about thirty miles we were told, in Stuttgart, and good conversation.

We caught up and talked about how we'd settled in Texarkana and had been farming there since we last saw him. We explained how a bad storm had interrupted that for a couple of years, but things had recently picked back up again, until. Charles didn't notice and said he was glad it seemed things were settled down again. But then he saw on our faces it wasn't so, when he asked why we were in town. We told him about the tragic death of Rachel—I had a hard time even saying it—and that Mama believed we needed a whole new start. We told Charles we remembered what he'd said about Keo years ago, about cotton and the railroad and all.

Not bypassing the tragedy of Rachel but seemingly wanting to get our minds off it, he said, "Well, I'm just glad you're here. It's so good to see you both. It really is."

Appearing to continue his distraction from Rachel's death, after supper Charles called the waiter over and whispered something to him. A minute later he came back with a fancy box, what he called a humidor, and offered us all a cigar. Uncle John declined and pulled out his pipe. I said that would be fine—I'd had taken up cigars back in Texarkana when working at Mr. Allen's cotton compress. Charles said, "These cigars come from Cuba. I like them a lot." I was a bit worried about the cost on top of the supper at this fancy place. But we enjoyed the cigars and continued the conversation about Keo, cotton, and the area. The waiter brought the bill and I reached to see what it all cost. Just as I did Charles grabbed it and said, "This is all on me." I didn't know how to respond. But he insisted. Uncle John and I were grateful and told Charles so.

Leaving, Charles said, "Let's meet in the morning and we'll show y'all around town and introduce you to some folks." This turn of events came out of the blue. It was so unexpected to see someone we knew. It was far better than I could have ever imagined.

We met in the lobby the next morning after breakfast and headed out. As we walked out the door, I could smell and briefly glanced at the remnants of the fire that destroyed the store next door. Charles turned right as we got out the door, and we started down Main Street. The first building we walked past was the Baptist church, which had also been destroyed by the fire. Charles and Mr. Lewis Gaston both commented on how lucky the hotel was, that it was the brick sidewalls and stone coping that saved it, they said, otherwise it'd be gone too.

We continued, past a restaurant, a real estate office, an apothecary shop, a couple of butcher shops, two doctor's and a lawyer's offices, and a feed store, all on the southwest side with the railroad on the northeast. Farther down were two blacksmiths, a sawmill and shingle factory, and two cotton gins. One is old Mr. Cobb's, Charles said. The other, Lewis said, was owned by Mr. J. W. Brodie and Mr. Dean Morris. We walked up to one and Charles approached a man who'd come out. They extended their hands to shake. "Hello, J. W.," Charles said to Mr. Brodie, and he introduced Uncle John and me. We talked a bit about cotton and the cotton business.

We were especially glad to get this and many other introductions that day.

We made our way back up Main Street of this small town. It seemed like Charles and Lewis knew about everyone. On the walk back to the hotel, we stopped at the cafe we'd passed on the way down and went in for coffee. There Charles said he'd like to ask me and Uncle John a question. Sure, we replied.

"I'm sure you saw the leftovers from the bad fire on both sides of the hotel."

We acknowledged we did.

"It looks like a total loss for the church and the store on the other side," I said.

"Yes, that's exactly what I wanted to talk to you about. Lewis and I bought the old store and we're going to rebuild it. Keo's growing and needs more than one store to support it. You said last night at supper y'all had come down to explore new opportunities. We could set up your papa, Claude, and you, John, with some farm work since that's what you're accustomed to doing. And as for you, Claude, what would you say if you came back and ran this new store for us?"

I was shocked, in the best possible way. In a moment, just as suddenly as the fire back in Illinois took our home and forced us to start a new life in Texarkana, we'd achieved what we came for—a path for a new start, this time in Keo. I couldn't believe it. It still astounds me. A true serendipity as they say. I told Charles and Lewis how grateful we were for their extraordinary offer.

We talked about things a bit more. Charles explained he'd teach me what I didn't know about running a store from his own experience back when we'd first met. And he talked to Uncle John about the farming opportunities for him and Papa. He told me what he'd pay me to run the store—I couldn't believe that either. We made a deal. I think this was the first one I'd ever made.

We walked back to the hotel and as we were about to depart, they said, "If you'd like to stick around another day, tomorrow we'll drive you around the Keo area." We agreed.

After breakfast the next morning we went out to the front of the hotel. Expecting a wagon, we were surprised. Charles and Lewis had one of those new automobiles we'd seen back in St. Louis and that Mama'd told the story about when Mr. Ford's car caught fire in Vandalia. They said, "Get in." We'd seen them more and more in Texarkana, but I was hesitant. I finally did and Uncle John followed. They first drove us north a few miles up through Toltec—that ancient settlement the farmer in Ward'd told me about and Charles had mentioned when we first met. And on up a few miles to the town of Scott, where we turned around and headed back south. We went through Keo down to England, a small town just a few miles down the highway. Charles wanted us to get a feel for the area. We turned around again and came back to Keo—but just before returning to the hotel, we turned up a small lane on the northeast side of the highway that was covered in a large grove of pecan trees. It was beautiful. That's when I saw an aptly named Pecan Grove Baptist Church and a big white house nestled back under some of those stately trees.

The trip around the area took a good portion of the day. When we arrived back at the hotel, we gave our thanks to both Charles and Lewis—and, Lord knows, we were *ever* so thankful. Charles and I exchanged addresses, so I could write to find a place for us to live and say when we'd be back. We departed and went up to our room.

This trip to find a new place for a new start could not have been more successful. We caught the early train back to Little Rock the next morning and from there to Texarkana.

When we got home Uncle John and I told everyone all the details about our trip. Most especially about Charles Alexander and Lewis Gaston and the great opportunity they'd offered us. They were all excited to hear about everything, the train trip, the hotel and fancy meal, and especially the ride in the new automobile. All except Papa. He tried to be excited. It just wouldn't come, but he knew it was for the best. The next day we started making plans to move.

I wrote Charles a letter saying we'd be in Keo around the end of February or early March. Papa and Uncle John went to talk to Mr. Allen. He understood and wished us the best. Mama, me, and the rest of the kids started getting things ready and packing things up.

We loaded the two wagons we came in from Illinois and headed off east, crossing State Line Avenue from Texas to Arkansas, and on to Keo. Being winter it was hard traveling, and cold. But all things considered we made good time. On the fifteenth day we arrived in Keo.

Fifteen—Small-Town Life and Close Encounters

Winter of 1914 to Winter of 1917

It jerked and bounced every time I let out the clutch and stalled. Standing just to the side, at a safe distance, Charles said, "Slower, let it out gradually." It jumped and died again, and again and again, and again. Papa, Mama, Uncle John, and the whole family stood on the boardwalk in front of the store. Half the town it seemed watched as I failed over and over. They all laughed. It was great fun . . . for them, not for me. Learning to drive that new motorized wagon called a Ford Model TT was hard because it was so new to me. With intense concentration I finally got it and drove a short way south on Main Street, turned around and came back. I got out and Theresa came and jumped into my arms and hugged me like I'd won a big race.

Charles and Lewis bought this new vehicle for me to haul merchandise and produce and make deliveries to customers from the store. The new macadam-type street pavement that County Judge A. J. Walls had provisioned for the road between Scott and England made it easier and faster to move around, all but eliminating the wagon and truck ruts even on wet days.

Learning to drive that new car kind of depicts my life the first few years in Keo. It started out disorienting but became a reliable routine, one that gave a new stability to our family.

Papa, Mama, and I found a small farmhouse for us all to live in on Community Street in Walls Township about two miles north and east of Toltec between Keo and Scott. Near there Papa and Uncle John got started at the old small eight-acre Scott Plantation settlement, and I worked with Charles and Lewis to make ready the opening of the new store next to the

Keo Hotel. We'd settled once again in a new place for another new start. There, just as in Texarkana we'd make a new life in a new place among new people. And it meant new experiences, education, and new encounters, especially for me.

* * *

The pattern I'd known for so long, getting up and going to the fields with Papa and Uncle John, changed in Keo. I'd still have Mama's usual breakfast with the family, but then I'd walk to work at the store—at first that part felt a bit like walking to work at Mr. Allen's cotton compress, but not for long. It was a whole new world for me. Charles and Lewis's store seemed far different to me than the little store I met Charles at nine years earlier. More likely they were similar, and my new job as store manager just made me aware of the endless details involved. I know for sure, starting a new store from the ground up made my head spin.

Charles and I worked daily, planning everything and putting it together, the suppliers, the facility, the inventory, and layout. Everything about it was thought through and had a purpose.

At its entrance, the Alexander General Store featured two screen doors that swung out and two wooden ones that opened in; they were kept open during store hours. On each side of the doors were two huge plate-glass windows. They allowed passersby to gaze upon displays that we'd change out weekly: displays of notions, jewelry, bolts of cloth, and finished premade clothing for women, including a papier-mâché mannequin (that's what it's called in French) with a featured dress, and other things. Sometimes we'd display boots and soft goods, hardware, tools, and tobacco appealing to the men, the town merchants and farmers and visitors.

Outside, on the side of each of the windows, there were two large metal advertisement signs painted with names and emblems and one above the door: Bull Durham tobacco on one side, Quaker Oats on the other. Above the doors in the red script emblem for old John Pemberton's elixir was a big sign for Coca-Cola, no longer sold as medicine but as a pleasurable carbonated drink. It'd become really popular since they offered coupons and sold it in bottles. We'd get crates of them delivered every other week by train from Atlanta, and folks loved them.

The inside was a place of endless items laid out according to the various types of merchandise. I'd been in many stores but, truth be told, I never really paid attention to the layout, only to what I wanted to buy. But as manager of Alexander General, I had to pay attention to it all. I remember how hard it was to keep track of it all.

There were buggy whips and harnesses, pans and ropes, some hanging from the ceiling. A wide assortment of nuts, canned goods, brushes, and combs on shelves, along with the pomade and other hair products, and an array of tilted baskets on the floor full of fresh root vegetables and garden produce, fruits, and melons. Behind the counter there was a whole section for nails, screws, and other hardware items stored in bins with special boxes to separate them according to type, size, and use. Also behind the counter there was a wide variety of household goods—soaps, medicines, spices, and such—and rifle cartridges and shotgun shells, small gardening implements, and sewing supplies. In the main open part of the store there were displays of bolt fabric and finished ready-to-wear clothes, and boots and shoes on wide tables.

The array of merchandise seemed never-ending. Right in the middle of the store on a big oak dining table, we had a center display featuring every-day plates and selected fine china, flatware, and serving dishes for women to buy or order from the catalogue. Items that until then I'd simply used to eat from and with or washed up afterwards, but never otherwise giving much thought to. Once I did, especially the fancy dishes, I was always reminded of the keepsake china and cups Mama lost in the fire.

It took all my time and attention from early morning to late at night to keep track of and keep straight the dizzying variety of merchandise. But the more I worked at it, the more fascinating I found it.

There was one thing I didn't have to learn. In the back of the store behind all the general merchandise, there was a small alcove that served as a small butcher shop. It was built specially for it, with an indoor water hydrant and a hose, a sloped tiled floor, and a plumbed sink-drain in the middle for easy cleaning. It wasn't a full-scale butcher shop like the others in town, but we offered select cut meats for sale. There I plied the trade I'd first learned back in Illinois, butchering Mama's chickens and the hogs in the way Uncle Jim had taught me.

Finally, running the full length from the back near the butcher's alcove up to the storefront there was a long curved-glass display case stacked on a flat, heavily varnished, wood countertop, with an open counterspace near the front where we'd conduct the business. There we had Sears, Roebuck & Co., Abercrombie & Fitch, L. L. Bean, and Filson catalogues for making special orders, and a large NCR cash register for check out. Just below the register was a newspaper rack holding the daily *Arkansas Gazette* and the *Arkansas Democrat*.

Those papers became part of my new daily routine. Before opening each morning, I'd pour a cup of coffee, light a cigar, and read the paper. Though the new job required me to learn so many new things and simply become aware of so many things I'd never noticed before, the daily newspapers always expanded my horizons beyond the day-to-day. My new morning habit helped me stay aware of the goings-on in the world and, like Papa used to do, pay attention to small, seemingly remote things and consider how they might be connected to our daily lives.

I distinctly remember one morning reading a small back-page news item in June 1914, our first year in Keo. It reminded me of the one Papa read from the St. Louis newspaper about the faraway land of Russia years ago. This one was about an event that year in Sarajevo, another place, then, I didn't even know existed. This story was about a Serbian nationalist who assassinated the heir apparent to the throne of Austria-Hungary, Archduke Ferdinand, and his wife Sophie. It astonished me how such a remote event made news in the local *Arkansas Gazette*, just as I had felt about the Russian protest Papa'd read at our campsite that night back in '05. As I read the paper that morning, I wondered if such a small story had bigger meaning for us in Keo. I thought about how a much bigger world always hovers over the local one where I was living.

I had learned a lot about the wholesale commodities business in Texarkana, especially cotton, but strangely in the bustling cotton-is-king town of Keo, I learned and worked in the retail business. I couldn't have learned all I needed to know without Charles. He'd become the bookkeeper for the Alexander Plantation, and from that experience and his earlier work at his father's store, he taught me how to run his new store in Keo. And about the area, too, so I could make all the deliveries in that old Ford Model TT to local and area merchants and patrons who'd bought more than they could take with them, and to folks whose special items shipped to the store from catalogue orders.

The first year I barely saw my family except in passing. I was constantly busy. But my new routine had become a good one.

* * *

Papa continued to be weighed down by the death of Rachel, as of course we all were. But for him all ambition was gone, and he couldn't recover it. I so often remember coming home at night, seeing him slumped down in his well-stuffed winged-back "grandfather chair," that's what they called it when we bought it in Texarkana, and smoke his pipe or cigar next to the fire. Even though I'd taken up the cigar habit, I could still smell the sharp tobacco aroma when I came in the house. The vision he'd had for a new start with new opportunities when we left Illinois for Texarkana had been eclipsed by the terrible tragedy that befell my little sister.

I thought about Papa a lot, and worried. The conversation I'd had with Mama about Grandfather Isaac weighed on me just like Rachel's death weighed on Papa. Mama doted on him even more than normal.

But he and Uncle John's farm work kept them busy day to day. That helped, even if with little prospects. Most of the time it yielded enough to pay the rent on the small house, and my work at the store took care of everything else, including school for my sisters and brother.

Occasionally I thought about and hoped to go back and finish school and go to college, but it hadn't happened. When I could find the time, I'd still read. But there wasn't much time for it except the newspaper. I learned a lot from the work I was doing and from the people I met. Though not school-based, those first three years in Keo were a never-ending education for me.

Beth graduated high school the first year we arrived in Keo, and over the next few years so did Maurine and Bill. They each wanted to go to college, and my work at the store enabled them to do that.

Beth and Maurine went to Galloway Women's College in Searcy, a Methodist-Episcopal school about fifty miles north of Scott. They had to wear common uniforms each day comprised of dark blue wool skirts and a matching wool cape coat during winter, white blouse, and a blue silk neckerchief tie. They both looked beautiful in them—I even believe that school and those clothes are what made Beth so conscientious about her appearance ever since. They both studied homemaking and secretarial training, and also took courses in music, art, and speech. As she grew up Maurine became less happy-go-lucky than she'd been as a little girl, and more nervous. I don't know why. Though not as striking as Beth, Maurine was a pretty girl, so I'm sure it wasn't that. She's a sweet-hearted girl, so it might have been the lingering effects of Rachel's death, all of us suffered from that. In any case, Galloway was good for her. It helped her come out of her shell again. And it was good for Beth too. They grew in their knowledge and life experience by attending concerts, recitals, and exhibitions that were sponsored by literary societies they each became a part of while in college. When Beth graduated, she came home and taught at the small primary school in Williams Township, near Toltec. When Maurine was home from school, she worked with me helping do inventory and the books.

Bill did well too. He was medium-sized but great at football. Once he graduated high school, he was recruited to Henderson-Brown College in Arkadelphia, about eighty-five miles southwest of Keo, a little over halfway back to Texarkana. He got a good education too, but his focus was on football. Until he took a terrible head-to-the-face hit playing in a game one afternoon. Because there were no helmets or face guards used, it was bad. He wound up losing an eye—we eventually had a glass one fitted to replace it. When he was home during school breaks, he worked with me at the store and with Papa and Uncle John on the farm.

Small-town life spent mostly in-town was new to me at first. But it allowed me to meet lots of folks, and being a town with multiple cotton gins owned by people I knew, it allowed me to stay connected to the cotton business that I'd learned so much about in Texarkana. Keo was a good new start for us. I learned on my first visit it was a place where serendipity can happen.

* * *

After about three years, we were well-settled in our new hometown of Keo. Charles and Lewis were pleased with the store and its business and growth, and so was I. The deliveries in the Ford truck gave an extended service to our customers, and they allowed me to meet many new folks in the area, just as I did daily when people came into the store.

One day late in the afternoon a fellow came in, a big man who I would come to learn was in town to preach at a revival that evening at the Baptist Church on the other side of the Keo Hotel—the church that'd burned back before Christmas in '13 but was now rebuilt and refurbished.

"Good evening," I said. "My name is Claude Howell. May I help you find something?"

The tall, big man—who kind of reminded me of Uncle Jim back home—responded pleasantly, "Hello, son, my name is William Crutchfield." We shook hands.

"I don't know," he said, "I'm actually just passing a bit of time before I go to the church for a service at 7:00."

"Is that where you go to church?" I asked. "I know quite a few folks who go there. Do you know Reverend Bogard, the interim pastor?"

Mr. Crutchfield said, "Why, yes, I do. He's the reason I'm here as a matter of fact."

"How's that?" I asked.

"I'm here to preach at the revival," he said.

"Oh, I see, so you're a preacher, so you're Reverend Crutchfield, is that right?"

"Yes," he said, "but please just call me Brother Crutchfield. I'm a Baptist preacher but not a full-time pastor at a church right now. I preach alternate Sundays at Pecan Grove Baptist Church just up the lane outside town, and I also do some farming."

"Oh, I see. My papa and uncle farm a small eight-acre section of the old Scott Plantation near the intersection of Walls, Williams, and Dortch townships. I grew up farming and was a farmer till we moved to Keo a few years ago and I started running this store. We were Baptists back home and even when we were in Texarkana. Now we go to the Methodist church."

"So, where's this home you speak of?" Brother Crutchfield asked.

"Illinois," I said. "Seminary Township, Illinois, near Vandalia. That's where we came from, first settling in Texarkana, Texas back in '05, and then we moved here in the winter of '14."

"Why'd you choose to move here?" he asked.

"Well, we moved because of a tragedy in our family, but we chose here for a couple of reasons. We'd learned in Texarkana that Keo had become a major railroad stop for the cotton business in this area of Arkansas, which is part of what we grew in Texarkana. But also because years ago when we were on the way down from Illinois we met Mr. Charles Alexander Jr. Meeting him in this area gave us a reason to consider here over other places."

"How do you like running a general store compared to farming?" Brother Crutchfield asked.

"Oh, I like it a lot. It's real different than farming, but I like it," I said.

"So, if you don't mind me asking, you mentioned a tragedy that happened that made you move. Do you mind telling me what that was?"

A bit hesitant, I decided to tell him; I mean, he was a preacher anyhow. "My little nine-year-old sister died," I said, "in a terrible accident. She accidentally pulled a large kettle of boiling water off the stove down onto her."

"Oh, my goodness," Brother Crutchfield said. "That's so terrible, Claude. I'm so sorry. Such tragedies are hard. I lost a daughter of my own, not that young but still way too young. I feel for you all and will pray for you and your parents. May the Lord be with you and your whole family."

"Thank you," I said, and it got quiet between us. Brother Crutchfield kept wandering through the store.

About that time two other people came in, an older woman and a young girl, about eleven or twelve years old I guessed. I heard her say, "Come on Papa, we gotta go over to the church, it's about time to start."

And he said, "Okay, Helen, let's go." He turned to me and said, "Nice to meet you, Claude. I'll be praying for you and your family. Come over to the church after you close up if you'd like. We'd love to have you."

"Okay, I'll try," I said. "Thanks for coming in and come again soon."

I did start closing the store soon after they left. I should have, I expect, but I didn't make it over to the Baptist church that night. I picked up one of the morning papers to read what I hadn't had a chance to finish.

My mind became preoccupied with questions about the bigger world that lay beyond my own small one in Keo. There was a lot about the war going on all over Europe, ever since August of '14 following the assassination of that regent and his wife in Bosnia in Eastern Europe. Every story I'd read about it was terrible. As Uncle John and I had talked about, all war is terrible but this one sounded unimaginably terrible, with heavy artillery, trench and mechanized warfare, and poisonous gases exploded to kill everyone in their path indiscriminately, and horridly.

Sixteen—Pleasant Days in Winter Belie a Coming Storm

Winter to Late Spring of 1917

I sat on the stool reading the paper. I couldn't get my mind off the goings-on in the world. The times were such a contradiction. On the one hand, for me, in Keo, the prospects continued to look promising. The headlines addressing our country seemed so too. There was a marked optimism in President Wilson's reelection campaign of progress. On the other hand, the paper was full of daily reports of the scope of death in a world falling completely apart in Europe.

I shook my head to get those things off my mind and stood up. I had to make my deliveries.

It was an unusually pleasant day that February of '17 and I needed a distraction. So, I drove up the lane Charles had driven Uncle John and me up when we first visited Keo, the road that went up past Pecan Grove Baptist Church and the big white house under those trees.

As I neared the big house, I saw a young lady out near the road. I slowed and pulled to a stop as she walked up to the Ford truck. I realized it was Brother Crutchfield's daughter—or, as I came to find out, his granddaughter, the child of the daughter he'd told me he lost at a young age when we talked about Rachel.

"Hello there," she said so cheerfully.

"Well, hello. I remember you," I responded. "You came in the store over in Keo where I work one evening before church, when you and your mother came to get your father to the Baptist church. You remember?"

"Oh yes," she said, "I remember that. Hi, my name is Helen. How are you? But they're really my grandparents, even though I call them Papa and

Mama," she said correcting my misimpression. "My real mama died when I was just four and a half years old, so they've raised me. What brings you up this way?" she asked.

I remember how I chuckled to myself. Helen said so much in such a short time. I also thought of Mama, how her mother died so young, leaving only vague cherished memories.

"Well, Helen, it's good to see you again," I replied. "My name is Claude. I'm out making deliveries to people who order things from catalogues at the store."

"So does something come to my house?" she asked.

I said, "I'm not sure; where's your house?"

"That one," she turned, pointing. "The white house underneath those pecan trees. See it?"

"I do," I said. "And I'll tell you, whether I have a delivery up here or not, I often drive up this lane just to see that house and those pecan trees. It's beautiful! But no, I'm afraid not. No delivery to your house today. I just drove up here today because it's such a pleasant drive. But I expect I'll have a delivery to your house sometime soon," I said.

"I hope so," she said.

About then I saw the sun fall to the tops of the tall pecan trees and realized how long I'd been away. I needed to head back.

"Helen, I'm sorry to rush off now," I apologized, "but I must get back to the store. I look forward to seeing you and your grandparents again when I'm over here or at the store. You have a good day now."

"Thank you, Mr. Claude. You have a good day, too. Bye," she said.

Such a pleasant girl, I remember thinking that day. So cheerful. And from such a good family I came to know. As time went along, I got to know them pretty well during those early days when my deliveries took me up by the Crutchfield place. When I'd see them out, I'd stop and chat with Brother Crutchfield and his wife, Mrs. Malvina, and with Helen.

I remember so clearly how beautiful it was as the sun descended slowly behind me when I drove the short way back to the store. What a wonderful day it'd been, almost springlike in the middle of winter. My mind drifted again to how the world was so full of contradictions.

* * *

I got back to the store just in time for the usual gathering. Charles and I had set up a table and six chairs and two benches under the awning on the boardwalk in front of the store. We'd put them there to encourage customers to stop by the store and come in, and it was a great success. Alexander General Store became a gathering spot in the center of town, sometimes for dominoes and always lively conversation. That day in early February of 1917 was special.

A. J. Walls, the US Marshall, was in town. Marshall Walls was the former Lonoke County Judge who had paved Main Street and the road between Scott and England that Charles had driven Uncle John and me up and down when we first visited Keo. He had recently become chairman of the Arkansas State Democratic Committee and he'd brought the newly elected Governor Charles Brough to town on a tour of the region. He said the governor wanted to assess the cotton economy, the reception of his Civitan Clubs program promoting good citizenship and his women's suffrage policies, and to check on race relations. They'd spent the day going all round, meeting with many different folks. Just as I arrived, I saw Marshall Walls and Governor Blough sitting at the table with Charles in front of the store. A group of the other local business owners were quickly gathering around them. I got back just in time to observe and, to my surprise, even be a part of the conversation.

There were so many pipes and cigars on the porch that day it made the front of the store look like a smokehouse. But how do you have a good conversation without good tobacco, I say? A few of the men quietly commented that it would've been even better if there was a keg o' beer on tap too, making the store entrance an outdoor pub. But there was no chance of that since the Bone-Dry Law had recently passed with the strong support of Governor Brough.

Mr. Brodie, the nice old fellow Charles and Lewis introduced Uncle John and me to when we first visited Keo, asked the first question. He asked the governor how he got into politics. And in a non-political way, the governor quickly responded that he never set out to. But that one question led down a winding path I never expected, a bit like pulling yarn on our wagon trip down to Texas.

The governor said he'd gone to school with plans to be a teacher, a professor in college. He got his PhD from Johns Hopkins University in Maryland, taught at several universities in Mississippi, and then came to the University of Arkansas. Where, he said, he taught many courses in his fields of European and American history, economics, sociology, ethics, German, and philosophy, including political philosophy. And while teaching there, he also went to law school.

That simple description by the governor of his original plans sparked my imagination. There on the porch in front of the store that day was not only a governor but a college professor. I imagined myself being at college. I'd so longed to go, but it was not to be back then.

My thoughts have returned to that evening on the boardwalk of the store so many times since, for many different reasons.

That Governor Blough taught history reminded me of how long I'd been interested in it, ever since I first read Mr. Edward Eggleston's book on the trip down to Texas, the many conversations I had with Papa, Mama, and Uncle John, and those endless nights when I read alone in the little house when they were in De Queen. But I was fascinated by his mention of the law too. Until the contracts and invoices I had to handle at the store, I'd never thought much about the law, and those activities didn't say too much about law itself but were connected to it.

So as Governor Blough waxed eloquently about politics and law that day, my mind faded back to the story about the mules and keeping promises Uncle Jim told me. I began to see I'd been exposed to things related to the law I'd never recognized. And I remembered what Uncle Jim and Papa told me, how the laws we pass don't make us do right or make us not do wrong, and that just because the law allows us to do certain things doesn't mean we should. I began to see there's something more basic, like what drove the Samaritan man who helped someone the local laws said he shouldn't. I began to see that the laws politicians write to help order public life sit atop a yet deeper law, one that forms the foundations of public life.

As I walked back and forth in and out of the store to get folks more drinks and snacks, Governor Blough began to answer Mr. Brodie's question directly. Yet as he did, it drew upon his education in economics, philosophy, and political philosophy—subjects I had no familiarity at all with then— and led to discussions about the big questions of what governments are for and the role they play in our lives. I'd never been exposed to or thought about such big questions.

Responding to Mr. Brodie's question about how he became governor, Mr. Brough explained that he taught about politics and got to know many folks in Arkansas politics. On their urging he considered a run when Joe Robinson vacated his governor seat to assume a US Senate seat. Then "Last year," the governor said, "I ran and won as a Democrat on a Progressivist agenda like that of President Woodrow Wilson."

Hearing this answer, I boldly blurted out a question. "What's a Progressivist agenda?"

Everyone turned and looked at me, including the governor. Being the youngest and the manager of the store, no one expected it from me.

"Well, son," the governor said, "that's a good question. Progressivism is a political philosophy that sees politics as a way to achieve social reform, to make life better for people."

"Isn't that what everyone thinks about politics?" I responded with sophomoric confidence.

"In a way it is, I suppose," the governor said, as he began to talk like a professor. "But this political philosophy is kind of new," he continued. "It takes as its model some of the ideas of the German philosopher, G. F. Hegel, who described history as a dialectical process," a word I'd never heard before. As if I was one of his college students, Governor Brough explained.

"That's a view where over time the world advances, gets better. We see this in the way science works, new scientific discoveries build on old ones. So, just as science advances, economies develop and social organization and life improves, and together the human condition is made better. The Progressivist politician believes the government is the primary means to facilitate this improvement of the human condition. But this philosophy of progress is not restricted to politics. It's even religious. You can see this in the Social Gospel Movement led by the great Baptist preacher Walter Rauschenbusch. It has been written about his view that politics and religion are both about applying "Christian ethics to social problems, especially issues of social justice such as economic inequality, poverty, alcoholism, crime, racial tensions, slums, unclean environment, child labor, lack of unionization, poor schools, and the dangers of war."

The governor stopped and looked at me. "You see, son, government is the tool to make life better for folks," he told me as the others looked on. I remember how stunned I was as it dawned on me that I was having a conversation with the governor of the entire state.

At the time I didn't understand all or even much of what the governor said, and I didn't know the people he spoke of and quoted. But I remember even then being quite sure he was wrong that the world is getting better. Sure, we've made great progress with great discoveries and new machines, and that's a wonderful thing. But is the world really getting better? I thought about Rachel and Papa's despair as a result, how his papa took his own life, and the conflict of the human heart and the Civil War that Uncle John and I had talked about so long ago. A Baptist preacher thinks the world is getting better? I'd never heard of such a preacher. Tragedies and brokenness never seem to slow. How could Governor Blough's idea of progress be reconciled with what I'd been reading in the paper—about the war going on in Europe, where I'd just read that morning that more than fifty thousand British soldiers were killed in a single day.

The conversation between the governor and the men in Keo who'd gathered was very interesting. That I was able to participate in it was amazing to me. That day is the first I can remember when I began to grapple and form some of my own views about political life.

Mr. James Cobb asked another question. "Governor," he said, "since you're so knowledgeable about politics, what about socialism, which I've heard some about, particularly the socialist party I've seen attached to Clay Fulks up in the Ozarks who has run for governor in Arkansas several times? What's socialism, and how is it different than the Progressivism you've been talking about?"

Governor Blough once again said, "Another excellent question. Let me try and explain briefly," still talking like a professor.

"Socialism is a socio-political and economic theory. There are different stripes of socialists but the common denominator among them is, they believe the means of production for a society's needs and surplus should be owned and controlled by the government, not by the private sector. In other words, they don't believe in a competitive, market-based economy but a controlled economy. This theory has its roots in German political-economy theorist Karl Marx back in the 1840s, who drew upon the other German I mentioned, G. F. Hegel. Marx rejected the kind of market-based economy we have here in America, saying private business ownership is inherently cruel and abusive to workers—and, he said, belief in God and religion is a delusion, something used by the government to control the people. Few people here in America give much thought to his theories, and certainly not the rejection of God. The very reason most people came here is for religious freedom and the opportunity for a better life, including the land they could get and farm and advance themselves on. Marx's theories arose in connection with the rise of the industrialized economy in the West, factories, and new technology. The only time this kind of theory is given much consideration is when the political and economic conditions people live in get so bad the people revolt. But what they don't realize is, after the revolt what all too often happens is one tyrant is simply replaced by another one, perhaps worse than the first."

When Governor Brough said this, I thought about the Russian Revolution Papa'd read about in the paper from St. Louis back in '05.

"Well, I'll tell you what, governor," Mr. Cobb said, "your progressivism and that of President Wilson best not move Arkansas and this country in *that* direction or you *will* have a revolt on your hands." Everyone laughed in agreement.

Governor Blough said, "Don't worry, Mr. Cobb; that's not gonna happen on my watch."

I wasn't sure about progressivism. But I was certainly with Mr. Cobb about socialism. I thought about Uncle Jim and our conversation about the land and about the deeds signed by the presidents Mama'd shown me. And about how folks have always come to America for freedom and opportunity, and for religious liberty. Not for the government to do everything for them.

That day on the porch made think more and more about how my little world fits in with the bigger one I'd been noticing in the newspaper, in the world of business, and politics—I'd taken more notice of politics and voting since I'd turned twenty-one. Ever since we got to Keo the small world I'd known had expanded by leaps and bounds. It'd become more complex. Especially so after that conversation about politics, economics, and war on the porch.

I was beginning to see how political philosophies, even remote, abstract grand philosophies like that of the German Mr. Hegel Governor Blough talked about, and the theories and policies that flow from them can change our daily lives. And how foreign affairs, also seemingly remote, are not so. I was seeing more and more how that bigger world that hovers over our daily lives all the time is far less in our control than we think, just as Uncle Jim said.

My mind returned to that small news item I read in 1914 and the many since about the war in Europe. Then to another newspaper article I'd read that morning by journalists Crowell and Wilson who wrote, saying, "The president continually told his audiences that the world was on fire, the sparks falling everywhere, and no one knew where the next blaze might be kindled."

What had once seemed remote didn't now.

Would America get caught up in the blaze?

None of us knew it at the time of that most interesting conversation on the porch but soon learned. A couple of weeks prior, Germany had violated the agreement they'd made with President Wilson—the *promise* they made, Uncle Jim would say—to keep the US out of the war. They'd agreed to stop using their new submarines to sink ships in the waters around the British Isles after the sinking of the Lusitania in back in 1915. Then suddenly they made an about face and declared that they'd openly use those underwater torpedo-machines in the war in Europe.

On top of that, a short time later we all learned Germany had offered a secret deal to Mexico to keep us out of the fight. They promised the Mexicans if they aligned with Germany, after the war they'd get back Texas, New Mexico, and Arizona that they'd lost in the Mexican American War.

These two events, hidden in the clouds high above my day-to-day world, above all of us on the porch that day, caused President Wilson to break his promise to keep the US out of the war.

Unknown to any of us on the porch that spring-like winter day, not even the governor, the president had been meeting with Congress. On February 3, 1917, President Wilson addressed the whole Congress to announce that diplomatic relations with Germany had been cut off. Then on March 20, the president held an emergency meeting with his Cabinet, and all agreed the US must enter the war. On April 2, the president met again with Congress and sought a unanimous declaration of war with Germany. The paper recorded his appeal, saying, Germany is already at "nothing less than war against the government and people of the United States." And yet "we have no selfish ends to serve. We desire no conquest, no dominion . . . no material compensation for the sacrifices we shall freely make," the *Gazette* reported. "We are but one of the champions of the rights of mankind. We shall be satisfied when those rights have been made as secure as the faith and freedom of the nations can make them."

Congress granted the declaration—America was at war!

Amid the winds of war in Europe and the now certain American involvement, a few days later as I sat on my stool with my coffee and cigar, I read another small news item. The *Gazette* reported that on March 15, 1917, Russian Czar Nicholas had abdicated his throne, the first step toward what later that year would be called Red October and the Bolshevik Socialist Revolution. I thought again about that piece Papa read around the campfire just outside St. Louis. And about what Governor Blough said about Karl Marx and socialism, and old Mr. Cobb's strong reaction to it. Once again, I wondered how the world was getting better.

But in America that year at that time, the focus was on Europe. On what the president called "war to end all wars." *Would it be?* I wondered.

On May 18, 1917, the Selective Service Act was passed. The US would raise a national army to fight in Europe against Germany.

At our small farmhouse on Community Street, I received my draft registration. It read,

> Claude Rama Howell
> Rt. 2 Scott
> b. June 12, 1895, at Vandalia, Illinois
> Occupation: Farmer at Walls Township; and General Store Clerk
> Single
> Description: Brown Eyes, Black Hair

Seventeen—In the Vortex of the Guns of August

Late Summer of 1917 to Winter of 1919

My sneaky nine-year-old sister Theresa got up earlier than everyone and quietly snuck into my room. Like a mountain lion taking its prey, she pounced on top of me and feverishly started tickling me. Completely startled, I almost shot up to the ceiling. She broke out laughing so hard it woke the whole house. I grabbed her, turned her over, and tickled her, and she squirmed and squealed like a little piglet. She was still laughing when the silhouettes of Mama and Papa appeared in the shadowed doorway, and they started laughing too. It was the first time I'd seen Papa laugh in four years.

"You got him, Theresa," Mama said. "You got him good! Good morning, honey," she said to me. "Welcome to the land of the livin'. Come on now T'res, let your brother get dressed."

Mama made a big breakfast that morning early before dawn, with those wonderful pan-drop biscuits and even apple-butter. Beth was there and Maurine and Bill were home from school, and everyone sat around the table. For a moment it seemed like we were just starting another day. I found myself imagining Papa and I getting ready to head out to the fields like we used to. Then I paused and looked at my family and was struck with an awareness of their faces and everything about them more than I think I had ever been—I needed to keep them with me as a left home.

I was deep in reflection, but there was no morning gaze at the moon on the porch with the excitement of Hoggin' Day. That morning was a different rite of passage, one of service to my country, and the way all Americans had come to think of it, to the world.

The Great War in Europe that began with the guns of August in '14 had a positive effect on the economy of Keo and the broader South due to an increased demand for cotton. But after the president's declaration of war, the whole country was quickly drawn into its vortex. One it was quite ill prepared for. Everything had to be built from scratch, including a new two-million-man army, and fast. It needed an endless array of things for the troops and the war effort. All this generated huge economic activity, with many new jobs and opportunities. But such benefits from war were shrouded by a cloud. Which everyone knew cast the shadow of death.

That morning I would not walk to the store. My walk would be into the enemy-facing part of the war machine.

Mama hugged me tight and kissed me like she'd done the night Papa and I came home to Grandfather Bill's place after the fire. She held me for a long lingering moment. I leaned back a little and looked into her eyes, which filled with tears, as did mine. Papa wrapped his arms around us both. And then Beth, Maurine, Bill, and Uncle John. Theresa snuggled through and hugged tightly around my waist.

We said goodbye and I stepped off the small porch. Slowly, one foot in front of the other, I started down the lane with only the lunch Mama had made me for the one-way trip.

Ever since Congress's declaration of war was published across the land, patriotism ran high. But the sacrifice interwoven with it was palpable. *Boston Herald* journalist Edward Van Zile captured the feeling in his poem, "RISE UP! RISE UP, CRUSADERS!"

> Rise up! Rise up, crusaders!
> Send forth a clarion cry!
> The race shall not be slaves to Huns
> Though you and I must die.
> A world at war?
> A billion men who arm and fight and slay?
> What are our blaring bugles for?
> Is Man insane to-day?
>
> Not we to whom the call has come,
> Not we, the unafraid,
> Now arming, God be with us, for the last, the great Crusade;
> Nor they who fight our fight with us,
> Across the surging sea,
> Where men are facing madmen
> That all peoples may be free.

We American boys mustered for war.

As I walked, I thought again and again about that picture of President George Washington hanging over the fireplace at Grandfather Bill's old log homestead in Illinois. Was this how Papa felt when he went off to the Spanish-American War? . . . *War?* My mind was saturated with patriotism and with the talk I had with Uncle John about war. Then I thought about the back-page piece in the *Gazette* about the assassination of that Austro-Hungarian regent that triggered this war and the one I'd read about 50,000 men killed in a single day.

There were six of us from the Keo-Scott area when we started out. We didn't talk much. Just walked. One-by-one we slowly added more to our journey the closer we got to Little Rock and Argenta. When we crossed from Lonoke into Pulaski County, I thought about how Polish Brigadier General Casmir Pulaski saved the life of General Washington at the battle of Battle of Brandywine, and by his actions possibly saved American freedom. In our silence we were sure it was our mission too.

What were we headed into? I suspect all of us wondered. None of us knew for sure. If it was as Mr. Edward Van Zile said, "where men are facing madmen," there was a very good chance we'd never see our families again. But our duty was so "that all peoples may be free."

Our small cadre from Lonoke combined with men from across the state. We arrived at Ft. Roots in early August of '17 where we were examined and inducted into the Arkansas Guard, just before the whole Arkansas Guard was combined to become the 18th Division. Once the induction was complete in early September, we were all transferred to Camp Pike.

When Congress declared war on Germany on April 6, I'd learned, the US Army had a total of 127,000 soldiers, officers and enlisted men combined. Even when the State guards became the *National* Guard, the whole US Army was still only 182,000.

Not always easy on base, I found and read every newspaper I could find. One reported that the German army had eleven million under arms, Austria-Hungary had 7.8 million, and the Ottoman Empire 2.9 million. The Ottomans and the Triple Alliance of Germany, Austria-Hungary, and Italy formed the Central Powers—although Italy switched sides by the end of 1914. The resistance was the Triple Entente, a friendly informal alliance between France, Britain, and Russia, and later Italy. Naively, both sides had thought the war that began in August of '14 would be over by the end of that year. But it was only the beginning. The combined losses were staggering beyond imagination, and it kept on getting worse. By the time the US declared war in April of '17, France's losses had climbed to over a million soldiers, and that month at the battle of Chemin des Dames they lost 40,000 the first day and more than 270,000 by its end. After that, the French army just quit, they wouldn't fight anymore. The paper reported French field commander Marshall Ferdinand Foch said, "We are holding the enemy—but for how long?" His British counterpart, Field Marshall Haig, said, "We are fighting with our backs to the wall." And not only in France. Russia's rising millions in war deaths plus famine and disease triggered social upheaval, the abdication of Czar Nicholas II, and by October Lenin's communist Bolshevik Revolution.

The whole world was disintegrating before everyone's eyes. Into this chaos I and my fellow soldiers-to-be walked. In about every way possible the US was unprepared for what was about to happen. And so were each of us who had come to be inducted and trained for this slaughter.

In response to Marshalls Foch and Haig, the US urged "Hold the line—We're coming, and we're aching to fight." By late October of '17 the first US troops saw combat in the Lorraine region in Lunéville near Nancy, France, just north and west of the Alsace region. In just over a year more than two million US soldiers fought in the war to end all wars.

We were soldiers. As we marched the eight miles from Ft. Logan Roots to Camp Pike, my mind drifted again to my conversation with Uncle John about war. How there are times when it's forced upon us. When it is, we must summon the courage to do our duty and remain at our post until we're relieved. That doing one's duty is a virtue even when it takes great courage.

I also thought again about what I'd read President Wilson told Congress when he sought their support for the declaration of war. And about how the best of courage is always in pursuit of goodness not evil. As we American boys mustered to our duty, we did so as champions for the rights of mankind. For "the Blessings of Liberty to ourselves and our Posterity" that Mr. Madison wrote of in the Preamble to the Constitution. Our duty was to help secure them by defeating the unbounded pursuit of imperial conquest.

As for so many before us, our hour of courage was at hand. Would it be enough?

The days were long, but as I had the time, I began a new practice of letter writing.

September 26, 1917

Dearest Papa & Mama,

I hope everything's good and everybody's doing well at home.

This is my first chance to write to you since I left, so it's a bit long. I just thought you might wonder what life has been like here.

I arrived at Ft. Roots August 8 and on September 2, along with everyone else, I was transferred to the new Camp Pike. By the end of the first day, we heard there were 1,500 men here. After being in the army now almost 8 weeks, I'm told there are about 10,000 soldiers in training.

All of us were required to quarantine in the new barracks for 10 days when we first arrived at Ft. Roots to avoid spreading any diseases. There's been quite a bit of sickness around, but I've been just fine.

After the quarantine we all went through medical and fitness exams. Those of us who passed were given vaccinations for typhoid fever and other things and issued uniforms and gear. The picture I've enclosed is me in my dress uniform. It consists of a white turtle-necked undershirt, "boxer" underwear they called them, wool olive-drab trousers with button fly. There's a cover tunic that fits snuggly with buttons from just below the waist to the neck, with pointed button flap-pockets on each side and button-flap shoulder straps to hold our gloves, wool gloves. And a round-brimmed army wool felt hat and boots. We were also given work dungarees, a jacket and hat. And everyone was given a helmet, a new Springfield rifle, and a gasmask.

For most, the day starts at 5:45 a.m. when the bugler blows reveille, not nearly as early or as startling as Theresa's alarm the day I left. Tickle her for me. It ends at 11:00 p.m. with taps. During the day we train from dawn to dusk, running ten miles through the eastern edge of the Ouachita range in full gear and backpacks, marching, firing range and bayonet drills, and trench warfare with gas masks. They say the terrain at Camp Pike is what it'll be like in France. Weekends allow for recreation, mostly baseball, football, boxing, and volleyball, and on special occasions dances and banquets sponsored by the citizens of Little Rock. But we can't leave the base.

I've been assigned to quartermaster duty, helping with ordering and managing supplies and preparing food for the ever-growing number of troops. We buy, receive inventory, and manage all kinds of things like hay, oats, grain, straw (for beds and pillows), gasoline, blacksmith's coal, butter, ice, and fresh beef—and lots and lots of it. In some ways it's like at the store, just with much bigger purchases and more to keep track of.

I don't know if this'll be permanent or not, but the good news is my duty will pay $36 a month, a little more than some other privates make. We haven't yet got paid, but when I do, I'll send home what I don't use, I don't need much, mostly just things from the Post Exchange, which is like the store in Keo, for basic hygiene, as the army calls it.

We've heard our Arkansas National Guard Division is being combined with the Mississippi and Louisiana Guards down at Camp Beauregard in Alexandria, Louisiana, and we'll be the 18th Division. We'll move there any day now.

I must say bye for now. I need to get some sleep before tomorrow morning comes. I get up an hour and a half before the other regulars to get breakfast ready with the other cooks.

I love you all and miss you too. Tell Uncle John, Beth, Maurine, Bill, and Theresa I said hello. If you see him, give Charles my greetings and my hopes the store is doing good.

I'll write again as soon as I can.

Claude, Pvt US Army

P.S., soon after I got to Camp Pike I met up with Heber McLaughlin from Toltec. I've seen him just about every day in the mess hall. He got his commission as First Lieutenant in the First Provisional Regiment in August about a week after I arrived, and he's shipping out to Britain today, then headed for France. Give his family my best and tell them we pray for Heber and all the Arkansas boys in the first US wave.

The move to Camp Beauregard took about fourteen hours. It was slow and tedious, but we finally got there. It seemed chaotic because there were so many men arriving at the same time from Arkansas and Mississippi, all merging with the Louisiana guardsmen. But surprisingly the chaos was well orchestrated. Everyone got settled into the new barracks, and in the next days the training resumed. All of us were slated to go to France within the next few weeks. However, that got delayed because many of the men were getting sick. There was a measles outbreak, and many got malaria from the Louisiana bayou mosquitoes. It was bad and some men died from each disease. Fortunately, I didn't get sick and continued my duty as part of the quartermaster unit. Then, a few weeks after I arrived at the camp, I received orders to go to New York City to attend a training program there, located at the Columbia University. I didn't really know what it would be, but I had orders.

October 31, 1917

Dearest Papa & Mama, and Everyone

I'm on the train and have a chance to write you again. We all moved to Camp Beauregard a couple of days after my last letter. It took 14 hours to make the move. There our 18th Division became the 39th US Army Division. There are about 25,000 men there now. But I just left and am on the train to New York City. Can you believe that?

I'll be short and mail this on one of the stops we make.

When I first boarded the train, my mind went back to my first long train trip with Uncle John when we first visited Keo just after Christmas in '13. This trip's different in many ways, first because it was a lot longer, almost fourteen hundred miles. But especially because all on the train are soldiers like me. Most are going to NY to embark across the ocean to France. I'll be doing that soon too, I've been told, but I don't know when.

I'm looking out the window just now and see lots of farms, cotton and corn mostly. They're flickering by, like a moving picture. Far faster than from the slow-moving wagons when we came down from Illinois, and far less painful on my backside, too, than the flat board seat on the wagons.

I'm being sent to NY for some training at Columbia University. Not to go to college there but where they've set up training both for some of the students for reserve officer training and for others, like me, being trained in other things. Because I did it back at Camp Pike, I've been assigned to the Quartermaster Corp. There are Quartermaster Units in each of the army, navy, marines, and airservice. We are a support arm for troops both at bases here in the US and those deployed to the frontlines.

All except those who are sick are ready and excited to deploy to France to help the allies defeat the Germans. But I'm leaving behind a lot of sick men at Camp Beauregard, many with the measles and some with malaria too. Sadly, some have died. I've been lucky so far, thank God. I've made some good buddies in a short time and hope they remain free of these scourges.

With Love,
Claude

When we arrived in Manhattan it was amazing. The city was bigger than anything I'd ever seen, so much bigger than St. Louis. It's really hard to explain how overwhelmed I was when we first got there. We all had to report to our duty stations, and it was busy nonstop. But a few times on leave, some buddies and I went out. It was so big and fast moving. Being small town rural boys, we could hardly take it in, all the lights and streetcars, and people. Truly it's amazing, people everywhere and the noise of the city is constant. One night at Christmastime was extraordinary.

December 23, 1917

Dear Papa and Mama,

Hi again. Merry Christmas Eve, Eve. This time from New York City, the biggest and brightest place I've ever seen. I've been here now almost two months. The training school at Columbia has been good. Kind of feels like I'm going to college, something I always wanted to do, even though it's not that for me. I've been temporarily assigned out to a navy submarine unit. The US is building new types of submarines as fast as they can, but for now they're only being used to guard the US coastline, not overseas. I don't know if I'll be transferred to the navy or not.

I must tell you about NYC. It's something else, always on the go, people everywhere all the time. So many soldiers are here ready for embarkation to England then on to France. Me and a couple of buddies from Camp Beauregard went out tonight to see the city. Two fellows who are from Lonoke County too, Joe Bond and Emmett Coleman. Joe's part of the First Arkansas Infantry and is headed overseas in the new year and Emmett is a navy man, a machinist headed down to Norfolk Virginia as a part of the Balloon Division at the US Naval Air Station there.

Everything in New York is lit up for Christmas, lights and garlands and Christmas trees all dressed in tinsel and colored balls, and Christmas music sung by carolers and even broadcast on speakers. It feels like one big Christmas festival. Broadway Avenue, which stretches up and down the length of Manhattan, was jammed with cars and streetcars, and thousands of people all bundled up and walking briskly down the sidewalks of the big avenue. Not only is this city crowded with people and activity but also with sounds. The city is always full of sound, even at night when we're trying to sleep. Right in the middle of town, a bowtie-shaped place they call Times Square, they were setting up that big 700-pound "electric ball" you read about Papa in the newspaper back in Texarkana for New Year's Eve.

It was an amazing night, and everyone we met gave us their best wishes and prayers for when we go to the front lines in France. But it was really cold out and the snow came down heavy. The temps have already dropped into the twenties and the forecast for the New Year's Eve celebration is 10.

It looks like I'll stay here at least through January. Don't know after that. I'll try and write again soon.

Merry Christmas to Everyone at home. With much love,
Claude

I stayed in New York and worked in the Quartermaster Corp with the submarine unit for the next six months, through June of '18. But I was never fully transferred to the navy. I got word I was being reassigned to my old 39th Division and would be deployed to France in August. But I couldn't tell Papa and Mama where I was going or when, because of restrictions.

We shipped out August 28 and arrived in England on September 14. We arrived in Champagne-Marne France on October 3. Our unit never saw battle. We arrived just after the Allied offensive in the Champagne-Marne Operation under Allied Commander Foch. That terrible successful battle that pushed the Germans out of France and Flanders. The beautiful land of celebratory Champagne was a graveyard. The vineyards were stripped bare, and the trenches were deep. The smell of death still lingered in the air. The Germans asked for an armistice. On November 11, 1918, the Armistice was signed at Le Francport near Compiègne, ending the war.

I stayed in France through mid-January of '19. It was a busy time. So many graves, so many wounded. We received new troops in and sent many home—demobbing, as the Brits called it. It was the work of clearing the battlefields, stabilizing a worn-torn country, and securing the new and fragile peace.

But strangely, in the middle of such carnage, there was extraordinary beauty. I remember standing outside the barracks one early morning as the sun came up. It was like white paint on a dark canvas. The soft sunlit beauty of the French countryside stood out against the barren ravages of war.

I even ran into a buddy I'd met back at Camp Beauregard, Foreman Kelley from Lonoke, who saw the same contrast I did. He said, "France is a land of poetry until you meet someone, then it's finished. The people are so poverty stricken that it's distressing. They live on corn bread, brown bread, milk and eggs, and of course wine. But the people where I was," he said, "are far better off than the ones nearer the front, like here—the people where I was, have a better chance to get things." He saw the contrast of dark and light separated by just a few miles.

I even saw it in the incongruous. One day several of us were jawing about old times back home, and Foreman told us a story about something he saw in the French countryside and thought it strange. He said, "Some time ago I was away from the company for a couple of weeks, and while away I saw something I will never forget. It was a Frenchman butchering a hog. I guess you guys are familiar with the method we use in the US; well, the French method is some different. First, he knocks said porker in the head, then he cuts Mr. Hog's throat, but not until said hog is stone dead. Next, in place of hot water and knife to do the barber act, he builds a fire of straw and proceeds to burn the hair off of Mr. Hog. The whole operation took time enough for an American butcher to have killed and cleaned a dozen such hogs. You see, everything is so primitive." Everyone laughed.

Though having laughed myself, I thought how necessary yet incongruous laughter is amid such terribleness.

I couldn't believe Foreman told that story, I really couldn't. It took me back, long, long ago, to when I enjoyed the happiness of Hoggin' Day in Illinois only to have it dashed by that tragic fire. It took me back to the stark contrast between the happiness of that day and the tragedy of the same day. So close in place and time, just like Foreman saw in the French countryside.

The contrasts and contradictions struck me: beauty in the middle of ugliness, triumph and destruction, the tragic and comedic in the same place. I'd thought about that strangeness so many times before, but I became acutely aware of it there in France. And one of the strangest of all I saw, sadly, as my unit was preparing to start home.

Just as we began pursuing the peace and swept the fields of the ravages of war, a new and terrible scourge was happening. More American troops were dying from a contagious, rapidly spreading flu than had in the war itself, the Spanish flu they called it. October 1918 was reported to be the deadliest month in American history from the flu.

We began the long journey home on January 16. Everyone was concerned about the flu, being all packed in the ships. Many got it and a bunch died on the way home. But not me. Why? I don't know, but again I was grateful just as I had been for so many blessings before. We got to Newport News, Virginia in early February 1919. It took me another month to finally get back to Camp Pike, where those of us who survived were mustered out of the army.

When I arrived at Newport News, I got a letter from Mama, one she'd written back in November.

> November 12, 1918.
>
> Dearest Claude,
>
> I hope you are safe and well wherever you are. I miss you so much, dear boy, your Papa too. We haven't heard from you in quite a while. Hope all is ok. Please write again soon.
>
> First, Claude, we just heard that Heber McLaughlin, the feller from Toltec you mentioned in your first letter, was wounded just shortly after you wrote. We saw his father and he said Heber was hit in the head by shrapnel and was gassed in a

battle in November of '17. It seems he was in command of some US soldiers when they were attacked by Germans near Nancy France. I don't know where that is. Mr. McLaughlin said three Americans were killed and eleven wounded, and Heber was the first US officer wounded in this war. Heber received the highest French military honor for his bravery and he was promoted to Captain. At first, he resisted being sent home but eventually his wounds took their toll. Now he's back home and about to be discharged. I hope you'll be coming home soon too, without injury.

But I must give you some sad news too, honey. Back in late August I got word my sweet papa, your Grandfather Bill, was deathly sick. So I traveled by train from Little Rock back up to Vandalia and out to Seminary Township, to the old homeplace, to be with him. I'm very glad I went. I got there just in time.

There in that old log house, on September 12, 1918, just two months before yesterday's Armistice announcement, my papa died. My heart is still heavy, honey. But at eighty years old he had a good long life, except for the stomach trouble he'd suffered from for many years, and that finally took him. Papa died in the same old house where he'd been born, where I was born too, you remember, honey. Where we all lived after the fire you remember. That old place has seen many births and many deaths. It's where Grandfather Raford died at the young age of forty-seven back in '56, and where my mama Mary died when she was only thirty-seven in '74, when I was just three and a half years old. And it's where Grandmother Carroll died at eighty years old in '92. So many memories. They're all together again now. I'm happy for that, but I miss them all so much.

Your Grandfather Bill had a good life but a lot of heartache too. You remember me telling you, honey? He and your Grandmother Mary had six children, me being the next to the youngest. You remember, first he lost my mama at that very young age, then he lost all my brothers, Charles, John, and Robert, in three years' time. I thought about Charles when you wrote about the measles outbreak at Camp Beauregard. And I think about John these days who most likely died of some kind of flu like we're going through now, and about Bob in a terrible gunshot accident. They all died so young, leaving your Aunt Ideana, me, and Aunt Ollie to grow up without our brothers, and their papa without his sons. Papa's passing and what's going on these days brings all this back. My heart is sad just remembering it all. But we'll all be together again someday in the hereafter and have a big banquet like we used to at the home place.

The oldest living roots to the home place are almost gone now. Only Uncle Jim's left and he's now eighty-six, and a few cousins. I had a good visit with him when I was up there. He's doing well and asked about you a lot. I told him you were good the last time we heard from you, in the army in New York. He's proud of you, honey. Papa and me are too. We're so proud!

Uncle Jim said to tell you that it's now up to you and your sisters and brother to get busy and carry on the Carroll family, even if through the Howell name.

Well, honey, I'm sorry to give you this news, but I knew you'd want to know.

We miss you so much, Claude. Hope you come home soon.

I Love You, Honey,

Mama

I was glad to get Mama's letter. But so saddened too. Though I hadn't seen him in such a long time, it hurt my heart to think Grandfather Bill was gone. I was especially sad for Mama at the loss of her papa and the many losses she's had to bear, back in Illinois and since we left. I thought about Rachel. But I was glad Mama was with her papa when he died. Death is so hard. I'd seen too much of it, way too much. I wished I could have been there with her. I missed not being able to talk with Grandfather Bill and Uncle Jim, especially during this crazy war—I think so much these days about the providence of God and his grace that Uncle Jim talked about. God bless Grandfather Bill, Uncle Jim, and Mama.

War is hell, it's often said. I know how true that is. I was fortunate not to have known it in the trenches like so many in that terrible war. The face of such terror like so many of my buddies knew, and the permanent wounds so many who survived suffer, like my friend Heber.

How fortunate I was to be going home in one piece. So unexpected. Home to the grace and beauty of my family.

Eighteen—Grace and Beauty

Early Spring of 1919 to Early Fall of 1922

I stared out the window of the Altheimer-Argenta line, the same one I'd ridden with Uncle John six years before. "There but by the grace of God go I," I whispered to myself, as off in the distance I saw Hanger 10 at Eberts Field when we crossed into Lonoke County—a ward and makeshift morgue for soldiers dying or dead from the flu at Camp Pike. I'd just read in the morning paper that of the 2,200 Arkansas soldiers who died during the war, over half was from illness, most of that from the Spanish flu. What a sad statistic. How but by God's grace hadn't I been one? Many of my buddies were still in France making the peace after that terrible war. I said a short silent prayer, that they'd be spared the sickness rampant there, on the trip home, and on the home front.

As my gaze pulled back from the distance, there in the foreground I saw those beautiful Arkansas fields, full with their bounty and ripe for the springtime harvest. A new day was on the horizon.

The train slowed, jerked forward and back, and came to a full stop. I heard the steam release from the valves. "Keo! Destination is Keo, this is your stop!" yelled the conductor. I slumped into my seat for a minute, completely relaxed for the first time since I left. I leaned forward slowly and stood up, grabbed my hat, and hoisted my duffle on my shoulder. I was home, finally home. I took the three steel steps down out of the coach planting my feet on the ground. I stared across the street at the hotel and the store just to the right. Then, from the corner of my eye I saw Theresa barreling toward me at full speed. About three feet out, she jumped. I grabbed her tightly with my free arm, and she buried her face in my shoulder. I dropped my duffle and looked up to see that everyone was there, Mama, Papa, Uncle John, Beth, Maurine, and Bill. We hugged as we did when I'd left a year and half before, but this time without hesitation and fear. This time only with satisfaction and joy. A kind I'd never known.

I'm home, I thought to myself again. *I'm finally home.*

* * *

Papa was doing better than he'd been in years. That fall he and I had started a new company, W. F. Howell & Son. Prompted by the renewed peacetime activity that year, Keo finally became an incorporated town. We had several discussions with the townsfolk, young Mr. J. D. Alexander (Delbert, we called him) at the Bank of Keo, and with Charles Alexander, J. W. Brodie, and Sam Cobb. Everyone agreed Keo could support another store. With the money I'd sent home and a small loan from the bank, we bought one of the old general stores that had shuttered. We refurbished and reopened it as Howell & Son General Store. I set it up very much like Charles and Lewis's store, and established relationships with the suppliers I'd maintained there. Papa and Uncle John kept farming but also worked with me at our own store too. We all shared the duties, Bill too, when he came home from college.

Beth was still teaching school over near Toltec, Maurine was still away at Galloway, and Theresa was doing well in the sixth grade. Mama had more time to be out and about than when we were all growing up, and since Miss Alice came to live with us—a wonderful negro woman who came to help when Theresa was young and had become a part of the family. So, Mama would often stop by the store during the day, sometimes by herself just shopping in town and sometimes with Theresa after school let out.

Just like at Charles's store, Howell & Son became a crossroads and gathering place for many in Keo. Following the proven path, we put out a table and chairs at the storefront. It offered a great way for me to reconnect with folks.

Ever since I came back from the war getting to know folks, really getting to know them had become far more important to me.

Brother Crutchfield stopped by one day to congratulate us on the new store. It was good to see him. He became a regular, and on occasion we'd sit out front and talk for a bit. Sometimes he came in with Mrs. Malvina, always dressed as a proper Englishwoman. And Helen often came in too. And I'd regularly stop by the big old white house under the beautiful pecan trees when I made my deliveries over that way. This time in a used Model TT we bought.

I locked up the store and headed out to make deliveries one day, and my last one took me to the Crutchfield's. Brother Crutchfield asked me to sit and visit for a while on his big porch, and since I'd already locked things up, I did. He asked Mrs. Malvina to pour us each a glass of iced tea. Though they'd become frequent patrons at the store, most of our conversations there were short with frequent interruptions—even when we sat at the tables out front there was always something to do. That day there was no rush, only pleasant distractions.

Mrs. Malvina came back with the tea, and I said thank you. I took a sip and looked out at those big pecan trees, noticing how they cast late afternoon shadows across the well-kempt lawn.

"I just love those trees, Brother Crutchfield. I've been admiring them ever since my uncle and I first came to visit Keo back in thirteen," I said.

"Yes," he said, "I do too. Most of them on the back property are native old growth, these up around the house I planted a long time ago. I replace a few every now and again. Speaking of when you first came to Keo, Claude, I vaguely remember you saying that you and your family moved here after your little sister died. Can you tell me more about that?"

"Well, yes sir. It was tragic and so very sad. Heartbreaking. My little sister, Rachel, pulled a kettle of boiling water off the stove over on herself, trying to help Mama, we think. She was just nine years old. My brother Bill and my other sisters were in the house, but in another room looking after my baby sister, Theresa. Mama was out in the barn gathering milk from the cow, and I was out in the fields working with Papa and my Uncle John. Nobody was in the little kitchen with her at the time. It happened so fast, the way accidents happen, you know?"

Brother Crutchfield nodded in agreement.

"It was so devastating to little Rachel's body. The shock and the burns took her quickly. And it took my Papa from us too, for a long time. His heart broke and he went into a shell, just going through the motions. We decided to come over here to Keo for a fresh start, you might say. I remember when I first mentioned this that night at the store, you said you lost a daughter too."

"Yes. I know how your father feels, Claude," Brother Crutchfield said. "I'm so sorry he and your mama, and you kids and your uncle ever came to know such a tragedy—and poor little Rachel, God bless her. For parents it's especially hard to lose a child, because it's so out of order. Your children are supposed to outlive you. But sometimes it doesn't work that way. It's all in the mystery of God's providence—those things we don't understand and must simply trust Him."

"So," I said, "your daughter who died, that's Helen's mother, is that right? She briefly mentioned that one day when I saw her while making deliveries up here back before the war."

"Yes, Violet Lenora. Nona, we called her. My oldest daughter. Her appendix burst, we learned, and she died from complications when she was just twenty-four. Helen was only four-and-a-half years old when she died. Just after Helen was born her father left. And though Nona had remarried before she died, that fellow left too just after she died. We took Helen in and have raised as our own, which she is, of course. Mallie and I have seven children of our own, but we lost two—Nona, and Mary, who died when she was a just a baby right after she was born."

"Oh, my goodness, Brother Crutchfield," I said, "that's so terrible. I'm so sorry."

"Well Claude, thank you, but life is like that sometimes. We never know what time we're given, for some it's short and others long. But each child's a gift from God for as long as we have them, even if along with it comes heartache through death or disappointment. We've had four daughters, Nona, Isorah, Mary, and Josie the youngest, and three sons, Plez—short for Pleasant, who now lives in Idaho—Frank, and Graves. You've met Isorah and Josie, I believe."

"Yes sir, they've come in the store, I met them both along with Helen several times," I said.

"You said y'all came to Keo from Texarkana. That's where Brother Ben Bogard was before he came to Little Rock. You remember him, he was the interim pastor at Keo Baptist Church when I came to preach the revival, the night we first met at Charles Alexander's store. Were you born in Texarkana? Remind me where your family's from," Brother Crutchfield asked.

"I do remember that night, and Pastor Bogard. But no, I wasn't born in Texarkana. My little sister Theresa was. I was born in Illinois, in Seminary Township near Vandalia in southern Illinois, just east of St. Louis, along with my other sisters and brother," I explained.

Helen came out the big screen door. She'd heard us talking. "Hi there, Mr. Claude," she said, looking quite grown up since I'd last seen her. "So good to see you again. Y'all need some more tea?"

I looked at Brother Crutchfield. "No, Helen Grace, we're fine," he said.

"Thank you though, Helen," I replied.

"What are y'all talking about, Papa?" Helen asked.

"Well," he said, "I was just asking Claude where he and his family were from before Arkansas. They came from Illinois."

"Oh," she said, "may I stay and listen?"

"Sure," I said, "if it's okay with your grandfather.

"Yes," he said and nodded, and Helen sat down on the big porch swing and started rocking.

"So, what brought you and your family to Arkansas, Claude?" Brother Crutchfield asked. I clarified, "Well we actually settled on the Texas side of Texarkana. But you know how Texarkana is; it doesn't make much difference. We came through Arkansas on our way down though. And it was because of that trip that we eventually wound up over here in Keo."

"We left Illinois because our home was destroyed by a big fire there. We had to pay off some debt, so Papa sold our land and we worked it for the new owner for a few months so we could have enough to travel down to Texas and start over. My Grandfather Bill, my great uncle Jim, and Papa had heard Texarkana was thriving from a new railroad crossing there and that it had good farming prospects, so we came down here. But we still have family in Illinois. In fact, my mama was just back there a year ago when her father died, my Grandfather Bill Carroll."

"So, Carroll was your mama's maiden name, is that right?" he asked.

"Yes sir, we're from a long line of Carrolls going back to Tennessee, North Carolina, Virginia, and Maryland in this country, and back to Ireland before that. On my Papa's side, the Howells, they also come from North Carolina and Tennessee and before that England," I replied. "Have you and your family always lived here in Keo?" I asked.

"Oh no," he replied. "We came from Tennessee, too, both my side and Mallie's, whose maiden name is Browne. But before that, like yours, our families both come from Virginia and North Carolina. And our ancestors on both sides hail from England. Most of my family comes from Worcestershire and Mallie's from Leicestershire. But both our families lived in North Carolina, like yours, before moving to Tennessee—mine in Fayette County and Mallie's in Haywood County, the county just north. That's where we met and members of our families moved to Arkansas, where Mallie and I were married, just north of here in White County."

"That's amazing," I said. "My great grandfather's family moved from Virginia to North Carolina, where he was born, then he moved to Tennessee where he met and married my great grandmother. They and most of Great Grandmother's family moved northwest to settle in Seminary Township in Fayette County, Illinois. Isn't it interesting how there seems to be a Fayette County in lots of places?" I asked.

"Yes," said Brother Crutchfield, "that's because of old Marquis de La Fayette, a famous Frenchman who helped General George Washington win the Revolutionary War."

"Wow," Helen said, "I didn't know any of that. So, we're all from the same place?"

"Well, sort of," I said, "from around the same areas or passing through the same areas. So, some of our kin probably walked the same ground. Maybe they even walked right past each other, Helen. What do you think?" I kidded with Helen. "Did I get that right, Brother Crutchfield?"

"You never know. What's for sure is, it's a pretty small world," Brother Crutchfield said. "I do like thinking about your family and ours coming from the same parts," he said.

What a great afternoon on the porch that day. We had many more. The Crutchfields even invited me over for supper on occasions, and Mama and Papa too. Over the next year our families became good friends. We saw them quite often, and Helen regularly stopped by the store when she was in town. We'd often talk across the fence of the small corral next to the store. That fall both families gathered under those big trees and harvested pecans. Mama taught Helen how to make pecan pralines over at our house. I began to see Helen in a whole new way.

* * *

I'd found my oasis after the terrible storm of war. Yet the trailing winds that followed swirled with change all round, in America and abroad. Whole new industries were born, and the prospects of prosperity bred a spirit of jubilation. The theme of "technology" heralded back in St. Louis was now real in day-to-day life. Wireless radio, automobiles, moving pictures, aviation, and so much more. And sweeping social and cultural change was afoot. The "Bone-Dry Law" that Governor Brough supported back in '17 became the law of the land in 1919 when Prohibition passed—though it didn't stop the use of alcohol, just pushed it into the shadows. But it didn't matter much in Keo, certainly not for Brother Crutchfield and the Baptists that attended his church. Women got the right to vote in August of '20. Every day I read of something new in the papers, often snippets lifted from *Harper's* and *Vanity Fair* about new ideas and "breaks with tradition," they called them, in about everything you can imagine. There were items on topics as varied as new music, art and literature, and philosophy: like jazz, that people were calling America's original music; painters, writers, and intellectuals in Paris and the "Bloomsbury Set" in England; and big-idea philosophy like Governor Brough had talked of that day on the porch of Charles's store—about a group of scientists and philosophers called the "Vienna Circle" who were trying to remake philosophy into a science. Change was everywhere and about everything. People started calling it "The Roaring Twenties." The world was no doubt changing rapidly after the war. A lot seemed very promising but there was plenty that was very strange too.

The papers helped me stay aware of the bigger world that always hovered over things. Much was exciting, some just local news and occasionally small things I just took note of, like the constant snippets about Germany that I always followed since the war ended. They were humiliated at the Armistice, I read. *Rightly so, by Gawd!* I thought. Even more since the Treaty at Versailles. And they were laden with debt. One back-page story I remember was about a fellow named Anton Drexler who'd formed a new political party called The German Workers Party, or the DAP. In early '20 I saw they'd changed the name to National Socialist German Workers' Party, the paper called it the "Nazi Party." Besides my persisting interest in Germany, the only lingering thought I gave to that small piece, then, was the word "socialist." It reminded me once again of Governor Brough on the porch. And it stuck in the back of my mind. As I'd learned, who could ever tell what those small stories might mean?

* * *

Reading and thinking about the current of constant change in the world normally tied me in knots. Strangely I was not. At least not in that way. It was my heart. Something all new to me.

I had been so busy working all my life I'd never given much thought to it. Maybe it's because I was never around too many girls who weren't my sisters. I certainly knew what I didn't want from that night in Texarkana. I'd never met anyone even to consider. Then the war came along, and well, it was very isolating. First down in Louisiana, then in the war-torn countryside of France, then just hoping to stay alive on the way home. The only time I might have met someone then was at the few dances at Camp Pike or maybe in New York the few months I spent there. But except for the few times I went out on leave with my buddies there, I was busy from before dawn until late at night.

In the back of my mind, I had always wanted what Great Grandfather Carroll left North Carolina to find, but the dream had gone dormant. Until, as I got to know her, unexpectedly my heart jumped. Slowly ever since it was my heart that had gotten all tied up in knots.

The more time I spent at the Crutchfields the more I was stricken. She'd grown up so tall and beautiful since I left for the war. Her wavy dark hair was like silk. And I got lost in those piercing hazel-green eyes. Helen Grace Wood had stolen my heart and there was only one thing to do.

If traditions were falling daily in the bigger world, it was not so in Keo, certainly not for the Crutchfields. There was no dating then, though that practice had begun in the big cities after the war. Courting was formal and required permission. Especially for me, a suitor eleven years senior to his teenage sweetheart, the granddaughter of a Landmark Baptist preacher, no less.

But other traditions helped. Our families had become close: those porch visits and occasional combined suppers with Mama and Papa, and of no little value that my little sister Theresa was Helen's good friend from school. These combined to make all the difference.

A little over two years after I got home from France, I asked Brother Crutchfield for permission to court Helen. He looked at me and gladly gave it, under the condition of chaperones.

It was a beautiful sunny but hot Independence Day in 1921. Red, white and blue streamers and banners were up everywhere. US flags were out in front of every store and business in Keo. The whole town gathered on Main Street.

Helen and I walked among the various booths through the crowd along Main Street, accompanied by Brother Crutchfield's daughter, Josie, and her husband Joe Foster. We stopped to play one of the games. For a nickel you'd get three balls to throw at dolls on shelves six or eight feet back from the counter. If you knocked three down in any combination of three throws you get your pick of the large stuffed animals made by the women of Keo.

"You should do it, Claude," Helen said. "I know you can do it."

"Well," I said, "I did play baseball back in Illinois, maybe so."

"Do it, Claude, I want to see you do it!" she taunted me, laughing just like she did when we competed to gather the most pecans the previous fall. I reached in my pocket and handed the fellow a nickel and he handed me the three balls.

I stood back, taking aim as other folks looked on to see if I'd blow it on my first formal outing with Helen. They all knew both of us and were really cheering me on. I reared back and threw hard like Boston's Walter Johnson. It flew off to the right hitting the edge of the shelf and bounced down to the ground. Strike one, no trophy. Palms sweating now, I reared back and threw again. Ping, I barely caught the edge of a doll full of sand in its torso. It tipped to the back and slowly fell—One down! Excited, I reared back one more time and let go. Swoosh, the ball went right between the dolls. *A terrible outing on the mound*, I said to myself. Embarrassment is a hard thing.

Is this how I'd provide for my sweetheart? Then I saw that beautiful smile. I was so smitten.

Helen said, "Do it again, do it again, Claude!"

"No," I replied in humiliation but also joy. "But why don't you try?"

Without hesitation, Helen says, "Oh Yes! Let me try!" I pulled out another nickel, and the man placed three balls into Helen's gathered hands. She handed me two.

She rears back and lets it fly. Boom! She hits right in the middle and three dolls fall all at once. She screams,

"Yes, yes, yes, I won, Claude. Can you believe it? I won all in one throw!"

The crowd standing round roared and clapped in astonishment and glee. I was both happy and embarrassed at the same time.

"Pick out your prize, Miss Helen, any one of them," Mr. Johnson said happily. "I'll take that one, the big bear." He hands it to her, she hugs it, and then hands it to me saying,

"Here's your prize, Claude. I won you a big bear at the Fourth of July celebration. Aren't you glad you brought me?"

Josie tried to hide it, but I heard her laughing behind me, Mama and Papa too, who had stepped behind us with the gathering crowd. It was hilarious.

I looked at Helen and hugged that bear with a big grin, as if I was hugging her.

We went on throughout the festivities the rest of the afternoon. It was a great day.

As the sun went below the horizon, everyone gathered at the flatbed wagons for the hayride. Helen and I got on, sitting next to each other with Joe and Josie next to us. I felt in heaven being that close to Helen. She leaned into my shoulder as the wagon made the loop down by the Cobb gin and back up in front of the hotel before coming to a stop—I already knew, but feeling Helen nestled next to me convinced me all the more; she was my girl, and I wanted her to be my girl forever.

Everyone had come together in the center of town to see the fireworks. Roman Candles and some small rockets shot off and burst, and you could see between the tall cypress trees in the background. The flashing light briefly awakening the darkened sky took me back to France. But this wasn't a war and those weren't bombs. It was a celebration of freedom. The freedom we went to France to preserve.

I walked Helen back down past our store. We said our goodbyes, and she and Josie and Joe walked on home. It was the best day of my life. Absolutely the best day of my life.

We had many more suppers in each of our homes with our families and many more chaperoned outings, and we got to know each other better and better. I learned many more interesting things about her family—including that Mrs. Malvina had an uncle who was a famous portrait painter and that "after his conversion" Brother Crutchfield went to Ouachita Baptist College in Arkadelphia, the same town where my brother Bill went to college and played football. I learned that "after his conversion" meant his life before was pretty wild—what he called a "profligate" life. I thought that might account for his sometimes hardness and sternness, though he was never that way with Helen. She was his angel, and I understood why. She had become mine too.

"You're awfully quiet this evening, Helen. Tell me," I implored in a whisper. "Please tell me what you're thinking about," I asked as we rocked gently in the big chair swing on the front porch until she stopped it.

"You," she said hesitantly, "and me. Us together. I was thinking about when you told me almost two years ago, joking I think, that I had to marry you."

We both chuckled. "Me too," I said as I looked deep into those beautiful eyes. "That's all I think about these days. I love you, Helen Grace. I love you with all my heart."

"I love you too, Claude. So much," she said leaning into me. "So much," she said again, as I lifted my arm up and around her shoulders and pulled her close to me.

I'd fallen in love with the most beautiful girl I'd ever seen, and finally I knew for sure she loved me too.

I went to Pecan Grove Baptist Church to see Brother Crutchfield. With the normal trepidation one expects on such occasions but compounded by the fact he's a preacher, I asked for Helen's hand in marriage. The so-often big-voiced Brother Crutchfield peered down at me over those dark round turtle-shell glasses and said . . . in a soft and gentle tone, "Claude, I couldn't be more pleased to give you my consent. May God bless you both together."

* * *

September 16, 1922

"Claude Rama Howell," Brother Crutchfield said, "do you take Helen Grace Wood to be your lawfully wedded wife, to have and to hold from this day forward, for better or worse, for richer or poorer, in sickness and health. Do you promise to love her, comfort her, honor and keep her, and forsaking all others to be faithful only unto her until death do your part?"

"I do."

"Helen Grace Wood," Brother Crutchfield said, "do you take Claude Rama Howell to be your lawfully wedded husband, to have and to hold from this day forward, for better or worse, for richer or poorer, in sickness and health. Do you promise to love him, obey him and serve him, honor and keep him, and forsaking all others to be faithful only unto him until death do your part?"

"I do."

"Having now made your vows before God and this company, I therefore pronounce you man and wife," Brother Crutchfield declared.

By God's grace I was spared from the many dangers, toils, and snares in wartime to come home to the beauty of the fields of Lonoke County. And by His grace I found my very own *Grace* and *Beauty*. And a whole new kind of satisfaction, far greater even than I felt when I stepped off the train in Keo after the war. My heart was full. My world, whole.

Nineteen—Be Fruitful and Multiply

Fall of 1922 to December of 1928

I couldn't imagine life any better. The world so recently full of conflict and death had settled down and was flourishing again. Papa was able to laugh again, and that made Mama happy. My brother and sisters were close by or underfoot. Beth still taught in Williams Township just up the road, and Maurine and Bill worked with me at the store, as did Papa and Uncle John when not farming. Howell & Son was going great. It truly was a family business. We were all close again and saw each other almost every day. It reminded me of the days when we were kids.

But most of all, married life was bliss. Helen and I found a small three-room house in town just behind the store. Our new home. And this new life soon came not just for me but for Beth and Maurine too who both married the year after me and Helen, in '23—Beth to Hayward Jackson, who everyone called Ward, and Maurine to Delbert Alexander, our banker. Bill wasn't far behind, marrying Letha Linn a couple years later. It took Theresa time of course—after high school she first went to nursing school, then decided to become a career woman, as people had begun to call it then. She moved down to Monroe, Louisiana to work for Mr. Berny Oakland.

I'm reminded of what Uncle Jim had told Mama to tell us kids when she saw him at Grandfather Bill's funeral. To get busy and carry on the Carroll family, even if through the Howell name or whatever names the girls have when they get married. We all took it to heart.

* * *

Helen and I ran the store day-to-day. It allowed us to be together all the time, which was wonderful. As I finalized sales at the cash register, I always found myself glancing at her across the displays as she worked. My God, how could I have gotten so lucky?

As had become our custom, that evening Helen had her arm wrapped in mine as we walked up the now familiar steps of the big white house nestled in the pecan grove. Mama and Papa followed behind as we all gathered for our new blended family supper, Brother Crutchfield, Mrs. Malvina and Helen's "sisters" Isorah and Josie (really her aunts) and their husbands. Josie was older than Helen but they were real close. She and her husband Joe were the chaperones when Helen and I first courted. Joe became the Marshall down in England for a time and after that an Arkansas State Representative. We also often saw Isorah, who was just a bit older than me, and her husband Homer Nelson. Homer was a commercial painter in Keo; he did houses mostly, but we often used his services at the store too. All of us saw each other as couples. But the big gatherings at the Crutchfields became our Saturday evening routine.

I don't know why it hadn't dawned on me before, but as we all stood in the big living room, it struck me that my marriage to Helen doubled the size of my family overnight. And with that, more stories too.

We all took our seats at the large mahogany Queen Anne table that sat twelve. It was draped with a violet linen embroidered-edged tablecloth, as it often was. Fine china and water glasses and large silver serving trays were elegantly displayed and full of fixins—that night with a large rump roast with white garden potatoes, heirloom Kentucky-wonder green beans, and glazed carrots like I had at the Keo Hotel the first night Uncle John and I came to town back in '13. I wouldn't have known the details of any of these elegances if Mrs. Malvina hadn't explained them to me.

I was reminded of the first time Papa, Mama, and I came to supper at the Crutchfields, before Helen and I were married. As I had that first night, I told Mrs. Malvina how pretty it all looked. And though by then I'd had supper there many times, for some reason that night I felt comfortable confessing just how little I knew about such fine things. Though in truth, I'm certain Mrs. Malvina already knew. I guess I told her because I really did wonder about those things and where she'd gotten them. So, I asked, and it opened into a new family story.

"Mrs. Crutchfield, do you mind me asking where you got these table things? I've seen some like them recently in the catalogues at the store. Is that where you got them?"

"No, Claude. I didn't buy them myself. They were a gift from my mother, part of my inheritance—Brother Crutchfield and I were able to build this house with the same inheritance. My mother got these wonderful place settings in England. That's where my family's from, in Leicestershire. That's an area like what we call a county, you see. It's in the midlands of England. I hold these dishes and silver dear in my heart, and when we use them, it's a way of honoring and remembering my mother. You understand?"

"Oh yes I do, very much Mrs. Crutchfield, I do," I said.

I looked over at Mama and saw her eyes fill with tears. She didn't say anything, but I knew what she was thinking. My mind went back to the day after the fire in Illinois when we were walking through the embers and Mama stooped down and picked up a few pieces of the broken china she'd been given from her mother's belongings after her death, the only keepsake she had from the mother she hardly knew.

"They're certainly beautiful," I repeated what I'd said the first time I came to supper. "Thank you again, as always, for inviting us to this wonderful table. It sure makes things feel very special."

It was. The Saturday night family gathering tradition was great. That first evening with Helen as my wife on my arm made it even more special, and less nervous to boot.

While I had always felt a little out of place in formal settings, I learned to settle in, even with the always thunderous prayers of Brother Crutchfield. As time went by, those Saturday nights became more relaxed. The conversations were always fun, especially the banter between the sisters kidding each other. And you might say engaging, from the sometimes deep and on occasion theological comments made by Brother Crutchfield. And there was always some new family story I had not heard. They were often triggered by recollections from the past. They always revealed new connections between our families that I never imagined.

Brother Crutchfield often asked Papa and Mama about home back in Illinois. They also talked about Tennessee and North Carolina and how he and Mrs. Malvina came to Arkansas.

That night I asked Mrs. Malvina, "Would you tell us about your uncle who was a portrait painter, the one Brother Crutchfield mentioned back when Helen and I were first getting to know each other?"

"Sure, honey."

When she said that, that way, I glanced at Mama and smiled. It sounded just like her.

"That's my Uncle Bill Browne, William Garl Browne Jr. That's my maiden name, Browne, you understand?"

"Yes ma'am, Brother Crutchfield told me that."

Continuing she said, "Well as I mentioned, my family came from England. My grandfather was a painter back there, a landscape painter. My Uncle Bill got his talent from him, I suspect. When my grandparents came to America, first to Virginia, Uncle Bill developed his talent and started painting portraits. He opened a studio in Richmond and was quite good. After a portrait he painted was hung at the National Academy he was invited to paint General Zachery Taylor, before he became President Taylor, you see."

When Mama heard this, she became fully engaged, saying, "That's interesting, Mallie. Zachery Taylor? When he was president, he signed the deed to one of the land grants my grandfather Raford Carroll received back in Seminary Township in Illinois."

I remember noticing how Mama said Great Grandfather Carroll's full name. When she does, she always pronounces Raford with a mixture of an o and e combined—like Raferd, the way folks say Herferd when talking about Hereford cows. I grinned.

"Oh, my goodness, Laura, that's so very interesting, I want to hear more."

But returning to the story about her uncle to finish it, Mrs. Malvina continued.

"Well, that National Academy showing launched Uncle Bill to quite a success at the young age of twenty-four. After that his portraits were shown in Washington, New York, Baltimore, and many other places."

That comment triggered another memory in Mama. She said, "Baltimore? That makes me think of our distant relation Mr. Charles Carroll of Carrollton, Maryland, Mallie. Do you know his name?"

"No Laura, I don't. Who is he?"

"Well, he's a distant relation as I mentioned. Our family connection to him is not in this country but back in Ireland. But he was one of the signers of the Declaration of Independence. I learned of this from my Uncle Jim when I was young, who learned of it from his papa, my Grandfather Carroll. It's the Carroll family connection, you see?"

"Oh my, Laura, that too is so interesting. There are so many great connections in this ever-growing family of ours. It's so wonderful."

"I love these connections, Mrs. Malvina," I said. "Ever since I was young, I've thought about the unexpected connections between so many different things. That's quite a story. You come from a very talented family," I told her.

Everyone enjoyed that story and the connections. It's so funny how conversations go.

But as much as I enjoyed that story, it wasn't the talent of William Browne that most impressed me. The best part of the evenings at the Crutchfields was after dessert and coffee. As she almost always did, that evening Josie coaxed Helen into sitting down at the piano to play. This hidden talent of Helen's astonishes me. I first learned she could play when we were courting. She told me her grandparents got her a tutor when she was young and took lessons for a few years, but mostly taught herself. She can read music a little, she said, but mostly she plays "by ear," as she calls it. She plays hymns from memory when we all gather at Pecan Grove Baptist to sing and hear Brother Crutchfield preach.

And boy could you hear Brother Crutchfield. On quiet summer nights with the church windows open, folks across the street used to say his big boisterous voice bounced through the big pecan trees on revival nights, and you could hear the gospel from your front porch.

Helen learned all the regular hymns and carols at Christmastime, by heart. We didn't have a piano at our home then, so she played only at church and at Saturday night suppers.

With Josie's gentle cajoling that night, Helen agreed to play. She sat down and started lightly picking out a few unconnected notes. First with her right hand, starting and then stopping, lifting her hand up quickly from the higher keys, followed by a few with her left hand on the lower ones in the same way, pressing and letting up on the right pedal below. No one could tell what she was doing, but she was remembering and picking out a new piece she'd heard. She stopped. Everything got quiet. Resting both her hands gently on the keys and her foot on the pedal, she began to play.

It was more beautiful than anything I've ever heard.

When she finished, everyone sat in stunned silence for a moment. The final notes seemed to hang in the air. I broke the silence asking Helen what it was, where she'd learned it. She said, "Something I heard on the radio recently. It's so elegant I think, don't you? It's by a French fellow named Claude Debussy. It's called "*Clair de Lune*." It means "Clear Moon Light," the radio said. It's so beautiful."

Later that night I asked Helen again how she learned it. She told me she'd listen to it when it was played on radio and pick out the notes on her knees as if they were a piano and memorize what she'd heard. Far more than the brightness of the moon that cast its glow before me as I stood on the porch back in Illinois so long ago, Helen had become my clear moon light. For me her glow was cast over everything. Helen Grace was my extraordinary gift and has been ever since. Her musical gift at the piano reveals a kind of beauty that's a pull on the human heart. My heart was full.

* * *

It could well have been that wonderful night or the feelings that lingered in me from the beautiful piece she played on the piano, or maybe that I just love Helen so much. God only knows.

It's certain that God alone gave us the gift that came from our love that night. Nine months later William Carroll Howell arrived May 26, 1924. Our first bundle of joy was beyond anything we'd ever known. William was the name given to him partly to honor my papa and partly Grandfather Bill. And Carroll carried Mama's family name forward. Papa was so proud and Mama so pleased. I think it was the first time I'd really seen new life in Papa's eyes since Rachel's death. It made me so happy. Mama wept tears of joy when she cradled him in her arms the first time.

"Oh, my goodness, William Carroll," she said rocking him gently, "you have entered a big loving family in this wonderful world. Your papa and mama love you so much," as she kissed him gently on his tiny forehead, "just as we all do. You're the first new member of the next generation. God bless you, dear boy," she said softly, tearful again with deep memories as she thought about his name and the connection it made to her papa and the Carroll family.

Becoming parents for the first time changed our world, all in a good way. Helen's time and focus shifted all onto Carroll, which is what we called him.

But not Miss Alice, who was like a third grandmother to Carroll. After he was born, she came over from Mama and Papa's daily to help Helen. For some strange reason she called Carroll Taboy. I don't know why, she's the only one who called him that. But she loved our baby boy as if he were her very own. Her nickname was endearing.

Helen and I were overjoyed. I didn't think our marriage could get more perfect, but it had. While there were many sleepless nights, and some scary and very exhausting ones when Carroll had colic, our joy remained full. We'd found ourselves staying up too late with him in bed with us just playing and listening to him make new sounds and watching his eyes discover new things.

Not only had our little family begun to sprout, so had Bill's and Maurine's. In October of the same year Maurine's first came along, James Delbert Alexander Jr., named for his father Delbert—they called him simply by his initials J. D. A year later Bill and Letha's first came along, little Barbara. Less than a year later, in June of '26, Maurine's second, Carmon, was born.

Then barely six months later, in late January of 1927, our first beautiful little girl arrived.

Your sweet mama, Laura Dean, son. What a wonderful day that was.

We gave her Mama's name and a shortened version of her aunt Ideana's name. Then, to our great surprise, we learned later she had another name too, Lenore. When Mrs. Malvina filed her birth certificate in the county register, she added that name—the middle name of her oldest daughter, Helen's mother.

At first, I was a little afraid when she learned what Mrs. Malvina had done. But in a subdued way, Helen was happy. She cried tears of mourning joy because now her oldest daughter had her own mother's middle name, the mother she barely knew, Violet Lenore.

Our little girl with three names had eyes so bright and a smile so big it made your heart melt. Helen called her Lauradean, like a single word. From the start, I called her "Sister" and I'd begun calling Carroll "Bubber." That began my practice of nicknaming all our kids.

Helen and I were in absolute heaven.

Now we had two young'uns to feed, care for, and play with. The days were busier, the needs greater, but all the fuller too. Our life was flourishing, and the store was going well.

That spring after Laura Dean was born, Bill's second, Norma Lee, came along.

Our big family was growing faster than we could turn around.

Now when we all got together, often at our little house and sometimes at Mama and Papa's or the Crutchfields, it was full of the sounds and play of little ones. Mealtimes were far more frazzled and informal, even at the Crutchfields. Mothers and grandmothers reached across each other tending to their kids and grandbabies. It was a symphony of sounds and a ballet of constant movement. So much fun.

For so long I'd thought only about farming or the store or the next new thing to pick up the pieces—especially after Rachel, then after the war. All my thoughts now shifted to protecting, taking care of, and ensuring the best possible life for our burgeoning family. In that spirit, sure I'd never need it but just in case, I did something I'd never even thought about before. A fellow named Mr. Davison Price came in the store one day. He presented himself as an insurance man who'd come over to Keo from Hot Springs. After talking for a short while, I decided to buy two small policies, one on the store—just enough to cover our bank debt and the inventory—and a small life insurance policy to protect Helen and the kids in case something happened to me.

The '20s were a wonderful happy time. The world was rapidly changing and ours was too—one could call it the "roaring twenties" like people in the big cities had termed the times. It was roaring for us but for very different reasons. Keo had weathered the downturns in cotton after the war, barely missed the ravages of the devastating Arkansas Flood the year Laura Dean was born, and continued to thrive. The pre-war optimism had returned across the country. It sure had for us. I'd struck gold with my wonderful Helen, and to top that off Carroll and Laura Dean filled our days and hearts with joy.

In a span of less than five years, Helen and I, and Maurine, and Bill added six new ones to the family. We had taken Uncle Jim's admonition to heart and God's to be fruitful and multiply.

It was only the beginning.

Twenty—Just When Things Were Going So Well . . .

January of 1929 to Christmas Eve of 1934

As we entered our seventh year of marriage the world could not have looked brighter.

After the catastrophes of the Great War and the Spanish Flu, for many if not most Americans the belief that the world was getting better and better had returned. For folks' daily lives, that is, not in some grand philosophical way like Governor Blough had talked about that day on the porch before the war. The sentiments held true in our small town of Keo and in our own family too. An unbounded optimism dominated the news as the new year dawned in 1929. Things were thriving. The twenties were still roaring.

But soon sad news came from Illinois. We got word that on February 13, Uncle Jim had died. James Monroe Carroll, the oldest son and last surviving child of Raford and Sarah Carroll, was dead at ninety-six. The news was hard, particularly for Mama, and especially for me. I reflected on how important he'd been for me ever since I was a boy. My heart was deeply saddened. I thought with such fondness about that formative and yet so crushing Hoggin' Day in the fall of '04. How a day that began with such great expectations could go up in smoke so quickly. I thought about how my towering Uncle Jim comforted and encouraged me when I was so down and taught me how to see the important and permanent things amid terrible times. I loved Uncle Jim and though I hadn't seen him in many years, I missed him so much. My heart ached . . . and oh how he would have loved Helen and Carroll and Laura Dean.

My mind swirled with memories. *What price, a good man? Invaluable.*

My cherished memories and sad reflections were overwhelmed by joy when four-and-half-year-old Bubber came barreling into the store with two year old Laura Dean waddling carefully on Helen's hand behind. How could I stay gloomy with such heavenly gifts in front of me? Uncle Jim would've loved the scene, and he would've loved seeing me find such joy in it.

Despite the sad news of Uncle Jim's death, it looked like only good times were ahead.

The early spring "planting" took root for a late fall harvest—Helen was pregnant again! Due in early December. Helen and the grandmothers spent all summer and into the early fall doing the normal nesting, preparing for our new little one, and that of course included tending to the two busy bees we already had.

Following my now evening routine, just as I closed the store I sat down and thumbed through the newspaper. I saw a few news items discussing the white-hot presidential race. When Herbert Hoover accepted the nomination for a presidential run in '28, he said "Given the chance to go forward with the policies of the last eight years, we shall soon with the help of God be in sight of the day when poverty will be banished from this nation forever."

The scope of the optimism was boundless.

When he took over from Calvin Coolidge on March 4, 1929, the now *President* Hoover saw only high prospects on the horizon. On inauguration day it was printed that "Hoover planned to immediately overhaul federal regulations with the intention of allowing the nation's economy to grow unfettered by any controls. The role of the government, he contended, should be to create a partnership with the American people, in which the latter would rise (or fall) on their own merits and abilities. He felt the less government intervention in their lives, the better."

The optimism that'd opened the year was now extravagant, especially in business. In a way, optimism was being sold as a commodity. Folks were selling pure speculation, it appeared. I read newspaper reports of Mr. Charles Ponzi and his investment schemes, and many Florida land speculators. And the US stock market was soaring. For good reason many said, on account of the country's productive output increasingly steadily. But lots of stock buyers were speculating too, using borrowed money, "on the margin," the paper called it. Borrowing from American banks was easy, then, and they and the US Treasury were carrying lots of foreign European WWI debt which had been loaned to help them recover and rebuild from the war.

I monitored the papers daily all year long. That fall, I don't know why but I remember it exactly. On October 3, 1929, I read that the British Chancellor of the Exchequer Philip Snowden undermined public confidence by calling the US stock market a "speculative orgy." The next day, on October

4, the *Wall Street Journal* and *The New York Times* further undermined confidence in the stock market by reporting Snowden's remarks and agreeing with him.

As I so often had, I thought about how small remote things can turn into big things and eventually arrive on your doorstep. This time the small remote thing was only *words* from an English fellow talking about America, but his words turned into a big thing.

On Wednesday, October 23, 1929, the newspapers and radio broadcasts reported that the day before the value of the stock market in New York fell by 20 percent from its September 3 high. What came to be called "Black Tuesday" was followed by a total disaster on Thursday. On October 24, 1929, "Black Thursday," the New York stock market tumbled by another eleven percent—losing almost a third of its total value in less than two months. The following Black Monday led to a near total collapse on Black Tuesday.

Those October events on the New York Stock Exchange came to be called "The Crash."

But as important as they were to many, for the moment they were still remote to most of us folks in Keo. Many reports I read said it was a "necessary correction," required for an "overheated market"—whatever that meant, I remember thinking. Most folks, including the president, believed it would all settle out by year's end. But just as so many folks naively first thought in 1914 about the Great War, that wasn't to be. By the end of November, the stock market had lost more than half its value. One news article said, all efforts to stem the tide of disaster were "tantamount to bailing Niagara Falls with a bucket."

Who knew then if that financial crisis would eventually affect us in Keo? I thought about something I read in Uncle Jim's diaries when Mama and Papa were in De Queen. About the economic crisis that followed Napoleon's defeat at Waterloo and the Banking Crisis of 1819 after the War of 1812. How those remote events contributed to the hard times that helped prompt Great Grandfather Carroll to leave North Carolina and make his way to Illinois. After reading that in Uncle Jim's diaries in Texarkana, I got a book from the library that talked about other such crises, the worst just two years before I was born. I'd learned to pay close attention to seemingly far-off unrelated things, including financial ones. They have a way of becoming close and related. I'd seen it happen so many times. My mind drifted. *Would it again?*

But the morning of December 6, 1929, I gave no more thought to any of that. It was another amazing day for Helen and me. Our second little boy was born. At Helen's urging, we gave him my name, Claude R. Howell Jr. I nicknamed him "Nicky," from Nikodemus in the funny papers. Christmas was wonderful that year. By God's grace, Helen Grace had graced us with another new son. Blessed first with Bubber, then Sister, and now Nicky, our family was growing by leaps and bounds.

Then despite not yet having been hit by the trials of the bigger world, just when things were going so well, our whole world in Keo changed in an instant.

When preparing breakfast before the other businesses were open, including our store, a fire broke out in the kitchen of the cafe next door. It quickly spread to the store. Though we lived only just behind, by the time I got there no one could do anything. The cafe, the feedstore on the other side, and Howell & Son were all engulfed in flames.

While "Black Thursday" on the New York Stock Exchange the prior fall hadn't yet directly affected us, "Black Thursday" in Keo on January 23, 1930, did. Our whole promising livelihood was taken from us all within the space of a couple of hours.

I remembered again the deep sadness that a fire can bring. This time, though, my cares were not for broken dreams on a rite of passage day. No. They were for my family, my beautiful wife and three kids, and Mama and Papa. A heavy weight of uncertainty set in.

* * *

I went to see Delbert at the bank. He had a phone. Not ever expecting to do so, from there I called Mr. Davison Price, the insurance man from Hot Springs who sold me the policy to protect against just such a disaster. He came over to Keo on the train a couple of days later and we made the claim. It was enough to pay off the bank and the credit I carried with a few suppliers I owed, barely anything more. But Howell & Son kept its promises.

Mr. Price and I went to our little house and spent the afternoon talking. We'd become friends. He'd taught me a lot about business, and I'd gotten to know his family a bit, since they'd all come to our area on occasion. He could see I was worried. I didn't have much to carry us for long and no regular income to provide for Helen and me and our three young kids. We discussed what I planned to do. I didn't know. I told him I supposed I'd look around in Keo, talk with some of my friends, that maybe I'd go back to farming with Papa. Mr. Price told me to stay in touch.

For the next couple of months I talked with everyone in the area. Including Charles Alexander and with Mr. Cobb and Mr. Brodie. Cotton prices were falling rapidly. I read that "commodity prices were sinking like stones—more than two and a quarter percent per month—with a big decline in April." By late spring the prospects of working in the Keo cotton industry were not good. The supporting businesses in town were also suffering with lower and lower demand. We stayed through the summer—with zero income. Then in August, it got worse. A severe drought hit the central US and it further drug down the agriculture industry. Our already very limited resources were draining fast. What was I going to do?

I went to the bank and called Mr. Price again and updated him as he asked me to do. We talked for a while and he said, "Claude, why don't you come to work for me, in the insurance business?"

I was taken aback. I told him I didn't know; that I didn't understand that business.

He said, "Don't worry, I'll teach you. If you're willing, I'll get you set up in our training group in Little Rock. You can learn the ropes there and then come over to Hot Springs and work with me. Let's do this, Claude. You don't have to do it forever, but it'll help you get on your feet."

I was overwhelmed at his generosity but also at the prospects of uprooting Helen and the kids.

That night I talked to Helen about it. And we decided it might be for the best. We had to do something. I hated to leave Keo, but what else could I do? Black Thursday in October had collided with Black Thursday in January. We were in a fix. I accepted Mr. Price's generous offer and told Papa and Mama and Brother Crutchfield and Mrs. Malvina. They all understood.

We let our little house go, and Helen and the kids stayed with Papa and Mama while I started training with New York Life in Little Rock in September—a six-week course. When I got back to Keo, Papa said he and Uncle John's farm at the Scott Plantation had shut down because of no place to sell their crops. So, now they were out of work and income too. My brother Bill got some work down in England but didn't know how long it'd last. Beth still taught school but was nervous—Ward's work had dried up. Theresa was still in Monroe, Louisiana working for Mr. Berny Oakland, who was in the new natural gas industry. For now, things were stable for her there.

I have often wondered about permanence and yet how fleeting the things we think are permanent really are. We continue to long for it, work for it, strive for it, and when things seem settled, we find contentment. Only to have the world turn upside down again, forcing us to face how transient things are—that word again that Uncle Jim used after the fire. There seems to be something in and through the impermanent that keeps drawing our heart toward something more, the truly permanent. I don't know. I just wonder.

Helen and I, along with Carroll, Laura Dean, and baby Nicky, gathered with Papa, Mama, Uncle John, and Beth and her husband Ward, and prepared to move. Maurine and Delbert and their two kids decided to come too—the bank in Keo was on the verge of failing and he lost his job. The kids' third grandmother, our wonderful Alice, stayed in Keo with her family. We all took the train to Hot Springs. What little I could garner there would have to sustain us all, at least for now. And it did, just barely. But despite the tailspin we were in, we were all still a family.

Helen was my solid rock, my constant encouragement. She kept me going, helping me to find new prospects to call on when she'd go to the market in Hot Springs, even if what we could buy was very little. The kids were an absolute godsend. Their simple and constant happiness was our sustaining joy.

I took Laura Dean with me to the office one day and everyone there just went nuts over her. After supper at home that night, holding her in my lap tickling and playing with her I told her, "Sister, everyone at the office says you've got a million-dollar smile." She turned that smile to me and looked up with those big brown eyes. I looked over at Helen holding Nicky, with Bubber under her feet, and we smiled at each other. No matter what kind of day it'd been, that was enough to make the whole world right.

We developed a new rhythm to life in Hot Springs. We found a big old house in significant disrepair but sufficient for our needs. Helen spent the days raising our young'uns—Carroll even started grammar school, growing up too fast, for me. Papa and Mama helped Helen and Maurine. Delbert looked for a banking job, and Beth's husband, Ward, looked for anything he could find, but neither were successful. We attended First Methodist Church there where Mr. Price was an ordained elder—I found myself at home in the church with him; and he even got me to teach a Sunday school class for kids, something I never imagined myself doing. Still, it was very different, and we never quite felt settled. It was a waystation, much as it'd been when we came through back in '05 on our way to Texarkana, just longer.

But with Mr. Price's help it became a bit more than that. He knew everyone in town and he and I spent a lot of time together. He became like a second father or Uncle Jim to me of sorts—I mean, Papa was always there, a constant encouragement, but his motivations were low. I had some success selling insurance. At first. But most folks I tried to sell to were like me. If they had anything they were holding on to it, focused more and more on what they needed for today, not insuring against what might come tomorrow. The calamity was worsening day by day.

Hot Springs wasn't permanent. I knew it and so did Mr. Price. I read the papers every morning like I used to, always with an eye for new prospects.

I'd long been in and around the cotton business. I kept a close watch on that market. Ever since I got home from the war, cotton had been volatile. In 1920, cotton had hit its peak at forty-two cents a pound, prompting Southern farmers to over-plant, resulting in the largest crop in history. Since then, cotton had fluctuated dramatically, mostly down. But it was getting worse and worse by the day. Price-per-pound had dropped steadily since early in '30, from over fourteen cents a pound now to a low of six and a half cents in '31. It was the worst it'd ever been. But finally, in '32 I saw signs of a possible rebound, not much but some.

That summer, two concrete rays of hope in the middle of our uncertainty gave promise for the future. Helen was pregnant again with our fourth and Beth, wonderfully, with her first. Hearing this good news, I thought about Uncle Jim and his encouragement to trust in God's providence especially in the face of difficult times.

But my sales in insurance continued to get worse. I gave my declining success in insurance and the small prospects for cotton some thought. I talked to Mr. Price about it. He completely understood. He knew I needed to try and find a way to build more—for this whole big family.

Maurine's Delbert and I decided to take a trip down to the coast in Texas to explore banking opportunities for him and, for me, to try and build something that could sustain us all selling cotton and other commodities around the Galveston shipping port.

At the train station in November of '32, just after the election I wondered if the new president Franklin D. Roosevelt would be successful at stemming the tide of the times. I sure hoped so. Everyone did.

I grabbed a paper at the train station to check on cotton and catch up on things on the trip down to the coast. There were two follow-up stories from earlier in the year that caught my eye. One about Japan, an important ally in the Great War, saying in February they'd won a war against Manchuria in northeast China and set up what the paper called a "puppet state"—I didn't know where that was or what it meant if anything important. And another story about Germany, always of continuing interest to me since the war. A month later, in March of '32, the paper reported, Paul von Hindenburg, president of the post-war Weimar Republic, had won a second seven-year term against a rising politician, Adolf Hitler of the National Socialist German Workers Party—the Nazi Party. I'd read about that new party back in '20 before Helen and I married. Both small stories were of only passing interest to me. My attention turned back to cotton, and the prospects for something sustainable for us down along the Texas coast.

Delbert and I found a place in the small town of El Campo, Texas, close to Galveston.

Much to his surprise, Delbert found a bank that needed some help in the small town of Wharton about fifteen miles from El Campo. It was a bit of a distance but workable with a car we got once we were settled. Delbert said he thought it would not be too bad—after all, it was work and we needed it.

I got to know some of the local cotton buyers in the area and was able to work out an arrangement to join them.

I wrote Helen a letter and told her. Delbert and I started to work and spent a couple of months to stabilize things. The prospects looked pretty good, at least the possibility of more money than what we had. We needed more to support the whole extended family.

Preparing to have the others come down from Hot Springs, I found an old house just on the edge of town owned by Mr. Jack Weaver—we came to call it the Weaver House, just across the street from the Methodist church. I rented the bottom floor where Helen and me and the kids would live. It would be a good new start for us I thought.

Delbert rented a small farmhouse just outside town within walking distance from our place. It had a good tin-roof that didn't leak, a small chicken coop, and a place for a garden—and the folks just across the way from it had a big old windmill that brought fresh water up from the well, and they agreed we could draw from it. There he and Maurine and their kids would live, along with Beth and Ward, Mama and Papa, and Uncle John.

I sent word to Helen by telegraph that it was time for her, the kids, and all the others to come down. I also sent a telegraph to Mr. Price explaining I'd be staying and thanked him for everything, and how grateful I was for his help keeping us all above water after the fire and the ever-worsening downturn. He sent one back saying no need for thanks, that he was very glad to help and hoped things would pick up for us all, and to stay in touch. I agreed I would.

Helen got train tickets for everyone. It wouldn't be long until I could see her again—I was so excited. I missed her desperately and longed to see Bubber and Sister and li'l Nick. It was a big reunion for all when they arrived, though a simple one with no extravagance except in joy. But that joy was extravagant! It was so great to be together again, and wonderful to see Helen's belly growing with our new little one.

When Helen and I got in bed that night she told me about their trip down. "Laura Dean," she said, "was fascinated with her little brother, Nicky, and she especially liked the old multi-colored Indian blanket I wrapped him in on the seat of the train, the one Mama gave me when we left Keo." I chuckled, looking over at Sister sleeping in the small bed I'd gotten for her. Nicky was asleep between us, and Bubber was on a small mattress of blankets on the floor.

It was a wonderful first night back together again. We'd learn a new rhythm again.

We were all hopeful, but the times were tough. I worked from El Campo most of the time, but regularly took the train to Houston and Galveston and port support towns along the coast. Delbert drove to Wharton each day in the rickety Model T we bought. Papa and Uncle John would gather eggs from the chicken coop daily and every few days take extras into town to sell. On good days they'd get ten cents a dozen, but it helped. Ward looked around and talked to folks but had no success, even as Beth was rapidly approaching her due date. Maurine got a job working as a bookkeeper at Redwine's, a small dry goods store in town. We combined our money, and it was enough, but not more.

Helen and Mama took care of ours and Maurine's kids while she worked. And Mama helped Helen and Beth as they each prepared for delivery. They all tilled and planted a new garden, mostly Mama, and they made bread when we could get wheat to grind flour. When we couldn't, Helen and Mama made cornbread from excess ears available from the local farmers, who couldn't sell all their crops due to the collapse in grain prices.

Helen said Laura Dean liked to watch Mama make flat cornbread, lacing the skillet with a thin layer of lard, pouring the mixture in it about an inch thick. When Mama would flip it to turn it over, "Laura Dean laughed and giggled," she said, "hollering 'Do it again Mama Howell, flip it again!'"

From early spring in '33, we had vegetables from the garden most days. On prosperous days Mama would take a fryer or two, wring their necks, and make fried chicken or chicken stew to fill us up. Because we had to buy it, having no cows or hogs of our own, we got beef or ham only on rare occasions—when I'd find a deal from farmers who were thinning things out.

My success buying and selling cotton for shipment was sporadic but enough. All of us living in two small places close to each other made things go far enough. There was no getting ahead, but we weren't completely sinking like so many. We were hopeful.

Until one night when Delbert didn't make it home. Everyone was desperately concerned.

Wharton County Sheriff Buckshot Lane knocked on our door around 5:30 a.m. Together we walked across to the little farmhouse. Papa came to the door and Maurine right behind him. The sheriff said Delbert was hit and killed immediately traveling home on the highway between Wharton and El Campo. Maurine buckled and almost fell as Papa and I grabbed her. It was devastating news. "Apparently," the sheriff said, "the old Model T had broken down and he was trying to fix it. Standing in front of the car with no lights on, a passing car seemed not to have seen him and hit the car. It drove over him killing him instantly, the Highway Patrol said. The driver of the other car didn't even stop," the sheriff said. It was so sad. Maurine was heartbroken. We all were. They'd barely been back together for a month and suddenly she was alone and young J. D. and Carmon would grow up without a father.

We buried Delbert after a small funeral at the Methodist church. Sadness hung in the air.

But as often happens, new life brightened the path forward. Just a few weeks after Delbert's death, in mid-March our third son, Charles Franklin, arrived. And three weeks later, in early April Beth gave birth to Chad, whose proper name was Charles John Robert, Mama's three brothers' names. These gifts of new life came to us in the face of death and gave new joy to the family. It temporarily lifted the grief of Delbert's loss, even a bit for Maurine.

But it was *only* temporary.

Less than two weeks after Chad was born, Beth awoke to find Ward gone. Her husband and Chad's father had just left. He abandoned them. And never came back. Just gone.

I tried to wrap my head around it. Maybe he just couldn't stand not having any work and now a new mouth to feed. "By Gawd, Ward! You son-of-a-bitch!" I whispered angrily to myself. I was so mad at him. It burned in my soul. How do you just walk away from your promises like that, just give up on your obligations? You don't just *give up*, even in the face of really hard times. You *stand up*. You *find a way*. *You don't just walk away*. But he did.

In a matter of a month, two of my sisters were left without husbands and three young boys were left with no dad to help raise and take care of them. One family rent asunder by a tragic accident and another by a man who just gave up and deserted.

After Ward left, we heard more stories of the same. Like those I knew in the army who went AWOL. The times were bad and getting worse. Uncle Jim would say, in such times you find out what people are made of. I guess we were finding out.

But the Carroll-Howell clan was doing okay. Even with two gaping holes, new life was flourishing in the face of loss. We weren't prospering, but the fabric of the family still hung together.

I was regularly away in Galveston and in and around Houston for several days at a time. One day later that fall I was out in the company-town of Sugar Land to broker a deal with the Imperial Sugar Company—like everyone else, they were struggling. As I drove my borrowed truck past the Imperial State Bank, I glanced and saw a strangely familiar silhouette of man walking along the street. Could it be? Surely not. But it was. That damned Ward Jackson who left Beth in the dead of night. I pulled over to the new concrete curb on the gravel street, stopped and pulled the brake. I made a beeline to Ward. I moved so fast that just as I got there, he felt my presence and swung around in a start. I got up in his face so quickly he was taken aback, scared even. I was furious, as much as when I first learned he'd abandoned Beth and baby Chad.

"By Gawd, Ward! By Gawd, what the hell are you doing here? Why the hell did you just leave . . . leave Beth and your very own son two weeks after he was born? Why! I ought to beat you to a pulp! By Gawd you, Ward!"

I could feel the blood fill my face. My anger, almost uncontrollable. I was about to hit him, I could tell. Right there in the middle of the street in front of the bank, I was about to have a fight.

"Wait, Claude. Wait! Wait!" he exclaimed.

I could see how shocked he was, and how he cowered in fear. I caught myself just in time, very different than with Jack back in Texarkana. I guess Papa's counsel all those years ago and my army training had some positive effect on me. I somehow got ahold enough to settle down a bit, to control my anger. As I've often thought back on that moment, I really can't believe I restrained myself. I was so mad.

But then I looked at Ward in the face. He was so pitiful. He was in Sugar Land looking for work, like thousands of others across the country. He had nothing but a knapsack. I later learned he was staying in the train cars nearby at night and looking for day-labor work each morning. He was so apologetic—he went on and on and on. I didn't know how to respond. My anger turned to pity—pity as pure as the cane sugar they made in the small town of Sugar Land. How can you not for someone, anyone, but especially someone who used to be your brother-in-law, the father of one of your nephews?

I wound up taking Ward to a coffee shop next to the bank for a short visit. In retrospect I can't believe this either, I found myself sitting across the table of the man who angered me as much as anyone ever had to that point in my life. But that short visit revealed something I had not considered or known. Not something that excuses his abandonment. There's no excuse for that as far as I can see. But still, considerations I had not seen, did not know.

"I loved Beth when we met and when we married . . . she was so beautiful, we fell in love, truly. I loved her," Ward mumbled to me, his face buried in his coffee cup. He couldn't look at me, almost never did.

"But she's a hard woman to live with, Claude. I'm sure you don't know this, especially since you've been so heads down working to take care of everyone. I've always been so grateful for that, and I want you to hear that from me. But she is, Claude. She has delusions, you see, and is suspicious. She goes from happy to sad in the same conversation. Sometimes she's gloomy for long stretches, and angry, very angry. Then suddenly, she's jubilant again. I never knew why or when. I couldn't please her. Nothing I did was good enough. And when the Depression hit and I couldn't provide, her depression got worse. Especially after Chad was born. She treated me like I was nothing, worthless. And I am, I know it. I feel it every day. Now I can't even provide for myself."

I listened. At first I became angry again when Ward said cruel things about my sister. But as he spoke, I realized I'd seen the signs in Beth that Ward talked about. Ever since we were kids, she'd had a habit of putting on airs, a kind of fake front, and even mood swings, but I never thought much about it.

I'd never considered that there might be deeper reasons to Beth's ways, maybe a connection to Papa's melancholy, and his papa's. Did Beth get a form of that from them? I thought about how Grandfather Howell's sickness got so bad he took his own life—I worried about my sister. Why are some stricken in that way and others not? Why not me? Maybe I just got more of Mama in me than Papa, maybe more of Grandfather Bill and Uncle Jim in me. Such things are still a mystery to me.

My anger softened on Ward.

I found myself thinking about love. How it comes to us, what it is, what it does and sometimes must endure. I'd been so lucky to find it with my dear sweet Helen, and how easy it is for us. I knew not everyone had what I had. I'm very disturbed when I see the problems so many families have. It confirms how lucky I am, have always been as far back as I can remember. God's grace, I must admit. As I listened and looked at Ward, I thought about how love is known by actions. Like God's toward us and how ours must be too. And how the easy path is to walk on by or away, like the priests in story of the good old Samaritan Papa read to me and Beth so long ago. How hard it is to stop and stay and help like the Samaritan man did. Surely that's the kind of love that holds families together, I thought. I also thought about something I heard Brother Crutchfield say, that God's love never fails, never gives up, even when we walk away like the prodigal son. Our love mustn't either. We just can't give up.

I learned something I didn't expect that day with Ward. I saw just how hard life is sometimes. I knew how hard it was for so many then. How even if you know the good and the true, how terribly difficult it can be to follow through. Especially when compounded with trials you don't understand, and your spirit is broken. I saw a pitiful broken man across the table.

My heart broke for Ward and for Beth and Chad. I understood things better even though I still strongly disagreed with Ward's decision to leave. As we left, I realized my anger was gone.

I urged Ward to come home. But he went his way, and I went mine. I never saw him again.

I didn't like going out of town, but it was necessary. That time was unusual. When I got home, after greeting the frenzy of the kids, Helen and I finally sat down at the kitchen table with some iced tea.

I told her about seeing Ward in Sugar Land. She couldn't believe it any more than I could. We talked about the whole thing, my anger and how it turned to pity. We talked about how lucky we'd been to find each other and how easy our love is and how hard it is for others. We were beyond grateful. We decided not to tell Beth right away, it just seemed best at the time. But we did many years later.

Our family was tattered but still intact, even if more frayed than we had known before.

Despite the hard times, there were happy times, even funny ones.

That night when Helen and I got in bed, we held each other close and were thankful for our love and our family. As usual we talked about the week and the day. I softly tickled her back, which she loved, but I loved even more. As we lay there in the twilight of the full moon outside, she told me another Laura Dean story.

"She's so funny!" Helen said. "Claude, you won't believe this," Helen started laughing before she even told me. "I was giving Laura Dean a bath in that big old tub, you know. I wondered about it at the time, at six years old she's growing up fast, but we needed to preserve the water, so I stuck Nicky in too. . . . you listening, Claude?" I gently nodded against her shoulder, and she knew I heard her.

"They were both playing and kicking their legs and splashing the water, and Laura Dean said, 'Mama, why don't I have one of those?' as she looked down between the legs of her little brother. I about laughed out loud when I realized. I could hardly contain myself. I simply didn't respond to her question but that'll be the last time they'll take a bath together."

I did laugh out loud and almost woke all four kids. "These little ones," I said softly to Helen. "They keep us sane even in the most insane times." We both laughed, then kissed each other and cuddled baby Charles between us and went to sleep.

Christmas was skinny in '33. Over the next several months in '34, cotton became more volatile, and the risk of trying to buy and sell it to make a margin was getting riskier every day. Corn and wheat weren't any better, and banks, merchants, and businesses were closing all across the country, and in south Texas. Folks everywhere were being laid off. The bigger the town, the worse it was. Things were getting worse and worse. I had to make another change.

Helen and I talked about it, and then we talked with Papa, Mama, Uncle John, Maurine, and Beth. I sent a telegram to Charles Alexander back in Keo. He responded saying the folks who ran the small bus stop-diner across the highway from the Keo town center had left, and he'd help me take over running it if I wanted. It wasn't much, but maybe it could stabilize us a little—I thought, people were continuing to travel to find work. Maybe it'd be something . . .

In a letter we'd learned that Brother Crutchfield and Mrs. Malvina sold that beautiful house in the pecan grove in Keo. Getting older and hampered to keep it up, they built a new smaller place in Little Rock, on State Street. My mind went back to the first time I saw State Street when we came through Little Rock on our way to Texarkana back in '05. I sent them a telegram telling them we were coming home and of our plans at the Keo bus stop. Brother Crutchfield sent back that Josie and Joe Foster still lived just behind there, and it would be a place for us to settle until we get on our feet. He checked with them, and they telegrammed back, "Wonderful! Can't Wait."

Heading to Christmas in late '34 we finished our plans to move back. Just Helen and me with our two youngest for now—Nicky, almost five, and Charles, whom I'd nicknamed Chafranken, just one-and-a-half. I say just Helen and me and our two youngest, but in truth it was us plus a new one on the way. Helen realized just before we left that she was pregnant again.

We'd get settled and see how things go and send for Carroll and Laura Dean when we could. Though we didn't want to leave the older two in El Campo, we considered it the best thing, at least for a time. I must say, to even think about leaving our two oldest behind, even for a time, took me back to when Papa and Mama had to leave me alone in Texarkana. I was worried for them. But they'd continue to go to school in El Campo and were looked after by Mama and Papa and Uncle John—they kept watch over all the kids, Maurine's J. D. and Carmon, who were Carroll and Laura Dean's age, and Beth's young Chad, while my sisters worked. Maurine continued to do bookkeeping and Beth got a job selling Luzier's cosmetics door-to-door to help a little. It wasn't the best situation, but it was necessary. Helen and I would send them as much as we could as often as we could to keep the family afloat.

Midmorning Christmas Eve everybody gathered to see us off at the small train depot in El Campo. It was an unusually cold day down on the

Texas coast. It felt like Christmas that year, but we couldn't stay. We had to get started. All wrapped up in their coats, Carroll and Laura Dean stood on the platform looking disoriented, and they were. How could they not have been? We had never lived apart. But they were close with their cousins. With Mama and Papa, and Uncle John, Maurine, and Beth, they'd be okay. We stood on the back of the last car of the train waving. Helen and I hugged each other and the boys, as they bunched Helen's dress wrapping their little arms round her legs and snuggled into her. Tears fell from Helen's eyes and welled up in mine. It was hard watching them all get smaller and smaller as the train got farther and farther away.

We were headed back to Keo. Part of us at least, for a time. How long? We didn't know.

Twenty-One—What Light through Yonder Window Breaks

Christmas of 1934 to Fall of 1939

It was a long train ride from El Campo to Keo that Christmas Eve. Arriving late that night we settled in with Josie and Joe and got a little sleep.

I stepped out early on Christmas day and looked up. Was it the first light of morning breaking on a new day? I wasn't sure, with the trees that towered above as I walked the short distance to the bus stop-diner. I saw a slight red hue. The light would break the darkness soon.

I inserted the key and opened the door to the small single-room old train-car diner on the highway I'd passed so many times before, just on the north edge of town. Not much of a diner really but a way station for passengers to arrive and leave. It had a small kitchenette with a Tappan cast-iron coal and wood stove, a cast-iron farmhouse sink, and an indoor plumbed water faucet. Charles and Joe had gotten the provisions we asked for and put them in the small fridge. We got it all cleaned up and opened up. Patrons sat on four rotating stools along the wooden counter or in two simple straight-backed chairs at two small tables. We served hot coffee, sandwiches, and Helen's chili, which rapidly grew in popularity.

That night as I cleaned and wiped down the tables, I looked over at her behind the counter like I used to across the span of the store when she straightened things up. She always makes me smile. *My Helen*, I thought . . . I noticed her face grimace, not a lot but I noticed it. She'd been standing all day long, starting early prepping the first batch of chili, and now cleaning up after the last batch just before we closed. All the while carrying our fifth new gift on the way. It was hard on that concrete floor all day long. Hard for anyone, but she's my Helen. I went over and took her in my arms and told her to take a seat.

The small bus stop-diner was a pretty good place for us. It offered a way back to Keo and something of an opportunity because more and more folks were traveling from place to place during those times to find work. It had steady traffic and offered a new if still uncertain foothold for us again. But the days were long, starting before dawn and ending late at night. We were so thankful to be staying nearby with Josie and Joe when we came back. Josie and her older kids took care of Nicky and Chafranken. We couldn't have done it without them.

* * *

"I caught them, I told him. Can you hear me? I caught them, the Bad Guys," Laura Dean wrote in her letter we received in late January after getting back, telling us of her and Carroll's days in El Campo. They were going to school and having fun. Helen and I looked at each other. "Those kids are growing up so fast, too fast," I said. God, how we missed them. We both laughed as Helen read the letter.

Mama and Daddy,

He said it was really dark in there, all except for a bit of light that came through a crack in the back. I'm glad Carmon's the Sheriff. I didn't want to sit in the privy out behind the house even though being Sheriff was the big job. The Sheriff told me to go out and catch those Bad Guys and bring them back to the jail and we'll lock them up. So I did. I went searching for them, I hid behind the chinaberry tree, pulled my gun. It's not a real gun it's a play one that we made of sticks and a rubber band. I jumped out all of a sudden and caught them. The Bad Guys, Bubber and J. D. were so upset that the Deputy (Me) did it. I caught them. I did it. I wrapped their hands behind, not really but with play rope, make-believe, ya know Mama. And I took them back to the jail where the Sheriff was. I knocked on the door, I caught them, I told him. Can you hear me? I caught them, the Bad Guys. We captured the Bad Guys and stopped them.

Mama Howell helped me write my letter, Mama. I hope you like it.

Hilarious! We both agreed. "Sister's so earnest," I said. "Yes. It's so funny but so sweet. She and Carmon, the Good Guys, captured and jailed Carroll and J. D., the Bad Guys. They're ridding the world of evil." We laughed again.

It felt so good to know our separated young'uns were doing just fine. Things were moving along but in such a new, strange, and so often very difficult way. Helen and I knew firsthand what Papa and Mama must have felt when they moved to De Queen.

But even as life had to go on as it did then, new life for us kept coming along too. Our beautiful fifth, Margaret Helen, was born that summer in July of '35. While the whole world was teetering on the brink, for us there was a constant: the growth and flourishing of our little family. Like clockwork, every couple of years a new gift came along. Those were hard but happy times.

Still in El Campo, Papa and Mama wrote us of their plans to stay. They'd learned that in August that year the Texas State Legislature was to pass the Texas Old-Age Assistance proposition. Papa was seventy-three and Mama sixty-five, so they were eligible. The fifteen dollars a month I sent them helped, but an old-age pension would double it. It required in-state residence half of each year, though, so they'd be staying. At least until, as everyone hoped, President Roosevelt's new Social Security plan passed and was implemented. The word on the street was it would provide a pension without state residency restrictions.

Late the next year, in the fall of '36 I sent word to Mama and Papa that it was time for Carroll and Laura Dean to come home. I wired them money for bus tickets at the Western Union office. It took them about ten hours to arrive just before Christmas, and of course the bus stopped right at our place.

The reunion was exuberant. Bubber and Sister both jabbered so fast and furious about what they'd seen on the trip up we could hardly get their attention to say hello. Carroll had turned twelve that year and seemed all grown up, and Laura Dean would turn ten the following month and looked too, too much like a lady, but so beautiful. Helen and I both grabbed them and held on tight. Laura Dean wiggled to get loose, saying, "I can't breathe, Mama." But we didn't care; our kids were home.

Back at Josie's, Bubber stumbled slightly as he stood up. He and Sister clamored for the attention of their younger brothers and their new sister. They tickled Nicky and Charles and traded holding Margaret, who we'd all started calling Boggie, the nickname of her second cousin and namesake, Margaret Josephine, Josie and Joe's oldest daughter. The night finally settled down. Everyone was tired and we got our brood to bed. After two years we were together again. It was a great Christmas that year. Things finally felt right again.

In January of the new year, I read in the newspaper that the US had "eased from the crisis at its peak in 1932," into what they were calling, "a national emergency." I thought that was a more-than optimistic way of putting it. Especially when the next sentence read, "Industrial production declines 47 percent, GDP falls 30 percent, wholesale price index declines (deflation) 33 percent, unemployment exceeds 20 percent." It had been bad times for seven years, ever since the store burned in '30 and we left for Hot Springs. It still was.

Helen and I were lucky, and our whole family in Arkansas and down on the coast in Texas. Lucky to have food on the table every day, a place to live, and some prospects of the same for the next day. The bus stop-diner in Keo had been a godsend to us so far. And living with Joe and Josie allowed Helen and me to send enough to Texas to help sustain Mama and Papa, Uncle John, and Beth and Maurine.

But I worried about our luck. While the diner was a godsend, it also took its toll on Helen—the grimace I'd noticed that night when we were cleaning up had become more regular. And the slight stumble I noticed when Bubber stood up the night he and Sister got home, was not just a stumble. We'd learn it was evidence of infantile paralysis, Roosevelt's dreaded disease. The doctors said they'd caught it early and with treatment they might be able to slow it. Early the next year we learned that the grimaces I saw on Helen's face were from an inflammatory disease called rheumatoid arthritis. Something she'd likely had since she was young, they said. It'd gotten worse with all the standing in the diner. Both diseases were progressive, they said, but should be manageable for a good long time. I grimaced myself at the thought of Helen in pain, and Bubber's disease sounded dangerous even if they'd caught it early. I was scared.

We took Carroll to the doctors in Little Rock regularly for aggressive treatment. He didn't respond well initially, so I also took him to a chiropractor, which seemed to help. He had to wear a brace all the time and he had to limit his activities. Helen suggested we ask the high school music teacher, Mrs. Shaw, to give him piano lessons while his movements were restricted. We did. She told us of a second piano at the school they didn't use much—an upright piano she called it—and said we could move it home for him to practice on. A couple of fellows and I moved it over to Joe and Josie's, crowding their place even more—they were so good to us. The teacher got the piano tuned, and Helen sat down to test it out. It was fun. As it turned out, Bubber got Helen's gift. He learned the piano quickly and well, and he learned to read music well too. He even wrote some pieces of music himself and played them for us. That piano and Mrs. Shaw were a godsend too. It gave Helen the chance to play now and again. And it opened a new world for Carroll. It brought joy to our home. But it didn't stop the disease. We all hoped and prayed.

It wasn't easy for us during those times. *But where was it for anyone?* I thought. We had each other and enough. That was as much as anyone could hope for then.

Everyone's gotta do their part. That's how I see it. It's just the way it is, I said to myself.

I awoke about five the next morning. My usual time, plenty early and well before the others. I thought. I poured a bit of water and washed from the bowl on the small dresser, dressed, put on my coat and picked up my hat. I grabbed for my keys. They were gone. I felt and looked around in the dark and slowly realized I might not have been the first one up. I woke Helen, trying to be quiet and not wake Boggie, and asked her to help. She got up and checked on the other kids and came back in a panic. "Charles is missing, Claude!" she yelled to me in a whispering voice.

"What do you mean?" I asked.

"Gone," she said, "not in the house anywhere." I was the one in a panic then. Where was Charles and where were my keys? I lit a lantern and glanced at where I always put the lockbox, the cashbox for the diner. *Gone!* Then I was in a real panic. Had someone broken in and taken both our four-year-old son, Charles, and the cashbox? I was terrified!

I hollered for Joe, and Helen for Josie. They jumped up and by then everyone in the little house was moving. But I was moving faster. I grabbed my rifle, the one I shot the deer with on the Trail down from Illinois. I opened the front door and looked out toward the diner. The lights were already on. Never! I started running, and Joe was right behind me. It took less than a minute to get there. The door was ajar. I shoved it open and raised my rifle. Then stopped! Slowly I lowered the rifle. The adrenaline began to moderate, and a momentary shock set in.

I saw him.

Charles was sitting atop a stool eating a donut and having a glass of milk with a man sitting on the other side of him. Joe and I slowly walked over to them. They were deep in conversation, it appeared. Charles Franklin looked up at me and said, "Hi Daddy," and went back to talking with the man. Then he looked at me again, saying, "Daddy, I knew you were tired, so I decided to open the diner for you. I got your keys and the money box and came over. But I couldn't reach the key lock in the door and Mr. Jefferson here helped me. He's such a nice man, don't you think so?"

He sounded so adult, my four-year-old.

I couldn't believe what I was hearing. About that time, Helen and the rest of the kids and Josie and her two oldest got there, with Josie's daughter

Margaret carrying our little Boggie. Helen ran over to Charles, grabbed him and took him in her arms, holding him tight. I said, "It's okay, Helen, he's okay. This will be one of the best stories ever if I don't wring your son Chafranken's neck." Still overwhelmed and not yet fully aware, she just held on to Charles. He didn't understand what all the fuss was about. As far as he was concerned, all he'd done was do his part to help out, which he said he'd heard me say. What I'd thought I said to myself I obviously said out loud and he heard me.

The risks of casual conversation with yourself, out loud, I thought—that time I was sure I only thought it.

Mr. Jefferson pulled Helen and me aside and explained he'd been standing in the dark near the bus stop pole waiting for the early bus when this little boy had come up and said, "Hi, my name is Charles. Can you help me unlock this door?" pointing to the diner. "I need to get inside and set up for the day to help my Daddy."

"I have to admit," Mr. Jefferson said, "I was startled. I mean it's pitch dark out here, and I didn't expect to see anyone, much less a four-year-old preparing to open his daddy's diner for the day." He laughed and we all did. I thanked Mr. Jefferson and said, "I don't have much but let me give you a small reward for taking such good care of our son."

But he said, "No, No. No need. I'd want someone to do the same for me if in the same situation."

The bus arrived. I saw him to it. Mr. Jefferson got on. And we never saw him again.

We really did have enough, especially with the drama of our four-year-old *doing his part*—plus, thankfully, a good man doing his part to care for our adventurous son. What more could you ever ask for?

Another year passed and Helen and I continued working the bus stop-diner—but I got her a chair behind the counter so she could stay off her feet. Carroll, Laura Dean, and Nicky were in school during the day, and Josie and her daughter Margaret (Boggie, the first) took care of Charles and our Margaret (Boggie, the second). Josie and Joe's house was full—with the constant activity, sounds, and people scurrying around, especially little ones. It was a busy time, and the routines were exhausting. We all slept well because of it.

There in the middle of one of the most daunting times in America, we were happy—dollar poor like everybody else but rich of heart. *What is wealth?* I wondered to myself again as I had when I was a boy. How wealthy we'd become, while yet poor. And we were getting wealthier: in July Helen told me she was pregnant again.

That Christmas of 1938 would be rich but sparse. As we had done the prior year, we gave each of the kids some of Helen's wonderful saltine-and-jelly "cookie" treats and small wrapped gifts we'd sent Carroll and Laura Dean on the bus to Little Rock to get at the Five-and-Dime. Each would get a comb and toothbrush and the same to wrap and give to their cousins. They were excited even though they already knew what the gifts were, the same as the year before. The gifts weren't expensive, but they'd remind us of the gift of Christmas and the season of joy.

But just before Christmas day a very wonderful and unexpected gift arrived. Beyond fortuitous. My baby sister Theresa came through the door of the diner. My littlest sister had grown into a beautiful woman; some said she looked like a movie star with her tall and elegant shape and shiny dark brown hair—same as Papa's—cut short and curled with the fashion.

I hadn't heard from her in quite some time. The last letter I'd received she was still in Monroe working for Mr. Oakland. When I looked up and saw her, her presence stunned me and struck me motionless. Then I rushed over, grabbed and hugged her just like she did me when I came home from the war. "Oh Sis, it's so good to see you, so good!" I said. She hugged me back and said the same.

Not two minutes later, my brother Bill walked through the door. I saw him more often since we got back. But not daily ever since he'd moved down to England for work just after the Howell & Son store burned and we'd left for Hot Springs. I quickly suspected he knew Theresa was coming to town and had come up to meet us. That was right, but as we sat down to catch up, it became obvious they'd talked and had something they wanted to talk with me about.

Beaming, Theresa exclaimed she and Berny Oakland had gotten married, just the month before in November. Then without a moment's hesitation, no time for me to take that extraordinary news in, she said she'd heard the old McLaughlin property in Toltec was available, and they'd bought it from the estate of Heber McLaughlin's family. *What!* I said to myself.

"It'd been in decline since Heber moved to Little Rock and became a member of the Arkansas Legislature after the war," she said. "When he died in '31 the whole estate became available, but due to the times it hadn't sold. Berny and I bought it, the whole thing. It included the McLaughlin farm, the big old plantation home that sits just off the highway at the main junction, the old gin, the general store, and some property across the highway."

My head spun. I was astonished at what I heard. Who could make such a purchase during these times? From her letters I'd heard her casually mention that Berny was fairly successful, but until this conversation I hadn't known how much. Theresa's boss, now husband, had been quite successful in the oil and gas business in Monroe, and they were moving to Toltec.

Theresa and Bill had talked. They'd come to tell me they thought, with the willing help and interest of Berny, we should start-up the old McLaughlin gin in Toltec and the general store too. They wanted me to help decide for sure if it was a good idea given my experience with cotton, ginning, and the general merchandise business, and given the times. The idea, an exciting one of course, came out of the blue to me. We sat down.

I looked at Theresa, reached across the little diner table and squeezed her cheeks in my hands like I used to do when she was young. "It's so good to see you, Sis," I said. "It's been way, way too long. I'm so happy for you. So happy you finally found someone and got married." She smiled and her eyes sparkled. The little girl who'd ambushed me the day I left for the army was all grown up and married—a bit later than the other girls, but she'd finally done it. I was glad.

I began to think about their business idea. It was beyond belief that in these times the old McLaughlin property was now in the family, and there was money to start a new business. It was certainly good fortune. But could it work, or would it be throwing good money after bad?

I told Bill and Theresa I thought we ought to think about it closely, and make sure Berny's in the loop all along the way.

"Consider for a minute President Roosevelt's New Deal. It has been good in many ways but very unsuccessful in other ways, especially when it came to the Agriculture Adjustment Act and the cotton business. It'd given a bump in '33 but since then prices," I explained, "have continued to be very volatile. That's why I left El Campo and came back to Keo. The price can and does fluctuate widely, and you can lose your shirt in a day, you see. Even though there was an occasional sign of rebound, the trend continues to be down most of the time—though it has stabilized more lately, but on the low end in the range of eight to nine cents per pound.

"Even at that, though, one place that might offer an opportunity is the part of Roosevelt's new Farm Security Administration that's focused on providing loans to tenant farmers to buy and equip their own places. That might open up a new sector for the cotton gin market here locally, because there are so many such farmers. Just maybe."

I explained that I'd recently read a report that said 65 percent of all farmers in the cotton belt are tenant farmers.

"With their own farms and lower cost of production, they might be able to sell at the low prices and make it work. I don't know. Maybe we could make it work."

I wasn't sure but thought it might make sense—particularly in Toltec instead of Keo where the bigger gins in the area were. Bill and Theresa and I, along with Berny, agreed to sit down and talk about the whole idea the following day. It was so good to be with my sister and brother again. I explained to them I thought it was an exciting idea, but it was risky—the gin piece anyway, I told them. I believed we should talk with Charles and Mr. Brodie and see what they thought. We all agreed.

After talking with the experienced cotton gin owners in Keo, and especially Charles who I trusted more than anyone, we all decided that with hard work it could work. It'd be a risk, no doubt, but we all knew America would come out of the slump sometime. Maybe now was the time to get in with the new government supports. Maybe we could be a part of the recovery. We decided to move forward.

Buying the Toltec gin for its real estate value, and because even those values were low given the current times, there would be very little start-up cost, and with Berny there'd be no debt burden. And Lord knows, available labor would be plentiful and not very expensive. The same with the general store. All that would be needed is to get the gin operational and the buildings back in shape, establish vendor relations, and some advertisers for the store—like Barq's Root Beer, Coke, and Bull Durham.

With Berny as the bank and a willing investor, we brought both the gin and the general store back up to working order, and we relaunched Howell & Son.

I wrote Papa and Mama in El Campo, and Bill, Theresa, and me all signed it. They were both very excited and proud. It lifted their spirits immensely. The family was back in business again.

Helen and I met with Mr. E. D. Wilson who owned the bus stop property, and we gave him notice of our plans to move to Toltec. And we expressed our deep gratitude.

Operations started quickly, and we had quite a bit of early success given the times. I ran the gin and the business side of the store, which Bill focused on running day-to-day. Theresa and Bill's wife, Letha, were a constant help, and Helen was too, as always. It was a family enterprise and a good one.

In addition to the gin and the store, we reestablished part of the old McLaughlin farm next to where Berny and Theresa built a new house—their "cottage" they called it, nestled in the pecan orchard on the edge of the lakefront that was part of the estate. There, with the help of so many folks in the area looking for work, we were able to plant small corn crops and raise a few cows, hogs, and chickens, mostly supplying our family but with some excesses to sell to locals to cover our cost.

In early February of '39 Theresa made another exciting announcement. She was pregnant. Everyone was overjoyed. I was so excited for my little sister.

One day I met a customer, Mr. Hazleton, outside the gin and was talking to him about a shipment that he needed to go to Pine Bluff the next day. We'd agreed on the price. It was a normal day's business and a typical conversation. That was the way the days went. I managed the day-labor crew to load the bales when they came in and strap them on the back of the old snub-nosed '36 International we had bought, so it'd be ready in the morning.

Just as I had that strange Chafranken morning, when I got up to go deliver Mr. Hazleton's cotton to Pine Bluff, I looked for my keys to the truck and they were gone. The shipment was due that day and I was concerned. I always put my keys in the same spot, hanging on a hook just inside the kitchen door. But they weren't there. Just as I had the morning of the earlier misadventure, I asked Helen. She didn't know. I quietly started looking in other places. And in the process I realized I was, once again, missing not only my keys but a son—this time an older one, Nikodemus. I got concerned, but a little less than with Charles because at least Nicky was ten. What would he be doing with my keys though?

Until I realized the loaded International was missing too. Was there a connection?

The sun came up and the day was in full swing, and we still had no idea where Nicky was. We told everyone and they were all looking around and putting the word out. We were all increasingly concerned. Helen was becoming distraught, again.

At a loss I stood staring down the highway, when in the distance I saw a speck on the horizon. The closer it got the more it looked like the International coming from the direction you go to Pine Bluff. It sure looked like it. Then I made out a small head bobbing just above the steering wheel. Yep, my boy. The truck pulled up and Nicky opened the door and climbed down from the top of four pillows he'd added to the truck-seat so he could see out. He'd left at 5:00 a.m., driven the thirty miles or so to Pine Bluff, made the delivery and drove back. I was beyond livid, but I couldn't help breaking out into a gruff and muffled laugh. Now I have two necks to wring. Helen came running as before with Charles and wrapped her arms around Nicky.

I slapped him on the back of the cap he wore. "You knucklehead," I said. "What were you thinking?"

He said, "Daddy, I heard you say we'd make this delivery today, so I decided to do it." *These kids hear everything, and act on it,* I thought.

"Let's get to work," I said. *What in the hell am I gonna do with these boys?* I wondered.

The times were getting better and better for Howell & Son and for us. Even Helen's arthritis was better, and Bubber was responding well to his treatment and braces.

Then one day Theresa and Berny came by and said, "Claude, get Helen, and let's take a walk across the highway." I didn't know for sure what they wanted to do over there, but I got Helen. They showed us the extra property they'd gotten with the purchase of the McLaughlin estate.

Theresa said, "Claude, we want you and Helen to have whatever piece of this you'd like, to build you a house."

I didn't think I heard her right, and said "What?"

She said, "Yes, take your pick from this unused property and build you a house."

Helen broke into a soft muted cry, and tears came to my eyes too. Overwhelmed and beyond grateful, my little Sis was taking care of us. That's not how I'd learned it was to be, but it was. And we were overjoyed.

With the plentiful workers available in Lonoke County, we planned and finished it quickly in the early spring of 1939. Our own home in Toltec, the first home on the first piece of land we'd ever owned. I thought about Uncle Jim and putting down roots. It was good for Helen and me, but the kids absolutely loved it. We were beyond excited, and beyond grateful.

The timing was good too, since Nona Ann, our sixth, was born that April, her given name chosen from the nickname Brother Crutchfield and Mrs. Malvina gave to Helen's mother.

Later that fall we brought Papa and Mama back to Toltec to stay with us for six months—what they were allowed on their Texas pension residency requirement. Maurine and her kids, J. D. and Carmon, came too. It was so great to all be together again—almost, Beth stayed back in El Campo with little Chad and Uncle John to take care of things there.

In those desperate times, we were rich beyond all measure. Not so much in money, though we were more stable than ever before, but we had the wealth that counts. The kind Papa had told me to strive for long ago, the kind that anyone can have, in virtue and the richness of family.

A new day had sure dawned for us since Theresa came home. And we were so grateful.

Twenty-Two—A Quiet Morning Erupts into a New and Violent Storm

Fall of 1939 to Summer of 1941

Porches are special places, or at least they've always been for me. They're gateways into the warmth and safety of home, a cool place to sleep in the summertime, a place to sit and have good conversations, and a good place to stand and look out through the crisp morning air.

Fall hadn't quite yet arrived when I stepped on the front porch of our new home and just listened. The Mockingbird repeated sounds of past and present, and my mind did the same. I wondered what the new day would bring, the same as I had Christmas morning five years earlier when I stood on Joe and Josie's porch just before heading over to the bus stop-diner for the first time. Would our glimmer of new first light of morning amid the Great Depression awaken to still brighter days ahead for us? Could it be a sign of a new day for the whole country? I didn't know. No one did. The times were precarious. All you had to do was look around. So many still lived on the cliff's edge clouded by a dense fog. God, we were so lucky. With not much more but better than most, our family was thriving, even Carroll was much better. What more could I ask?

But I knew the frailties and perils of life were never far away. Not just the kind that come from the rhythms and burdens of daily life, though they came as sure as the sun comes up. It was the bigger world that hovered over us that worried me. The gathering storms of war in Europe were on the horizon. For the past year I'd followed news reports on Nazi Germany and fascist Italy. *Surely not*, I thought. Who could forget the horror just twenty years before? If it happened, I knew too well how the turbulence from a violent storm far away could draw us into its swirl.

I sat on the stool at Howell & Son having my coffee and cigar reading the new *Time Magazine*. "The telephone in Franklin Roosevelt's bedroom at the White House rang at 2:50 a.m. on the first day of September, nineteen thirty-nine. In more ways than one," the magazine said, "it was a ghastly hour, but the operators knew they must ring. Ambassador Bill Bullitt had just been called by Ambassador Tony Biddle in Warsaw. Mr. Bullitt told Mr. Roosevelt that World War II had begun. Adolf Hitler's bombing planes were dropping death all over Poland."

World War *Two*? I exclaimed to myself! Had the world learned nothing? Had not Germany? As any reasonable person would have at first, British Prime Minister Neville Chamberlain sought to stop it with words. But no. His no-action appeasement reaction to Germany taking Austria and the Czech region the year before was an open invitation for more. When bombs fell on Warsaw the world was at war. President Wilson's "war to end all wars" had been a pipedream.

I worried. When will we be pulled in? God, I hope it's over before Carroll's of age to go.

My mind went again to Governor Charles Brough's German Mr. Hegel and his progressive march of history. Sure, we'd progressed in making the world less burdensome, as the St. Louis Fair celebrated. That's the wonder of human cultivation we marveled at. But we had not progressed in cultivating ourselves each to our proper end, as Uncle Jim urged. We had not improved in virtue, and we hadn't taken wise counsel. The Great War hadn't taught us anything. Adolf Hitler had only progressed in the ability to brainwash his people with his own distorted "struggle" and to kill with greater horror, speed, and scale. He was showing we hadn't made any progress in all the ways that matter. I was sure we'd only progressed down a deeper rat hole.

* * *

Helen startled me out of my foreboding when she walked in the store. It was the best distraction one could ever want. She had Nona in her arms, Mama had Boggie by her little hand, and the ever-industrious Chafranken wandered along behind looking at what he could get into next. They'd brought lunch, but their presence alone nourished me and lightened my heart. I cleared a place on the small table in the back and took Nona. I lifted her above my head and whizzed her around in the air. She laughed and laughed. We went on a tour of the store and I talked to her all along the way. Her eyes darted back in fourth from the shiny candy jars and buckles to my eyes. Staring into those bright brown pools of endless curiosity made my heart full and I began to sing . . . that's not something anyone but a baby would want to hear. I sang that meaningless chorus of The Umbrella Man, a cheerful song that had become popular on the radio.

> Toodle-luma-luma
> Toodle-luma-luma
> Toodle-aye-ay
> Any um-ber-rellas, any um-ber-rellas to mend today?

> Pitter patter patter, pitter patter patter
> Here comes the rain
> Let it pitter patter, let it pitter patter
> Don't mind the rain
>
> . . .
>
> Toodle-luma-luma
> Toodle-luma-luma
> Toodle-aye-ay

"Toodle-aye-ay," I said. Helen looked at me. "That's it. That's her name, Toodles! Like the other kids, she needs a nickname," I told her. "I've been looking for it. Now I found it," I said to Helen and Mama.

They laughed. "You are so silly, Claude. You're such a clown sometimes," Helen said.

She came and wrapped her arms around us both, whispering in my ear as she took Nona, "I got your Toodle-aye-ay. Go eat your lunch."

Maurine came out from the little office at the back of the store where she kept the books for both the store and the gin, and Bill came over from the gin where he was working that morning. We all had lunch together. It was a great break in the day.

Late in October more news came to brighten our days. My little sister Theresa gave birth to her first child, beautiful Albertina—a new ray of sunshine.

My heart still lifts just thinking back on that day and those times. They were good and simple, yet such happy times. For a moment it seemed they would just go on forever.

But the clouds rolled in not four months later. In February of '40 Berny died suddenly of a heart attack. A wave of grief washed over my little sister and the whole family. It took me back to Delbert's tragic accident, when Maurine was left alone to raise J. D. and Carmon without their father. Theresa and I took Berny back to his hometown of Monroe to be buried. Many folks gave him tributes and spoke of his success in business. It was a good memorial, as good as a funeral can be. But Theresa was heartbroken, and I was for her. She came to stay with Helen and me when we got home. Little

Tina didn't know her daddy was gone, of course. And as all four-month-olds do, she demanded constant attention, but she smiled all the time. That helped bring smiles to Theresa. The pleasant yet constant demands of motherhood plus our big family surrounding her gradually allowed my little sister's spirits to lift and her joy to return.

Then not two months after Berny's death, barely time for one tide of grief to recede, more sad news interrupted our halting joy. News that reminded me of the letter Mama had written to me about Grandfather Bill. Helen's papa died in Little Rock, also from a heart attack at the age of seventy-six. When Mrs. Malvina's neighbor came from Little Rock to deliver the news, Helen was at the house with Mama and the kids. It was hard to hear. I wish I had been there with her. Mama kept the kids, and Helen came to the store and told me—I held her as she cried and cried. That night we drove to Little Rock to stay with Mrs. Malvina. The next day the three of us followed the hearse back to Keo to bury Brother Crutchfield. That Sunday about the whole town gathered at Pecan Grove Baptist Church for his funeral. It was hard for her, but Helen played "Amazing Grace" on the piano. He was laid to rest in his beloved pecan grove at Keo Cemetery. Just like Grandfather Bill and Uncle Jim, he'd had a good long life. There was sadness in our hearts but celebration too for a life well lived, for the life of a Good and Faithful Servant.

I never cease to be amazed by the rhythm of life. The extraordinary joys and the deep sorrows, followed again by the return of joy. Like that wonderful "*Clair de Lune*" piano piece Helen played that night after supper so long ago. It starts out so soft. There's even a hint of pain or sadness in it, it seems. Then it brightens and gets brighter and brighter and until it's as if you're on pristine waters sailing into the wind and the joy will never end. It speeds up, and for a moment it feels like a disaster is coming. But then it lifts again like a hawk catching a thermal. Until it gently lands as if a lullaby sung to one of my little babies. And sung again to those we love who go to sleep for the last time. What a mixture of joys and sorrows life is.

By the time everyone left the small church fellowship hall, the sorrow at the loss of Big Grancy, as the kids called him, seemed all but gone. Sharing good memories and funny stories serves as a salve on grief, especially for someone who had a good long life. Everyone laughed with the goodhearted jokes about the preacher's long boisterous prayers and sermons heard by neighbors across the street from the church during summer revivals. Mama comforted Little Mammie, as the kids had come to call Mrs. Malvina, and Helen's heart hurt. It was her daddy. But they too found some laughter in the good stories. Joy always seems to come again to wash away the grief if only like gentle waves at the beach. By God's grace it always finds a way. For

Helen, and for everyone really, it was those cherished memories mixed with the ceaseless activity of life's demands that kept her from living in sadness. Just as with Theresa, the demands and joys of our kids were for Helen like a thermal lifting her heart again.

Theresa moved back home and Mrs. Malvina stayed with us for a while. But soon she wanted to go home too, back to the bungalow house in Little Rock she and Brother Crutchfield bought when they moved from Keo. Our world had gotten back to normal.

Six kids were a lot to handle. The younger ones, Toodles, Boggie, and the ever-industrious seven-year-old Chafranken demanded constant attention. Bubber'd made amazing progress with the braces—they straightened his legs, and the therapy was really helping. He was sixteen and much better, he'd even started working at the store, mostly with Maurine keeping the books. We felt the goodness of God for him. The docs said it looked like he'd fully recover. Then there was Nicky. Well, eleven-year-old Nicky was like one of the engines powering the gin—he wanted to work all the time. He'd rather work than go to school and was a big help. I loved working with my boys. It reminded me of Papa, Uncle Jim, and Grandfather Bill working with me when I was their age. Sister, at thirteen, was a huge help to Helen taking care of the younger kids. She's the dream child; I don't think I'd ever said one cross word to her. Our life was a family affair.

I'd take the older ones to the movie house down in England every few weeks. They loved it. It was good entertainment for them and got them out from under Helen's and Mama's feet for a few hours. I began staying too, to watch the newsreels before the picture show started—it was one of the best sources to track news of the war in Europe. By mid-year the effects of Carroll's infantile paralysis, what they'd started calling polio, was all but gone. He began driving the crew back and forth to England, and he and Sister went to dances down there too—they'd been especially close ever since the two years they stayed in El Campo, and going dancing was something they'd grown to love. It even helped make his legs a lot stronger.

Every night we'd all sit down at the table for supper together. It was our daily ritual, like chickens gathering for their evening repast. And it was a good one.

That table, yes, the same one that sits in our small dining room back in Little Rock. It's special. A wonderful gift from good old Mr. Price. We hadn't seen or heard from him in a long time, when one morning to my great surprise I got a call from him at the store. He said he was coming to visit and wanted to bring Helen and me something, at the house. At lunchtime he showed up in a big truck and on the back of it was that big oak claw-ball table he and I used to sit around and talk about insurance and life. He also brought the beautiful, curved glass china cabinet. It was so good to see him. I shook his hand and Helen gave him a big hug. Once we got inside, he told us his lovely wife, June, had recently died. We expressed our deep condolences, and he was grateful. Then he said they'd both talked about it and wanted us to have the table and cabinet. Then we were the grateful ones. The boys and I got the cabinet and the table in the house. He and Helen and I sat around it in those familiar chairs and talked for a while. It was so good to see him. He was pleased to learn of our good fortune and our settled life in Toltec. After a good but short visit Mr. Price said he'd better start back. With roads much better then, he could make it to Hot Springs in about an hour and a half. We said our goodbyes and he drove away. What a wonderful surprise that day. What a good man, Mr. Price. He'd rescued us at a really dire time. We've had so many good fortunes, big ones like when Mr. Price gave me a job and helped keep us from sinking and when Theresa and Berny unexpectedly came to Toltec. But there've been so many smaller ones, like that beautiful old oak table that holds so many memories . . .

The table became a centerpiece in our little home. It's where we gathered each night for supper. There was never a night with just our brood around it, it always included one or two of the kids' cousins or friends. Always ten or twelve every night. It was festive.

After supper Helen would get the little ones to bed, then we'd all bunch up in front of the Motorola stand-up radio box we'd gotten. We all listened to the serial programs, *One Man's Family, Our Gal Sunday, The Lone Ranger,* or *Fibber McGee and Molly,* and later Bubber and I ended the night listening to CBS radio commentator H. V. Kaltenborn.

Our life in Toltec was so good even with the demands of the gin, the store, the farm, and the kids. Around Carroll's birthday in late May, Mama, Papa, and Maurine, J. D., and Carmon left to go back to El Campo to meet Mama and Papa's residency requirements for the Texas old-age pension.

Cotton prices had not rebounded much, still hovering at 9.9 cents and we were never able to exceed 50 percent of the gin's capacity. It was more of a drag than a help, for us at least, and the war in Europe was full tilt. No one knew what to expect. So around Christmastime of '40, Bill, Theresa, and I got together and decided we'd try and sell it. I talked to Charles Alexander, and he said he thought James Cobb's son, Sam, was about the only one who could absorb our small operation and make it work. We approached him and he visited, inspected our operation and the books, and decided he'd take it over. We reached a deal and sold the gin. But we kept the store.

That simplified life even more, but it left less money to cover for Bill and Letha and their four and Helen and me and our six. And the brokenness of the world never seemed far away.

For three mornings straight I'd noticed a bunch of produce and some other things missing from the store. We had a regular burglar. It made me mad! But when Helen settled me down and we talked about it, we both wondered if it might be a fellow just trying to survive in the times. I really did wonder that. But dammit, if so, if he'd just asked, I'd have given him what he needed.

I couldn't let it go so I decided to set up in wait for him one night. Carroll and I'd brought over two of the chairs to Mr. Price's oak table to place in front of the door just inside, as an unexpected obstruction. The burglar came in about 2:00 a.m. as I watched. He stumbled over the chairs, and I jumped out and hollered "Stop!" In the dark I saw the muzzle flash. He'd shot toward me but missed. I was so damned lucky! In the pitch dark I quickly raised Grandfather Bill's old Winchester centerfire that I'd brought just in case and returned fire. I missed too, and he ran out the door. I chased after him for a short distance, but he got away. When the sun came up, I surveyed things and noticed my rifle shot had gone straight through the center of the top slat of one of the oak chairs, leaving a perfectly round hole in it. All morning I felt shaken inside. The same feeling I had with my early rifle training back at Camp Pike when they told us to picture the enemy in our sights. I didn't like the memory.

My mind wandered away from our simple, all but settled life and back to the bigger world.

* * *

I recalled the news of the war I'd followed all year long, the news reels at the picture show and with Bubber each night listening to Mr. Kaltenborn's report on the radio. He'd reported that France surrendered to the German army on June 22 of '40, "With great irony," Kaltenborn said, "in the same railroad car at Compiègne where Germany had surrendered in 1918." Less than a hundred miles from where I'd been stationed in WWI.

That September he reported that "Three hundred German bombers raided London, in the first of fifty-seven consecutive nights of bombing." What, as it turned out, was only the beginning of eight straight months of bombs dropped on London and other cities across Britain night after night, what the British press called "The Blitz."

The same month Kaltenborn reported, "Japan signed the Tripartite Pact with Nazi Germany and Fascist Italy, in which they agreed to assist one another should any of them be attacked by a country not already involved in the war. Japan sent troops to occupy French Indochina that same month, and the United States responded with economic sanctions, including an embargo on oil and steel."

I thought back to the two small back-page news items that I'd read about Hitler and the Nazi party and Japan's invasion of Manchuria when Delbert and I took the train from Hot Springs to El Campo. I was struck again by how such seemingly remote, small events can swell beyond all proportion to haunt the world and shake its very foundations.

My mind went again to the beautiful red-sky morning back the year before. It became clear to me that what had been the dawning of a new day after a long dark night for my family in the small hamlet of Toltec, was now showing the bolts of lightning of the descending storm on the world. And just as President Wilson had hoped back in '14, at Christmastime in 1940, most Americans still hoped the storm was off in the distance and would dissipate before it got to us. But Kaltenborn's reports suggested otherwise. My own experience told me otherwise.

Then one night, Kaltenborn gave a commentary on the war that brought back more memories of my time in the Great War and took me again to that day on the porch with Governor Brough when he talked about German philosophers. Kaltenborn explained that "Hitler rose to power playing on the German people's sense of humiliation and the economic devastation following World War I." And that, according to a philosophy expert named Scott Hendricks, "Hitler imagined himself to be the great savior of Germany—the Übermensch," which Kaltenborn said means "Overman. A term coined, he said, by the nineteenth-century German philosopher Friedrich Nietzsche, whom Hitler had become enamored of." Kaltenborn said, "Hitler is not content to be a mere politician. As the Overman he plans to separate the wheat and chaff and create a pure German race of Higher Men."

What the hell? I wondered. What is it about those damned German philosophers?

"If there's one philosopher the fascists love," Kaltenborn continued, "it's Nietzsche. He's so adored that Hitler gifted Mussolini the complete works of Nietzsche for his birthday. The Nietzschean ideal of the Overman, and his Will to Power, wielded by Hitler's propaganda machine inspired the Germans to act, and thousands were dying because of it. They adore his ideas and anointed him as the prophet of their ideology." Kaltenborn said that "Hitler hijacked the fame and philosophy of Nietzsche to rally the German people to embrace with a religious fervor the idea of a superior

Pure German race. A pure race and a new empire, the Third Reich, destined to rule the world by the will to power, with him as its great savior. On the back of this ideology," Kaltenborn said, "Hitler had begun instituting formal policies of hatred of Jews, Poles, Gypsies, people with disabilities, Afro-Germans, political dissidents, Jehovah's Witnesses, and homosexuals. Anyone blemished and not of the Pure German race. With Hitler," he said, "the blood-dimmed tide has been loosed upon the world again."

I could hardly take in the twistedness of what I was hearing. I thought back on my conversation about war with Uncle John. About the dense dark maze of the world of war and of the human heart. How war opens the door to bad and even evil things. How it allows the underbelly of our nature to be seen, how we're bent the wrong way, to Cain's way. Unlike when the power and strength of a broken horse can guide toward the good, Hitler was deluding his own people and releasing unrestrained evil. As far as I could tell, Hitler's reason for war was no reason at all. It was his own outrageous, evil delusion. It seemed to me, Hitler had not only hijacked Mr. Nietzsche, as Kaltenborn said. He was trying to hijack the Lord God himself.

While our life in Toltec was simpler and more stable, the bigger world that hovered all round us was not. I was very concerned.

Bubber graduated from Scott High School in June of '41, the month after the bombing stopped over London. One night shortly after, we listened together to Kaltenborn as he reported that on June 22, 1941, Hitler launched an invasion of the Soviet Union, violating their non-aggression pact. Hitler's war in Europe now extended from Russia through Europe, the Middle East, and Africa, and Hirohito's war was expanding in Asia. WWII had reached three corners of the globe.

More surely than the shattered hold-out hopes of avoiding war back in '17, it was clear to me and almost everyone that it was only a matter of time before the US would be fully engaged.

The day after we listened to Kaltenborn's report about Russia, Carroll came to Helen and me and said he wanted to join the navy. I'd taught each of the boys to be patriots just as I had been taught. Carroll knew I served in the Great War. And he knew the legendary story of local Toltec hero Heber McLaughlin in that war. He watched other boys in the area enlist. He told us he felt he had to, too.

I'd sensed it coming for some time. I was proud of him for it but because of the times I feared for him. The distance between the raging war in Europe and America had been closing for a long time. And while not yet on our shores, for our family it had arrived.

On the morning of July 20, 1941, our firstborn son William Carroll Howell stood on the screened-in porch of our little house in Toltec. The same one I'd stood on and watched the sun come up two years before, wondering if it foretold better days ahead for our family and our country. I looked at Bubber, standing tall, one leg slightly shorter than the other, and proud. As I looked at my boy all grown up, my mind went in different directions. I saw myself standing in his shoes. Everyone gathered around him and hugged him to say goodbye, just as Papa and Mama and my brother and sisters had done for me twenty-four years before. But I also saw myself holding him in my arms, helpless and completely dependent on Helen and me. Helen's eyes filled with tears just as Mama's had for me. Mine did too.

As Carroll stepped off the porch that July morning, it struck me how porches are not only places of comfort and conversation and a doorway to step into the safety of home, but they're also places to step off from into danger. I recalled being the one left standing before when Papa and Mama and everyone left me when they went to De Queen. But this felt worse, a lot worse.

We watched our son walk to the bus stop to report for duty, a slight limp from the polio still there. *Would it keep him from passing his physical?* we wondered. It didn't.

Twenty-Three—Waking a Sleeping Giant

Summer of 1941 to Fall of 1945

Not since I entered the quietness of our small house in Texarkana after Mama and Papa moved to De Queen could I recall such a sound of silence. It was strange, though, since the silence mixed with the other kids' voices around the supper table. Carroll's empty chair shouted at me. Like Rachel's had, but I couldn't, I wouldn't let my mind go there. For the first time I sensed how Mama and Papa must have felt when I went into the army. How Helen must have felt when I left Hot Springs for El Campo to explore new opportunities, and when I'd leave for business traveling down on the coast. I knew how to go and do to keep things going or start over again. Those feelings I knew. Proud of him or not, and I was, I didn't know how to watch my boy go away and just wait, especially given what I was reading in the papers each day. I worried.

A month after Carroll left, we got our first letter. He wrote he'd become an SK after basic training. That's short for Storekeeper, he said, explaining SKs are responsible for ordering, stocking, and issuing repair parts, clothing, and general supplies, and they maintain financial records, accounting systems, and inventory records for supplies in shore-based warehouses and the ships' storerooms. His primary job was accounting and keeping financial records and tracking inventory. It was so providential how Bubber's bookkeeping work with Maurine at our store in Toltec had prepared him for his navy duty. Just as my work at Charles's store had prepared me for my quartermaster duty in the army.

How mysterious, God's providence? The families we're born into set us on the path we take in life. What we learn to do to make our way in life grows from the soil we're planted in. Whatever gifts and good fortunes we're blessed with waters the sprouts of our dreams and allow them to flourish.

Some are lucky to be planted in rich, cultivated soil where the weeds of life's necessities and events don't impede the growth so much. But they are few. Most take seed among the thatches and thorns and are forced to twist and turn in constant reach for the sunlight. Yet, even when covered in dark shadows, the good light of God's providence finds its way through. I hoped and prayed it would be so for our Bubber.

I was glad Carroll's preparations at the store helped land him a good job in the navy. But I feared for him during the times he was set on his path. I hoped beyond hope that the same providence that'd prepared him for his new path would strengthen him for the difficulties he'd face and protect him against the dangers.

In November we got a second letter. He told us he'd been sent to Treasure Island Naval Base in San Francisco Bay and was helping with procurement at the US Naval Hospital there. But he ended saying he'd only be there for a short time. We didn't know what that meant.

Helen and I looked at each other that night after reading Bubber's second letter. Her eyes filled with tears. I took her in my arms and held her close. The truth is we held each other close. We were so thankful he was on the West Coast doing what he knew and was good at, on a hospital base far away from the raging war in Europe. There was some comfort in that.

Daily life for us in Toltec remained steady but not unchanged. Bubber was always on my mind, at home and work. I tried to come to grips with how life continues on when families are separated by military service. Mostly because it must. But it helped to think of Bubber in defense of our country, that noble service that allowed our routines at home to go on. So far. Helen and I prayed each night for our brave son and all the American boys. That somehow, they wouldn't be drawn into that terrible war in Europe and would come home to us safe and well.

Though the storm of war had not yet let loose on us directly with full force, the thunder clouds were all around us. Those conditions came as a blessing from a curse for America, just as had happened during the three-year run-up before American involvement of WWI. Ever since the bombs fell on Poland in September of '39 there'd been a steady increase in demand for US commodities, including cotton for uniforms, and finished goods and war materials from those countries fighting against Hitler and Mussolini— though the demand was moderated somewhat due to compromised shipping lanes resulting from the war. But the country needed all it could get, and badly. The Depression raged on. Still, America's blessing came with the stench of death from Europe. No one wanted the war. President Roosevelt kept supplying all kinds of support to the Brits and French, but despite their pleas to join in the fight, like Wilson he wouldn't. Not yet anyway.

* * *

Monday morning Joe and Josie came by the store and urged us to turn on the radio at half past eleven to hear the president speak. My normally upbeat and always politic brother-in-law, Joe Foster, spoke with resolute sternness. "There's news, very important news," he said. We all gathered around the radio at 11:30 a.m. as President Franklin Roosevelt delivered a speech before a gathered Congress to the whole nation. It was printed in the paper the next day, and certain things kept reverberating in my head.

> Yesterday, December 7th, 1941—a date which will live in infamy—the United States of America was suddenly and deliberately attacked by naval and air forces of the Empire of Japan. . . .
>
> As Commander in Chief of the Army and Navy, I have directed that all measures be taken for our defense. But always will our whole nation remember the character of the onslaught against us.
>
> No matter how long it may take us to overcome this premeditated invasion, the American people in their righteous might will win through to absolute victory. . . .
>
> With confidence in our armed forces, with the unbounding determination of our people, we will gain the inevitable triumph—so help us God.
>
> I ask that the Congress declare that since the unprovoked and dastardly attack by Japan on Sunday, December 7th, 1941, a state of war has existed between the United States and the Japanese empire.

The violent storm of tyranny and evil had finally let loose its reign of terror directly on America. Without warning, a hellish barrage of torpedoes, bombs, and machine guns rained down on a quiet unsuspecting island thrusting the United States headlong into World War II.

Not from across the Atlantic as before, though it seemed clear enough we'd wind up there too, and soon. But from across the Pacific. Those Gawddamned Japanese! When they'd first locked arms with Germany and Italy, it seemed far, far away in Asia. But like Hitler, Hirohito and his military religious zealots imagined a World Empire. Their first almost silent step when they invaded Manchuria back in '31 had trampled over large parts of China. Their visions of conquest had become their national religion with Hirohito as their god. Suddenly and deliberately, as the president said, the empire of Japan turned west and unleashed their bombs.

Dear God, Almighty. Why can't more small, good stories be writ large instead of those of hubristic demigods? Why can't we learn from the past, find release from the shackles of our arrogance? If a question lingered that there's no real evil in this world, World War II removed all doubt. It's a disease of the human heart, as Uncle John warned. Capable of so much good, yet when yielded to corruption and twisted into deluded imperial dreams, it can become pure evil.

It had. The world had gone mad, completely mad. Led by three madmen, Hitler, Mussolini, and Hirohito. The whole civilized world had no choice but to stand up and fight.

We would come to learn the Japanese are a very symbolic people. Even while still in peace negotiations in Washington, the empire chose to strike Pearl Harbor. Not just as a strategic target but as symbol of their strength. It enraged President Roosevelt—and the whole country soon after at his rallying cry—and he'd offer a symbol from America in return. Just three and a half months after Pearl, the president sent Lieutenant Colonel James Doolittle and a small group of airmen on an extremely high-risk bombing raid directly into the heart of their empire.

Symbols *are* powerful. And Japan got the message. That raid proved what Don McNeill of NBC news said after the attack on Pearl Harbor: "You can strike a giant who is dozing momentarily, but when the giant is awakened, look out." Doolittle's raid was a yawning stretch. Momentarily caught asleep, even crippled by the blow, soon America and all its united strength and ingenuity would be fully awake. And Japan would come to see its fury unleashed.

But the fury of war is terrible no matter whose bombs burst. It rains down on all. When we first heard Carroll was stationed out west, Helen and I thought, or at least naively hoped, our boy would be shielded from the frontline ravages of war. And he was for a moment. But after Pearl Harbor, our worries skyrocketed. There was little doubt he'd be pulled into the new Pacific theater. We just didn't know when and how. He was, and we soon found out how.

In January we received another letter, dated December 7, a short one. Carroll said just after he sent his letter from San Francisco he'd been sent to Bremerton, Washington. Where the navy had attached him to the aircraft carrier Saratoga in dry dock.

I vaguely remembered that ship from something Joe had said a few days after he and Josie came to listen to the president's speech. Back in '38, he said, the Saratoga and the Lexington carrier groups mounted a successful attack exercise on Pearl Harbor from the north, an exercise designed to help defend against the very approach the Japanese took using the same advanced air warfare tactics. Now our son was on that very same carrier.

Carroll's letter described how they'd left drydock in Washington early the morning of December 6 and all was calm. Just as they entered San Diego harbor on the morning of the seventh, they got their first reports of the attack, and orders to head out to Pearl. He explained his letter had to be brief because everything started moving very fast. He told of how they hurriedly loaded US Marine Corp aircraft, refueled, and gathered supplies to get underway. At Pearl they'd refuel again, he said, and immediately head to Wake Island—which had been in a constant battle since being attacked simultaneous with the attack on Hawaii. Carroll said he didn't know when he'd be able to get us another letter but would write every day.

That letter he penned on December 7 was the last one not censored. After that, each one we got while he was on the Saratoga was redacted.

God, could it be any worse? I wondered. The silence between letters was horrible—our minds' wanderings and all our worries had become more than real. The world was at war, and our little boy was steaming straight into it on a ship with a big target on its back.

I sat in front of the radio on December 9 to listen to President Roosevelt's fireside chat to the American people. His candor that night came to worry me all the more, especially one thing.

> So far, the news has been all bad. We have suffered a serious setback in Hawaii. Our forces in the Philippines, which include the brave people of that Commonwealth, are taking punishment. . . .
> The reports from Guam and Wake and Midway islands are still confused, but we must be prepared for the announcement that all these three outposts have been seized.

Wake! From another letter postmarked at Pearl Harbor, we learned that they arrived at the severely wounded Pacific base on December 15, eight days after the attack. Through the redactions we could still make out Carroll's descriptions of the devastated still smoldering port. We learned later from the newspapers the Saratoga refueled there and set sail with Task Force 14 to Wake Island, one of the most isolated islands in the world. On the way over to Pearl the Saratoga heard some good news. On December 11 the marines on Wake had repelled an amphibious assault by the Japanese and sunk two of their ships. But the battle raged on. Wake became one of the first sustained US battles in World War II. But the outcome was unclear.

The Saratoga steamed full speed ahead for the island, but harsh weather slowed them along with support ship crews with too little experience refueling on the high seas. Just as they got to Wake Island, the Saratoga launched air support and fresh marines were dispatched to the island under heavy siege. They'd not been there long when news came that another Jap carrier group was on its way. At 9:00 p.m. on December 22, Vice Admiral William S. Pye—the acting commander in chief of the US Pacific Fleet—called them back to Pearl. The US lost the battle of Wake Island. That was hard to hear, but I was sure glad Carroll was okay.

In a letter written soon after Christmas, but which we didn't receive until February, we learned the Saratoga had been temporarily assigned to patrol the American Hawaiian Islands. That made me feel better. For that moment it seemed they were not in the thick of the battle.

But then, in another letter we didn't receive until March, Carroll wrote they were heading for a rendezvous with the USS Enterprise, just 500 miles southwest of Oahu, when the Saratoga was hit by a deep-running torpedo fired by a Japanese submarine. "It was scary business," Carroll wrote, "being that close to Pearl and all." But he didn't say any more about it. Just a week after we received that scary letter, we received another one. He began by saying he was back in Bremerton, Washington for repairs. But as we read on, it was clear from that latest letter he'd held back in his earlier one. He told us about when the torpedo hit.

"There were six crewmembers killed, and three firerooms flooded. The Saratoga managed to reach Oahu under her own power. After temporary repairs were completed, our ship made way to the Bremerton Navy Yard for permanent repairs and the installation of a modern antiaircraft battery."

That scared us to death, of course. And worse, we didn't get another letter until August. Our fears were justified. He said they "left Bremerton, stopped in San Diego, then departed for Pearl again on June 1 and arrived on June 6, the last day of the Battle of Midway."

I'd read about that battle in the newspaper and saw pictures of it on the newsreel at the movie theater in England one Saturday when I took the kids over there. Carroll wrote again while still at Pearl Harbor, saying they'd be leaving in early July headed to the Southwest Pacific. He didn't specify where because he couldn't, he said.

We didn't hear from him again until early October, when he wrote a very short letter with very few details. All he could say is they were near Guadalcanal and the Solomon Islands. As we later learned about those places, it became clear the Saratoga was right in the middle of it. Then after Christmas of '42 we got another short letter. He was back at Pearl Harbor again. He said "while we were engaged in battles in the Eastern Solomons, the Saratoga was struck again on her starboard side by a torpedo from a Jap submarine, and that's why we are back at Pearl Harbor. But no one was killed."

My God! I thought. I might have even said it out loud to Helen by accident, I'm not sure. Our boy's ship, struck by another torpedo, and this time

way down in the South Pacific Ocean. Our combined worries for Carroll
froze us both as we read. It was one thing to hear Mr. Kaltenborn recite the
terrible goings-on of the war night after night. It was even a bit surreal to see
the newsreels at the picture show. But seeing it in his own hand, reading that
our son was right there in the middle of the battle, his ship taking torpedoes,
that was unimaginable. Helen and I stared at each other. I gathered her in
my arms, and we just sat for a few minutes.

The war was not at all over *there* anymore. It was sitting in the center
of our living room. As the war in Europe raged on, the war in the Pacific
was getting worse and worse. I became more and more worried that WWII
could be the war to end all wars, and the civilized world might be the losers.
At that thought the hair stood up on the back of my neck.

In February of '43 we received another letter, written in January.

January 2, 1943

Hi Daddy and Mama,

I'm writing you just after Christmas, a long one this time. I don't
know when it'll get to you.

Just wanted to let you know the Saratoga set sail again from
Pearl Harbor just before Thanksgiving, headed ███████████
███████████████ That's about a thousand miles farther south
than we'd gone during the battle of Guadalcanal. But I stayed on
shore this time. I remained at Pearl through Christmas because
I'm being transferred.

As I stood on the dock, I hated to see my buddies go, especially those I'd known since I first joined the crew at Bremerton
in '41 before Pearl. They were headed back into it, and I was
staying ashore. It felt strange. There's something about working
and living together day-in and day-out and especially fighting
real battles together. It binds you in a way I can't fully explain.
All the men aboard work separately together like a symphony—
everyone has a job, and everyone does it. Everything is constant,
it never stops because if it did the ship would stop. But when
the battle starts, everyone goes from general quarters to battle
stations at once. It's crazy fast. For many below deck, like me,
that means keeping the ship going—but everything moves a lot
faster. The noise level rises to a fever pitch for everyone. Horns
blowing, orders barked, airplanes taking off and landing, guns
blazing. It's deafening, not just from the Saratoga but from the
surrounding battleships, escort cruisers, destroyers, and frig-
ates firing their big guns and dropping their depth charges,
and around the islands the fast-moving PT boats, quick lethal

weapons against the enemy. It's scary but so busy you can hardly think, at least that's how it was until we took those torpedoes. Wow we were lucky, at least most of us—my heart goes out to the families of the six boys we lost.

I'll miss my buddies but this is the navy. You go where you're told and do what you're told. I did cherish the R&R, especially in Hawaii and especially at Christmas—though I'll tell you, Christmas in Hawaii just ain't quite the same as back home. It's beautiful and all in an island way but I like Toltec.

I've been reassigned. Off carrier-duty and onto hospital duty, the US Naval Hospital Base Unit, No. 4 in New Zealand. I'm about to leave Pearl and head back stateside, to San Francisco. Hurrah! But only for a short visit to pick up supplies. That's my job, ordering, organizing, and accounting for everything. I'm afraid the trip will be too busy and too short to get home to see everyone. I really hate that.

Once everything's gathered up, we're headed back down under to help move the hospital from Wellington up to the tip of the country at Auckland. They're preparing the hospital for the move now and expect it'll take through March—it takes that long. We're told the prep and the move will take close to the rest of the year. It's a big job, the logistics, new construction, supply and set-up, then the move itself. All this while caring for the existing patients and receiving new wounded daily. And we've been told there are lots of them, many from combat but right now even more from a terrible outbreak of malaria among the soldiers fighting on the islands in the South Pacific. We might make one more trip back to San Fran sometime later this year. After that, I'm told to expect to be in Auckland 'til we beat the socks off the Empire of Japan.

Tell Sis I got her letter and I'll try and write her soon. I love you all so very much,

Bubber

After receiving that letter, Helen and I took a deep breath. Carroll looked to be out of harm's way again. At least out of it directly for the moment. But everything I saw and read about the war in the Pacific and in Europe told me it was getting worse, not better. We could only hope and pray Carroll could find shelter from it in New Zealand on a hospital base.

* * *

The country had shifted to a war economy ever since the attack on Pearl Harbor. The month after the attack President Roosevelt set up the War Production Board. Its job was to convert manufacturing facilities from making peacetime products like automobiles, appliances, and toys, to weapons and military equipment for the fight. It also called for conserving materials like metal, and petroleum products, rubber, paper, and plastic, "which soldiers, sailors and marines would need for the fight in such things as guns, ordnance, tanks, ships, aircraft, tactical vehicles and so on," Kaltenborn had said. The war was putting people back to work again. Along with the earlier increased demand from Europe, the US economy was experiencing a long and much needed bump.

But none of this gave Toltec much of a bump, not for us anyway. It made things harder at the store, less access to some products we stocked compounded by fewer customers due to so many young men heading off to war. The effects on the store crimped an already tight number of dollars for Bill and me to split. The store just didn't have the ability to carry two large families. The tighter things got, and the closer Bill and I worked together, the more the tensions rose. To my great distress, it was creating a rift between us. It bothered me a lot. I talked to Helen about it. I just couldn't let it become a festering permanent breach in our family. Like a small crack in the chinking of Grandfather Bill's old house, it had to be fixed. I just didn't know how.

Every time I thought about Bill and me and thought about the money necessary to take care of the family in those tenuous times, and every time I read Bubber's letters and listened to the news, I knew things had to change. I needed to do something different. Taking care of the family was uppermost, and that meant solving the rift with Bill too. I talked to Helen about it some more, but I still didn't see how to resolve things.

I regularly talked to Joe and one day when he told me his son, Bill, had enlisted in the navy, it gave me an idea.

That night I talked with Helen again and told her I saw a way that might work. If I sold my share of the store to Bill, that would solve our conflict, and it would supply a small cushion to tide us over. But only temporarily.

The war was getting worse. I thought I should do more, in a concrete way. I felt I had a duty. If I enlisted, I could take care of the family and do more in the war effort. Helen listened to me quietly. She hung her head down as we talked. She didn't want me to go and told me so. But she agreed. I don't remember another time I've ever asked Helen to support me in something she was not fully behind. She laid her head on my chest and assured me that they'd be okay. What an extraordinary woman, my Helen.

We talked to Bill and Theresa, and Joe and Josie. It was clear to all of us it would be a sacrifice—a huge one for Helen. They agreed to support her and the kids while I was away. I'd send back all I could from the service pay I got.

On May 5, 1943, I enlisted in the US Navy, and reported to the US Naval Repair Base in New Orleans in late June. Back in the service in Louisiana, in a strange way I felt like it was 1917, except this time in the navy. I wrote to Helen for the first time on stationery from the Roosevelt Hotel, where the navy had put up the new recruits.

July 1, 1943

Dearest Sweetheart & Babies,

Well I'm still in New Orleans but expect this will be my last letter until you hear from my new address.

We heard in several meetings that we might need some cash because it's likely we won't get a pay day for 2 months. I wrote a check on Worthen for $25.00. Probably won't need it but thought it wouldn't hurt.

Have been pretty busy the last day or two and will be until the zero hour I suppose. Am going to another Masonic lodge in downtown N.O. tonight.

Wish I could see my sweetheart & babies but don't think I'll be able to—Sorry!

No need to write here but send a letter in a few days to the new address.

Lots & Lots of Love & Kisses,
Daddy
New Address:
Mora 76
Navy #82
C/O Fleet P.O.
San Francisco, California

Things began to move fast. Several of us loaded on the train the next day headed for San Francisco. Others headed to New York, Norfolk, and Newport News, and many others shipped out to Britain directly from New Orleans. The whole basic training and deployment process was so much different than what I'd experienced back in '17. The train ride brought back memories of my trip to New York, but it was so different too. In every small town on our way to San Francisco, on every platform we stopped at, there were lines of well-wishers waving flags and new recruits hopping on. The number of new inductees in the US military reached its peak in '43.

I had been in San Francisco for only a couple of days when I received orders to report to the USS Heermann, a destroyer docked in San Diego Bay. The war was in full swing everywhere and war was on everybody's mind, those at home and those of us headed into it. No one had a sense of how it was going. Until one night in late July when all aboard ship gathered to listen to the president's latest fireside chat.

He announced the fall of Mussolini! Who, he said, "came to the reluctant conclusion that the 'jig was up'" and "he could see the shadow of the long arm of justice." Everyone cheered, you could hear it echo through every nook and cranny. The president said America had begun to make good on its promise to free the people who "have been reduced to the status of slaves or chattels . . . to restore these conquered peoples to the dignity of human beings, masters of their own fate, entitled to freedom of speech, freedom of religion, freedom from want, and freedom from fear." He talked about how the war machine of the American economy was building and supplying the world to stop Hitler and Hirohito and bring the world back to order again.

Then unexpectedly the president began talking about how the country would help take care of all the soldiers and navy men when we came back home after the war was over. It felt strange to everyone on board that he'd be talking about things to occur after the war just as we were about to ship out. But it also offered something to look forward to. He urged Congress to act on his policy to get mustering-out pay, unemployment insurance, education paid for by the government, and improved veteran's medical care and in particular disabled veterans.

None of us listening that night heard hardly anything other than that Mussolini surrendered. Maybe the war was turning our way, we thought. What he said about education that we all let pass by would become very important later, to Carroll and me and millions more.

The president ended his fireside chat with a charge not to let up, saying,

> It's not too much to say that we must pour into this war the entire strength and intelligence and will power of the United States. We are a great nation—a rich nation—but we're not so great or so rich that we can afford to waste our substance or the lives of our men by relaxing along the way.
>
> We shall not settle for less than total victory. That's the determination of every American on the fighting fronts. That must be, and will be, the determination of every American here at home.

And so it would be for Carroll and me and for everybody back home working together.

Like ships passing in the night, Helen and I exchanged letters about the same time.

October 10, 1943

Dearest Claude,

I got your short letter and loved it. Am writing you back quickly in hopes that you get it while still here in the States. Laura Dean received a letter from Carroll just yesterday, dated September 28. He is in San Francisco. I'd hoped somehow you could both meet up while in California. He tells that he's back in the US for a supply run, to gather up things for the hospital base down in Auckland, New Zealand. As soon as they get what they need, they'll be heading back.

His letter is funny too. He says that he "just came back from another one of those miserable Red Cross dances. And as usual," he says, "my feet are as sore as ever; believe me." I noticed his proper use of the semi-colon, how like Bubber is that? He goes on, "I'm dancing with the most delicate and fragile thing in the house. These cows," his word, "are really hard on the feet and invariably I ended up with the biggest creature at the dance. The name of the gal I spent most of my dancing hours with tonight," he says, "was 'Violet'. But goodness knows, she was far from being a violet."

I almost laughed out loud when Laura Dean read this to me. I think our Carroll wants to find a wife. And I don't think he's attracted to fuller women, do you? I think he was spoiled by Laura Dean when they go dancing and have so much fun. Remember? She misses her big brother and so do I . . . and I miss you too, darling, so much.

Oh, and by the way, J. D. and Carmon are both in the Navy too—Maurine signed for Carmon since he wasn't of age yet. And on his way to his duty station, J. D. came through Little Rock and took Dean out dancing just last week. It was so good to see him. It made me think of Papa and Mama Howell, and Beth and Maurine down in El Campo.

Carroll apparently knew he would not be able to see you while there. He told Dean in the letter to tell me he was sorry. And that he was disappointed he wouldn't get to see you. I hope somehow y'all can see each other somewhere else.

Things are going pretty well here. Bill's taking care of the store—he's happy and I'm glad to see that. All the kids are well, too, and funny. That helps a lot.

Toodles still has her imaginary friend, Mrs. Bolster. She keeps us in stitches, giving plays with her. We also got her good the other night. You know how she hides her desert until all the others are finished? Well, we all did that to her. Everyone set their dessert in their lap until Toodles was finished. She hadn't realized because she was carrying on about Mrs. Bolster, then just as she finished her dessert, we all lifted ours up to the table and began to eat. She was beside herself. At first she was really mad, but then she liked it—she was still the center of attention. Our Sweet Nona Ann!

Well, I'll stop for now. Wish you were here. I miss you so much, darling. We all do.

Be safe. All My Love,
Helen

October 20, 1943

Dearest Sweetheart & Babies,

I got your letter sweetheart, through San Francisco where I told you to write. I love it, everything about it. It was wonderful to hear about the kids, and about Carroll in San Francisco. I'm sure he'll find someone once this tragic war is over. I sure hope so. It's a shame to have been so close and not be able to see him. I miss you and all the kids so much—Tell Mrs. Bolster I said hello, miss her too. Give them each a kiss from Daddy and keep a special one for yourself!

The address I gave you is still the right one for future letters. Letters sent there will get to me even when I'm in different places, but it'll take a while. The day after I wrote from New Orleans I shipped out to San Francisco. I was there only a day and was sent to San Diego, where I was assigned to a new ship, the destroyer USS Heermann—DD-532.

Because I have a few minutes right now and because to write this makes me feel like I'm talking to you, I'll tell you a little about things, what I can anyway. I hope it's not boring.

I was given the rank of Seaman Machinist Mate (MM) 1st Class. As soon as I got to San Diego, we started what they call "shakedown" exercises. That's where new ships are tested out getting them ready for duty, at least that's part of it. In our case it was to do that but also get the crew to work together and ready for war. It was close to all-day and all-night 'til the end of August. Everything was tested, the ship's speed, all the huge guns and anti-sub depth charges, and making sure all the machinery worked. And all that to pull the whole crew together to work as one. Most of the crew are young like Bubber, and green except for our basic training—though there are a few like me who had WWI experience, and in some ways that seemed to help. But by the time we finished the shakedown cruise on August 26, the ship and crew worked together like a Swiss watch. The next day we set sail in heavy fog from San Diego back to San Francisco, where final repairs were made at the Bethlehem Steel Corp. Dock. Out of San Francisco we stopped a couple of days in San Diego again, then on ███████ we set sail for Pearl Harbor. It took us about a week to get here.

The Islands are exceptionally beautiful, like you sweetheart. The temperature stays the same all the time, the sun rises with a golden glow most mornings and it sets the same way. But yesterday when there were big thunder clouds the sky turned a deep orange just as it dropped below the horizon. It was so beautiful. And the water, wow Helen! It's like nothing I've ever seen before, not in the Atlantic, not even on the shores of France. It's a pure azure blue, that's what some of the fellows call it. I don't know what to call it, but it looks like the deep blue color on the edge of some of the porcelain dishes your mama has. But then it changes to a crystal-clear light green color right at the shore . . . in calm water you can see your feet until you're almost shoulder deep. I'd so love it if you were here with me, especially under different circumstances.

But the remnants of the devastating Jap attack are still everywhere. Commander Agnew ordered us all on deck and to attention at salute in our whites as we came into port near the eerie silhouette of the Arizona, resting a mere forty feet deep as a kind of memorial.

For the last two weeks we did daily firing exercises, and I've just learned we've been assigned to the Fifth Fleet. Any day now we're headed to the South Pacific. I can't say exactly where, but it's closer to Bubber than here. I'm not sure how, but I hope to meet up with him if I can.

I make only $66 a month. I've arranged to have most of it sent home to you and the kids. I don't need much on board ship.

Lots & Lots of Love & Kisses –

Claude

P.S. Tell Carroll I'll hope to see him down under. Use the same address as before, sweetheart.

From Pearl Harbor we shipped off to the South Pacific. The first memorable moment was crossing the international dateline. My buddy Hal Brook captured this rare fun time we all remember, writing,

The highlight of the trip came on the twenty-fifth of October when we crossed the equator and King Neptune, and his entire court came aboard to convert all the Pollywogs into honorable Shellbacks. This ancient ceremony, which takes place upon the "crossing of the line," is a little difficult to explain. About the closest thing to it is the initiation of a freshman into a college fraternity, except that it's more violent if anything. The Pollywogs were washed down with salt water, shocked with electric current, submerged in fuel oil and all received a sound paddling, all this after being made to do sundry foolish things for the amusement of the old shellbacks. This process completed, all were welcomed into the ranks of Honorable Shellbacks.

And he was right. Becoming a Shellback was the last bit of fun I remember until much later when I was transferred to Brisbane, Australia for a month to work with the Red Cross—and got leave and free transport from them to New Zealand for a day and a night.

After crossing the date line, we joined the Fifth Fleet and steamed to a little place in the New Hebrides islands on our way to Havanah Harbor, Efate, which is part of the Vanuatu islands northeast of Australia. It was uneventful, except for a mysterious sound our communications crew picked up one day. They first thought it was a submarine and everyone went to battle stations, and we dropped several depth charges. But as it turned out it was a signal from American survivors in the water, from a reconnaissance plane assigned to the battleship Indiana. We picked the crew up and got them back to their ship.

In November we separated from the Fleet and took up with another destroyer, the Hazelwood, to escort a couple of oilers to Nandi, Fiji Islands. Then we returned to Fila Harbor and joined back up with the task force as the fleet made its way towards the Tarawa Atoll, Gilbert Islands Group. Around there we saw our first small battle, sinking a 200-ton Japanese ship just before it could reach ground on the island. From there we rejoined the task of providing cover for the fleet. After a couple of strafes by Jap bombers, being so close in, just before midnight we ran aground ourselves—a dangerous situation. But only for a short time, and the commander got us out of it.

Soon after we entered the lagoon to provide close-in fire support for US troops assaulting Tarawa. That night and into the next day we bombarded the island to suppress Japanese troop movements. At one point we annihilated a large number of troops and a machine gun nest. Though we were low on ammunition stores, we continued to operate in a fire support capacity well into the next evening.

After that we headed back to Pearl to replenish and get some repairs. There we stayed through Christmas. In mid-January we got a short shore leave in Hawaii. I wrote Helen every day.

After our leave, in late January we headed out to support the US assault on the Marshall Islands in the North Pacific Ocean, about halfway between Hawaii and Australia. We stayed down in and around the Marshalls through early spring, and then we received orders to head to the Solomon Islands. There we stayed doing runs and lots of training through late summer of '44.

In August we were sent to Noumea, New Caledonia. The whole crew got leave, but I was sent to Brisbane, Australia on short-term duty assignment with the Red Cross there. I was disappointed at first, but then I had a thought. The New Zealand Base Hospital came to New Caledonia regularly, so I left with them headed to Brisbane. I was there for less than a month. While there I became friends with the head of the Red Cross. At the end of my duty, I got my delayed leave, and I asked him for a favor, a big favor. I asked if he could he get me over to Auckland, New Zealand to see my boy, and back in time to catch my flight to New Caledonia by September 4—to catch up with the Heermann headed back to the Solomon's. It was a huge thing to ask, but he worked a miracle. I only had four days and most of that would be taken up by travel. But it was enough time.

Unbelievable! I landed early in the morning at the US Naval Hospital Base Unit, No. 4 in Auckland and found my boy. *Truly a miracle*, I thought. War all round and I'm able to see my boy. God, it was so good to see Bubber, and while we were both in service to our country. Carroll showed me around the base hospital and where he worked. It was a very busy time for him, and not just with his strict navy duty, but also with raising the morale of the wounded and base troops. I had only that day and that night and had to catch a flight back to Brisbane early the next morning to make my flight back to the Heermann. It was such a wonderful night. I learned it happened to be a very special night for Bubber and his buddy, Ralph, from Kansas.

Carroll had written a musical, and he and Ralph had staged it for all the patients and base crew. A whole musical. *Unbelievable*, I thought. He wrote all the music, the songs, and directed it all including a small orchestra and everything—Helen would be so excited when I could write and tell her . . . those piano lessons when Bubber was stuck at home with polio had really paid off. Drawing upon base and local talent, they performed the musical that night for the whole base. It was an enormous success, everyone loved it, especially one song he wrote, "Long Remember," a song of love and longing, which took everyone back home to their loved ones. It was a superb night in every way. It was so wonderful to see Carroll all grown up, doing his duty and a whole lot more. He had things to give the world I hadn't realized. I was so proud of him.

At 0600 the next morning I hugged my boy on the tarmac, loaded onto the US Air Transport Command plane and headed out. Back to the Heermann and back to the war. I was glad Carroll was in a place that seemed safe and where he could thrive. I couldn't wait for the day when the long arm of justice, as the president called it, had corralled the evil let loose on the world, when the war would be over and Carroll, Helen, my babies, and I were all together again back home.

I caught up with the Heermann at Purvis Bay, where she'd been docked and redocked for recurring mechanical repairs. But just two days after I got back, on September 6 we shipped out and became an escort and support for Rear Adm. William D. Sample's carrier group for the invasion of Palau, a small but important archipelago in the middle between Micronesia, Indonesia, and the Philippines. We continued giving screening support for various ships and battles through the first part of October. Then we were called to support planned landings in the Leyte Gulf in preparations for a major invasion of the Philippines.

Surprisingly so far, we had met no serious resistance from the Japanese fleet. That was curious. We were getting so close to their mainland. Why so quiet, everyone wondered. The weather was terrible on our way up to the Leyte. The shipped rocked hard and constant. It was difficult to get anything done and hard to keep anything down. We learned later we'd come upon the edge of a typhoon that wreaked havoc across the area. We were lucky, suffering little to no damage, but many other ships didn't fare so well. Our area of operations was Samar Island. There we stayed for weeks. In relative calm. Then, as my good buddy Hal Brook later wrote—see here, in his recollections for the war history of the USS Heermann—he says,

> There we were, steaming innocently along, much as we had for weeks—six baby carriers, three destroyers and four destroyer escorts of the northern carrier group. All of a sudden, all hell broke loose. The general alarm started to ring and the word was passed, "All hands, man your battle stations!" Before we left those battle stations again one phase of the greatest daylight surface engagements in history would be finished. It looked as if the whole Jap navy was on top of us. It wasn't really the whole Jap navy, just four battleships, five heavy cruisers, and eleven destroyers. But it felt like it.
>
> We saw mysterious splashes in the water all around us and other ships in the fleet. We couldn't tell where they were coming from, but surmised they must be from high level bombers. The

squalls were relentless, which was both good and bad. They gave some protection, but we couldn't get a fix on the enemy. All the fleet protection vessels kept maneuvering this way and that, to avoid aerial assault and torpedoes and to protect the fleet and give time to get planes off the carrier decks. In the squalls and all the maneuvering, some of our ships ran into each other, and we barely missed one ourselves. We were constantly laying down smoke for cover, firing on a cruiser and trying to get in position for a run in. We did finally and the battle really began. We sent our first salvo of seven torpedoes headed toward a huge Japanese battleship, then just as we did we turned and saw another. We let go a second salvo of four, all while using the big guns and small ones for close quarter encounters.

The way Hal remembers it:

"We were so close that we could smell the rice cooking in the Japs galley. One torpedo hit right under the No. 4 turret of the lead battleship with a terrific explosion, and she was out of the fight for the rest of the day."

And he was right. It was scary. The problem after that was, we were out of torpedoes and two of our other ships, the Hoel and the Johntson, were sinking. We were the only destroyer left to help protect the carriers, and one of them had been hit and was listing about twenty degrees. We went full speed ahead to get there. But as we did the Japanese battleships and torpedo bombers saw us and turned their attention to us. That's when our real troubles started. Listen to Hal again:

As soon as the Japs saw us, they stopped firing at the carriers and took us under fire with everything they had. How so many shells could miss, we'll never know. Even with our small guns, we were hurting them more than they were hurting us. Our shells started a big fire on the fantail of the leading cruiser, and she dropped out of the formation. It was too good to last though; one of the other cruisers finally hit us with a salvo of eight-inch shells. One shell went through the base of the number one stack, the rest went through the bow, down low, causing the forward part of the ship to flood. In addition, there were shrapnel holes everywhere. It was at this point that we suffered most of our casualties.

We lost three sailors when the shell plunged through the pilothouse, and sadly another fellow who later died of his wounds. We took two more shells forward, flooding several compartments, then a third near the keel. We were limping when the battle ended but still afloat.

I remember that day so well, but it is one I wish I could forget. I've never talked about it with anybody except Helen. While the noise had been deafening during this battle and the others, that explosion was unimaginable. I was fortunate to have been in the stern. Otherwise, I wouldn't be telling this story. We guessed the Jap fleet saw our fire and thought it best to pull away. Crippled, we began to make it back to our position. As we did, we realized the battle was not over yet. We discovered a new Jap weapon of war, the kamikaze. The first plane buried itself into the St. Louis, and it started to sink. We were successful taking out a couple of other dive-bombers on their way in, and we rescued as many crew as we could from the St. Louis. It was a terrible sight, the dead and wounded. Terrible.

Another buddy wrote, "Somehow our small number of ships and tin cans had fended off the bulk of the Japanese battle force." And it was true. We were small of stature against a big foe in that battle. Commander Hathaway and those of our whole task force saved our lives that day—along with everybody aboard doing their part. Carroll was right about everyone on board ship working together like a symphony. It had to be that way. And even when it's at its best, the enemy can still break through as they did that day. But we escaped with our lives, most of us.

The fleet headed out and we were left to catch up. We buried the dead in the navy way—God Bless those brave men, God bless them even today. We transferred all our wounded to the USS Bountiful, a hospital ship. We got temporary repairs from the tender USS Prometheus, headed to Manus, and from there on to Pearl. We stayed at Pearl only a couple of days and received orders back to the Mare Island Navy Yard just north of San Francisco for a major overhaul.

All anyone aboard heard was *San Francisco*. We were going home. We arrived November 26, 1944, quickly reloaded ammunition, and got the Heermann in dock. Then came what everyone had been waiting for—we were all released on leave.

I got home to see my sweetheart and babies for Christmas in '44. God, it was incredible. I was a middle-aged man when I joined the navy, so much older than most. But when I got home to hug and kiss Helen and the kids and tell them about seeing Carroll down in New Zealand, I was like a teenager. It was so good to lie in bed with Helen that night and tickle her back the way she loves. And it was so good to see the kids and how they'd grown. Laura Dean, such a lady, would turn eighteen just after Christmas, Nicky and Chas becoming young men, and Boggie and Toodles. Wow! So good to see my babies. It was the best Christmas I could remember . . . except Carroll's chair was still empty. I hoped we'd all be back together again soon.

But my time in the navy wasn't over yet. I reported back to the Heermann on January 5. We'd soon ship out again. On the eighth we left Mare for San Francisco, and then left there for Pearl on January 14. On February

1, we headed back down to the Marshall Islands, to Eniwetok, and took up a screening station with our task force that steamed south of Honshu, Japan. We were getting closer and closer to the heart of the empire every day that went by. There we supported aerial attacks on Tokyo through February and then shifted to support the battles for Iwo Jima and Okinawa in the spring.

On April 14, our commander came on the comms and told us of the death of President Franklin D. Roosevelt, the commander-in-chief. The colors were lowered to half-mast. That brought back so many memories to me. He'd been president for twelve years, a tremendously difficult twelve years. I didn't agree with everything, but he'd seen us through it. I remember thinking how close we were, almost in Tokyo Bay, and he didn't get to see it.

I stayed on the Heermann through the end of the war, and Carroll stayed in New Zealand.

On May 5, 1945, Commander Hathaway spoke from the bridge again and announced V-E Day! Germany had surrendered, and Hitler was dead. The war in Europe was over. But, he said, "In his speech to the nation on V-E Day, President Harry S. Truman cautioned that Allies must work to finish the war by defeating the Japanese in the Pacific."

Three months later, the commander came on the broadcast system again. He announced that on August 6 and again on August 9, 1945, the "Allies dropped atomic bombs on Hiroshima and Nagasaki, respectively." No one even knew what that meant. No one could believe the descriptions. But the effect was immediate. On August 10, Japan communicated its intention to surrender. On August 15, Emperor Hirohito made a radio broadcast announcing Japan's surrender. The Heermann stood protective guard while General Douglas MacArthur and Admiral Chester W. Nimitz began preparing forces to occupy the Japanese mainland. On September 2, 1945, the formal surrender occurred aboard the battleship USS Missouri in Tokyo Bay.

On September 16 we entered Tokyo Bay, where we received repairs for about a month.

World War II was over.

Twenty-Four—Sweet the Rain's New Fall

Fall of 1945 to Late Summer of 1954

The Heermann left Tokyo Bay October 7, the day after the Nuremberg war crime indictments were handed down against the Germans in Europe.

The whole crew sighed with relief. Newspapers were available in the commissary on board, so I grabbed one. And the captain showed newsreels on our way back across the Pacific to San Pedro Bay at the port of Los Angeles, visual evidence of the discoveries in the aftermath of the war in Europe. What I read and saw was beyond comprehension. Stories and films of "death camps," they called them. Places where the "impure," according to Hitler, were taken to be studied like animals and killed en masse in gas chambers. The flickering moving pictures were unimaginable. Gaunt, bone-thin people barely able to walk came toward the gates opened by allied Russian soldiers at a place called Auschwitz. Later, during the Nuremberg trials, the newspapers reported there was "a complex of over forty concentration and extermination camps operated by Nazi Germany in occupied Poland during the War, where German ethnic cleansing and holocaust deaths took place." Those trials revealed that there "were as many as 6 million Jews, 1.8 million non-Jewish Poles, 3 million Soviet prisoners of war, 300,000 Serbs, 250,000 Gypsies, and more." Though we didn't know the full extent of all that then, I still had to try and take in what I was seeing and put it together with what we'd all seen in the battles of the South Pacific. It became clear that no matter what, the Japanese just wouldn't give up—the Soviet Russians didn't believe they would, they declared war on Japan just days before the bombs were dropped, and the very day Emperor Hirohito surrendered Japan, we had to shoot down a Kamikaze pilot diving toward the Heermann.

What evil in this world? War is insane! The only just cause for it is to stay the hand of evil.

I remember thinking when Carroll enlisted and when I did, that this war was another one of those unavoidable fights that Uncle John and Papa had talked about—like the Great War, to defeat tyranny and preserve liberty. But seeing those newsreels it became obvious it was far more than just that. It was clear that something else had taken hold in the world, a kind of pure evil. One I'd never known existed. In the paper I'd picked up, I saw something that General Eisenhower had said in a speech: "War is a grim, cruel business, a business justified only as a means of sustaining the forces of good against those of evil." We'd stayed the hand of this evil, I'm sure of that. God knows, I prayed, I hope it never gains such a foothold ever again. God knows, I hoped.

To be truthful, for a fleeting moment I wondered if he did. Did God really know? After seeing and reading those things, I wondered if God really was there. If so, how could such evil ever be allowed? Then after only another moment's thought it dawned on me. If He's not there, why would I even care? If not, Nietzsche and Hitler were right; it's all about raw ruthless power. But that I and the whole civilized world did care assured me there is a *True* good. That God really is there. That it's God in his providence who makes us cringe and push against evil. That's why we went to war. Not because we wanted to, but because we cringe at evil. In doing so we confirm the True good even when some are seduced away by evil. The Good God is why.

We docked in San Pedro Bay November 1. It took us a week or so to muster out. I was finally on my way home again. If I was lucky, by Thanksgiving, and this time for good.

The train from LA swayed gently side to side, the steel of the wheels clicked monotonously on the tracks below as I silently read from the navy-issued pocket New Testament in the early morning light.

> In the beginning was the Word, and the Word was with God, and the Word was God.
> The same was in the beginning with God.
> All things were made by him; and without him was not any thing made that was made.
> In him was life; and the life was the light of men.
> And the light shineth in darkness; and the darkness comprehended it not.

I remember lifting my eyes from the page and thinking about Miss Jennie so long ago, about how I should read from the Bible as part of my education. I hadn't in quite a while. But on my final leg home, I was still overwhelmed by the deep dark tunnel we'd all been through. I looked back down and thought how similar those words in St. John's Gospel are to those at the beginning of the Bible.

> In the beginning God created the heaven and the earth.
> And the earth was without form, and void; and darkness was upon the face of the deep. And the Spirit of God moved upon the face of the waters.
> And God said, Let there be light: and there was light.

Darkness was upon the face of the deep. Let there be light, and there was. In him was life and the life was the light of men, and the light shined in the darkness and the darkness didn't consume it but was consumed by it. Thank God the terrible storm was over and there was light again.

I was lucky. On November 15, at the main station in Little Rock, the train stopped. I grabbed my duffle, got off and became consumed by the light of my life, sweet Helen Grace, and our wonderful kids. God, it was good to be home.

* * *

Just before New Years I held her as we lay in bed in our new bungalow in Little Rock—I've always loved those early mornings with Helen in my arms. I'd barely been home six weeks and the whole world was back to how it was supposed to be. Muffled and softly, with her cheek against my chest, she said hesitantly,

"I'm pregnant."

"What!" I said, sure I didn't hear right. "What?" I asked Helen again. "Are you sure?"

She lifted her head and stared at me in the twilight. After a prolonged pause she finally said,

"Claude, don't you think I'd know after six kids? Yes, I'm pregnant. At thirty-nine years old I'm pregnant."

We peered into each other's eyes saying nothing for a moment. Then, at precisely the same time, we broke into laughter.

"Wow," I said. "I'd planned to come home to start over but we're *really starting all over again*. I bet this is happening all over the world."

Love has a way of replenishing the world, like how sweet the rain's new fall is after a long drought. Our love has certainly multiplied the harvest. Helen and I had and were doing our part to replenish the earth. We'd taken Uncle Jim's admonition to heart, over and over and over again. I was overjoyed and so was Helen, even if she was a little embarrassed to be pregnant at thirty-nine. That sense of embarrassment would become more palpable to my sweetheart.

* * *

The world changed a lot and fast after the war, both in the Howell family and beyond.

Twelve million American service men and women made their way back home all at once. Most were young people who wanted to get married and start a family. And everybody needed a job. Some would pick up where they left off and start again but for most there was no good place to pick up from. The war itself had put the world back to work. It's a great irony that such a tragedy would pull the world out of the Great Depression. The challenge after the war was to convert the war machine into a productive peacetime economy. It would be an extraordinary feat.

For us it meant a big change too. Before the long train ride home from Los Angeles I'd called my brother Bill at the store in Toltec and arranged to talk to Helen. Her mama had been alone in Little Rock since Brother Crutchfield died six years earlier. She was eighty-four then and needed help. Helen and I talked about it and decided we'd move into the city to be near Mrs. Malvina. She and Brother Crutchfield had bought two extra bungalow houses on State Street next to theirs when they moved to Little Rock, so we took one of those.

Carroll had gotten home early in September before me, so just before I got home, he and Nicky moved our things from Toltec, including Mr. Price's big oak table.

Since things were still a bit unsettled at Thanksgiving, it was Christmas that year before we all finally sat around that table again—for the first time in almost five years. God, it was good. That table was a wonderful sign of home whatever house it was in. And as had long been the custom, there was always at least one guest. That night was no exception. Laura Dean had invited Miss Elaine Coleman, a friend of hers from when she'd worked for Principal L. O. Baker at Scott High School after she graduated. Elaine taught there.

I learned that night that Dean had invited Elaine for supper back in September, the first night Carroll was home—at our house in Toltec, before we moved into Little Rock. And wouldn't you know it, they fell in love almost at first sight.

That table, as it turns out, was not only a family gathering spot, it was also a matchmaker.

Just after the new year, Carroll and Elaine were visiting at supper again—Carroll stayed in Toltec at our home there, and Elaine lived in Little Rock with her parents and each day drove out to Scott High School to teach. Soon after they got there when things were still settling down, they looked at each other, and Bubber looked at everyone with a huge smile and announced,

"We're engaged! We're gonna get married in June."

Everyone was excited and cheers rang out. I glanced at Helen with excitement and saw quite a strange look on her face, a strange mixture of happiness and fear. I didn't understand why until later that night. She was excited for Bubber, but she knew that by June she'd be "showing," she said. "I can't go to the wedding of my oldest son pregnant with another child. What would people think?"

I couldn't help chuckling under my breath, but I soon realized that wasn't a good thing to do. Helen started crying. I'd hurt her feelings. Her "situation" was a very serious problem for her, and I had treated it lightly. I wrapped my arms around her and kissed her. "It's okay, sweetheart. It's okay. Carroll will understand, and so will Elaine. It'll be okay," I assured her. And it was.

Since we'd moved into Little Rock, and since I'd sold my half of the store to Bill, I needed to find something new to do. I reestablished the insurance license that I'd first gotten under Mr. Price—this time selling property and casualty insurance as an independent agent, mostly targeted to businesses. And after selling our house in Toltec I decided to take the real estate broker's test to start selling real estate too. Taking that test made me think of school, something I hadn't thought much about for many years.

With the Service Readjustment Act that President Roosevelt had first talked about in the fireside chat back in '43 when he announced Mussolini's surrender, I had a wild thought. Many veterans were thinking about school—taking advantage of what was by then called the GI Bill. The government would pay for veterans to go to school as a part of the initiative to train or retrain a new workforce to meet the growing peacetime economy. Carroll had already applied and got into the University of Missouri at Columbia. And Laura Dean, who was working in Little Rock, was also going to Little Rock Junior College. And though I'd never finished high school, I applied to the same junior college and got accepted. I was more than surprised and very excited, though I wasn't sure how to work it out. But selling insurance and real estate offered enough flexibility to go to school too.

My mind went back to Texarkana when I was fifteen, when Papa and Mama moved to De Queen and I had to quit school to work. And to when I was twenty-one that day on the porch in front of Charles's store in Keo when Governor Charles Brough explained things and "taught" like the professor he was before running for governor. As a result of the GI Bill, at fifty-one, I was finally going to get a formal education. The pace of life change increased dramatically.

The year after the war was a very busy but a very exciting one. Carroll and Elaine married in June—Helen reluctantly stayed home.

Then on September 8, our new bundle of joy came along. We named her Mary Kay, and I nicknamed her Kay Baby. We were young again, noticeable one night when Laura Dean came home late from out dancing with friends, knocked on the door to our room as she always did, and opened it to see Helen and me lifting, laughing, and playing with Kay Baby at 1:00 in the morning. The light into our renewed life was bright. And it would grow brighter still and quickly.

Almost to the day a year after they married, in June of '47, Carroll and Elaine had their first child, our first grandchild, sweet little Laura Ann.

Nicky married his sweetheart Jimmie Sue the following summer of '48. And Laura Dean met her sweetheart, Warren, a good navy man, on a blind date in August that same summer.

We'd all thought she might marry her regular dancing partner, a fellow named Ed she been seeing for a long time, someone she'd met through Josie and Joe's son-in-law. But no. Your daddy swept her off her feet. Warren was a good Arkansas boy, born in Little Rock, and navy man. But when he got out of the navy he took a job with Dallas Power & Light Company. They had a whirlwind romance. Sister and Warren only saw each other a few times before they married the day after Christmas, not quite five months after they met—and they had a luxurious honeymoon on the train to Dallas because Warren had to get back to work.

When Helen and I saw and experienced all these joys develop, we were overjoyed ourselves. It was everything we'd ever hoped for our kids. The world was at peace and our family was flourishing. What more could we ask for? Our blessings overflowed.

Amid the fast-paced changes in the family, I plugged away at school. It was everything I'd always thought it would be. With formal instruction I was able to read and learn more fully a lot of the history and ideas I'd pieced together on my own like a patchwork.

I even read and heard about some of those philosophers Governor Brough mentioned that day at Charles Alexander's store, including even something of Friedrich Nietzsche and Hitler's favorite anti-Semitic composer Richard Wagner. I studied many things in college, of course. But I mention this because I've always been interested in history and politics, and we've talked of them so much relating to the war. These things were talked about a lot in colleges after the war.

It is said the "nineteenth-century intellectual figures de Gobineau, Richard Wagner, and Houston Stewart Chamberlain," my professor said, "all greatly influenced early Nazism with their claims of the racial and cultural superiority of the 'Nordic' (Germanic) peoples over all other Europeans and all other races." And there was an emphasis, particularly in Hitler, on "political romanticism," the professor called it, and the "proclamation of the rights of Nietzsche's exceptional individual, the Übermensch, or 'Overman,'" he called it. Whose "Rights," he said, were "over all universal law and rules." I thought back to what I'd heard Mr. Kaltenborn say about Nietzsche and Hitler on the radio before the US entered the war, and the incomprehensible havoc that can be perpetrated by someone with such a political philosophy.

With the professor's help, I began to recognize how Nietzsche's ideas were in many ways a reaction to eighteenth-century Enlightenment ideas that so emphasized what he called "disinterested reason."

"During the nineteenth century," the professor said, as I wrote in my notes, "the new ideas and narrowed practices of reason slowly settled into new intellectual patterns, cultural practices, and ways of living. The flow of this undercurrent would lead to a profound cultural vertigo soon after the turn of the twentieth century." He went on to say, "Pure disinterested reason and pure intuitive romanticism are each a dangerous thing. Especially," he said, "when coupled with a rejection of God. In the first, morality and virtue are sacrificed on the altars of modern social and political science in pursuit of an imagined utopia. In the second, virtue and *truth* itself are sacrificed on the altar of unconstrained passions evoked through sentimentalism and propaganda. Eventually both reduce to raw power, as seen in Adolf Hitler on the one hand and Josef Stalin on the other."

Hearing this I began to see more clearly how seemingly abstract, remote ideas can have huge consequences. And how dangerous certain ideas are especially when combined with a charismatic leader focused on persuasion through propaganda. Learning about such things gave me an educated foundation for my long-held belief going back to Uncle Jim, Grandfather Carroll, and even our distant relative, Charles Carroll of Carrollton. That for a society to flourish it must be based on liberty and law, but that foundation must itself be underwritten by virtue, and virtue, by God.

Prompted by my studies in history and political philosophy, on a lark after junior college, I decided to apply to Arkansas Law School. And to my even greater surprise this time, I was accepted. I really couldn't believe it. It just goes to show, if you don't try, you'll never know.

I was excited to study the law. It was demanding, especially with work and the family. But it also helped shape and inform my views on even more things. I remember deciding, finally, how I felt about old Governor Blough's "progressivism." I came to understand the history of its development, and how, if at all, I favored Teddy Roosevelt's version over President Wilson's. But now I'm not very keen on that either. But I agreed with President Teddy Roosevelt that "wise progressivism and wise conservatism go hand in hand." The central government can and must do some things that state and local governments just can't. Of that, I am sure. But it can't and shouldn't do many things it often tries to do. I'd initially favored President *Franklin* Roosevelt's policies, but I knew firsthand how many didn't actually work. I came to believe he went too far. His policies made the American people feel too entitled. It made too many look to the government for solutions that we ourselves should handle. I became concerned we were moving to a Welfare State like the kind Britain and West Germany adopted after the war. And some at the extremes promoted communism, the very thing James Cobb had warned Governor Blough against back before WWI. A communist state like the Soviet Union, where the government owns all means of production and uses the power of the state to force its will.

By Gawd, this has never been the American way and must never become our way.

These were among the very things we'd fought a war against. And though they'd been an ally in World War II, and though they lost more people in that war than any other country, we've since come to learn the Soviet Union has become the worst kind of tyranny. If you can believe it, ever since Red October back in 1917, they've killed more of their own people than the Germans did in WWII. And they support communist expansion in China, Korea, and Indochina—that remote place the Japanese sent troops back before the war. The risks are even higher now in the "cold war," with the terrifying idea of a "nuclear arms race."

I wrote in a paper in college that "In America, the Constitution and the law are underwritten by moral and civic virtue," as President Washington had urged Congress to remember in his farewell address. And that these virtues "include the virtue of hard work and the prospect of advancement in a free economic order. Together they combine to make our system work. The federal government's primary role," I said in the paper, "is to protect the liberties that allow this system to work." Law school helped me clarify my political views even more sharply.

I was able to sustain Helen, Toodles, and Kay Baby with insurance and real estate, even while I continued in law school. And before our eyes the family was expanding more and more.

In early '49, Nicky's wife Jimmie Sue became pregnant and your sweet mama, Laura Dean, announced the same in early spring. Nicky and Jimmie Sue gave us our second grandchild, beautiful Theresa Gail. And Laura Dean gave us our first grandson, James Michael Roseman.

"You know who that is, Jimbo?"

Seeing our kids make their way in life was beyond satisfying for Helen and me. The year 1949 was a happy one. Until it was interrupted with very sad news in October.

I got a telegram from Mama in El Campo. "Papa is ill, very ill, Claude," she said. "Come now so you can say goodbye." I did. Papa died November 8, less than a month after his second great grandchild Theresa Gail was born. My heart sank. My papa was gone. So many good memories, and some sad ones too—he'd had better seasons, but Papa never recovered from Rachel's death. With seven of my own I understood why. *He can be with Rachel again,* I thought to myself, *and we'll all look forward to a happy reunion some day.* Mama was so sad. But Papa had been sick, and she knew it was coming and had prepared as much as anyone can. She knew she and Papa had a good life together, and she cherished the good memories. But her heart was broken. We brought Papa back to Little Rock, and buried him at the Pinecrest Cemetery, not far from where we first came through back in '05.

Despite Papa's death, Mama continued to thrive at the ripe age of seventy-nine. Because of Papa's death in November, Mama was allowed to stay with us through June of the following year—extending her allowable pension absence from Texas by a couple of months. She had cataract surgery while with us, and it went well, but the recovery turned out to be difficult. She had to lie completely still on her back for a whole week. She finally healed and could see a lot better, but it didn't end her aching heart—whenever she heard Papa's name her eyes glistened.

* * *

I graduated from law school in '51 with a concentration on real estate law. That same year, Charles married his sweetheart, Dolora, and the next year Boggie married her honey, J. C. Pierce. The family kept expanding. I never took the bar exam but used the law degree to expand my real estate business, focused on commercial properties, with the bread and butter in residential.

In 1953 there was a particularly lucrative deal I'd come across through Mr. Charles Simon, a man who represented himself as a licensed broker. In November of '52 Mr. Simon explained he knew and represented an executive of a company needing to acquire property for a large corporate development project. The opportunity was to aggregate properties along Center Street and the corner of Ninth Street and Louisiana Street in Little Rock for the new headquarters of Arkansas Power & Light Company. We were engaged to acquire the properties.

Everything went very well, and I was even allowed to buy a small 1,400-square-foot residential house located on one of the properties, on the condition I relocate it. I closed on that house before we closed the larger deal and moved it to a small, inexpensive lot I'd purchased up in the Heights.

It took about a year, but we closed on all the properties for AP&L in early '54. Mr. Simon wasn't able to be at the closing, so I had the title company hold a check for his half of the fees. It would be my largest commission. All the hard work had been worth it. One of the best days ever.

Until it wasn't.

By omission, Mr. Simon had lied to me and to the title company. He didn't have his real estate broker's license. When completing the paperwork, the title company discovered it and called and told me. Since I was the lead broker, I was responsible. I should've checked but didn't and I got branded with the lie Mr. Simon told and I had my license suspended. I was really depressed when it happened. I did make a claim, and we reached a settlement, though not big and it could not give me my license back. That would take quite a while, but I eventually did.

In the meantime, I was in a quandary. Like so many times before, I had to start over again.

You Are What You Love

Late Summer of 1954 to Fourth of July 1967

Wherever we go and whatever we do, it is our loves that move us and take us there, especially in our pursuit of happiness. Consciously or not, in our brokenness and pain, we attach our loves, affections, and desires to people, places, or things with the hope that we will finally find the felicity we have been searching for all our lives.

DAVID NAUGLE

Twenty-Five—Howell's Highway Grocery

Late Summer of 1954 to Late Winter of 1960

We got a call from Josie in England, where Mrs. Malvina had moved a few years earlier, to live with her and Joe—Joe and Josie had moved from Keo down the road to England before the war when Joe became sheriff there. I answered the phone and Josie asked for Helen. I knew. As she listened tears began to fall from Helen's eyes and roll down her cheeks. I wiped them away and wrapped my arms around her and held her tight. I took the receiver as she said goodbye and laid it back on the cradle. Helen raised her head and looked in my eyes, then buried her face into my chest and sobbed, just as she had when Brother Crutchfield died fourteen years before. Helen's mama was gone. It doesn't matter if they're young or old, losing your papa or mama is hard—even if your grandmother is the only mama you've ever really known. We drove to Josie's that Friday so Helen could say goodbye.

The *England Democrat* was late getting out that week, so the family was able to post a short obituary, which read simply, "Isorah Malvina, 'Mallie,' Browne Crutchfield, born September 17, 1861, in Rutherford County, Tennessee, died August 20, 1954, at 92 years old. The funeral will be Sunday at 2:00 p.m. at Pecan Grove Baptist Church in Keo after regular services. She will be buried in Keo Cemetery next to her beloved husband, Reverend William Crutchfield."

Everyone in our family who was still in the area, and all those still left who knew her, came for the funeral. It was a sad occasion but again, like at Brother Crutchfield's, sweet Mallie's funeral was a celebration too. It was so good to see so many familiar faces.

Being back at Pecan Grove Baptist where Helen and I were married and just being back in Keo again evoked so many memories. The day Uncle John and I stepped off the train, why we came from Texarkana, the long trip down to Texarkana from Illinois, and good old Charles Alexander and his brother-in-law Lewis Gaston. I thought fondly of the store that Charles and Lewis opened next to the Keo Hotel and the Baptist Church on the other side, which prompted Brother Crutchfield to come in the store that wonderfully fateful day back in '14. Followed by the Great War, the one the president foolishly thought was the war to end all wars. Then that wonderful return home to start Howell & Son's store with Papa, and best of all, marrying my sweetheart, and those wonderful suppers and evenings at the Crutchfield's in that big old white house. Only to be uprooted after the store burned and the weight of the Great Depression that took us to Hot Springs, El Campo, and back to Keo and the bus stop-diner—short two kids for two years. Oh, that other fateful day when Theresa walked through the door, allowing us to get the gin and a new store in Toltec, only to be pulled away again by another World War. After which we moved to Little Rock to take care of Mrs. Malvina, "Little Mammie," as the kids called her. Like so many before her she now rests in peace—the matriarch on Helen's side of two great families who came from Virginia through North Carolina, to Tennessee, to Keo, Arkansas.

But another memory flooded my mind that day too: my current situation. It weighed on me. I didn't like myself for thinking about it, especially right there in the middle of Mrs. Malvina's funeral, but I couldn't get it off my mind. The loss of my real estate business due to a lie and my own improvident mistake resulting in the death of a dream—another one of those broken dreams like Uncle Jim talked to me about all those years ago. I was angry at Charles Simon and at myself. The very thought of a new start again depressed me.

* * *

The family kept flourishing through our children. Carroll and Elaine had had their second daughter, Helen Susan, named for my sweetheart. Nicky and Jimmie Sue had their second, Rama Sue, named for me and her mama. And your mama, Laura Dean, had your brother, Ricky—Richard Warren, named after your father. He's such a good man, your daddy. He's become like another son to me. That same year Charles and Dolora had their first, Lila, and Boggie and J. C. had their first, your cousin Debbie. Time is marked so much by the kiddos. I could see that all the more as our sweet Kay Baby was growing up too fast.

I saw through them all that I had nothing truly *worth* complaining about. And seeing that through the lens of my festered anger made me feel even worse. How could I allow the most important things, the permanent things, to be overshadowed by scratching at a wound that needed to heal? The most important thing was still the most important thing—the family! I needed to get out of my stupor and find new ways to help take care of them.

Nicky was just getting his legs under him in his new construction business, so I suggested that he and Jimmie Sue and their two young'uns stay at the small house I'd moved up on I Street in the Heights. They stayed there for a while before getting their own place. After we sold Mrs. Malvina's place, we moved up there for a short while from down on State Street, so Toodles could finish high school at Central High, which she did in '55.

To get Helen and me by while Toodles and Kay Baby were still at home, I kept selling P&C insurance, using the license I'd renewed after the war. But to add a little, I started selling landscaping plants and materials to many of the corporate real estate contacts I had. But these meager efforts were unpredictable and just barely kept us afloat. I needed something steadier.

Then one day a thought crossed my mind while making a delivery of plant material out on US Route 70—the old Southwest Trail that held so many memories from our trip from Illinois to Texas. That fateful road, where at a particular bend, in Lonoke County, I was introduced to Charles Alexander. I drove past the old store where we first met. It was boarded up. Might it be possible?

As I drove on down the highway a bit, I looked across the fields of tall corn and white cotton on the north side and the towering cypress on the south—the scene took me back to when I was a boy. I slowed and pulled to a stop on the shoulder just next to the turn: that long straight tree-lined drive leading to the big old Alexander place where Lewis and Margaret Gaston and their daughter Mary Carolyn lived. Lewis had run the Alexander farm for many years by then. My mind was awash with thoughts as I turned and started down the white gravel road, listening to the crackles from the turning of the tires. I pulled to a stop in the circle in front of the big old antebellum home, got out, and walked up on the porch. A little hesitant, I gave a rap with the large knocker in the middle of the door. After a short delay, Lewis opened the door. We both stood silent for a second or two, then he began to speak excitedly.

"This can't be! Oh, my goodness, Claude Howell! Oh, it's so good to see you, Claude. My goodness. Margaret!" he yelled. We shook hands vigorously. "How've you been? Come in; how are you doing?"

It was the reception I'd hoped for. It was so good to see Lewis after such a long time.

"Let's go sit in my office and catch up."

We walked back to his office. The old, finished-oak plank floor creaked like old places do, and the slight noise echoed a bit in the ten-foot-wide main hall and twenty-foot-tall ceiling. The familiar sounds and the surroundings brought back more fond memories.

"Have a seat, Claude. Margaret!" he yelled again, "guess who's here. It's Claude Howell. Would you mind getting us some tea or something?"

Margaret came to the office door opening and stuck her head in, and when I stood up to greet her, she came over and gave me a great big hug.

"So good to see you, Claude. So good!"

"You too, really great to see you and Lewis."

"Sure, let me go get you some iced tea. I'll be right back," Margaret said.

"So, Claude, tell me what's going on. What brings you out this way?"

"Well, I was making a delivery of some plants and equipment to another old estate. They're doing some relandscaping, and I'm supplying them with some of the things they need."

"Is that what you're doing now, Claude, landscaping?"

"Well, yes, something like that. I'm selling various plant materials and equipment for landscaping, but I'm also selling property & casualty insurance too. Remember Mr. Price from Hot Springs? I'm an independent agent now. I renewed the insurance license I first got when I worked for him a long time ago when our store in Keo burned and we moved to Hot Springs."

"Yes, of course I remember that. So, have you been doing this for a long time now?"

"No, only for a short while. After the War, I had a chance to go back to school on the GI bill, and even went on to law school at Arkansas Law School."

"You're kidding? That's terrific. Really, Claude, that's terrific. So do you also practice law?"

"No," I said. "I never took the bar exam. I never intended to practice law. When I was going to school and after I got out in '51, I used the law degree to help me with my real estate business. That's what I was doing until last year."

Margaret came back in with the iced tea, along with their daughter, Mary Carolyn. I stood and said hello to her too.

"Great to see you, Mary Carolyn. I hope you're well."

"I am, Claude," she responded. "I got married back in '46 and have two children of my own now."

"Oh my, that's wonderful. I'm so happy for you—and for you, Lewis and Margaret. I know how wonderful it is to be a grandparent. Helen and I have six of our own now—but it's been a few minutes, I may have more and just don't know it yet."

We all laughed. "Great to see you," Margaret said again, as she and Mary Carolyn left the office.

"So, you're not doing real estate now?" Lewis asked.

"No, I'm afraid not. Not for a while, I'm afraid. I'm embarrassed to admit it but a large deal I did last year for AP&L, a good real estate deal, resulted in me getting caught up in an attempt by a business partner of mine to skirt the state real estate laws and take a commission when he didn't have a license. I got my own license suspended. I don't yet know how long. I didn't actually do anything wrong myself and certainly didn't intend to, but since the real estate deal was conducted under my broker's license, I bear the responsibility. It's my fault for not double-checking. But it's such an obvious thing I never thought to ask the fellow who didn't have his license. He should have said something early on, but it's my fault for not asking and verifying. I hate it, but that's the law and I have to bear the consequences. I'm confident I'll get it straightened out. I just don't know when."

"Wow, I'm so sorry to hear that, Claude. It sounds like things were going well for you only to have a major setback, once again, I sadly remember," Lewis said.

"Yes, but that's the way it is. I must live with it and find a way to pick up the pieces. In fact, that's what made me stop by. I drove by the old store, the one up the road where Charles worked so long ago, and noticed it was closed and boarded up. Any chance you'd like to open it up again? I mean, not that you'd like to, but would you be willing to let me get it back in shape and open it again? I think running the old store would allow me time to work things out with the state real estate commission, make a living, and have a place for Helen, me and our two youngest in the living quarters. It'd bridge me over for the next few years before I qualify for Mr. Roosevelt's Social Security. What do you think Lewis? Think such a wild idea might work for you?"

It took less time than when we stood staring at each other when he first opened the door for Lewis to say yes.

"Of course. Absolutely. Let's get to work on it," Lewis said. "It'll be like old times. Like when we first met in the old Keo Hotel and struck the deal to start the store there. You've always been a trustworthy stand-up fellow. I have full trust in you," he said.

"Now, Lewis," I said, "I'll be the one to fix the old place up and stock it and get it operational. I'm not asking you to do that. You understand? Your family has been so much help to us through the many years, and I don't want you to feel like I'm asking you to put me in business again."

"Yes, yes, I understand what you're saying. And I'm willing to go along with that. But our family has never given you a handout, only a hand-up.

This is no different. But if you need any help along the way, I want you to promise me you'll ask," Lewis said.

"Okay," I agreed.

Just like so many more times than I can count, in a flash I had a new way to start again. I don't know why. I never have understood why such fortuitous things happen at just the right time. But one thing I know for sure, good friends are worth their weight in gold.

When I drove back, I stopped at the old store and got out to look around. I looked at the place we camped that night back in '05. Where we got to know Charles when he ate supper with us. It was a great night. One I can never forget. It was a providential evening. One that'd led me back to Lewis fifty years later.

I thought about Uncle Jim and God's providence again. My Lord, how good is providence? Who can know the ways?

When I got home, I told Helen about the day and my conversation with Lewis. At first it was a shock to her. We talked about it, about moving again so soon, and going through another startup. I could see Helen was unsure. But we continued to talk about it.

Then I saw a change. I didn't grasp it then, but I later realized how much more insight Helen's wisdom had than mine. She saw it not only as a way to stabilize things, which we needed of course, but as a project for me to take my mind off losing my real estate business. Helen's so smart, and she loves me so much, even in ways I can't fully see until the effects of her love have worked their magic on me. What does Proverbs say about a good woman, that "her price is far above rubies"? That's certainly true with my sweetheart. We continued to talk about it, and she shifted away from whether we should do it to how it would work. To things like how to stock up with items that would sell in a plantation store, and how to space the things out to make a beginning inventory look like the store was full, even though we didn't have much to invest at first. She'd given some initial shape to my new dream, my new healing distraction.

It would be a lot of work, Helen agreed, but by then she was urging me on.

"Yes, let's do it, Claude," she said. "We can use the small inheritance Mama gave us to get started."

That's Mrs. Malvina, you see, Little Mammie. When she died, she still had that original old bungalow house on State Street she and Big Grancy bought when they moved into Little Rock. When we sold it, the small amount of money was distributed between the surviving families of her and Big Grancy's five kids, including one-fifth to Helen for her mama's share. It wasn't much, but it was enough to get us started.

"We can do it. We can!" Helen said with determination and excitement. We decided together it was for the best. So, we started making plans.

As it turned out Lewis decided to have two gasoline pumps added to the old store, which became a big attraction for motorists. I had a stand-up facia with a sign put on the main building above, displaying "Howell's Highway Grocery." And I had a big, huge Barq's Root Beer mural painted on the plank board side, to draw in patrons as they rounded the curve of the two-lane, black-topped highway—far different than the dirt one when we first came down. The store was a simple place, especially the living quarters, only about one thousand square feet. But when we got it all fixed up, we were very proud of that store.

I know you remember the store, Jimmy, where I gave you and your brother jobs to do. You, throwing down the sawdust-and-oil sweeping powder I made as I came behind you with a broom. And Ricky, the job of straightening can goods. Jobs required of you before I let you go out and play and explore the surroundings out in the country. It was a different kind of world than you boys knew in Dallas, and you liked it.

Reopening Charles Alexander's old store turned out to be a good project, and it made for a pretty good place to live and work for several years. It was hot in the summer, so we put four of those large flat black-colored buzz fans in the main store area, one high up in each corner, and two mounted in the residence, one in the back bedroom where Helen and I slept, and one in the other bedroom where Toodles and Kay Baby slept. We kept warm in the winter with cast-iron radiator heaters—one in each bedroom, one in the living room and bathroom, and three bigger ones in the store space. Even with that, we had no choice but to wear extra layers. It wasn't quite cozy, but it made for a good place to get started again.

We moved all our belongings into the small residence that ran length-wise on the east side, cut into two small bedrooms, a bath, a kitchen and a small living room—that's where we stored Mr. Price's old oak table and china cabinet in the corner because of limited space. The long side-room living space reminded me a bit of the similar one we stayed in after the fire at Grandfather Bill's old Carroll homestead cabin in Illinois.

Opening Day for the store was in late '55 just before Christmas. We lived and worked there for five years. Everything was thriving again.

Helen took Kay Baby back and forth to Little Rock so she could finish her third year of grade school there. The following year after we opened, Toodles moved into Little Rock and started to work at Camp Joseph T. Robinson, the successor of Camp Pike where I mustered for the Great War. Later that same year, Toodles met her beau, Mickey Fitzgibbon, who'd soon become her husband. Charles and Dolora moved into the I Street house for a short time before Charles got a job with the National Guard and moved to DeWitt.

Your mama and daddy brought you and Ricky for that Christmas of '56 and back again the following February for Toodles's and Mickey's wedding. J. D. and his wife Ruth brought Mama up for it and that began her six months in Arkansas, before Carmon and his wife Winnie came and took her back to El Campo—J. D. and Carmon and I traded bringing Mama back and forth from Texas and Arkansas, sometimes stopping at your house in Dallas, as you know.

Before the decade ended, all our kids except for Mary Kay were married. And they were all being fruitful and multiplying. Carroll and Elaine's third, Kathy, came along in '55. Charles and Dolora's second, Chris, came in '56 and their third, Gary, in '58. Your brother Bobby, and Boggie and J. C.'s second, Dana, in '57. And Toodles and Mickey's first, Vicki, rounded out the decade in '59. It was so wonderful when we all got together, seeing all you young'uns.

The Carroll-Howell clan, as Uncle Jim had called it, has been a prolific contributor to what people had started calling the post-war baby-boom generation. Late at night, Helen and I would laugh and place bets on who'd be next to deliver a new bundle of joy.

In those days the newspapers were filled with stories of the picket fence dreams of the millions of boys who came home from the war wanting a simple, stable life. Journalist Michael Dolan said Frank Capra captured that "postwar paean's most optimistic dream" in his 1946 *It's a Wonderful Life*. In so many ways that was the American dream. A simple quiet life. It was certainly what Helen and I wanted. I thought I had gotten it, then I lost it. At first, I was depressed about it. But just as Helen had imagined, with the store I found it again. Like Harry Bailey toasted to his older brother George in Capra's movie, I felt like the richest man in town.

But such wealth never seems to satisfy the ever-hovering bigger world. In truth, the international order never allows for stability. By the end of the 1950s the Cold War was in full swing and competition between the US and the Soviet Union took on a new dimension when they launched Sputnik in 1957, when the "space race" began. The range and character of the Cold War became manyfold and still is. But the greatest concern in the West is over communist expansion. I remember reading one of those portentous small news pieces in the paper the same year as Sputnik. It said, "South Vietnam's President Ngô Đình Diệm visited the United States and was acclaimed a 'miracle man' who had saved one-half of Vietnam from communism." No one had any idea then how things would develop. Most in America, if they even knew anything about it, saw this as a telltale sign of containment.

And while the docile picket-fence dream was real for some it was not for others. During the same time the Cold War was disrupting the world order, the American social and cultural order at home was also changing, and fast.

The 1954 Supreme Court decision in *Brown v. Board of Education of Topeka* forced the issue of public-school integration in the US. And it was hardest to swallow in Southern states where separate but equal was still the standard way of life. The implementation of Brown led to a Constitutional crisis in the 1957–58 school year, played out at Toodle's alma mater, Little Rock's Central High.

When this ruling came down, I remember thinking of my time in college and my law school days, when I studied both political philosophy and the law and when we all discussed such laws. And I remember thinking back to when Uncle John and I talked about how, because the founding fathers couldn't eliminate slavery at the beginning, it became much more difficult to do it later. I knew many in Arkansas couldn't stomach Brown. Most really, and many hated the prospect of school integration. It was a tumultuous time. I sure hoped it wouldn't lead to violence.

Then I read a story by Elizabeth Huckaby, who taught for twenty-eight years and was vice-principal for girls in 1957–58 at Central High School. About how "Initial plans for orderly integration were foiled when Governor Orville Faubus called out the National Guard to maintain segregation. And Eisenhower dispatched the 101st Airborne to get the Little Rock Nine into school." It was a Mexican stand-off, as they say. But I knew, and I think most everyone else knew who would win. But it was clear we'd have to go through the ordeal anyway. As expected, Eisenhower won. But just like after the Civil War, winning the peace was far harder, if less bloody. The country had to change.

That now infamous weekend, your uncle Charles came home for a visit from DeWitt, where he and Dolora lived. He wanted to talk about it—everybody was. The events in Little Rock were plastered on the news across the country, including on the new TV Nicky had just gotten Helen and me. We watched it together, as CBS news reporter Howard K. Smith reported from the steps of Central High.

"Little Rock waited through a tense weekend to see what would happen on Monday when classes resumed, and nine Negroes tried to enter Central High. The worst happened," Smith said.

"Encouraged by the stand taken by Governor Faubus, the anti-integration forces rioted outside the school. Some even enjoyed what they saw," Smith went on. Then he interviewed some of the protesters on the street.

"'Well, I just saw the cars as they was passing here and the rocks flying. I don't know who was throwing them, but some of them was hitting the new automobiles, hitting people. Everybody was having a good time,'" a man said into Smith's microphone.

"'We destroyed about seven new car windshields and busted windows and everything, hitting niggers on the heads with sticks,'" a boy said.

"'Everybody was hitting niggers with rocks,'" another boy said.

"The prejudices and fears of the parents were transmitted to the children," Smith reported.

"'I'm not going to school as long as they—the niggers go to white schools. 'Cause the niggers, when they go, they might have some dangerous weapons put on them,'" another boy says.

It was hard to watch and hear what became a violent riot. Reflecting back on that day, Walter Cronkite said, "Images like these ended all rational debate about race in the United States. Moderates seemed to vanish, and zealots became the symbols of Southern resistance."

As Charles and I watched the TV in the small residence of the store, he asked my thoughts on it all.

"Faubus is a fool," I quickly told Charles. "He's nothing but a politician. He's never considered the idea seriously having grown up in Madison County, where I'm pretty sure not one black man lives. There's no matter of principle at stake for him on this. Obviously, for many in Arkansas it's a good political position to take—you can probably get reelected by his stance.

"I mean, no one's so naive to think this'll be easy, though in the long run I think it's probably the best thing for the country. But the Supreme Court has ruled. And Faubus is wrong."

Charles nodded in agreement. He didn't think much of Faubus either, but he was still young and hadn't fully formed his own opinions on a lot of things. He asked, "Daddy, how did your views on this and the matter of negroes and whites in general come about?"

"Well, Charles, in my experience," I told him, "all my life whites and blacks have lived largely separate but parallel lives. But we've always easily and comfortably done commerce together and lived without conflict, except when laws are broken and mischief and crime are perpetrated—then the law holds us all accountable whether white or black or any other color, as it should. Though I admit, the law hasn't always been written or applied fairly between whites and blacks like it should be—like in the Plessy case which Brown overturned—and that's wrong.

"I've always known life this way and have always been taught that all human beings are created in God's image and are equal in that way because God made it so. I learned this from my Uncle Jim back in Illinois. And I remember Uncle John telling me about how old William Wilberforce in England used this principle and his Christian faith to eliminate slavery there. Wilberforce was a young politician when he met Mr. John Newton, a former slave-trader in England who was converted to Christ—he's the fellow who wrote the great old hymn, 'Amazing Grace.' Anyway, Newton's faith so influenced Wilberforce that he set about to end slavery in England, and eventually succeeded three days before he died. And Wilberforce's pursuit influenced the US Congress to outlaw bringing new slaves into this country in 1807. This is how principle and politics should work for the good. Not the way Faubus is doing things."

"That sounds right Daddy. But it also sounds hard, and hard to get people to live that way," Charles said.

"Yes, son. It is. But it has a lot to do with how you grow up, what your experience is. I've always known blacks and whites could live together, ever since I was a boy from my friendship with my negro friend, Sally. Her great grandparents came to Illinois after they were freed by their slave owner in Virginia and given resources to come and live there and work and get an education. They'd been in Illinois almost as long as my great grandfather by the time Sally and I came along. We saw each other often and played together when we were kids and were good friends. When you're a kid you just don't think about differences like when you get older.

"That's just what I've always known. It's also what I knew in Toltec, and you did too, where the vast majority of our customers at the old gin and store were black sharecroppers who'd bought land with the government's help. And here too, at this store.

"But I also knew by experience that whites and blacks in this country didn't seem naturally to live together or in completely the same way—there are cultural differences. This, to my mind, is not bad, just different.

"I think old Abe Lincoln was probably right when in his first debate with Mr. Stephen Douglas, he said there are real differences between blacks and whites, so much so that they will probably never live together in perfect equality, but we all share in the right to life, liberty, and the pursuit of happiness. That's what Mr. Lincoln said, and I think he's probably right.

"My point, Charles, is that the laws of the land should reflect the principle embodied in the Declaration. Whether that means everybody lives together in the same way, that's a different question it seems to me. That's the point Mr. Lincoln was making about social equality when he said, 'it becomes a necessity that there must be a difference.' I'm not sure if that's the right way to look at it. The times are changing right now and maybe I need to change too, but change doesn't come so easy for me . . . I expect not for anyone. But that's what I believe."

"So, what about school integration?" Charles asked. "What do you think about that?"

"Well, that's where Faubus is flat wrong. This is a country of laws. Yes, there are state laws and federal laws. But when they conflict, the US Supreme Court decides. That's the final say. The Court can change its mind and that happens. That's what the Brown decision shows. With that decision, the Jim Crow laws came to an end. With it the question of separate but equal schools has been ruled on. It's the law of the land. No governor has the right to defy that law on his own. If he disagrees with it, he must go through the Congress or the court process as with all other disputes. That's how the US system works. Faubus is wrong, Eisenhower is right. Faubus must get out of the way.

"As for the rest of society," I told Charles, "we have no choice but to figure out how to live within the law, even if it's strange to us. And this one will be for a long time, I expect.

"Son, that's where I expect old President Teddy Roosevelt's principle might be right," I told your Uncle Charles that day. "'Wise progressivism and wise conservatism go hand in hand.' Change is hard and I admit I don't accept it easily. But I accept the US system of laws. Even at that, though, as my Uncle Jim and old Charles Carroll of Carrollton would say, there is a foundation on which the laws we write sit, a deeper law, the law of virtue and religion. I accept that law first even before the US system of laws. We would be better off if we recognize this when writing our laws."

Charles and I had a glass of tea and just sat and talked about his kids for a while. That old back room at the store had become a special place.

Those five years in the store were surprisingly good, in every way. Much better than I'd ever expected, and in more ways than I expected. I loved it when Helen and I looked at each other across the span of the room and smiled like the old days. By 1960, she said she could tell I was relaxed, even despite my political rants about Governor Faubus from time to time.

I've thought about it a lot. There was something about that old store. Where it was located, there on the old Southwest Trail. Howell's Highway Grocery had become more than a waystation, more than a place to start over for me. It had roots—roots not found just in that store but that reached back to the others and to the ups and down in between. It became a prism to me, a refracting looking glass through which I could see the beautiful colors that made up my whole life. Those that captured the memories I recalled so fondly after Mrs. Malvina's funeral. It did give us a place to start over again, but the project of the store and running it also worked as a kind of salve on my anger, which I desperately needed at the time, and I guess I'd needed for a long time. I learned to let go and know the fresh feelings that come from that. Helen somehow knew all along it would happen but like for most men, it took several years to dawn on me. And the simplicity of life at the store helped me see that it was truly that picket-fence life so many came home from the war looking for. And our plantation patrons and our neighbors, the Tillmans, in the shanty beyond the pond behind the store—you remember Mrs. Tillman who taught you and Ricky to fish with a cane pole and bob—well they reminded me that if we'll live out the virtues of the good old Samaritan, the boundaries that divide us crumble, even if we never live together in the exact same way.

I think even Mary Kay found that store a pretty good place too. She became good friends with Mrs. Tillman's daughters and especially Mary Carolyn's daughter who was close to her age. But when she turned fourteen and soon headed into high school wanting her wider group of friends and things to do after school, I thought it might be time for a change. My baby girl was growing up.

I turned sixty-five in 1960 and began to think about moving back in the city.

"These have been good years, sweetheart. Don't you think?" I asked Helen. "Stable ones too, a good thing, don't you think?"

"They have been, Claude, they really have," she said.

"The store has been a good living, a simple one but a good one," I said. "I've enjoyed serving the Alexander-Gaston farm and the many surrounding sharecroppers and small farmers like we did in Toltec."

"Yes, it's been more than we'd first thought. It's helped you, too, Claude. You know it, don't you?" she asked.

"I do, honey. I really do. You were right all along as you always are. But I'm thinking it's time for a change. Do you?" I asked Helen. "We can start drawing Social Security now. None of the kids are staying up on I Street any longer. Maybe we should go up there and make ourselves a new home. I can continue to work doing small jobs buying and selling, and if I want, I could even look into real estate again since I have my license back. Coupled with Social Security it should make life comfortable for retirement. What do you think? Do you think it might be time for another move?"

"I do," Helen said.

We started making plans.

Twenty-Six—I Street, a Settled Place in Unsettled Times

Winter of 1960 to June of 1966

Two men from Nicky's construction crew maneuvered the new chair into the house. The chair the boys bought for Helen. They sat it to the left near the back wall in the small living room, just out from the stand-up piano. Then they took in the Price's old oak table and curved-glass china cabinet and put them in the compact dining room. I watched as the movers stepped down the stone pavers that led to the front door—Nicky's mason crew had put them in while he and Jimmie Sue had lived there. The stones made me think of important and permanent things.

Memories had become my most constant habit of late. I stood up on the gray gravel road looking down at our little house in the quiet hamlet of the Heights—what most folks by then were calling Hillcrest, just over the hill from the grand mansions of Pulaski Heights. I thought about the first time we came through Little Rock. About how Mr. A. F. Auten from Chicago bought the whole high-hilled section that very same year back in '05; and developed it and named it for the old Polish calvary officer Casmir Pulaski—who saved General Washington at the battle of Battle of Brandywine. God, what a connection. That year we looked up at the hills from the flats below, where we camped on our way to Texarkana. Then I thought of how I got that little house from the AP&L deal, and how promising things looked at first, only to go awry, leaving me in a stupor and so angry. And how that led Helen and me back to Lewis Gaston and the store for the last five years, what turned out to be a necessary therapeutic that allowed me to let go of my anger, and truly rest. There I stood in front of our little oasis at 3412 I Street.

I've come to see that in all the seemingly random lines of life, there's a picture. It's true for all of us, I think. But for whatever reason you can only see it as a picture when looking back. For some folks seeing a picture is really hard—or seeing any beauty in it can be too painful because life is so damned cripplingly sad. But I think it's still there. Not to diminish anyone's difficulties, and I've had my share, you just never know for sure. Even through the darkest thicket some light gets in. I didn't understand it when Mama read from Uncle Jim's diary so long ago, but I do now. As Great Grandfather Carroll told him, we're always journeying through a bigger story. I can only say, despite my ups and downs, I'm satisfied with my painting.

What a mystery? God only knows. Does he turn bad things into good like an alchemist? I'm not sure. I only know he has for me. Our little house on I Street is a stone-solid marker of it.

How amazing life is. How amazing the journey.

As we settled into our little house in the Heights, I had hopes that the bigger story of the world around us would also settle down. But I didn't yet know. No one did.

* * *

We met Carmon and Winnie in Dallas to pick up Mama and bring her home to Little Rock after Thanksgiving that year. We had only a small celebration with Mama on her actual ninetieth birthday, December 11. Just Helen and me. But it was a big party when all the kids and you grandkids came home that Christmas of 1960. We made a big fuss over her, and she was so excited—a great time of festivities, food, and of course desserts, Mama's favorite part.

Beaming like a little girl again, Mama was happy. It brought back so many good memories of her telling funny stories and laughing. I was so happy for her. With everyone there, it was the perfect christening of our new home.

That first year of the new decade showed real promise, though warning signs never seemed too far away.

I kept my habit of reading the paper and watching the news on TV to stay abreast of the bigger goings-on in Arkansas, America, and the wider world. With less work to do and less need for it with Social Security, I spent more time reflecting deeply on events and happenings.

There was no "hot war" as people called it. That was a good thing. But the Cold War, as Walter Lippmann popularly referred to it, was raging and that concerned me. Who's to say what that might bring—the advancement and expansion of nuclear weapons was a daunting thought.

On January 20 of '61 President Kennedy took office. I'd voted for Nixon, but we got Kennedy. He was an eloquent fellow, who'd grown up in New England, not too far from where Little Mammie had gone to school in upstate New York. I liked what Mr. Kennedy said at the inauguration: "Ask not what your country can do for you—Ask what you can do for your country." *That's a good way of thinking, a very good one*, I thought; we'd have to see how things go for the new president. I hoped well.

The relative tranquility of the '50s seemed to have carried over into the new decade. It sure had for our family. With no crisis demanding it, I'd now go shopping at the farmer's market just for fun—where I'd find good deals and do a little reselling and bring the rest home to distribute to the kids. They were all doing well, and we heard from them often even though spread out—Carroll and Elaine were in Wichita Falls. Laura Dean and Warren were in Dallas with you boys, and Boggie and J. C. were just west over in Fort Worth. Nicky and Jimmie Sue and Toodles and Mickey lived nearby in Little Rock. And Charles and Dolora lived just across the river in North Little Rock, a stone's throw from where I did basic training for WWI. At fifteen, Kay Baby was happy and thriving in high school and had her own room with us for the first time ever. She was growing up so fast—she'd even found her a beau, Ken Polk, a star football player at Hall High.

All my babies were grown up, or almost. It was hard to believe, especially since Helen and I started all over again after I got home from the War. Time keeps moving and the family keeps expanding—that year in April, Toodles and Mickey had their second, Terri Kay.

There've been many times I thought should just stop reading the newspaper. But the more I read and listened to the news then, the more I knew the relative tranquility and promise of the 1950s hadn't carried over to the '60s. Certainly not in the Cold War and Russia's communist expansion. And there were growing signs that the core of American culture was losing its way. The surface sense of peace and calm after the war masked simmering problems below. And simmering problems are never a good thing, I'd learned long ago. It's been confirmed too many times. And you can't predict when simmering problems will erupt into volcanic explosions.

It didn't take long for the Cold War risk to arise. It came terrifyingly close to becoming a hot one—one that with nuclear weapons would have fulfilled old Woodrow Wilson's war to end all wars in the worst way. Kennedy's '61 "Bay of Pigs" CIA operation was a debacle. He'd sought to topple the communist revolutionary, Fidel Castro, in Cuba under the radar. But the best laid plans, as they say. Well, they went awry. And shortly after, in '62, there followed the almost certain launch of WWIII during those 13 Days of October. A crisis created by the Soviet communists when they installed nuclear warhead missiles in Cuba, just ninety miles from Florida. The US could not allow it. It would not be allowed, the Kennedy brothers said.

By Gawd they'd better not, I said to myself, the same sentiment old James Cobb expressed to Governor Blough about progressivism and social-ist communism on the porch in Keo that day before WWI. I remember him saying, "Well I'll tell you what governor, your progressivism and that of Mr. Wilson best not move Arkansas and this country in that direction, or you will have a revolt on your hands." *Precisely!* I thought. The Soviets had been pursuing and supporting the spread of totalitarian communism for a long time, especially since the end of WWII. After Castro ousted Batista in '58, he made way for Russian missiles in our own backyard. They were provoking an American response and pressed to see if it would come. Fortunately, it did, and with sufficient fortitude they finally backed down. You can't pussy-foot around with that kind of thing, as England's Chamberlain and France had learned with Hitler. I didn't want another war by any means; no one did. Who in their right mind would? But you can't be too careful with the communists. I wondered if Russia would have ever stepped foot in Cuba if Truman had let MacArthur cross the Yellow River back in '51. Who knows?

The decade that'd started out in a quiet picket-fence way, quickly be-came riddled with risk.

The same year as the Cuban missile crisis, I began to worry about dif-ferent risks. Not about war but risks afoot *inside* America, affecting the way we live and what we believe, born of advancing technology—it reminded me of the theme of technology at the St. Louis World's Fair back in '04. While it's brought us so many good things, ever since Truman dropped the atomic bombs on Hiroshima and Nagasaki, a necessary evil I still believe, I'd begun to worry about the unintended consequences of technology advance-ments. The Cold War confirmed that. But with what I'd recently read, much subtler supposed "advancements" were changing the world in less obvious but maybe more profound ways. In '62 one of those small back-page pieces I read was about "progress" on birth control—what the papers called simply "The Pill." That technical advancement began to change how we live in a fundamental way. On the surface it seems like an advancement or just in-nocuous. But to me, it's like letting the genie out of the bottle—and once out, you can't get it back in again.

Don't misunderstand me, son. I'm fond of sex. It's the most natural thing. It gave me and Helen our seven wonderful babies and now an ever-growing number of grandbabies, including you, you see. But I've read about how you kids in college these days talk about "free love," as if there's no brackets around it, no responsibility. This new so-called advancement separates sex from procreation and procreation from marriage. It allows it to be a mere recreational activity. It worries me. Especially for the way young people live. You understand? Self-control has never been easy, especially self-restraint. They're hard virtues to practice for everybody. But with a "birth control pill," all the natural supports for sexual self-restraint are gone. That's a high-cost proposition. I've thought so ever since I read about it. And look at where we are now.

The culture is changing fast these days, son. And not in a good way, it seems to me.

That same year I read about another so-called "advancement." It wasn't about technology but was a supposed advancement in wisdom. The Supreme Court ruled out school-sponsored prayer in all public schools. *Advancement? Really?* I mean, I agree with the founders that America shouldn't have an established religion. And I'm no preacher like Brother Crutchfield was—I'm not even a regular churchgoer too much these days—but I still see the world the way Grandfather Bill and Uncle Jim did. God is always with us, woven in and through the fabric of our lives. How could he not be? How harmful is it to students to urge them to acknowledge that? Seems to me the harm is *not* to urge them to do so. I'm worried we're working tooth and nail to remove God from life altogether. As if we could.

I've thought about how it's one thing to be pushed into a battle by an outside foe, like the Nazis and the Communists. But it's another thing altogether to corrode from the inside out. I'm afraid I see signs we might be headed that way. At least that's how I see it.

But as it had so many times before for Helen and me, right in the middle of the renewed fears of war and the dramatic social change afoot, in our little world we got two new signs of life the following year. Toodles and Mickey's Stacy came along in April of 1963. And barely three months later, Charles and Dolora's sweet little Judy was born in July. These two miracles, as they all certainly are, seemed to right the scales, at least for the moment.

But the moment didn't last long. Not four months later all hell broke loose. I was out buying and selling produce when just after lunch, at 12:30 on November 22 of '63, I heard a CBS news bulletin come on the car radio. Walter Cronkite reported: "In Dallas, Texas three shots were fired at President Kennedy's motorcade in downtown Dallas. There has been an attempt, as you probably know now, on the life of President Kennedy. He was wounded in an automobile driving from the airport into downtown Dallas along with Governor Connelly of Texas. They've been taken to Parkland Hospital there, where their condition is as yet unknown." It continued, "We have just learned that Father Huber, one of the two priests called into the room, has administered the last sacrament of the church to President Kennedy." And after a short pause, Cronkite continued. "From Dallas, Texas, the flash, apparently official, President Kennedy died at 1:00 p.m. Central Standard Time."

Oh, my God! My mind at once went to Laura Dean and Warren and you boys in Dallas. But then to a bigger world concern. Will this be the trigger for another World War, like the assassination of Archduke Franz Ferdinand by that Serbian nationalist back in 1914? Those damned Communists bastards. I was sure it was them, payback for Cuba? Oh, my God! I rushed home to be with Helen.

By the time I got there, there'd been news of an arrest. A man named Lee Harvey Oswald. Initially arrested for killing a cop in Dallas and later for killing Kennedy. Early the next morning, he was arraigned for the assassination of the president. And beyond all belief, the next day, on November 24, when being transferred to a more secure jail in Dallas, Oswald was shot and killed!

The world had gone mad, I thought. Everyone I talked to thought so.

Only one day later, on November 25 church bells tolled before what the TV called the Requiem Mass at St. Matthew's Cathedral in Washington, DC. The president, a navy man who'd fought in the Pacific like Carroll and me, was buried at Arlington National Cemetery in Virginia.

For a month, and much longer for most, America was in shock and a long and dreary period of national mourning. Regardless of who you voted for, Mr. Kennedy was our president.

The country was on edge. So much had happened in just three years. It was a tenuous time. It all weighed so heavy on my mind.

* * *

Christmas was subdued that year. But it was still bright for us with our two newest ornaments, Stacy and Judy, and an old one, Mama, who was doing great at ninety-three.

We took Mama back to Texas in January of '64—and when your mom called to check on us when we got back to Little Rock, we got a momentary lighthearted respite from the times.

Laura Dean had just received a letter and card from Mama wishing her happy birthday—Mama's always been good about the kid's birthdays. Her letter began on a sad note. Mama had learned her cousin Juno Evans in California died just before Christmas. Hearing that sure made me think about Uncle Jim. But as Laura Dean read the letter to Helen and me, she saw something funny in it.

> You know, honey, at 93 I'm the oldest member of the Carroll Family now—dating back to my Grandfather Raford & Grandmother Sarah Carroll. Not too many of the old cousins left. Just from Uncle Andy Carroll's family—he was Ella Hammond's father, you see. I just mailed a card to Ella's brother George. He is about 76 years of age & Reesie tells me he is almost deaf and real feeble. So maybe I had better not complain too much.

"Mama," Laura Dean asked Helen, "what do you think about her not complaining too much? She never complains."

Helen and I chuckled. Then Helen told Dean a cute story about Mama,

"No, she never does complain, Laura Dean. Never. But she certainly intimates what she wants. This is how subtle she is. One night when we were washing clothes just before we took her back to El Campo, rather than just saying, 'Helen, would you mind washing this handkerchief?' she says, 'Do you think you might have room in there for my handkerchief?' Now, really, Laura Dean, do you think a single lace handkerchief was going to tip the washer over?"

We all laughed. We needed it—even if at the expense of one of Mama's funny endearing habits. Who doesn't have them? The times seemed to make laughing even more important.

But all the lightheartedness ended abruptly a day later when Mickey called . . . a deep dark shadow descended over our world. Mickey and Toodles's precious little Stacy had been rushed to the hospital with a severe illness. Then not long after, came the most devastating news since Rachel. Despite the doctors' desperate efforts to stabilize Stacy's little body, she was gone. The little one who'd so brightened the world just the prior April died suddenly on January twenty-sixth at only nine months old. It was earth-shattering, heaven-shattering. No words. "How could the world go on?" I could hear Toodles and Mickey saying to themselves. "How? The world must stop, it has stopped. Why?"

Our hearts broke for our sweet Nona and for Mickey, as we quickly headed to the hospital. My mind went to that terrible day so many years before. But this time, my own little girl's heart was breaking for her little girl, and that broke mine even more. I knew the pain would not go away; it couldn't. I knew that somehow some way, over a long, long time, they would only find a new way to live again, that we all would. I just hoped they could do what Papa couldn't. Just as we entered the hospital, from the entrance we saw Nona sitting in one of those cold chairs in the hospital waiting room, Mickey standing next to her with his large hand softly caressing her tilted head. I felt the same feelings I had before as we walked the distance to be with them. I just wanted to hold my little girl as she mourned her little girl.

As I recall this, I can hardly even keep telling you my story. The whole family came to Little Rock for little Stacy's funeral. It was heartbreaking, just as it was with Rachel.

All too sadly the world doesn't stop at such losses, as it seems it should. It never does. The tragedies of life force us to face them, even in the throes of inconsolable grief. Or crawl up in a ball like Papa'd done, and that's a double tragedy. Helen and I always prayed for our kids—more and more constantly for Toodles and Mickey then and for their other little ones. They are only now beginning to feel life again, and as it always goes, they have good days and bad. Grief is a heavy burden—I can't imagine how heavy it would be to lose one of my babies. Only by God's grace can we go on.

* * *

Too often when we awake from the stupor of grief, we face new dangers. And later that year I read about one. A news item in the August 3 *Arkansas Democrat-Gazette*—not on the front page but not completely buried in the back pages. It told of an attack on a US warship in the Gulf of Tonkin in Southeast Asia. I looked it up and saw it was north and east of where I was at the battle of Samar in WWII, about the same distance from there as it is between Little Rock and New York City. The article described how the US had been in the waters off Viet Nam since 1954 monitoring and offering intelligence gathering to contain communist expansion—pursuing the Truman Doctrine, it said. Multiple incidents had occurred in the past, but they had been escalating a lot of late. Unprovoked, "the USS Maddox came under attack by three Democratic Republic of Vietnam (DRV) patrol boats," the small article said.

I could see where this was leading. The day after I read about it in the newspaper, it became clear what it meant. And as expected, on August 4, President Lyndon Johnson came on national television to tell the American people more about it and the US response—see here, the paper printed it on August 5. He says in part, "My fellow Americans,

> as President and Commander and Chief it is my duty to the American people to report that renewed hostile actions against United States ships on the high seas in the Gulf of Tonkin have today required me to order the military forces of the United

States to take action in reply. The initial attack on the destroyer Maddox on August 2 was repeated today by a number of hostile vessels attacking two US destroyers with torpedoes. . . .

But repeated acts of violence against the armed forces of the United States must be met not only with alert defense but with positive reply. That reply is being given as I speak to you tonight. . . .

I have instructed Ambassador Stephenson to raise this matter immediately and urgently before the Security Council of the United Nations. Finally, I have today met with the leaders of both parties in the Congress of the United States. And I have informed them that I shall immediately request the Congress to pass a resolution making it clear that our government is united in its determination to take all necessary measures in support of freedom and in defense of peace in Southeast Asia. . . .

It is a solemn responsibility to have to order even limited military action by forces whose overall strength is as vast and as awesome as those of the United States of America. But it is my considered conviction, shared throughout your government, that firmness in the right is indispensable today for peace. That firmness will always be measured. Its mission is peace.

After serving out Kennedy's remaining term, with this response and running as the "peace candidate," Johnson won the election of 1964.

Despite saying he was the peace candidate, the paper reported "in the month of the election, the Viet Nam War was escalating day by day." It sounded a lot like Wilson all over again.

Considering the events of '62 and '63, while reading and listening to the news of Viet Nam in '64, I wondered if it would become a powder keg of global war like 1917 and 1941 had been. I prayed not.

Amid the terrible grief-ridden and increasingly uncertain times of '64, life moved forward, and new light dawned for our family.

In June Kay Baby and Ken both graduated from Hall High School, and Ken got a football scholarship to the University of Arkansas—that reminded me of my brother Bill. All my kids were out of school and grown up now. That August we got another new light of joy when Charles and Dolora's fifth, Jana, came along. Ever since Helen and I married in '22, even in the midst of the brokenness of the world, new life kept renewing our hopes.

That same summer, a new kind of day dawned for many, something so many had so longed for. With Congress's passage of the Civil Rights Act, the American dream heralded in the Declaration that Mr. Lincoln had talked so much about, moved closer to a reality for all. Like most things in politics, not everybody liked it. But it was the right thing to do.

As we went into '65 things looked promising again. But just about every time I found signs of hope to grab and hold onto, some new and crazier thing happened. In October of that year I saw something in *Time Magazine* that really took the cake—it convinced me the decade of the '60s was driving off a cliff. It simply relishes chaos over calm. The article was investigating what it called "a trend among 1960s theologians to write God out of the field of theology." I literally scratched my head. What, *theologians* are writing God off? That makes no sense at all. Brother Crutchfield is surely rolling over in his grave. What's the point? Some weird theologians have swallowed the strangest of all "progressive" pills. How is theology without God a form of advancement? Progressing, moving forward, advancing has lost all meaning. In fact, I thought, without God how do you know if you're moving forward or backward? Without God what does advancement even mean except raw movement, change as such? What does "forward" and "backward" even mean if there's no purpose, no good, no end toward which we reach? What about truth? It's just crazy!

I cringed every time I picked up the paper or a magazine, and turned to the news on the radio. Protests were everywhere, especially on college campuses. The culture is going crazy, it seems.

Once again though, as had so often happened for Helen and me, at Christmas that year a pleasant surprise pulled me out of my stupor. Kay Baby and Ken announced they were engaged. Their wedding would be the following June. A big affair that everyone in the family said they'd attend—at the church for the wedding and up at 3412 I Street for a big celebration.

My excitement remained high despite confronting a follow-up *Time* piece the following April in '66, asking, in huge red block letters set appropriately on a black background, "Is God Dead?" It attributed the crazy notion to Hitler's old friend Nietzsche. I thought to myself, it's strange how ivory towers can make otherwise smart people go crazy. I wondered how many of those so-called radical theologians have ever lived in the trenches of the real world or gone to war. There, such lofty absurdities don't last long.

So far as I know, in our small circle of the world, no one has yet given up on God. Which is not to say with no doubts—most everyone has doubts, especially in dark times. But the way I see it, that's when God simply carries us. He's never given up on our family, I'm sure of that! The shores of our family still seem strong even as the crazy storms of these times beat against them.

Despite the vertigo of cultural chaos and of war, I still see and feel the stability of our home—our family. I'm confident we can weather the storm.

What I've come to see in my years, such as they are, is that this world is a broken place, a dangerous place, full of sound and fury, and always treacherous, as if standing on a precipice. But at the same time, it's a beautiful place, so rich with new possibilities every morning, even after the unimaginable tragedies and misfortunes of life. When I was a boy so many years ago, I had the nascent hopes and dreams of most kids then: to follow in Papa's footsteps and have the settled life he and Mama seemed to have. But life didn't turn out that way. The tragic fire in Illinois set us all on a different path. It took us to Texas and through a series of so many other moves and events. But in the end, it brought me to this little house on this small piece of land. I got that dream of a settled life, just not as I'd imagined as a boy. I've gotten so much more . . . of the truly important and permanent things, those essentials that are necessary to make it through the harder times.

The thread of faith and family weaves the rope that holds things together. I'm sure that's what Uncle Jim meant all those years ago, urging me to remember where I come from and to make the virtues that were passed down to me, my own; and in turn to pass them along to my own family. In a strange way, I think that might be part of why I couldn't resist buying that big thick rope that I hung in the tree just up the street for the bag swing, so maybe just by swinging on it, you kids would realize how important the thick strong binds of faith and family really are.

Kay Baby and Ken tied the knot in June and made the bonds even stronger. Their wedding was wonderful. It was so great to have everyone home.

Because everyone came to the wedding, I knew most wouldn't make it back for Thanksgiving and Christmas later that year.

I knew the next big gathering would have to wait until the following spring, at Easter.

Twenty-Seven—The End and the Beginning

January to Easter of 1967

After Christmas, in late January of '67 we drove to Texarkana to meet Carmon and Winnie to pick up Mama. While there, we drove out to visit Rachel's grave. Mama moves cautiously now, having just turned ninety-six. I walked her over slowly so she wouldn't fall. The cemetery was kept up pretty well. She stooped down and put the small bouquet we got on the simple gravestone. It reminded me of when she stooped down to pick up her mother's broken china in the charred remnants of our home back in Illinois after the fire. Just like back then, I saw tears fall from her eyes. This time, though, not for broken china but for her little girl. My little sister. After visiting Rachel's grave, we said goodbye to Carmon and Winnie, and told them we looked forward to seeing them at Easter.

They did make it back and everyone else did too. It was a great Easter weekend.

"You remember Easter, don't you Jimmy?"

With a big grin on my face I responded, "Of course, Daddy Claude. How could I not? That's how all this started."

"The house was bustling, and Mama was resting back in our room, you remember?"

"I do, Daddy Claude. It was so crowded. It was such a great and unexpected day."

You almost delayed lunch. I remember because I went through the hall and Kay Baby's old room, then stopped to see how Helen was doing and asked if everyone was there. She said, "Most everyone. We're just waiting on Jimbo. Laura Dean said he should be here soon."

269

I'd been cooking all morning and the ham was just about ready to slice. I heard the door open and saw you come in. I stepped out of the kitchen, and tapped Charles and told him to go get Mama. Charles came through the doorway from the bedroom with Mama, just as I sat the ham on the table. You and your brothers stood next to her. I called everyone to attention and said the blessing. We had a feast.

After dessert, those who lived in Little Rock filtered out and things quieted down. Then I heard Warren back in our bedroom, and remembered he wanted to talk to Mama about the past. I stuck my head in and noticed you stretched out on the floor beside the bed as Mama and your dad talked and he recorded her on the tape machine he'd brought. I listened for a few minutes, and it brought back so many memories.

After quite a while, when I was back in the kitchen, I heard Helen begin to play "*Clair de Lune*" on the piano—I was taken back to the first time I heard her play it that night after supper at the Crutchfields, in the living room of that beautiful old house nestled in the pecan grove in Keo.

Those family's stories and that beautiful melody capture my whole life in a way.

Carmon and Winnie came by the next morning for a last visit before heading home to Houston. I saw them off and told them we looked forward to seeing them again on the Fourth, when they'd come back to get Mama and take her back to El Campo.

* * *

Fourth of July Weekend 1967—Where the Saga Began

"Hi, Daddy Claude," I said as I pulled up in front of Uncle Charles's place.

"Hello, Jimbo," he said working on something on the side of the house. "Good trip?"

"Yes, sir," I said as I grabbed my bag and books out of the front of the Volkswagen.

It was Independence Day weekend, and I was out of school for the summer. Some of my college mates had urged me, as they had earlier last spring, to go with them back to San Francisco, to Haight Ashbury for "The Summer of Love." But I didn't go. As I did at Easter, I went back to Arkansas to be with my family. This time to Uncle Charles's lake house a short drive out from Hot Springs on Lake Hamilton—a man-made reservoir drawing from the Ouachita River, built by Arkansas Power & Light Company to make power for the state.

It's a truly beautiful spot, about four acres on a quiet cove that looks out across placid waters to the busy main channel. A small island densely forested with hundred-foot-tall grand Arkansas pines and hickory trees protects the cove from the winds across that channel. Making a smooth place for newbies to learn to water ski on a calm, glassy surface, as I had years before.

Uncle Charles had worn himself out driving the boat over the weekend for all of us grandchildren. We exhausted ourselves on water-skis and inner-tubes from the early morning to midday.

Late Tuesday morning on the actual Fourth of July, Uncle Nicky and Uncle Carroll took over boat duty from Uncle Charles, allowing him to get things ready for lunch.

On the big screened-in porch I set up the reel-to-reel recorder, the same one my dad used to record Mama Howell in Little Rock at Easter. I looked forward to hearing Daddy Claude continue the stories Mama Howell started. To hear him talk about his life growing up in Illinois, going to Texas, and coming to Arkansas.

He helped Mama Helen out on the porch. I walked over and kissed her on the cheek and helped situate her in the chair next to the one Daddy Claude would sit in, next to Uncle Jim's old trunk. She said, "Hi, Jimbo, where are your brothers?" I told her I thought they were down skiing or tubing.

Carmon and my dad helped Mama Howell out. There they sat, Daddy Claude, Mama Helen, and Mama Howell in three big wicker chairs on the comfortable cushions. My mom, Lauradean as they all called her, and her sisters brought all kinds of food and drinks out and put them on the long tables draped with Independence Day paper tablecloths. They worked together like a symphony, all playing their parts with different instruments, chattering constantly all along the way. It was fun to watch.

Uncle Charles called the rest up from down at the dock. It was time for lunch. They came running, and the youngest, wettest ones wiggled and dripped and slopped lake water on the floor as their parents grabbed them and wiped them with towels. Since this was Uncle Charles's place, he returned thanks. "Not quite as short as Daddy Claude's blessing and nowhere near as long or as loud as Big Grancy's," my mom said, referring to Brother Crutchfield. Everyone chowed down. It was a great meal of Fourth of July fare: hamburgers, hotdogs, chips and Cokes, and plentiful desserts to cap it off.

Many of the kids were quickly back down at the dock, supervised by the older cousins. For the rest, the conversations became languid on the porch. After a short time, the parents called the young kids up and things settled down—naptime for many after a hard day of fun and festivities.

Daddy Claude helped Mama Howell back inside the lake house to rest, too. When he returned, he stopped just outside the door onto the big porch. He looked across at Mama Helen and smiled. I glanced at her in her chair and saw her smile back at him. Daddy Claude walked over and helped her up—her rheumatoid arthritis was so bad now she had to sit most of the time. It'd been getting progressively worse for years, especially since they reopened Howell's Highway Grocery. Now Daddy Claude did almost everything, to relieve her from the pain of standing for very long. He kissed her and helped her inside, and came back out again.

Silently, he stood and stared out across the lake through the screen walls on the porch . . . and relit his half-smoked cigar. I wondered what he was thinking.

He came and sat in his chair, and we got situated. I asked Daddy Claude,

"Are you ready?" he began.

Twenty-Eight—Reflections in My Diary

Fall 1967

Back in my dorm that fall I wrote feverishly in my diary.

I'm overwhelmed by the door Mama Howell opened into my past last spring. I loved her frontier stories. Then, beyond all expectation, I discovered in Daddy Claude's story, as if from a philosopher's stone, how good habits of the heart are formed and how important they are amid life's perilous storms.

Staring from my window at the students protesting, I find myself thinking about Daddy Claude's curiosity about important and permanent things after that terrible fire on Hoggin' Day. And about those flowers along the highway when I drove to Little Rock at Easter.

I'm struck again by the contrast of the lilies in the field cared for by God and the "flower power" and protests against all-things-traditional across campus. I'm especially struck by the contrast of the Summer of Love in Haight Ashbury and my summer of love at Lake Hamilton. My mind drifts to the thick rope that holds the old bag swing on I Street, and the enduring ties that bind my family, as so many around me grab at what seems driftwood in today's cultural storm.

Dylan is right, "the times, they are a changin." But it's clear to me now that our mothers and fathers can understand. Listening to Mama Howell and Daddy Claude, it's clear they too went through times of dramatic change, far more tumultuous than mine. While Dylan's right that the "old road is rapidly agin'," I've come to believe that, unless he was being ironic, he was wrong to suggest that aging means passé. The rebar of the virtues buried in the "old road" that Daddy Claude's story reveals is the strength we need now. They're the rope cast to us in the rising waters, so we don't "sink like a stone."

Daddy Claude is an ordinary man. But not a "common man" of the kind Ortega described. I'm pretty sure he'd call my grandfather an "excellent man" because he's lived a life of essential servitude—a sense of servitude that seems to come not from within himself but as a call, a pull from a standard beyond himself, superior to himself.

Listening to Daddy Claude, I discovered it was a standard given to him as an extraordinary inheritance. Bequeathed to him by his mama and papa and his Uncle John, and especially Uncle Jim and his Grandfather Bill, and even from his Great Grandfather Raford Carroll and others in the Carroll family he never knew. Those virtues then became his own, forged on the unyielding anvil of life through the many travails that he's endured. In that standard, it seems, are hidden the truly important and the permanent things. A bequest that has enabled him, like those before him, to live an extraordinary life—not perfect but extraordinary.

Before he told me his story, I hadn't seen this. I couldn't. I'm not even sure he did. But in the telling, his inheritance came alive. I can see it now, and I think he did too.

The contrast is bright between his world and mine. My generation's constant cries for freedom, for release from all restraint, constraint, and convention, and from war. And who in their right mind wants war? Our cries seem to be for a complete release from the past and the knowledge and wisdom embedded in it, discovered only when the stories are told. It is so easy to jettison faith in things we've never heard, believing it offers false answers to what an extraordinary life is. In some ways it does seem clear we've lost our way. I wonder to what end today's experiment in search of untethered freedom will lead. Or if its vision has no end in view, turning, turning of our widening gyre, wandering in search of the falconer but declaring there's none to be found. If, as Dylan suggests, "the order is rapidly fadin'" with the march of time, I fear things are breaking apart under the centrifugal force of Yeats' center that cannot hold.

All I know is, if anyone really listens to the past as I've heard it and sees the kind of extraordinary life I discovered in my grandfather, and there are many others like him I'm sure, the past tells a different story. That freedom with no standard becomes an albatross. True freedom is a transcendent call upon us. A call I only now begin to hear, as a bequest found buried in the folds of his inheritance.

The kind of manifest destiny that pulled him along was not the pursuit of conquest or an elusive idealistic dream, but of necessity and the simple fulfillment of life as a moral adventure. His life is extraordinary not because of great genius, achievements, or wealth, nor from some new brand of freedom, but because of the man he became having been given treasures surer than gold. The virtues of wisdom, courage, justice, and self-control that gave him the strength to endure and overcome the tragedies of his life, and the heavenly ones of faith, hope, and love—a self-sacrificial love that contrasts the self-absorbed kind celebrated in the Summer of Love. Virtues that guided him even in the darkest times, with a north-star assurance of God's providence and a confidence that as important as this life is, it's not all there is.

I discovered as Daddy Claude talked, that virtue itself, while grasped for in the practice of the virtues—which he succeeded at more than most—is not found in their mere repetition. Virtue, it became clear to me as I heard his story, is something toward which we yearn. It's not something we ourselves weave into bolts of fabric to fashion a finely tailored garment. Nor is it something we can go to college and learn from a textbook. It's not a destination found in this life but in that toward which we journey, the object of our heart's deepest longing. One implanted in us by God, as Uncle Jim would say. In Daddy Claude's story I came to see that virtue can be bequeathed as a seed planted from generation to generation—often buried in the space between the notes, as Debussy might say. But growth in virtue must be cultivated and showered with the gifts of grace in response to the faint voice calling from far away. Only then can it yield the fruit of good habits of the heart.

It did in Daddy Claude. He found in his inheritance what's truly important and permanent, and it bore the fruit of love that flowered in and through the crevices that are the triumphs and tragedies of this mortal coil. His inheritance nourished his soul to step into the darkness, humbly accept, and when necessary, release life's transient triumphs. It allowed him to live an extraordinary life.

By telling me his amazing life story, I began to realize Daddy Claude had bequeathed to me his important and permanent inheritance.

The question that lingers for me is, can I live up to my inheritance?

[Moral precepts] were once at home in, and intelligible in terms of, a context of practical beliefs and of supporting habits of thought, feeling, and action. . . . It is only because human beings have an end toward which they are directed by reason of their specific nature, that practices, traditions, and the like are able to function as they do.

ALASDAIR MACINTYRE

Epilogue

The Carroll-Howell family matriarch, Laura (née Carroll) Howell, "Mama Howell" died in El Campo on February 17, 1971, after a fall. She was one hundred years old. The whole family came to her funeral as she was buried next to her beloved husband Bud, William Findley ("Papa") Howell, at Pinecrest Cemetery in Little Rock, AR.

Claude ("Daddy Claude") and Helen ("Mama Helen") continued to live at 3412 I Street in Little Rock until Helen got sick, when he moved in with Nona ("Toodles") and her husband Mickey. He died there suddenly at eighty-two years old on August 4, 1977, one day before Helen was released from the hospital. Carroll ("Bubber") and Charles ("Chafranken") brought Helen to Claude's funeral at Little Rock National Cemetery in a wheelchair. Laura Dean ("Sister"), Margaret ("Boggie"), and Mary Kay ("Kay Baby") stayed and cared for her on I Street through the mourning period. After that Claude Jr. ("Nicky") took her home with him. She stayed there and with Toodles for the next two years but never stayed in their little house again. Helen died on September 4, 1979, two years and month after her beloved Claude, a week and two days shy of seventy-three years old.

Claude and Helen's seven children continued to multiply and thrive as Uncle Jim had urged. There are so many grandchildren and great grandchildren now it's hard to keep up. If he were still around, Daddy Claude would repeat what he told Lewis and Margaret Gaston that day they talked about reopening the old store on the Southwest Trail: "It's been a few minutes, I may have more and just don't know it yet."

It seems to me Claude gave everyone in this ordinary family the extraordinary inheritance he received from his family before him: good habits of the heart and the wealth of family.

Author's Note

A Bit about Me

I'm a business guy who became a writer after I retired. I spent a career in banking and management consulting, and I still do some consulting with small to mid-sized companies. But I spend most of my time now writing, lecturing at local universities, teaching at my church, and serving on the board of two nonprofits.

In college and grad school my heart and sights became fixed on the big questions of life. I became infected with what G. K. Chesterton described as education not as a subject or series of subjects but as a "transfer of a way of life." This fixation led me to a life of philosophical reflection, literary and artistic wonder, and religious affection—in my case, my deeply held Christian faith. It never went away while I pursued my business career. I've tried to live in the practical work-a-day world of business while pursuing what Dr. Louise Cowan called life shaped by the "poetic imagination." The modern world tends to separate the pragmatic worlds of politics, economics, and commerce and the worlds of ideas, history, literature, poetry, and the arts. It often treats them as parallel worlds that don't touch. But they do and are integral. We are shaped by the prevailing myths and big ideas that we live in at any given time and that are communicated through the images, sacred stories, and practices we partake of—this is what philosopher James K. A. Smith calls our "cultural liturgies." *Habits of the Heart* is a standalone story but is also a narrative picture of how this shaping force occurs in the life of Claude Howell.

Habits is my second book and my first foray into the world of historical fiction. My first book, *Rediscovering God's Grand Story: In a Fragmented world of Pieces and Parts* (Wipf & Stock, 2017), was more philosophical and explicitly religious.

How *Habits of the Heart* Came about

It is a child of COVID-19. The first year of that dreadful pall, my thoughts were so often fixed on my mom, Laura Dean. To help protect her, my wife Janet and I hardly went anywhere except to the grocery store, and to deliver Mom hers. The only other regular outing we had was our daily trail walks alongside the east fork of the Trinity River.

I thought about how my then ninety-three-year-old mom was barely three years younger than her namesake, Laura (née Carroll) Howell, "Mama Howell" (my great grandmother) in 1967, the year this book opens (Mom is now ninety-six, the same age as Mama Howell then). I thought about how Mama Howell and her son, my grandfather "Daddy" Claude, and her husband "Papa" Howell and their other children lived through the Great Influenza epidemic of 1917–18.

My mind drifted to a conversation my dad had with Mama Howell that portentous year of 1967 as I sat transfixed listening to them for almost two hours. The reel-to-reel tape-recording of that conversation got lost for twenty years. I found it a few years after my father died in 1984 and I set up the recorder and listened to it. It was wonderful to hear once again the voices of Mama Howell, my dad, and the muted voices of other cherished family members in the background.

As Janet and I walked along the quiet river, I told her my thoughts, which I so often do. But that day was different. We had a long talk about our parents, grandparents, great grandparents, and others further back as much as we knew—imagining what it was like when they were young, and all they went through before we came along. A seed was planted. I wondered how many in the generations behind me know any of this. Not many, I guessed.

Arriving home that day, I went straight to my office and began transcribing the 1967 tape of Mama Howell. Could this be the doorway into a story? I wondered. Something for the family.

I roughed an outline and took it on our walk the next day and asked Janet. Is there a story here? Maybe, she said. That was August 2020. I got a very rough draft done for the family by Christmas and gave a copy to my mom and sent it to her three sisters (their three brothers are in heaven now), and to my brothers Rick and Bob.

That's all I had in mind, something for the family, never a book to be published. But the family readers urged me to publish it. Later, a few readers outside the family thought so too. I decided to consider it. That became the three-year-long project that is *Habits of the Heart*.

The result is what you have in your hands. A historical novel drawn from and based on my own family's saga. In so many ways it is a quintessential

American story. But one easily lost in the noise and chaos of '67 ... *and even more so now.* A story of an ordinary man of essential servitude forged on the unyielding anvil of life. A narrative picture of the good "habits of the heart" Alexis de Tocqueville saw when he visited America. Of how they are formed and passed from generation to generation and woven into the fabric of life, and how important they are in life's perilous storms.

   This has been a labor of love. I hope my family enjoys it—even more, I hope you do too.

Acknowledgements

My most important acknowledgements go to my mom Laura Dean (née Howell) Roseman ("Sister," now ninety-six), and to her younger sisters, my aunts, Margaret (née Howell) Pierce ("Boggie"), Nona (née Howell) Fitzgibbon ("Toodles," the true family historian), and Mary Kay (née Howell) Polk ("Kay Baby"). They each helped me in endless ways, including with hilarious anecdotes. I cannot thank them enough. And I give posthumous credit to their brothers, my uncles Carroll, Nicky, and Charles, whose strong opinions, stories, and jokes echo in my mind.

To other family members: Thank you to my then nine-year-old grand-niece Willa Rose Freeman—the same age Claude was on hoggin' day—for helping with the opening line of his story. To my brothers Rick and Bob for reading the early family version and encouraged me to write one for publication. And to my niece, Laura Nicole (Nicki), for reading a serialized chapter-by-chapter version on her iPhone in a distant land and found it to be an encouragement in a difficult time. Special thanks go to my cousin Laura Ann (née Howell) Bauman, the oldest daughter of my Uncle Carroll Howell ("Bubber"), who helped me with his story during WWII, and to my cousin Judy (née Howell) Pratt for helping to uncover important documents from one of Daddy Claude's old filing cabinets. I thank all my many cousins with whom I grew up, exploring the Indian mounds near Toltec, the cornfields and waterholes next to Daddy Claude and Mama Helen's 1950s grocery store, and flying high on the bag swing at the corner of Midland and I Street in Little Rock. Those memories were inspirational.

I must give special thanks to my dad, George Warren Roseman (d. 1984), who by his unwitting foresight reopened the door to Mama Howell's story through that 1967 reel-to-reel recording. The stories Mama Howell told in her wonderful country-girl cadence and spontaneous laughter and excitement at ninety-six-years-young, became my muse.

Family stories rely on family lore and old documents, and genealogy work by somebody. *Habits* is no exception. One such important source is Juno Evans Pierce and Andrew Jackson Carroll's *Carroll Genealogy: A Brief History of Raford Carroll* (Vandalia, IL: Fayette County Genealogical Society, 1932; revised 1982), which Mama Howell had in her lap during the 1967 interview with my dad. That piece includes James Monroe Carroll's ("Uncle Jim") "A Brief History of The Carroll and Elam Families," which provides the formative elements of Uncle Jim's story about selling the mules in this book. More current and accurate genealogical work on the Carroll family is by Greg Lamberson (a distant Carroll cousin still living in Illinois)—I want to thank Greg for his help and for reading an early manuscript of this story.

But making a family story into a historical novel requires creative fiction and a great deal of historical research. I have relied on many different sources to create characters, events, times, and views. These include social and political views which though fictionalized are consistent with real times, places, and people—including Claude's. But to be clear, this story is not a political one and has no political agenda. Some points of view, rhetoric, and words may be offensive—they are kept to reflect the characters and the times—but no offense is intended. See an annotated list of key sources used for the novel in "Just for Reference" below.

I want to extend an extra special thanks to associate librarian Cathy Smith with the Evans Public Library, Vandalia, IL and to Sherryl Miller with the Lonoke County Historical Museum. Without their invaluable help I would have been merely speculating on important connections, key characters, places, events, and on crucial historical details, especially in Seminary Township and Vandalia, Illinois, and Pulaski and Lonoke Counties, Arkansas.

* * *

Most books require an outsider's perspective. I want to thank my longtime friend and author Dan Taylor for his insights from reading a very early partial manuscript. Thanks to Robert Cantrell and Ann Kline, too, for reading an early draft and providing critical and constructive comments. And to my good friend Fred Durham who read and commented on a near final draft.

Similarly, I extend my special thanks to Ann Howard Creel for her invaluable published-novelist and specialized historical fiction editorial expertise.

I also extend my special thanks to Dr. James Patrick, chancellor emeritus of the College of St. Thomas More for reading an early draft and a near-final one and for his constant encouragement.

I extend an extra special thank you to my now very good friend Dr. Larry Allums, executive director emeritus of the Dallas Institute of Humanities and Culture, for providing his unique eye toward great literature (which I in no way presume this book to be) and his editorial expertise to make the book better. Even more so, I thank Larry for his gracious friendship and constant encouragement to me in this project.

And definitely no outsider, I give more than an extra special thank you to my wonderful wife, Janet, who is always my first and last reader and best critic (constructive mostly). She walked next to me when the book was conceived and has helped me all the way through.

Despite all this help, whatever errors and weaknesses that remain are all mine.

Special acknowledgement and thanks go to the Lewis Tolkien Society. I hope this book contributes in a small way to the Society's tagline, "for the renewal of the common tradition." Without the Society's gracious financial gift this book would not have been possible.

* * *

Final Note: As with all works of historical fiction, I have taken literary license with some real historical figures and developed them into characters or adapted them into this story in ways that did not actually occur. This includes selectively changing the names, age, birth order (including my own as the character Jim, whose story opens the book in chapter 1), and the date of death of a few historical figures, including family members, to allow the story to work. To establish historical context, in certain places I have construed actual words from selected sources to be dialogue, writings in publications, or comments by a character; where workable as a natural part of the narrative, I give attribution in the text; otherwise, I give it in Just for Reference below.

I have used the content of actual letters—e.g., from Claude to Helen, from Uncle Carroll ("Bubber") to Laura Dean, and from Mama Howell to Laura Dean; and actual WWI and WWII letters from public records. Some I created as if written by these and other characters.

Late Discovery: though Mama Howell declares proudly on the 1967 tape, "Grandfather Carroll had some of the blood of the Carrolls of Carrollton in his veins," with some personal regret, it has now been determined by DNA tests that he did not. For this story I have kept the Raford Carroll family lore that Charles Carroll of Carrollton is a blood ancestor.

Special thanks to Rick Roseman and Joseph Burns for the exceptional artistic sketches in the book and for artwork on the book cover.

Just for Reference

While *Habits of the Heart* is a historical novel and not a work of history, I have tried hard to make it as historically accurate as possible—in times, ideas, places, events, and people, with a lot of fiction as the ligaments holding things together. To achieve this, I have relied on a host of resources and sources. Below is a lengthy but non-exhaustive list of the most important ones, with a few annotations describing how I have used them and where I have taken literary license.

Alexander, Charles Newton, Sr. *Biographies*. Pulaski County, Arkansas Genealogy and History. https://genealogytrails.com/ark/pulaski/bios.html.

Ambrose, Stephen E. *Undaunted Courage*. New York: Simon & Schuster, 1996.

Archaimbault, Delores, and Terry A. Barnhart. "Copperheads," Northern Illinois University Libraries. https://www.lib.niu.edu/1996/iht319615.html.

Aristotle, *Politics*, Book 8; and *Nicomachean Ethics*, Book 2. Perseus Digital Library. https://www.perseus.tufts.edu/hopper/.

"Arkansas National Guard during World War I." https://en.wikipedia.org/wiki/Arkansas_National_Guard_during_World_War_I.

Ballotopedia. "Texas Old-Age Assistance, Proposition 3." https://ballotpedia.org/Texas_Old-Age_Assistance,_Proposition_3_(August_1935).

"Birth Control in the United States." https://en.wikipedia.org/wiki/Birth_control_in_the_United_States. (Parts of this entry are construed in the book to have been a newspaper article in 1962.)

Birzer, Bradley J. *American Cicero: The Life of Charles Carroll*. Wilmington, DE: ISI Books, 2010.

———. "The Last of the Romans: Charles Carroll of Carrollton." *The Imaginative Conservative*, June 14, 2016. https://theimaginativeconservative.org/2016/06/last-roman-charles-carroll-carrollton-bradley-birzer.html.

Blatt, Daniel. "Descent into the Depths (1930)." *Futurecasts Magazine*, March 1, 2001. http://www.futurecasts.com/Depression_descent-beginning-'30.htm.

"The Blitz Begins as Germany Bombs London." https://www.history.com/this-day-in-history/the-blitz-begins.

"Casimir Pulaski." https://en.wikipedia.org/wiki/Casimir_Pulaski.

Christ, Mark K. "William Heber McLaughlin." *Encyclopedia of Arkansas*. https://encyclopediaofarkansas.net/entries/william-heber-mclaughlin-13558/.

City of Keo. "Our History, Arkansas Heritage/National Register Write-Up." https://keoar.com/our-history.

Cronkite, Walter. "Civil Rights Era Almost Split CBS News Operation." *National Public Radio*, May 30, 2005. https://www.npr.org/templates/story/story.php?storyId=4672765.

Crowell, Benedict and Wilson, Robert Forrest. *The Giant Hand. Our Mobilization and Control of Industry and Natural Resources, 1917–1918* (1921). New Haven: Yale University Press, 1921. https://archive.org/details/gianthandourmobiloocrowuoft/page/n11/mode/2up.

Cryptology Information Warfare. "Remembering the Gulf of Tonkin Incident (August, 2–5 1964) and Honoring the First POW of Vietnam, CAPT Klusmann, USN." https://stationhypo.com/2016/08/02/remembering-the-gulf-of-tonkin-incident-august-2-5-1964-and-honoring-the-first-pow-of-vietnam-capt-klusmann-usn/. (I selected parts of this essay to construe a fictional article in the *Arkansas Democrat-Gazette*.)

Dalton, Lawrence. "History of Randolph County Arkansas." https://argenweb.net/randolph/books/daltonintro.htm.

Dougan, Michael B. "Charles Hillman Brough (1876–1935)." In *Encyclopedia of Arkansas*. https://encyclopediaofarkansas.net/entries/charles-hillman-brough-89/. (Brough was also governor in January 1919 when the Elaine Massacre of 1919 [in Elaine, Arkansas] occurred—one of if not the worst race riots in American history. He also supported the Arkansas "Bone Dry Act," proffered by his predecessor Gov. George W. Hays, passed in January 1917—a state act that provided national momentum for the passage of the January 1919 passage of the 18th Amendment and October passage of the Volstead Prohibition Act. See: "Elaine Massacre of 1919." In *Encyclopedia of Arkansas*; Ralph Bradley Hoshaw, "A Study of the Role of Churches in the Enactment of the Arkansas Prohibition Law of 1917.")

Eggleston, Edward. *A First Book of American History: With Special Reference to the Lives and Deeds of Great Americans*. New York: American Book Company, 1889. https://archive.org/details/firstbookinamerio3eggl/mode/.

Encyclopedia of Arkansas. Multiple references. https://encyclopediaofarkansas.net.

Falvey Library. "Newspaper Scrapbook, World War I, 1915–1917." https://digital.library.villanova.edu/Item/vudl:353147.

Fayette County Genealogical and Historical Society. Vandalia, IL, Historical Society.

Fischer, William, Jr. "Lincoln Travels to the Capital 1834." *The Historical Marker Database*, https://www.hmdb.org/m.asp?m=42527.

Foisy, Gloria Cardwell Stachurski. "History of Keo, Arkansas," 1999. https://keoar.com/our-history. (The town of Keo was originally the Cobb settlement, named after Lafayette Cobb. Rumors of the railroad extension prompted J. W. Brodie to purchase property in Dunham Station, renamed after Miss Keo Dooley, daughter of Judge P. C. Dooley, and namesake of the town.)

Foster, Jeremiah D. "Heermann (DD-532) 1943–1975." Naval History and Heritage Command, September 30, 2019. https://www.history.navy.mil/research/histories/ship-histories/danfs/h/heermann.html.

"The Great Depression: 1929–1939." https://web.archive.org/web/20230320000602/https://www.fdic.gov/about/history/timeline/1930s.html.

Great Missouri Birding Trails. "Southwest Birding Trail." http://greatmissouribirdingtrail.com/Wordpress/birding-trails/springfield/.

Hendricks, Scotty. "How the Nazis Hijacked Nietzsche, and How It Can Happen to Anybody." *Big Think*, December 16, 2017. (I have construed excerpts of this piece to have been reported by CBS news radio reporter H. V. Kaltenborn in the lead-up to WWII. I obtained Mr. Hendricks's approval to use in this way.)

Hickman, Kennedy. "World War II: USS Saratoga (CV-3)." *ThoughtCo*, April 5, 2023. https://www.thoughtco.com/uss-saratoga-cv-3-2361553.

"Hirohito." https://www.history.com/topics/world-war-ii/hirohito-1. (A quote from this article is construed to have been reported by H. V. Kaltenborn.)

Holocaust Encyclopedia. "Victims of the Nazi Era: Nazi Racial Ideology." Authors, United States Holocaust Memorial Museum, Washington, DC. https://encyclopedia.ushmm.org/content/en/article/victims-of-the-nazi-era-nazi-racial-ideology.

Hood, Michael. "The Original City of Little Rock." September 11, 2016. https://www.littlerock.gov/media/2110/original-city-historical-firsts-illustrated.pdf.

Hoofman, Judy. "A Day in the Life of a Texarkana, U.S.A., Homemaker from 1900–1917." *East Texas Historical Journal* 32 (1994) art. 5.

Huckaby, Elizabeth. "Crisis at Central High: Little Rock, 1957–58." *Kirkus Review* (1980). (Construed as an article the main character reads. Credited in text.)

"H. V. Kaltenborn." https://en.wikipedia.org/wiki/H._V._Kaltenborn. (I have taken literary license, construing Kaltenborn, speaking on the radio as he did in the 1930s and 1940s, to be saying words actually written by others, e.g., from "How the Nazis Hijacked Nietzsche, and How It Can Happen to Anybody," in *Big Think*, and "Victims of the Nazi Era: Nazi Racial Ideology," in United States Holocaust Memorial Museum—*Holocaust Encyclopedia*; and "During WWII, Industries Transitioned From Peacetime to Wartime Production," David Vergun, March 27, 2020, DOD News, U.S. Department of Defense).

Johnson, Lyndon B. "Gulf of Tonkin Incident." https://usa.usembassy.de/etexts/speeches/rhetoric/lbjgulf.htm. See also "Tonkin Gulf Crisis, August 1964," Naval History and Heritage Command.

Lamberson, Greg. Greg Lamberson's Genealogy Website and Raford Carroll Origins Blog, https://freepages.rootsweb.com/~glamberson/genealogy/index.htm; Raford Carroll Origins Blog, https://rafordcarrollorigins.wordpress.com/; and personal correspondence.

Lincoln Home, National Park Service. "The Lincoln-Douglas Debates of 1858." https://www.nps.gov/liho/learn/historyculture/debates.htm. (I have the character Uncle John say that "Mr. Lincoln never suggested that the negro and the white would or should live in political and social equality—he didn't think they ever would—he did suggest slavery was wrong." This is a very close paraphrase of what Mr. Lincoln says in the first debate with Douglas. This is a historical novel, and as such represents the times in which it takes place. This is in no way intended to promote social inequality between the races today.)

Lurie, Jonathan. *William Howard Taft: The Travails of a Progressive Conservative*. New York: Cambridge University Press, 2012; review at *Journal of American Studies* 47 (2013) E104.

Lyford, Joseph P. *The Talk of Vandalia: The Life of an American Town*. The Fund for the Republic, Inc., reprinted by permission from McNally and Loftin Publishers, Charlotte/Santa Barbara, 1964.

MacIntyre, Alasdair. *After Virtue: A Study in Moral Theory.* 3rd ed. Notre Dame, IN: University of Notre Dame Press, 2007. https://archive.org/details/4.Macintyre.

Mayo, Mary Carolyn Gaston. "The Charles Alexander Family." In *Temple Mounds and Plantation Bells: A Historical "Happening"*, edited by George Alexander Brown, n.p. Ashley Mills, AR: N.p., 1989. (I have taken literary license with the Alexander family. Margaret Alexander (b. ca. 1898), was actually the older sister of and Charles Alexander, Jr. (b. ~1908). I am construing Charles to be the older brother (and b. ~1888) rather than the younger. I am thus construing Charles and Margaret's parents, Charles N. Alexander and Blanche Pemberton, to have been married in ~1887, whereas they were actually married in 1893.)

Miller, Sherryl, director of the Lonoke County Historical Museum.

Moss, Robert. "The 1904 World's Fair: A Turning Point for American Food." https://www.seriouseats.com/food-history-1904-worlds-fair-st-louis.

Naugle, David K. *Reordered Loves, Reordered Lives: Learning the Deep Meaning of Happiness.* Grand Rapids: Eerdmans, 2008.

Naval History and Heritage Command. "USS Saratoga (CV-3)." https://www.history.navy.mil/research/histories/ship-histories/danfs/s/saratoga-v.html.

"Nazism." https://www.britannica.com/event/Nazism. (I have construed excerpts of this piece to have been reported by CBS news radio reporter H. V. Kaltenborn in the lead-up to WWII; and I have Claude's college professor speak from this source.)

Netherland, New, and Rodney, Caesar. "Charles Carroll of Carrollton." https://www.revolutionary-war.net/charles-carroll/.

"1957 in the Vietnam War." https://en.wikipedia.org/wiki/1957_in_the_Vietnam_War.

Ortega y Gasset, José. *The Revolt of the Masses [Rebelión de las masas].* 25th anniversary edition of authorized English translation. New York: Norton, 1957. https://archive.org/details/TheRevoltOfTheMasses/mode/2up?view=theater.

Paterson, Pat. "The Truth about Tonkin." *Naval History Magazine*, February 2008. https://www.usni.org/magazines/naval-history-magazine/2008/february/truth-about-tonkin.

Pemberton, John Martin. *Biographies.* Pulaski County, Arkansas Genealogy and History. https://genealogytrails.com/ark/pulaski/biosp2.html.

Pollock, John. *William Wilberforce: A Man Who Changed His Times.* Washington, DC: The Trinity Forum, 1996.

Polston, Mike, project director. *The Arkansas Great War Letter Project*; specific citations of "Joe Bond," "Emmett Coleman," "Foreman Kelley." https://chsarkansasgreatwar.weebly.com/contact.html. (Used as dialogue. I construe the main character, Claude, to be friends with each of these historical figures, though there is no evidence they were.)

"The Presidency: Preface to War." *Time*, September 11, 1939. https://content.time.com/time/subscriber/article/0,33009,711734,00.html.

Rasenberger, Jim. "1908." *Smithsonian Magazine*, January 2008. https://www.smithsonianmag.com/history/1908-7683115/.

Reynolds, John Hughes. "History of Pulaski County." *History of Pulaski County*, SMC.012.014. Arkansas State Archives. https://digitalheritage.arkansas.gov/reynolds-john/7.

Roosevelt, Franklin D. "Pearl Harbor Address to the Nation." December 7, 1941. Transcription by Michael E. Eidenmuller. https://www.americanrhetoric.com/speeches/fdrpearlharbor.htm.

———. "Presidential Speeches. 'December 9, 1941: Fireside Chat 19: On the War with Japan.'" https://millercenter.org/the-presidency/presidential-speeches/december-9–1941-fireside-chat-19-war-japan.

Russell, Stefene. "In 1905, the World's First Education Museum Opened, with Amelia Meissner as Its Lead Curator." St. Louis Magazine, August 16, 2018. https://www.stlmag.com/topics/stefene-russell/.

Schrag, Zachary M. "Abraham Lincoln, First Debate with Stephen A. Douglas at Ottawa, Illinois, August 21, 1858." https://mason.gmu.edu/~zschrag/hist120spring05/lincoln_ottawa.htm.

Shields, Charlene. "The Fascinating Dunkards." Notes from the White County Historical Society. https://white.illinoisgenweb.org/wchs_04_20_02.html.

"Southwest Trail." https://encyclopediaofarkansas.net/entries/southwest-trail-2305/. (This reference is merely indicative of many sources consulted about the Southwest Trail.)

Stanton, Carl L. They Called It Treason: An Account of Renegades, Copperheads, Guerrillas, Bushwackers, and Outlaw Gangs that Terrorized Illinois during the Civil War. Bunker Hill, IL: N.p., 2002.

"The Stock Market Crash of 1929." https://openstax.org/books/us-history/pages/25-1-the-stock-market-crash-of-1929. (Except where otherwise noted, textbooks on this site are licensed under a Creative Commons Attribution 4.0 International License.)

Taylor, Alan. "Photos of the 1904 St. Louis World's Fair." The Atlantic, September 9, 2019. (I construe some of the main character Claude's recollections from visiting the Fair in 1905 from this piece.)

Taylor, Daniel. Tell Me a Story: The Life-Shaping Power of Our Stories. St. Paul, MN: Bog Walk, 2001.

Tocqueville, Alexis de. Democracy in America. Translated and edited by Harvey C. Mansfield and Debra Winthrop. Chicago: The University of Chicago Press, 2002.

U. S. Navy, Bangor Community. "War History of the U.S.S. Heermann" (1946). World War Regimental Histories, 159. http://digicom.bpl.lib.me.us/ww_reg_his/159. (This is a true account but has no identified author in this source; the Bangor Public Library cannot find an author, and suggests it might have been written by one or more of the commanders: Dwight M. Agnew, Commander July 1943–April 1944; Amos T. Hathaway, Commander April 1944–August 1945; William K. Yarnall, Lt. Commander, August 1945 through the end of the war. In my story, Claude cites his fictional shipmate "Hal" recalling comments made in this source material, as if they are the character's words.)

Van Zile, Edward. "Rise Up! Rise Up, Crusaders!" In Patriotic Pieces from the Great War, edited by Edna D. Jones, 61–63. Philadelphia: Penn Publishing, 1918. https://en.wikisource.org/wiki/Patriotic_pieces_from_the_Great_War. (Text is free for use under the Creative Commons Attribution-ShareAlike License.)

Wilson, Woodrow. "Wilson's War Message to Congress, 2 April, 1917." https://wwi.lib.byu.edu/index.php/Wilson's_War_Message_to_Congress.

9 781666 7733